ANORAK IN FENLAND

Retired teacher Martin Brady's interest in footpaths leads him to investigate a run-down Fenland farm – which turns out to contain illegal immigrants and to be linked to a national neo-Nazi Organisation. His amateur sleuthing (whilst his wife is away on a course) leads to his being shot at, but not before undertaking a hair-raising river trip, causing a spectacular plane crash and discovering a Bunker which contains a photo of a rather special U-boat.....

i

John Nicholson

Descended from the Nicholsons who farmed in the nineteenth century at Grimblethorpe Hall in North Lincolnshire, the author has lived for many years in the Fens where this tale is set. Retired now from a career in teaching, he has also worked for the Hong Kong Shanghai Bank, in Paris, and as a Second Secretary in the Foreign Office. He and his wife, Angela (a retired French teacher) have long shared a love of the culture and language of France.

After attending the Stamford Endowed Schools, their children, Patrick and Lucy gained places at the universities of Cambridge and Oxford respectively – he to read Russian and French, she History. Their present Golden Retriever, Toffee, would like to point out, however, that she is in no way related to or similar in character to Sherry, who figures in '**Anorak in Fenland**' – and that goes for members of the author's family as well.

Also by
John Nicholson

*

Contemporary Problems of Foreign Exchange and Trade
(Ginn & Co Ltd, 1971)

Modern British Economics
(George Allen & Unwin, 1973)

ANORAK

IN

FENLAND

by

John Nicholson

WRITERSWORLD
A SELF PUBLISHING RESOURCE

Published by WRITERSWORLD

Copyright © John Nicholson 2002

Cover design Alan Taylor

The moral right of the author has been asserted

Printed and bound by Antony Rowe Limited, Eastbourne

ISBN 1-907181-03-2

WRITERSWORLD
15-17 Maidenhead Street
Hertford SG14 1DW
England

www.writersworld.tv

For
Patrick Brady Nicholson
Счастливого пути!

CHAPTER ONE

"Bloody Hell! These books get worse and worse." There was a thud as Martin's action thriller hit the floor.

"Do calm down, dear. I'm trying to finish this marking."

"But it's ridiculous!" expostulated Martin. "Here we are on page 18 and he's already fondling her small firm breasts, contemplating her flat buttocks and hard at it. He only met her on page 15! And the bloody book didn't start until page 10!"

"You don't *have* to read escapist rubbish all the time. Why don't you take up a hobby or do an evening class or something? Lots of retired people do."

"That's not the point," said Martin, picking up the book again. "The publishers insist on bad language and graphic bonking – I remember an article or an interview with Dick Francis when he said he had to write a few steamy scenes in, just for the sake of it. Those bits just stand out like... like... sore thumbs."

"I wondered for a moment what graphic image you were going to use," said Jennifer, whose mind had been broadened over thirty years of marriage and a few more of teaching. "Why don't you make a cup of tea, get my case down from the roof and make a list of what I shall need to take on this course?"

Martin's wife was shortly to leave for three weeks in France on a language refresher course, designed to better equip her – or, rather, better to equip her – to guide her reluctant students to ever higher exam grades, using currently fashionable 'target language' approach. Whether, thought Martin (whose growing disenchantment and cynicism had led him to seek early retirement from his post of Head of Economics) the approach would still be approved of by the time she returned, was another matter. However, it meant that he would have plenty of time to catch up on his reading, and could at long last tidy the garage. He might even decorate the dining room, one of several items on the notional list, hopefully prepared by Jennifer.

1

"You're always on about footpaths," said Jennifer when the tea eventually arrived, after much banging and crashing from the roof and a lengthy search for the sweeteners, "so why don't you join the Ramblers or get up an action group?"

"Action? Round here? You must be joking – it's dead. The Fens used to be famous for eels and wild-fowling, but that was before the seventeenth century. It's gone down since then. All there is now is sugar beet, and rape – and even that's a far cry from what the Vikings understood by the term."

"Yes, well, while I'm away, I suggest you practise both defeatism and decorating – the dining room and the front bedroom both need doing, and the books need sorting, and...."

Martin hurriedly revised his negative approach at the prospect of endless useful tasks and interrupted to say that he had been thinking of writing to the County Council about the removal of footpath signs, the culprits being in his view more likely to be the landowners than layabout teenagers. The latter were much too busy fulfilling their output norms in terms of lager-swilling, drug-taking and copulating – the last being undertaken in remarkably draughty locations, if the evidence provided by used condoms was to be believed. During the ensuing conversation, Martin agreed that it was silly to suspect respectable farmers, and agreed that it was, in any case, none of his business, and that he would think about seeing whether they needed someone to patrol and effect minor repairs.

Jennifer had her mind on other things, such as the packing, her husband's feeding arrangements, emergency telephone numbers, etc., as a result of which she failed to register how unlike him it was to be so reasonable. In fact, Martin had just had a very productive thought, leading to an idea which he knew would not commend itself to his wife – especially when she was going to leave him on his own. The thought related to the removal, or rotating, of footpath signs, and the fact that he did not know who was doing it – but it was not related to the notion that it was none of his business. Martin had decided to do some investigating, to try to catch the culprit(s) in flagrante whatsit – and to decide on a plan of action as soon as he returned from taking Jennifer to the station. It was a decision which was going to have far-reaching effects.

On his return from Peterborough, Martin made himself a coffee and contemplated irresponsible behaviour – thereby demonstrating (although the thought did not occur to him) that some boys remain at the 'difficult age' well beyond their teens. To be fair, Martin did not plan to confront any youths if he found them – indeed, he expected to confirm that they were not to blame. He intended to hide in the hedge near to one of the signposts which he had had to relocate a few weeks previously, on one or two likely nights, and use the lack of action as a form of 'evidence' to support the theory that those with the greater motive and opportunity – the landowners – were the most likely culprits.

Having taken their Golden Retriever, Sherry, for her walk earlier – and been reassured by a lengthy telephone call that his wife had arrived safely – Martin set off as dusk fell. He went shrouded in dark clothing, without Sherry and also without his face blacked, as he was afraid of looking silly if discovered. He planned, in such an eventuality, to claim a desire to look for owls and bats. He remembered to take the dog lead, however, which could enable him to appear to be searching for Sherry, a torch 'just in case' and a thermos of soup, as it could be a long wait.

Martin stepped out briskly, his gumboots making little noise, his senses more acutely aware than was usually the case, conscious of the sound rather like distant surf from the main road a mile or so to the east. The lights of an occasional plane or helicopter winked above, as much a part of the Fenland scene as the odd tractor, ploughing by headlights or the softly gliding owl and flickering bat. Having arrived at his chosen spot, Martin settled himself down well hidden in the hedge which bounded a wide track, accessible by car, with two 'suspect' footpath signs just visible by the intermittent light of the moon through the scudding clouds.

It was about 10 o'clock when they came, stepping carefully in single file, silent and watchful, only visible to someone at a lower level, causing the graceful beasts to be silhouetted against the backdrop of the lighter night sky. The small herd of deer disappeared almost as soon as Martin spotted them, however, put to flight by an approaching car. He sank back into his hiding place as the courting (for want of a better word) couple drove on past to the end of the track, from where, to his now heightened aural awareness, came the intermittent sounds of copulation in the cramped confines of a Carina. As Martin had suspected, neither party was interested in footpath signs, so he decided to wait about another hour before calling it a day – or rather night.

He settled down to consuming the soup, hoping to see a badger or a fox, and wondering whether he could, on subsequent such occasions, bring a personal radio if he kept it at a very low level. A few minutes after midnight, Martin decided to return home and set about gathering up his 'things'.

He was about to step forward onto the path when he heard a faint padding noise coming not from the direction of the lane along which had come the car, but from his right. To his amazement, three darkly clad, silent figures moved across his line of vision, proceeding at a brisk walking pace. There was something faintly menacing about the patrol (for such it seemed to be to Martin, perhaps on account of his own somewhat strange behaviour). The air of faint menace, however, gave way to one of a definite threat when, a few metres behind the main party, Martin heard the low growl of the sort of dog whose bite is even worse than its bark.

The handler paused, emitted a quiet but penetrating hiss to warn his colleagues, and, to Martin's horror, allowed the dog to lead the way. That way would shortly result in the discovery of a watcher who would find it difficult to convince this sinister group, particularly when speaking between the jaws of a less-than-friendly neighbourhood hell-hound, that he was only there because he was interested in nature and not at all in their nefarious activities.

As the dog pressed on, drawn by the scent of its prey, Martin could only crouch lower, unable even to think that he had every right to be where he was and would do better to go on the offensive, to step forward and confront them with their behaviour.

Somehow, even if he had had the time to reason logically, Martin perceived this group to be likely to operate outside the law. To the extent that he thought at all, it was to regret that he had ever put himself in such a dangerous situation. The dog growled again, now within a couple of metres of his hiding place, and Martin grasped the vacuum flask which had contained his soup, hoping to repel the beast for long enough for the handler to bring it under control – always assuming that he wish -shhhhhough!.... The explosion caused Martin to drop the flask, clutch himself and fall backwards. It also caused the dog to start violently, pulling over his handler, who let out a curse – just the sort of reactions hoped for by the pheasant, which had lain undetected for several hours and now made good its escape, having erupted out of the thicket with the maximum of momentarily paralysing noise. Anxious not to cause any more disturbance which might draw attention to the silent group, the handler pulled the protesting animal away, leaving behind an elderly gent whose heart raced and whose one desire was to get home and recover – but not until he was convinced that the coast was completely clear.

Conscious of his lucky escape, Martin waited until he had recovered his nerve and then emerged from his hiding place. As he was about to depart, his eye caught the gleam of a small object on the track. On a brief inspection it looked sufficiently interesting to take home, particularly as it had almost certainly been dropped by the handler when he was knocked off balance. He was not prepared to use his torch to check for anything else, but thought he might return in daylight, if he felt up to it. It was, after all, a public right of way, so there could be no problem in walking along it, especially if accompanied by one's dog.

Before going to bed, fortified by a bath and a large whisky, Martin had a look at the object he had picked up and found it to be a form of identity card bearing a three letter, three figure identification, a photograph and the letters H F C. Finally, despite his fright – and helped by the alcohol – Martin drifted off to sleep, vowing never to eat pheasant again and reliving the moment when the handler fell back, masking any noise that Martin himself might have made.

CHAPTER TWO

Martin felt surprisingly brisk in the morning – livelier, in fact, than had been the case for some time. Perhaps the surge of adrenalin had done him good, for he set off after breakfast with Sherry, to check out the spot where he had hidden and see whether the file of mysterious men (or, he mused, men and women) had left any other clues. The footpath signs had not been disturbed and there did not seem to be any other artefacts lying around. He wondered just how close he had come to being discovered, and found, as he peered into the hedge, a perfectly formed footprint, made, he thought, by a walking boot or trainer with solid notched grips. This was not surprising, given the silent approach and nature of the ground they had been traversing, but as it was under two metres from his hiding place, and the dog would have been about a metre in front of the man's foot.... it had indeed been a very near thing.

As these people were not a threat to his beloved signposts and had him no harm, there was no reason whatsoever for Martin to concern himself with the two matters which now occupied his mind. These were, of course, from where the group had come and to where it was going.

Some form of 'night hike' was a strong possibility, but scouts did not normally move as quietly as that – and were most unlikely to be accompanied by 'Baskerville' and his blaspheming handler. The army, or young offenders? The alternative of other pensioners behaving just as oddly as himself did not cross his mind – and in any case they had moved sufficiently fluently to set him thinking on the lines of a younger, paramilitary probability.

The answer was to follow their route and try to find out their destination, to set off in an easterly direction and see what transpired. It was reasonable to assume that they had followed the track, but after a few hundred metres it came to a lane forming a T-junction, with no means of knowing which way they had gone. After casting about for a bit, to no good purpose, Martin decided to return home, get on with some of the chores, and consider what, if anything, he should – or rather could – do to discover more.

The list of jobs, suggestions for meals, etc., included fish and chips for lunch, and as he had arrived home, he had seen the travelling 'chipper' trundling down the road to the next port of call. Martin decided to cycle after it, partly for the exercise and partly because it was possible to take the odd short cut through a housing estate if one heard its electronic chimes calling the faithful. Having cycled in vain for about twenty minutes, Martin gave up and considered the best return route.

As he got his breath back, he saw a van turn out of a road to his right and proceed slowly to the junction ahead. With a burst of energy, Martin accelerated after the vehicle, having noticed that it advertised fresh fish daily – perhaps because 'fresh fish weekly' had less of a ring to it – and there was no reason why he shouldn't cook his own rather than rely on the considerably more fattening version, nice though that might be. Jennifer would be suitably impressed, he thought, as he banged on the side of the van to stop it driving off, and cycled to the driver's window. Martin heard the driver reply briefly to his colleague, before winding down the window to see what the elderly cyclist was on about.

It transpired that he had no more fish to sell and was just on his way home, so Martin broke off the conversation and wheeled his bicycle forward. Then it occurred to him that it might be useful to discover when they delivered and whether one could order in advance. As he turned back, however, he caught sight of the driver's identity card, lying just behind the windscreen. The driver wearily wound down the window again:

"Well?" he asked, none too politely.

"I – er – just wondered – er – whether one could ... that is. ...When do you deliver?"

Martin found himself sounding like some doddering old fool, an 'act' which the driver seemed to find entirely in keeping with his appearance, which was perhaps as well, for the real reason lay in the nature of that identity card. It seemed to be exactly the same as the one dropped by the dog handler the previous night! Martin did not pay much attention to the driver's somewhat unconvincing explanation as to why it was not possible to order, partly because he was both disconcerted and excited by having picked up the trail again – and partly because he was reading the company name, which was blurred by a film of dirt on the side of the van. He apologised to the driver (in that typically British way which leads one to apologise when one is trodden on) and withdrew, having deciphered 'H F C FRESH FISH DAILY', which left him little better off.

Martin returned home without incident, without fish, but with a growing unease concerning the company he seemed to be keeping. As he rummaged in the cupboard for a tin of baked beans, he wondered how many were involved in this..... whatever it was. There had been three or four on the midnight trail and the van driver did not look like the photograph on the identity card that was now lying on the table, so that made five – plus the colleague to whom the van driver had spoken..... unless he had been the dog handler, of course. It then struck Martin that on returning to the van he should have gained some impression of the passenger's appearance – young, old, the same as this photograph, male or female. He had, however, no residual impression, and it was pretty clear why that was so: because the passenger seat had been empty. That meant that the voice Martin had heard just after he had banged on the side of the van had come from the back..... and the most likely explanation of *that* was not a talking cod, but a clandestine human cargo. There was, indeed, thought Martin, something very fishy about the van – and about the firm H F C. Martin decided to see what he could find out, and resolved to start by raising with Jennifer, when she rang that night, the topic of travelling delivery men.

His wife was pleased to hear that he had tried to buy and cook some fish (as opposed to purchasing the ready-fried version) and explained that there were plenty of suitable beans, which only needed soaking overnight. Martin shuddered at the word 'only', but pressed on to see whether his wife had ever actually bought any fish from Messrs H F C. It transpired that she had not, as she was never in when they called round, but that she had heard quite good reports of them from her friend Alison, who understood that they regularly visited Wothorpe Castle (a large feudal establishment some miles to the north). Martin was not certain that being known as a 'supplier of fresh fish to the gentry' was quite the same as a good report, but he found the information intriguing and only just stopped himself from conveying that impression down the phone.

"Where do they come from?" he asked.

"Oh, they always come from Hull," replied Jennifer. "There was one a few years ago, but he stopped – said it wasn't worth it in our area. Now remember you promised to pop down to Mother's to see how she is while I'm away. When are you going? And make sure that Sherry doesn't get into the hall, she likes to lie on the carpet and she's moulting at the moment."

By the end of the conversation, Martin found he had agreed to go down to Essex the next day. He also, somewhat belatedly, and to the animal's evident surprise and indignation, moved Sherry from her comfortable spot in the hall back to the utility.

That evening, Martin considered his next move. He could stake out the Castle, and try to follow the fish van, if it came; he could try to find out more about H F C; he could return to his original spot – or somewhere near-by – where he could make an intelligent guess as to the route the mysterious group had followed. Perhaps the answer would be to climb a tree to avoid the attentions of the canine scout. He did not fancy another encounter with the dog, however, and it could well be that no-one came for several nights. In the end, he telephoned an ex-pupil who lived in Hull, asking him whether he knew anything about the reliability of H F C as a supplier of fish. He also wondered whether any other of his scholastic contacts, built up over many years, could be of use. The local representatives of the aristocracy were not included in that list, for they were socially out of reach, as were most who lived in the shire counties and came from families whose origins lay far back in history – so far that they considered the present Royals to be upstart Continentals and regarded the feudal system as having been merely modified, rather than abolished, by the various events over the centuries. The ex-pupil was not surprised to learn he had retired, as he recalled a man of 'very mature years' some twenty years previously (when, in fact, Martin had been under forty!) but he agreed to ask his wife..... and then rang back half an hour later, with the disappointing news that there was no such company listed in Yellow Pages.

CHAPTER THREE

The next day, Martin set off, with Sherry moulting happily in the back, towards the Great North Road – or A 1, as it was rather less romantically marked on the map – and thence south to the M 11. As he drove, he reviewed his progress – or, rather, lack of it – and resolved to try to find a way of forcing the pace, regretting his failure to capitalise on having spotted another H F C identity card in the fish van.

This recognition of his feebleness on that occasion was still in his mind as he registered the presence of a white van, parked on the hard shoulder just south of Cambridge. He slowed, noted that the driver was in the process of changing a tyre – and noted, too, the name on the side, visible now because it had been washed. It read 'H F C' – or something sufficiently like it for Martin to feel once again the adrenalin rising, as he drew away down the motorway, wondering how he could follow it. He slowed down to about thirty miles per hour, feeling somewhat conspicuous as an even more elderly man, wearing a hat (a sure indication, he always considered, of a doddery driver) had to pull out to overtake him, his octogenarian wife showing a need not so much of Help the Aged as Help the (Road) Raged. The turn to Duxford was signalled ahead, so Martin decided to leave the motorway, lurk with the bonnet up where he could see approaching southbound traffic, and thus be in a position to follow whether the van turned off or not. This ruse worked quite well and he was soon in pursuit of the H F C van, whose driver (always supposing he had something to hide) could have no reason to be suspicious.

As the miles passed, Martin began to wonder how far he would have to go: London? Dover? Budapest? No, there was no GB plate, thank Goodness. The van signalled its intentions in good time to turn off as if for Stansted airport, but then took the A 120, going east towards Dunmow and Colchester. It was less easy to follow without alerting the quarry, particularly as Martin lacked the necessary training and had no 'back-up' team. Whether or not the driver was aware of being accompanied, he took no evasive action, presumably reasoning – if indeed he bothered to think about it – that it was not so surprising if another vehicle was going the same way as himself. The trail continued beyond Colchester until it became apparent that it would soon have to stop – at the North Sea. Martin was not inclined to push his luck by following the van to its ultimate destination, but at Harwich it carried straight on at the turning for the cross-channel ferries, making for the old town. Martin, although wary of making himself conspicuous, followed, deliberately driving on when it turned left towards the church and the quayside. By this time, Martin was in fact intent on finding his own destination – the nearest 'Gents' – followed by a cup of coffee and a pause to take stock, consider his next move and concoct some suitable tale to explain his late arrival to his mother-in-law.

The last was not difficult. He invented a flat tyre and added that he would have to wait until it had been repaired before resuming his journey, thus giving himself time to do some sleuthing. Restored by the coffee and a filled roll, Martin asked the cafe owner for a local telephone directory and looked up H F C in the business section. There was nothing as such, but there were, not surprisingly, several firms with those initials: Harwich Flooring Co.; Hardman, Fletcher and Charles, Solicitors; Harwich Fishing Co.; Harwich Ferry Contractors ..... . There were a few others, but Martin decided to try the Harwich Fishing Co., given the supposed nature of the business conducted by the van's owners. The address was in East Street, the whereabouts of which Martin easily discovered by asking when he filled up with petrol. He parked well short of his target and set off on foot, accompanied by a sprightly Sherry, towards the quay.

The search was made easy, however, by the presence of the H F C van outside a run-down corrugated iron building which carried no identification. Martin walked on past, not merely to disguise his interest, but also because he found that he now had no idea what to do. There was no sign of activity – no sign of fish, for that matter – and he felt that to call in on some pretext might prove counter-productive, should he be recognised in the future. It seemed to be another occasion for his secret weapon – local intelligence – supplied, in this case, by an ex-colleague.

Stephen had spent three years in Martin's department, before going on to 'higher things'. He was now Head of an 11 to 16 Community College in Harwich, and, as luck would have it, could spare Martin half an hour or so before setting off on the 'night shift', as he described it. There was to be a Governors' committee meeting, discussing the curriculum, including an input from the Humanities department. Stephen reflected philosophically that the governors (for whose benefit this was supposed to be) would probably be out-numbered by the staff and expressed envy of someone who had 'escaped' before the era when the early retirement rules were changed, known cynically throughout the profession as 'taking prisoners'.

"So, what can I do for you, Martin – looking for some supply work? Or are you into selling a textbook designed for a syllabus which has since been radically altered?"

"Well, it's a strange request, really, concerning the Harwich Fishing Company. Do you know anything about them?"

"Such as what?" asked Stephen. "Two of their lads have been through the school. No great shakes academically, but no problem – and the father was very supportive."

Martin considered making up a tale about a 'scratch and run' minor vehicle accident, but then decided to put his friend in the picture, outlining briefly the reasons why he had gone so far as to follow the van to its destination. He left out the bit where he had hidden in the hedge, as it made him look even more ridiculous, but said he had found the identity card whilst 'out walking'.

"Quite the little Jack Slipper, aren't you?" laughed Stephen. "I'm glad to see you've not lost your sense of adventure – even if the sense of proportion is a bit shaky! No, I can't think of anything which indicates the Harwich Fishing Co. is up to no good."

Martin was conscious that he had taken up sufficient of a busy man's time, and felt a bit embarrassed as he contemplated the thin series of coincidences which passed for 'evidence'. The knock on the door provided a suitable moment for him to take his leave, so as Stephen called out 'Come in!', Martin gathered up his anorak.

The member of staff who entered was introduced as Harry Bartlett, the Careers Master and, to Martin's mild consternation, Stephen asked him if he knew anything about the Harwich Fishing Co., adding, with the facility for instant mendacity possessed by all good Heads, that Martin was doing some work on the history of the local industry. Mr Bartlett gave a similar vote of confidence in the firm, adding that one of the lads had done his work experience there, reminding his boss that when he had been to visit, he had gone, by mistake, to the building next-door, where a very surly chap had eventually opened the door, holding a vicious looking Alsatian on a short lead.

On an impulse, Martin fished the dog handler's identity card out of his pocket and showed it to Mr Bartlett.

"Yes. That's the chap! But how come you ......?"

"The less you know the better," said Stephen smoothly. "You've been very helpful. Martin is in fact involved in a bit of positive vetting for the Foreign Office and it looks as though this H F C and the Harwich Fishing Co. may have been confused with each other again."

"I don't know if it's of any help," said Mr Bartlett, who was clearly nobody's fool, "but after that reception, I did a little checking on the establishment with the dog. It seems to be known as H F C, thought to stand for the Harwich Factoring Co., but seems to exist in order to do a bit of fishing and a bit of diving – especially the raising of sundry artefacts, occasional gold coins, et cetera, from a Spanish armada wreck a few miles off shore. They don't find much, or don't declare much, but seem fairly innocuous – apart from what might be seen as an exaggerated desire to discourage casual callers. Oh! And they're ex-directory, as are, of course, many eminently respectable people.... including headteachers!"

After thanking the two men, Martin set off towards his mother-in-law's place in Leigh-on-Sea, pondering the new information he had acquired and revisiting his idea that he would have to make some positive move rather than rely on chance encounters, valuable though those had proved to be.

Shortly after arriving in Leigh, he set off with Sherry for a walk in Belfairs Park, earning black looks from other dog owners, as he was too abstracted to pay proper attention to the whereabouts of his dog in relation to others. He did manage, however, to decide on a course of action, which made him rather better company on his return to the meal which, several hours delayed, awaited him on the table. He had resolved to compile a reasonable imitation of the H F C identity card, substituting his own photograph, and pay a visit to the local seat of feudal power, which, his wife had claimed, was known to be visited by the so-called fish-vendor. It might not throw anything up, but it was possible.

Having completed one or two minor jobs around the house, Martin took his leave, gratefully loaded a cake and several pots of jam into the car and set off back to Lincolnshire.

CHAPTER FOUR

Despite having arrived very late the previous night, Martin was up early and, with the connivance of David, the caretaker, had used his wife's school's photocopier and a plastic wallet designed for student identity cards, to compile an effective-looking version of the H F C card.

On his return home, he had a cup of coffee, checked on the times when one could visit Wothorpe Castle, and then strode briskly in the direction of a stretch of woodland which should contain plenty of interesting smells for Sherry. From time to time, Martin whistled the dog in, a task made easier by the almost total silence within the wood, whose tall, bare trees masked the distant background hum of traffic and prevented the sound from being snatched away by the wind. The effect within the ancient woodland was either peaceful or eerie, depending on one's mood. In the past, on such walks, Martin had productively pondered the best way of explaining the Theory of Comparative Advantage to his older students, and the best way of outwitting the efforts of the younger ones to learn as little as possible.

On this occasion, the image of pupils past – whose falsely innocent faces and earnest lies had long been replaced by equally inaccurate assurances that the product they were now selling was ideal for the purpose – faded from his mind, as Martin considered how best to approach his forthcoming visit to a seat of inherited wealth. He was reluctant to face the obvious, namely that he would neither see, hear (nor smell in the case of the fish connection) anything which would give him a lead.

These thoughts were interrupted by the realisation that he was approaching the edge of the wood and ought to bring Sherry to heel. She was gathering intelligence via her nose at a thicket by the side of the track and as he bent down to slip on the lead, Martin noticed, just inside the brambles, a perfectly formed footprint in a patch of yellow clay. Two things could be described as significant about the footprint. One was that it was, if his memory served him correctly, exactly the same as the one he had found so close to his hiding place, when he had gone back to have a look on the following day. The other was that it was underneath the brambles in such a way that they had to have been placed there *after* it had been made.

Martin grasped the vegetation in his gloved hands and – rather as he had suspected – it came away easily to reveal a sort of tunnel through the undergrowth along which one could proceed at a crouch. It led to a deep ditch which ran across the fields at right angles to the border of the wood, showing distinct signs of fairly frequent use by various animals, including the two-footed variety which walked upright. Intrigued, Martin carried on for a hundred or so metres, feeling rather like a would-be tomb robber in the Valley of the Kings. The sight of a heron rising lazily ahead of him, long legs trailing, long neck carefully tucked in, dispelled the Egyptian image and substituted one of a mediaeval messenger to Hereward the Wake, hiding out on a remote island, surrounded by sky.

The dog still on the lead, Martin clambered to the top of the ditch and surveyed the bleak landscape. Had he been further west, on what passed for a hill, he could have seen as far as Crowland Abbey in one direction and the church tower known as Boston Stump in another. As it was, there was nothing apart from a collection of run-down buildings and an old brick-built farmhouse about a quarter of a mile away. To one side, the high bank of a river could be seen above the level of the surrounding land. From the other side, there ran a line of old-fashioned telegraph poles, along what was presumably the access road, and the ubiquitous high voltage electricity pylons cut across the fields, running north to south.

It was an isolated spot, sheltered to the east by a belt of woodland, and it was the only possible goal for those who chose to tread the route which Martin was following. Convinced that he had found the destination of the mysterious midnight walkers, Martin returned to the seclusion of the wood, regretting his lack of a pair of binoculars, and wondering where the access lane joined the main network of roadways. Once back at home, Martin turned his attention to making himself look respectable, and preparing lunch, prior to the afternoon visit to the Castle.

Having decided to leave the Audi and take their other car, an old blue Renault, Martin set off, thinking that at least he now had another lead if (as was only too likely) nothing transpired when he contrived to show his forged H F C card. He was quite pleased with the look of the card, and with the simple way he had been able to alter the number on the first photocopy and then re-copy the result. He had changed one of the letters, an E, to a B, by inking in the joining sections, and adopted the reverse technique with one of the numbers, using Tippex to convert an 8 to a 3. He was, however, to come in due course to regard that aspect of his forgery as having been a mixed blessing.

Martin drove up the gently curving, mile long carriageway, towards the imposing, beautifully maintained buildings, parked near the stables (now containing a café and various 'museum areas' of transport and implements of a bygone age) and strolled towards the main entrance.

The average age of the other visitors was about forty, but Martin did not feel out of place, apart from being a man on his own, as the average encompassed about half being under seven and the other half over sixty. He hoped not to be noticed in one way, but in another he was conscious of attempting a bit of lion's tail twisting – or at least provoking some reaction to his H F C identity card. He had already practised removing a ten pound note from his wallet in such a way that the card fell face up and felt very happy with the way the manoeuvre was accomplished. He was disappointed by the lack of reaction, however, for the lady on the till welcomed him exactly as she had the others, asking whether he had been before and offering him a booklet. He replied, truthfully, that he had been before and, in answer to her further enquiry, expressed his admiration for the Grinling Gibbons carvings.

"Yes, I thought you might like those," she said. "You'll find a particularly interesting example in an alcove at the far end of the long gallery."

Martin thanked her, picked up his change, the ticket and his H F C card and set off for an anticlimactic tour, taking in the portraits of haughty ladies and, in this case, chin*ful* wonders, painted next to their much more intelligent and, if the truth were told, rather better bred, gundogs. Despite the real purpose of his visit, Martin gazed with genuine interest at the many exhibits and felt uplifted by the magnificence of the proportions of the rooms.

As he was about to leave the long gallery, he remembered the ticket seller's comment concerning the woodcarvings executed by the incomparable Grinling Gibbons. He had already seen the one he remembered from his previous visit and turned back with interest to examine the alcove. As he peered at the panelling, he was amazed to see it move before his eyes, disclosing a narrow passage, leading to downward spiralling stone stairs, which appeared safe, if ill-lit, and were clearly part of the oldest section of the house. Intrigued – and not a little apprehensive – Martin stepped cautiously down until he came to a small door on his left, giving a choice between it and continuing down to the lower levels of the ancient spiral stairwell. He tried the door, which opened smoothly to reveal a small windowless room, lighted by two wall sconces, once designed to hold torches (in the more literal sense), now adapted for electricity. As he entered, a young man rose from behind a modern, utilitarian desk, greeted him briefly and asked him to be seated.

"I'm afraid I don't yet know everyone, as this is my first day on this job," he apologised, "so I shall need to make a note of your number."

He held out his hand, into which Martin placed – on the reasonable assumption that this was the number to which he referred – the forged identity card. To Martin's surprise, the young man practically sat to attention at the sight of the card, giving a low whistle of almost awed approbation.

"That's some number," he said. "Were you on it? Or on the other one?"

Martin tried to hide the fact that he was appalled that he had contrived to forge the one number which would guarantee he was remembered, and thought frantically how best to answer a question which meant absolutely nothing to him. Fortunately, the young man came to his rescue, apologising this time lest he be thought impertinent.

"With a number like that," he added, "I suppose you're used to us youngsters being impressed!"

Martin reassured him that no harm had been done and agreed that it had happened before. In fact, he was dying to ask what was special about the number (which at that particular moment he could not even call to mind).

"I presume you've come for these in place of 584," continued the clerk, anxious now to make amends for his gaffe. "He had some problem with the van on the way to Harwich, didn't he?"

Martin felt sufficiently confident at this point to agree that the van had had a flat and was not as reliable as it once had been.

"Yes, and I heard he thought he'd been followed by some old boy in a white Audi, all the way from the M 11 to the Shell garage where you turn off in Harwich."

Martin had just about recovered from his consternation when his number had caused so much interest, but this piece of information left him thinking it was high time he departed – with or without the package which was now being pushed across the table.

"Well, that was probably just a coincidence," he opined, hoping to damp down the Organisation's interest in both Audis and 'old boys'. "I must be on my way, anyway."

"Yes, of course, Sir. Follow me!"

This time the slight awe in which he was held had caused the 'Sir' to be slipped in, and Martin hoped fervently that it would prevent any further conversation or check on his bona fides. They emerged behind a hedge which enabled Martin to slip, unremarked by the other visitors, back to the car park. There he lost no time, albeit without making his mounting concern apparent, in setting off back down the long drive. Among several wildly spinning thoughts in his head, there arose that of his departure being watched on CCTV, combined with heartfelt thanks that he was in the old blue Renault, and not the Audi.

In fact, Christopher, for such was the young man's name, entertained no suspicions concerning his distinguished visitor, who had to be one of the top men to possess a number like that, and who was clearly taking the opportunity to check systems under the guise of standing in for Gerald. Should he say anything to anyone? To the Agent? Would it be better to pretend he had not noticed, and to get the credit later for being discreet? His desire to share the news vied with his desire to prove his reliability and ability to keep a secret and avoid gossip. The latter won the day, which resulted in Martin gaining a useful breathing space.

The real courier drove up to Wothorpe Castle, supposedly to enable them to restock with fresh fish, about 36 hours later. Another hour or two was wasted checking their story that the papers had already been handed over – and checking on the description of number 534, who had seemed so familiar with the procedures and the problems experienced by the van driver. Eventually, they were forced to the conclusion that the two 'old boys' must be one and the same and that they were under serious investigation, possibly by the security forces, or an enterprising reporter. Christopher was interviewed and questioned closely as to what had been said: in particular, what the impostor had said concerning the number 534. He insisted that the visitor must have been genuine and indignantly rejected criticisms of his gullibility when faced with what must have been a forged I D card.

CHAPTER FIVE

Meanwhile, lying low as the rain teemed down, Martin busied himself with some domestic tasks, while trying to decide what he should do. He had opened the packet and discovered three sets of documents, which he had concluded must be forgeries made for sale to illegal immigrants. Martin had recently read about this lucrative trade and rummaged in the pile of newspapers which were ready to be taken to the skip, to remind himself. The more he read, the more convinced he became that this was what he had stumbled upon. The Fenland connection was there in a reference to the illegal immigrants being found jobs with 'gangmasters' who supply cheap labour to farmers. This system was quite common in the seasonal horticultural trade, with mini-vans setting off from as far away as Sheffield, and a high proportion of foreign-born (although not necessarily illegal) workers. The deals resulted in would-be immigrants paying up to £10,000 for transport, forged documents, legal assistance and a job on arrival. An immigration minister was quoted as saying that there was increasing evidence that organised crime was heavily involved as the profits were greater than those from drugs and prostitution. The numbers slipping through the net were estimated as thousands and the wretched people were often held prisoner in this country until further moneys were paid over – or they were forced into bonded labour to pay off the debts. More ominously, reference was made to the prevalence of violence if debts were not paid. Kidnap and murder were not unknown; members of both Triads and the Mafia were included in the international ramifications which spread to Russia, China, Colombia, Turkey, Brazil, Nigeria and the Indian sub-continent.

With mounting concern, Martin read about a 'forgery factory' run by a Turkish group in Islington, a Derbyshire lorry driver jailed for trying to smuggle 24 Asians through the Channel Tunnel (claiming he was threatened at gun-point in Germany) and a Romanian family of 22 found wandering by police in West Thurrock, Essex, at about three o'clock in the morning. Martin gazed thoughtfully out of the window at the pouring rain and considered his position. He could – nay, should – take the documents to the police and voice his suspicions, even if aspects of his own behaviour made him seem a little ridiculous and even if it meant that he would almost certainly never hear the full story, which, he reluctantly admitted to himself, would always be a nagging disappointment. Also, he continued to muse, what could he say about the isolated Fenland farmhouse, for which he felt certain the original midnight group was making? Was a footprint, now washed away, likely to be seen as significant? Perhaps the best thing would be to see if he could find out a bit more – and then decide what to do. This scheme commended itself to him as much for the fact that it put off any real decision as for the concept of keeping him in the hunt. He was reminded of a discussion he had had with his wife some years previously. It had concerned whether he should try to become a headmaster and the qualities needed. At the same time they had been considering where to go on holiday, something he tended always to leave until everything was booked. He recalled the thoughtful and essentially supportive way in which she had agreed that he was academically well qualified, relatively literate and numerate, willing to work long hours, and good with people of all ages, from stroppy teenagers to experienced governors (even if the greater need was an ability to get on with stroppy governors and terrifyingly experienced teenagers). Jennifer had then added that he had one other attribute which should stand him in good stead, namely that of flexibility and the ability to weigh the pros and cons of any situation. As they had returned to the holiday brochures, she had qualified this statement by saying that no headmaster she had ever come across had been able to take a decision and stick to it. Headmistresses, on the other hand..... .

Reasoning that he might have a little more time before the Organisation went onto full alert, Martin decided to stick to his earlier idea of checking out the isolated farmhouse. He did not fancy plodding through the mud to within effective range of his binoculars, so set off in the Renault to find a road which would get him as near as possible. There were several remote-sounding settlements marked on the map, such as Moulton Seas End, Gedney Drove, Tongue End, Marshland St. James, but the nearest minor road appeared to be called Marby Dyke Drove, off which there ran a thin line culminating in a small un-named mark near to the river Glave. It seemed likely that the mark was the building in question, so, uncertain just what he would do when he got there, Martin climbed into the Renault and set off.

Crossing the bleak, windswept terrain, Martin thought that one had to have drawn the short straw to find oneself earning a living in such a spot, fertile though it might be. There seemed to be little by way of a really significant windbreak, not merely as far as the eye could see, but right across the North European plain. The wind continued to blow from the south west, bringing the rain, but if it were to swing round to the east this would indeed be a grim spot to be exploring on foot.

The unmarked, narrow, pot-holed lane was not in fact difficult to find, but after four or five hundred metres, Martin came to an open gate with a weather-beaten, faded notice, which informed the reader that he or she was about to move onto a private road, the property of Hall Farm Cultivators. The addition of 'Trespassers will be prosecuted' did nothing to encourage a would-be customer, and the thought flashed across Martin's mind that, given what he suspected, it could be that 'prosecution' would be the least of an intruder's worries. The buildings were just visible from this point but they were partially hidden by the belt of trees which Martin had seen when he had first discovered the probable goal of the dog handler and his companions.

Martin drove on past until he ran out of road (as he had expected) at the edge of a vast stretch of land from which sugar beet had fairly recently been harvested. He made a pretence of studying the map (just in case he was under surveillance) whilst deciding where to spend a few hours observing, in the hope that a person or a vehicle would arrive or leave, thereby giving some indication of the nature of the inhabitants and their business.

This time Martin had brought his binoculars and as he drove back he spotted a likely piece of cover for himself from where he could keep the farm access in view. He had to leave the car further away and make his way back on foot, feeling slightly exposed, hoping to rely on the binoculars as evidence of an intention to birdwatch, should he be observed. After two hours, he was feeling stiff and cold, and bored. There had been some activity – a post van which stopped a short way along the 'private road' to leave the mail in a rusty box set on a post, and a figure wearing a non-descript anorak with matching accessories, who walked down to collect it. Admittedly, it indicated a desire to keep people away, if not even the postman was permitted to approach the buildings, but he had not been able to see the face of the person who collected, as he (for that much Martin assumed from the walk and general build) kept his head down, looking neither to right nor left. The other unsatisfactory aspect was his failure to get a good look at the buildings from this approach, for they had appeared to be quite extensive when he had seen them first – although on that occasion he had had no binoculars.

Martin regained his car and sat thankfully in comparative comfort for a few minutes, before setting off home. As he sat, he noticed a light plane approaching from the south. This was not remarkable in the Fens, where a number of wealthy farmers had their own airstrip; neither was it remarkable that it was flying low – around 1000 feet. What was remarkable, however, was the fact that it flew lower, and slower, until it disappeared behind the line of trees, which was all that Martin could see from this distance to mark the spot where lay Hall Farm.

Martin felt certain it had landed at the farm, and cheered up at having gathered further evidence that things were not all that they seemed. That such a derelict looking business had a landing strip (and possibly its own plane) was certainly of interest. It encouraged Martin to renew his efforts to get a better look at the place, and forced to the surface a thought which had been lurking in his mind, as yet unformulated: the best approach route had to be the river. Martin drove slowly back, mulling over the best way to use the river in order to get close without being observed. In the loft they still had an inflatable boat which had seen service on many a holiday when the children were small; it should still be usable and, if he could take advantage of a moon-lit night, it should be possible to allow the current to take him right to the spot. As the craft was rather unstable and likely to overturn if it hit a floating branch, Martin decided to be well prepared for everything by borrowing some suitable gear. As fishing was the country's major participator sport (a fact unknown to many) and as Lincolnshire was one of the major counties in which it took place, it would not be difficult to borrow a form of 'wet-suit', with waders which went up to the neck, on the pretext that he wished to bath his dog in the river.

At this point the word 'dog' reminded Martin, as he drove homewards, that he had a book on dogs in the car which he had promised to return to the people from whom they had borrowed it. A detour in the direction of Stamford would not take long, and it would mean that at least one of his many tasks would have been completed.

Unknown to Martin, the pilot of the light plane circling above, tailing the car whose presence he had reported on landing at Hall Farm, now radio-ed back to his base that he was still able to follow its progress, and might even be able to report where it came from without having to organise any back-up. Normally, Gerald Gridley, who ran Hall Farm, would not have reacted in quite such an alarmist fashion as to order the plane to take off again and check on a parked car, but they had just spotted a man walking near the edge of the property, so it seemed worth it. In fact it was very easy for the pilot to follow the car home, note that it had parked in the drive, and even see what he took to be the owner disappear round the back and enter the conservatory. He duly reported back that the car came from a house at the top of Lark Hill, circled for a few more minutes, then set off back to base.

Having established that his friends were out, Martin spent some time searching for some paper and a ball-point with which to write a brief note of thanks and then left the book in the 'lean-to', round the back. He was vaguely aware of a light plane moving away from him in an easterly direction as he returned to the car, but not, of course, of its significance.

The small van which set out shortly after from the nearby Road Maintenance depot arrived just too late to find the blue car which had been followed from the air. Neither the two men in it, who waited for about an hour, nor those despatched to carry out surveillance throughout the evening, witnessed its return (not surprisingly, as it was by then in Martin's garage). That night a file of men, complete with dog handler and dog, set off purposefully from Hall Farm, following back lanes and bridle paths to the top of Lark Hill. Entering the property from the back garden, they searched the empty house (whose owners were away on holiday), finding nothing which was, from their point of view, suspicious.

There was, as it happened, a blue car in the garage, so they contented themselves with disabling it, and passed the name of the eminently law-abiding inhabitants back to their superiors for evaluation – and appropriate action. During the search (a detail which was not contained in the report) one of the men pocketed an attractive, but not in fact very valuable, brooch when the others were not looking, unable to resist the easy opportunity, and keen to build up some capital for the day when he was given his documents and allowed to disappear into society.

Unaware of his narrow escape, Martin busied himself at home with household tasks, reassuring telephone conversations with his wife.... and acquiring the necessary equipment to investigate Hall Farm. The weather forecast looked quite promising for the following night, so Martin set himself to plan the exercise – for he was coming to think in quasi-military jargon, unaware of just how appropriate it was, given the attitude of his quarry.

Having decided how to go, what equipment to take and where to leave the car and to join the river, Martin allowed himself the luxury of considering what he hoped to achieve, indeed *why* he was going. The idea of getting close was all very well, but if it was a night-time approach, he was not going to see the layout, and would find it difficult to decide where to snoop, apart from watching a lighted window (if there were one) which might give some idea of how many people lived there, and their nature.

Martin decided to delay the aquatic expedition and return to the spot where he had found the second footprint, this time with his binoculars, and then work his way round, still at a safe distance, to survey the establishment in daylight.

CHAPTER SIX

The next morning he set off early with the dog to give her a short walk before following, alone, his earlier route to the edge of the wood from where the farm buildings were visible. It was a bright clear day, and promised to stay the same overnight – excellent conditions for the river approach. He found the hidden pathway without difficulty, but continued along the edge of the wood for a hundred metres or so, until he came to an ideal angle from which to observe. The main building was constructed of brick, ground floor plus two storeys, with about eight windows at each level, indicating a substantial number of small rooms. The tiled roof was covered in lichen, the window woodwork had not seen paint for years and the doors looked as if they were seldom, if ever, opened. There were various open sheds, a long, low strawstack, covered in a plastic sheet, weighted down with old tyres, and some brick-built sheds with concave tiled roofs. The inevitable corrugated iron, both as a roofing and a walling material, blended with rusting farm machinery, sprinkled with old tumbled hay bales between which grew a selection of hardy weeds, docks, nettles, and self-seeded scrubby trees. The whole was not untypical of a certain type of Fenland property, although one which had an airstrip was normally a total contrast, well maintained, including smartly painted fences, gleaming silos and an environment in which a weed would feel extremely conspicuous. In the morning sunlight, the property looked shabby rather than picturesque, and little could be discerned behind the uncleaned windows, other than matching curtains. It could be said to lack a woman's hand.

As he studied the outbuildings, Martin suddenly noticed the figure of a man standing near the long strawstack, although he had not noticed him arrive. Presumably he had come from round the back, the side on which grew the belt of trees, which (Martin knew from his earlier surveillance) screened the landing field. The man walked, carrying what looked like a clipboard, towards the back of the house and was lost to view, so Martin swung his binoculars back, and concentrated on an interesting shape in one of the upstairs windows. It was a triangle, about head height and...... With some embarrassment, Martin lowered his binoculars, as it occurred to him that what he was looking at was a person looking straight at him, also through binoculars. The sides of the 'triangle' were the arms, and the apex was the face. Too late, Martin realised that the bright sunlight must have given away his only partly screened position, by glinting on his lenses. It could be argued that only someone watching out for 'spies' would have seen him, but this was no time for quibbling. Rather, it was time to leave.

Inside Hall Farm, the watcher, in fact the man 'on watch', for the Organisation had been sufficiently alerted by recent events to post a look-out, put down his binoculars and spoke into a 'walky-talky'. Very shortly after, two quad bikes fitted with containers for crop-spraying – and as such quite innocent tax-deductible farm vehicles – set off from a dilapidated barn, driven by capable, athletic, unsmiling 'labourers'. Their instructions were to catch up with the unknown observer and at the very least find out who he was and where he lived, but not to flinch from bringing him back to the farm against his will if his actions showed him to be sufficiently suspicious. The boss had added that if this person fitted the general description of the impostor who had called at Wothorpe Castle and the driver of the car which was thought to have followed the van to Harwich, he should definitely be brought in. With this last eventuality in mind, one of the quad bike drivers was armed, but warned that on no account must other, genuine, members of the public see or hear anything out of the ordinary.

In addition to the two men despatched swiftly to the place where the glint of binoculars had been spotted, Gerald mobilised other forces. A helicopter pilot was contacted to go immediately to take off from Peterborough Business Airport, about twenty miles away, to look out for anyone breaking cover from the wood, and another member of staff from the farm, accompanied by two reliable Asian 'customers', hidden whilst awaiting documentation, were sent to patrol the eastern edge of the wood. Through the Organisation's links with the local 'gentry', it was not too difficult to summon up equestrian assistance (mainly female, but none the less effective for that) to stand around at strategic corners, covering the western and northern edges, although very few could be in place in under an hour. They were told to look out for a lone anti-hunting saboteur, take a mobile phone with them and telephone in if they saw anything. This time, Gerald was determined to find out who was on to them – and neutralise the threat.

Martin had departed rapidly back the way he had come, but had not gone far before hearing the noise of motorbike engines, which he had no doubt were driven by people anxious to make his acquaintance. All the thrillers he had ever read or seen on film combined to conjure up packs of martial arts experts, nets placed among the leaves under his feet to close and whisk him up towards the canopy of tall trees – and silenced firearms which, on this occasion, might be aimed rather more effectively than was normally achieved by the average 'B-movie baddy'. After a few minutes, however, reason reasserted itself and Martin stopped to hear the sounds of pursuit sufficiently distant as to cause no immediate problem, providing he kept moving towards the wood's western boundary, which was well away from Hall Farm. He also persuaded his head to overrule his heart, reminding himself that this was the Fens, not Viet Nam or Eastern Europe, and that he was a respectable (not to say boring) retired teacher out bird-watching, who had every right to focus his binoculars on a run-down farmhouse if he so wished.

On reaching the edge of the wood, Martin emerged carefully and surveyed the open countryside. Apart from two people on horseback approaching from the west (a common enough sight), the coast seemed clear, so he moved off at a rapid walk away from danger. In fact, of course, Martin had allowed himself to be driven, like a deer or pheasant (but not a fox which was altogether much craftier!) by the 'beaters' towards open country. In this case, things were made worse because he failed to recognise the danger represented by the horse-riders, who had now split up, circling to cover the other two sides of the wood from which he had just emerged. On seeing a lone figure who fitted the profile she had been given, the horsewoman, who ran a local stables and regularly rode to hounds, acted calmly and cleverly. She stopped and turned away so that the fact that she was using her mobile phone could not be seen, and then continued slowly towards a different part of the wood.

Quite unaware that his goose was virtually cooked, Martin continued, somewhat relieved that there was another member of the public in the offing, as it would prevent his pursuers from trying anything physical. Not, of course, that they would, but one nev.... Martin's thoughts were broken into as he became aware of the unmistakable phutter-phutter-phutter of a helicopter which could now be seen approaching from the south, flying at about 500 feet. The coincidence was too great and Martin's earlier (as he had thought) wildly exaggerated fears of a hi-tec chase, reminiscent of spies coming in from the cold, returned and caused him to turn back in panic towards the comparative safety of the wood which, he now realised, he should never have left. As the report came in from the jubilant helicopter pilot, Gerald could only curse the element of 'over-kill' which had resulted in one searcher over-turning the good done by the other.

"You bloody fool!" he shouted into the radio. "You've spooked him now: we were just closing in and he thought he was safe. Get that noisy lump of iron down here before you do anything else stupid. You can at least help to search the wood."

"You asked for the bloody chopper," retorted the pilot, who had been less than pleased to be turned out at such short notice, and felt he had done all that was asked of him and more. "You didn't say it had to be invisible as well. What am I supposed to do? Make smoke?"

"Oh! Shut up and bring her down here. We can still get him: he can't get out once I've got everyone in place, unless he has the sense to wait until dark, and even then the dogs should be able to sniff him out."

Martin stumbled, gasping from the effort of running, into the short term safety afforded by the trees and undergrowth and crouched low in dense cover to get his breath back and allow his pulse rate to slow. What now? Should he try to get to the horse-rider and ask for help? If only he had brought his mobile phone, he thought, followed by the realisation that it would probably not work amongst the trees – and who should he try to contact anyway, the R A C?

31

Before he had managed to think out a sensible plan of action, he heard the sound of approaching voices coming from his right. It was clear that they had abandoned all attempt at stealth and were now openly communicating by their walky-talkies, guiding each other to his last known position. Martin crept deeper into the wood, hoping to lie low and let his pursuers move past him: there did not seem, as yet, to be any dogs nearby. Whether this strategy would have worked – or how the hunters would have acted had they reached the edge of the wood and realised he was lurking somewhere behind them – was never put to the test. Instead Martin, with growing horror, became aware, as he approached the main central footpath, of a line of people blocking his eastwards route. As he peered, still unnoticed, through the undergrowth, he saw that they were waiting for those in front, who were at a junction in the footpath system, to decide which way to go, consulting efficient looking maps. They appeared, at first sight, to be respectable to the point of total harmlessness – but that could have been said of the fish van, thought Martin, as he waited for them to make a move. The lead pair turned, after a couple of (agonisingly slow) minutes, and called back:

"Take the left-hand fork and keep going until you reach the edge of the wood. We'll pause there for everyone to catch up."

Martin was so intent on not being seen that he almost missed his opportunity, indeed almost failed to realise what he had found – a group of respectable ramblers all dressed (and mostly aged) exactly the same as he was. He stepped out onto the track and hurried after the last of the group, pulling a woolly hat from his pocket, and removing his glasses, hoping that this simple attempt at disguise would be sufficient to make it impossible for the Hall Farm gang to work out which one was their quarry. Martin also relied on the fact that not all those who had set out on that day's ramble would know each other, would realise that he had just joined them – or even mind if he had. After about two hundred metres, Martin had positioned himself fairly centrally within the line and had passed a few words with several of the walkers, thus enabling him, should it prove necessary, to engage in more animated conversation. In due course, they emerged from the wood, passing two young, 'unrambly-looking' men, whose eyes Martin was careful not to meet.

It was in this fashion that Martin escaped from the wood, finished the walk and departed for the nearest telephone box to ring for a taxi, a ride in which, he reasoned, would prevent his pursuers from spotting, whether by air or by horse or by car, one of the group who had to walk home a suspiciously long way, having no means of transport. Martin asked the taxi-driver to wait whilst he went indoors to get some money, having explained in response to his friendly interest, that he had developed a blister so did not feel up to walking all the way home. As he handed over a fiver, Martin thought that it was money very well spent, as was the additional 'price' of appearing to the taxi driver to be a bit of a wimp, having failed to complete a ramble which some who could give him at least ten years had found no more stressful, indeed less so, than a visit to Queensgate Shopping Centre in Peterborough, just before Christmas.

CHAPTER SEVEN

As Martin immersed himself in a deep, hot bath and began to take stock, things were much less tranquil across the Fens at Hall Farm. At each level the fear and insecurity of the superior resulted in the inferior(s) being blamed for their failure to discover the identity of the elderly investigator. When at last they got around to doing something more productive than blaming each other, they, too, took stock and called a conference, including the Area Commander, John Dalton, who flew in from Colchester.

Firstly, there appeared to be one person involved with no back-up. Secondly, that person seemed to be remarkably naïve and lacking in tradecraft, easily panicked, unable to conceal his actions. Thirdly, however, he had acquired the means to penetrate the Organisation and demonstrate considerable knowledge about its origins and activities and was now in a position to make a connection between the Fens and Harwich – and they did not know how far beyond those two 'cells' his investigations had taken him.

"He knew about the 534 and the 'Retter', so he knows our real allegiance."

"So he must know what's been going on at Harwich."

"And he knows about the illegal immigrants, because he collected the documents."

"He'd already made the connection with Wothorpe Castle, so he probably knows about the Scottish dimension – or can make a guess at it."

"And he probably knows about Thorpe Tunnel."

At this point another, less alarmist, voice joined the discussion, reminding the group of the other aspect of the enigmatic investigator, namely his naïveté and lack of professionalism.

"I am not convinced," said John, "that he has put all this together yet .... but I am convinced that if he were to retail it all to the wrong people in Intelligence, they would very soon put two and two together and make not just five but fifty-five. This old fool must be stopped before he does any real harm."

"When you say 'the wrong people' in Intelligence, do you mean we have some 'right people'?" asked Gerald.

"You would do well to forget you heard that, and have more sense than to ask," came the reply. "You know what curiosity did to the cat."

Gerald had merely been going to suggest that, if they did have sympathisers in British Intelligence, they could be asked to keep an ear to the ground so that any move in that direction could not only be headed off, but could also be turned to advantage in discovering his identity and associates. Faced with the thinly veiled threat from his superior, however, Gerald did not put forward this eminently sensible suggestion, reverting to the rôle of bumbling local commander who was not paid to think, just to do as he was told. The conference broke up on the more positive note that the 'old boy' was sure to try again and that his luck could not hold for ever. They were to be vigilant, swift to act and remember not to under-estimate an opposition which, to date, had eluded detection in ways which showed an element of resourcefulness, even if there had been a heavy reliance on what could only be described as very good fortune.

Blissfully unaware of the forces which were being mobilised against him and lacking virtually all the knowledge ascribed to him by the mysterious Organisation which he was discovering as he followed up his original quest for midnight footpath sign removers, Martin luxuriated in his bath, considering his next move. He had borrowed some gear suitable for a night approach to Hall Farm by river, which he planned to undertake as soon as the weather was suitable, and was considering how he could cause 'them' to make an expedition from Hall Farm which would lead him to the other destination – the place from where that original group with the dog handler had been coming. In addition, Martin ran over in his mind the strange conversation at the Castle. What had the young man said? 'Were you in it – or the other one?' And was he not deferential, almost reverential? Was there even more to this than a bit of illegal immigrant-running, presumably via the port of Harwich? Just how extensive was the organisation if it could call up light planes and helicopters, and get its forging done courtesy of the aristocracy? Where else did the fish van call, and what other rackets were they involved in?

Martin got out of the bath, dressed and studied the map to determine the best point at which to embark. That was fairly obvious, there being a section of by-passed road which carried a bridge, providing a secluded spot where a parked car would attract little attention and a geriatric would-be member of the Special Boat Service could clamber unnoticed into his inflated craft. Martin had been turning over in his mind the best exit route after his reconnaissance – especially if a rapid departure seemed called for. To paddle upstream was not an option, especially as the river was in spate, although that same condition would help if he could carry on downstream. The answer was to leave one of the cars at a point two or three miles away, where a road came close to the river, return and set off in the other one. With appropriate timing it should be possible to walk a mile or so to a point where he could catch the local 'Delaine' bus back to near his home. His lack of a team – or at least a partner – was beginning to prove a problem (but who else would join him in such an escapade, other than someone who only had his straight-jacket removed at weekends?). Martin put away the map after spotting a single track 'drove' which ran to a point about fifty metres short of the river some three miles downstream from Hall Farm. He then climbed up into the loft to get the old inflatable which he hoped was still serviceable enough to carry him down the Glave to a point close to the farm buildings. The little dinghy proved quite easy to find, although it took longer to locate the pump and some time to inflate it sufficiently for test purposes.

Martin had taken the dog out and fed her and himself by the time his daughter rang to make sure he was not fed up and bored (bored!). He reassured her that he was coping quite happily, eating proper food, getting plenty of exercise and sleeping well. Putting down the phone, he decided on an early night in order to make a prompt start in the morning to set up the 'getaway' car, return and prepare for an early evening departure.

Having slept well, Martin rose full of keen anticipation. The morning's activities worked out satisfactorily. He parked the car, secreting a spare key under the offside wing in a magnetic holder which he had had for years and never bothered to use and stepped out briskly towards the main road after climbing up over the high bank and down to water level to mark the spot with a 'flag' made from an old dishcloth. Having walked back just over a mile to the main road, Martin only had to wait about half an hour before the familiar blue bus hove into view, precisely on time, to bear him westwards across the bleak Fenland countryside.

Once it was dark enough for his purposes, Martin stowed the half-inflated boat and paddles into the car, and pulled on the all-over waterproof fishing waders which he had borrowed, covering them with an old anorak lest he be noticed as he drove off. A thermos of soup, torch, elasticated tape (used when playing tennis) to stop his glasses falling off, spare clothing and a balaclava completed his equipment. After a final look at the weather, Martin set off to a point well up-river which was accessible by road. He had often taken the dog there for a swim, and as an afterthought once again included her lead, so that he could pretend to be calling her if discovered walking nearby. He felt that he might pass as merely an eccentric (how right he was!) to a passer-by, even if the dog handler and his friends were unlikely to be similarly impressed. Once again, the adrenalin was flowing and Martin's movements were more fluid and his senses (but not, it must be admitted, his powers of judgement) were sharper. He drove without incident to his chosen launch site, parked the car in a secluded spot and completed the task of inflating the plastic boat.

After several days of rain, the water was flowing very rapidly, and he had little need of the paddles, other than as a means of fending off from the bank as he sped effortlessly downstream, overtaking branches which rode lower in the water.

Although one could see more at river level from the light reflected on the water, the speed at which he was travelling made the spill inevitable: the boat bumped violently into a heavy, half-submerged log, tipped its crew overboard and moved off, gathering pace, into the night. The current was strong, but the river was still shallow enough to walk with one's head out of the water – except right in the middle, and

Martin had had the forethought to put his few supplies (the thermos, etc.) into a canvas bag which was attached to his wrist.

Hoping to catch up with his transport, Martin set off to wade down river, stumbling on the uneven surface and cursing his failure to attach a line to the boat against such an obvious eventuality. In the dark and with the high retaining banks cutting off the immediate view, it was difficult to work out exactly where one was, and had he remained on board Martin might well have been swept beyond the farm. As it was, he decided to climb the near bank in order to get his bearings. He was nearing the top when suddenly, less than fifty metres ahead, both banks were flooded with light. The surprise and fear of exposure felt by Martin, however, was as nothing compared to that experienced by the fox which had unwittingly triggered a hidden alarm. The unfortunate animal stood silhouetted on the top of the far bank, looking across (although from where he was Martin could still not see them) at the darkened windows of Hall Farm.

Suddenly the fox crumpled to the ground and lay there motionless. Martin raised his head cautiously above the bank and looked towards the floodlit buildings. The alarm triggered by the fox had done him a great favour, as he was well away from the light, invisible to them, but able to observe the inhabitants' reactions. As Martin watched, he saw an opening appear in the long low strawstack covered in old tyres. Light spilled out and shone on the figure of a man in his shirtsleeves, looking towards the river bank. Another man emerged from the house, carrying...a rifle. It was not possible to hear what was being said, but Martin had the impression from his gestures and the second man's body language, that the latter was the subordinate, being given orders to go and check up. The boss also asked for the gun and, as it was handed over, Martin could clearly see the telescopic sight and a wider shape at the muzzle which seemed strangely familiar and had to be (as he recalled the sudden collapse of the fox) a silencer.

"And raise the sensors while you're there!" Martin heard the instruction as it was called after the departing guard, who was striding towards the river. This last order made sense to Martin, as he could see that they would be keen to avoid a false major alert – still more, he suspected, unnecessary use of illegal firearms. Leaving the door into the strawstack open, the senior man went into the house, carrying the rifle, so Martin searched for a lighted window to see where he went. As he peered intently at the darkened building, he saw a slight movement at one of the top windows, which was open, making it clear where the shot had come from.

Martin now turned his attention to the riverbank. The first man was pulling himself across to the far side by means of a line attached to a small rowing boat – in effect, a sort of chain ferry. Once at the far bank, he climbed up, threw the dead fox into the river and then bent down among the bulrushes. He straightened and moved up river until he was almost opposite. This area was dark, but there was enough light to see him bend down again among the undergrowth. The sensors – that's what it must be, thought Martin, and he looked cautiously around. The man returned to the left bank and continued with the task of adjusting the height of the sensors. It was not until the final one, less than ten metres from where he lay just below the top of the bank, that Martin saw what he was adjusting. It was made to look like a bulrush – invisible to the casual glance (which is all the average person gives a bulrush!) – but, when you knew, could be detected as the only one in a clump which did not sway in the wind. Somebody had spent quite a lot on the security of Hall Farm, and was even prepared to arm a guard to keep out intruders. When that guard moved on round the remainder of the defences, Martin raised himself, being careful to keep below fox level, to continue his inspection of the premises.

Within Hall Farm, however, another person had been on the move. He had taken advantage of attention being confined to the area where the fox had been killed, and of the temporary absence from the strawstack bunker of the boss, to slip inside the open door. Somewhere in there, he was sure, could be found the papers he had been promised, for which his family had paid so much. He was fed up with being an unpaid – and effectively imprisoned – member of this organisation for which he was forced to work. He was expected to help to steal vehicles, moving by night from one hidden base to another either on foot or in a closed van, unaware even of his destination. Once inside the Bunker (as it was called), Ahmed paused to look for a filing cabinet or desk which might contain the papers. To gain access, he had gone down a short flight of steps into a small, bare room, containing only a desk, phone and three chairs. It took a moment to establish that there was nothing to interest him there, but his eye was drawn to the far end where another door, followed by a further, longer, flight of steps, led into a larger room containing a bank of television screens, one of which showed him a guard about to return from the far side of the little river. With mounting panic at the thought of being caught in the act, he looked round the room, taking in the red and black hangings, the black and white photographs of men in naval uniforms and, across one end, a blown up print of a warship moving rapidly through the water. Hurriedly, he pulled open drawers and lifted up piles of papers, hoping to find those vital documents. Choking down a cry of frustration at his failure to find what he wanted, he turned and scrambled up the steps, expecting at any moment to be confronted with his captors. His only thought was to get away – to where he did not consider – before they found out that someone had seen the inner room and tried to steal the documents.

On the long, often freezing journey across Europe, Ahmed had been in no doubt about the ruthlessness of those whose assistance he had sought. To stay now, he was convinced, meant death – a death easy to cover up, for officially he, like others before him, did not exist, and his family would assume that he had perished somewhere along the hazardous route. As silently as he could, bending low, he moved away from the buildings, seeking the cover of the dark and the undergrowth and praying that it would be some minutes, at least, before his escape was discovered.

Martin heard first, and then saw, a figure coming towards him. The furtive nature of his movement, the way he stopped to look behind and the lack of guile had he been trying to sneak up on the hidden watcher, convinced Martin that this was an escape in progress – an escape that was about to fall foul of the bulrush sensor which lay between the fugitive and the river bank. Taking care not to raise his body, Martin wriggled forward and whispered loudly:

"Stop! There's an alarm sensor near you."

Fortunately, despite the panicky nature of his departure, the terrified Asian froze. Martin crawled closer and whispered:

"Follow me – and keep close to the ground. There's a sensor hidden in the rushes."

It was no time for explanations. Neither party knew quite what to expect of the other. One had little to lose and the other felt that anyone who feared the Hall Farm hierarchy deserved help – and might throw valuable light on the whole organisation. Slowly and carefully, they worked their way back to the level of the river, which Martin knew to offer their best chance of undetected escape. Martin lost valuable time persuading his new partner that the best route lay downstream, back towards the farm, but eventually they slipped into the water and half swam, half floated in the rapid current, expecting at any moment the sounds of discovery, which, they both well knew, could be followed by extreme action.

It took Paul, the guard, several minutes to complete his tour of the sensors, after which he reported back to Gerald, who had remained on watch at the upper window. The latter remained for a minute or two looking out at the night when he returned to the Bunker, then stepped inside. The howl of rage coincided with all the perimeter lights coming on as Gerald discovered the intrusion. All the inhabitants, illegals and legals (if one could use such a term for those who worked for the Organisation) were quickly mustered, resulting in the discovery of one significant absentee. Search parties quickly despatched and the dogs were woken from their slumbers and provided with an article of Ahmed's clothing.

From his vantage point, Paul unconcernedly noticed what appeared to be a fairly large log floating past the 'ferry', considered taking a pot shot at it, but restrained himself, remembering the lecture he had recently been given on that subject, and continued to search the night for the missing Ahmed. The dog soon led them to the river bank, where the trail ended, calling into question the direction of flight thereafter.

"Which ever way he went, he can't get away quickly," reasoned Gerald. "It's dark and he doesn't know the area. More importantly, he's got no transport or contacts. He'll move more rapidly if he went downstream, but we can go round by road and have a good chance of spotting him if he tries to hitch a lift."

"He'll be sopping wet, too, so no-one's likely to pick him up," said the other assistant, Henry. "He'll look as if he's on the run, which'll help, too."

"He may be struggling upstream – more than likely, as he'd have had to come back towards the farm otherwise – so I'll take the dogs and see if we can pick up his trail where he comes out of the water. You drive round and work your way back up river from Moulthorpe Drove. Once it's light, we'll get the chopper airborne and I'll have a word with one or two coppers I know."

"If he does get away, surely he won't say anything? He won't want to draw attention to himself."

"There's a problem there," replied Gerald, grimly. "He got into the bunker while I was upstairs, and ...."

"You didn't leave the inner room door open, did you? You don't mean he knows about the ....?"

"No, of course not. He probably didn't even realise he was looking at a U-boat, still less what it was used for. But if he were to tell the wrong people, someone might put his two with their two and make five. I want that young man back, Paul, alive or....not."

CHAPTER EIGHT

In his all-over waterproof outfit with a balaclava, Martin was able to float past the floodlit section giving a good impression of a log, and contrived to shield his companion from the watcher in the top window. To their relief, they were swept along unnoticed (happily unaware of the passing thought of a casual shot by the guard who had shot the fox) and soon gained the safety of darkness. At a bend in the swollen river, a branch had stuck, and various items of floating debris were building up behind it, one of which was the inflatable dinghy.

Martin grabbed his companion's arm and pointed to the boat. They scrambled on board, not waiting to disentangle other flotsam which had attached itself to the line and rowlocks, for a rapid escape was essential. Once in the boat, they speeded up and, less than ten minutes later, Martin spotted the marker flag he had prudently planted near his parked car. There was no time to deflate the boat, so it was allowed to float off in the general direction of the North Sea, and the two men, wet, cold and not a little frightened, still crouching although there was no immediate danger, ran to the car. Ahmed (as Martin had discovered him to be named) was by now beyond being surprised that there was a get-away vehicle. He waited patiently while Martin searched for the key (which turned out to be under the offside rather than the nearside wing, as he had at first thought) and eagerly got into the back, changed into the spare clothing and crouched down on the floor as instructed.

To begin with, Martin drove slowly, without lights, but on gaining the main road, he speeded up and relaxed, allowing himself to start thinking of the implications of his virtually knee-jerk reaction in aiding the runaway – and remember to remove his balaclava. Occasional cars passed in both directions just after he joined the main road and then his headlights picked out a white van, parked in a lay-by on the near side. The quick glimpse he had of the letters H F C painted on its side as they swept past was sufficient to raise his heartbeat and it was all he could do not to speed up and draw

43

unwelcome attention to himself. Fortunately, all that could be seen from the van was an elderly gent, driving soberly home, manifestly not accompanied (or likely to be accompanied) by an Asiatic on the run. His somewhat unconventional garb was not discernible, although it did make Martin think that he had better not take a route which caused him to stop at traffic lights (particularly in an area where he was known!). His mind ranged over the scenario of him explaining to one of his more bourgeois friends why he was dressed in a tight-fitting rubber suit, accompanied by a young semi-clothed Asian, who preferred to travel in a crouched position, next to a heap of wet clothing, both of them smelling of river mud.

In fact, they arrived home without further incident, and in due course had cleaned up, donned dry clothing and were facing bowls of soup which had arrived on the table by way of the freezer and the micro-wave. As the meal progressed, Martin listened with mounting sympathy to the story told by Ahmed, whom he now perceived to be quite young (eighteen, he claimed, but Martin thought that sixteen was more likely). Others with whom he had set out had not survived the terrible conditions, including, at one time, twenty hours in the back of a refrigerated lorry, next to boxes of frozen chips. His main worry was that in running away he had lost his chance of getting false papers which would enable him to get work, save and send money home to repay the thousands paid to the organisation which ran the smuggling – and make it possible for the family to survive. The tears of frustration, shame, anger even, flowed as he related the tale.

"The papers must have been there somewhere," he said. "I got right into the inner room but there was not much time – and if I'd been caught....." He shuddered and then turned to his rescuer: "Can you get me papers? I'll steal for you, work for you, I'll even.... ." His voice died away and he lowered his eyes.

"Even what?" Martin asked, thinking mainly that he needed to draw Ahmed out on the contents of the 'inner room' and other aspects of H F C and their wider connections.

"It was why I decided to go," came the reply. "It was because of Gerald. He... he....."

"He had it in for you? He made you work too hard?"

"No, no. It was the opposite – he liked me, he gave me extra food, and he wanted to ...."

"Bugger you, you mean," said Martin sadly, realising he had been a bit slow-witted.

"Yes. They told me when I left home that I could earn money this way, if all else failed, that I was only ...."

"Eighteen?" Martin interrupted, with a smile. "Never mind that – or stealing. You can help me by telling me all you know about the set-up, particularly in this area. We'll start where I started. There's a regular route through the woods, going west from the farm: where does it lead to?"

"To the other, much bigger, bunker. They call it Thorpe Tunnel and there's a hidden door, leading into a large underground area, with electric lighting, cooled air, telephones, and several locked doors we never go into. I think that's where they keep the stolen goods. They grow mushrooms there as well, and there are bags of something called 'peat' – explosives we think – and ....."

"Hold on, hold on. Is it an old railway tunnel, with a security fence and a road running over the top of it?"

"Yes! I thought it might be a good place to escape from – to get a lift. There's quite a lot of traffic."

Martin searched his memory for something he knew about Thorpe Tunnel. It had been built in the late nineteenth century and the line had been closed in the 1950's, but there was something about it ... . Yes, he remembered now. He had, for a brief period, been acting senior teacher some years previously and liaison with the Civil Defence had been delegated to him. As a result, he had attended a meeting called to familiarise everyone with the procedure when we received four minutes warning of the arrival of a Russian rocket bearing a nuclear bomb. The main concern of most of those attending centred on the list of people who were adjudged sufficiently important to the continued running of the country to be allowed into the nuclear bomb-proof Area Government 'bunker'. To some this might have seemed of little interest, given the nature of the devastation and the remote chance of finding oneself both within 200 metres of the entrance and in a position to receive the warning. However, it had soon become clear to Martin that the rules of precedence were extremely important as they reflected *status*. Was the Mayor of a small town more important than the Chairman of a parish council? Both were third tier authorities, neither had any significant power (unlike, say, their French equivalent) but neither was willing to be left out if the local Cadet Force Captain was allocated a place. Yes, Thorpe Tunnel – that was it: the bunker which, rumour had it, had started its 'clandestine' life as a base for the local (anti-German) resistance movement, during the second world war. Now *there* was a well-kept secret, thought Martin: all those poachers recruited to slit Nazi throats if *they* had won the Battle of Britain!

"Right! Thorpe Tunnel. Let's have a look at the map," said Martin. "Yes. Here it is – and there's Hall Farm, with the river running along to the south, and your cross-country route through the woods about here.... and along this track... here."

"You know the route well!" Ahmed sounded surprised. "If you are this chap we were trying to catch, they are making a mistake: they think you have not much idea. Gerald said you were a 'bumbling old busy-body'. What does 'bumbling' mean? Is it busy, like a bee? Are you a policeman – or a secret agent?"

Martin, privately thinking that Gerald was not far out in his assessment, tried to look enigmatic and avoided a direct reply to the lad's desire to improve his vocabulary.

"The less you know about me the better, young man. Carry on telling me what you know. You say you got into this 'inner room'. What did you see? You mentioned a picture of a boat: what sort of boat?"

It took several questions and recourse to an illustrated Encyclopaedia before Martin was satisfied that (a) it was a submarine and (b) it had a number rather than a name painted on the sail. This latter forced him to the conclusion that it was a German craft, for the English equivalent would have had a name, such as Ursula, Utmost, or Upholder. Further questioning concerning the red and black décor pointed to an interest in, if not an actual connection with, the Third Reich and the Nazis. Martin might not yet be at a point where he could make two and two make five (the development feared by the senior men in the Organisation), but he was beginning to let his imagination stray beyond suspicions of mere smuggling and forgery.

"And what is there at the farm? How many work there apart from those like yourself who have been smuggled in by this – er – the 'Organisation'?"

"I've only seen three, but Gerald is in charge – and sometimes, as happened recently, others fly in by plane or helicopter to see him. They make sure we don't meet those people."

"What else can you tell me?" asked Martin, eagerly. "What do they do? What happens to these stolen goods? What do you know about H F C, or visiting local country houses?"

At this point, a calculating look crossed Ahmed's face, and Martin remembered that, whilst the lad might be grateful to his rescuer, his main aim was to get the papers with which to obtain work – and money. It had clearly occurred to him that he possessed knowledge with which he might bargain.

"I can't remember anything else. They kept everything hidden from us," Ahmed mumbled.

Martin noted the mood of mulish stubbornness and reflected that, whatever cultural differences there might be between the continents, adolescents bore remarkable similarities. Was it not an ex-head of Eton who had said of the boys that they would either let you down or do you down? As he pondered how to use the potentially powerful weapon which Ahmed represented, in his investigation of the dog handler and his colleagues, Martin suddenly remembered the package he had been given so trustingly by the clerk at Wothorpe Castle. He had only glanced at it but now was the time to take a closer look. He made an excuse to leave the table and nipped upstairs to the drawer under the bed, where he had placed it, along with other important documents, such as passports, his will, etc. It took only a few minutes to discover that the batch he had been given included some for Ahmed – with a different family name, but bearing his photograph. The lad's opinion of the meaning of 'bumbling' would be even higher, Martin thought, if he was told that documents could be provided. More importantly, he would be willing to co-operate fully if, as a result, he received the papers. If he knew that they were in the house, however, there was a risk that he might try to steal them – even to the point of using violence to do so. Martin debated with himself the propriety of aiding and abetting an illegal alien. Should he not turn him over to the police, drawing their attention to the possibility of the presence at the farm of firearms, and of stolen goods in the bunker? Ye-es ..... but on the other hand he had not rescued him in order to turn him in and he was very conscious of the enormous sacrifice made by the Asian family. The main crime was committed by the Organisation which made hundreds of thousands of pounds, casually causing the death of many of the desperate human cattle whom they 'helped'. Ahmed at large (and believed to be still in the area, but increasingly fearful of discovery either by 'the law' or themselves) could be a potent weapon.

Martin returned to the kitchen, just in time to see Ahmed moving away from the telephone, holding a scrap of paper.

"What are you up to?" demanded Martin, his mind full of theft or betrayal. Had he been about to ring the farm to tell them where their persecutor was, he wondered?

Wordlessly, Ahmed showed him the piece of paper, on which was written Martin's telephone number.

"I'm s-sorry," he stammered. "I thought I might want to ring you in the future or..... ."

A thought suddenly struck Martin, causing him to interrupt:

"You will have done the same in the bunker. Is that right? You can give me that number in return for keeping mine."

He could hardly stop him remembering the number anyway – and it was not such a great crime. One could call it sensible and, a pound to a penny, he had done the same at the farm.

"I – er – I'm not sure I can remember it," said the lad, unconvincingly. "I think it was something like 3424, or 4324."

"Right!" said Martin, firmly. "Let's get something clear. I can get you some papers, but my bosses are going to need something from you. You've no money, but if you co-operate fully, and I *do* mean fully, I'll recommend that we help. Is that clear?"

To Martin's consternation, Ahmed burst into tears and flung his arms round him, promising he would do anything they wanted, and would be forever in his debt.

Pushing the young man gently down onto a chair, Martin cleared his throat, and renewed his quest for useful information. First of all, he asked for the number on the telephone in the farm bunker. Ahmed had written it down and went to get it from his pocket, before realising that the paper had become sodden during the escape by river.

"Never mind!" said Martin, seeking to calm the lad's tendency to panic. "Just take your time and imagine yourself back in the bunker. Now close you eyes and tell me all you remember: the furniture, the pictures, other doors, the floor – everything."

Other items in the inventory were not particularly useful, although he described a swastika in the midst of the 'red and black' mentioned earlier, and said that the local boss, Gerald, was one of the men on the U-boat. Martin was intrigued by this, but did not wish to break Ahmed's concentration, so he let him carry on. It did, however, seem unlikely that Gerald would be pictured on a vessel which was presumably destroyed either in battle or by scuttling over fifty years previously. By now in an almost trance-like condition, Ahmed continued reporting what his inner eye saw – including the all-important telephone number.

"I put the paper into my pocket," he continued, "with the keys, and then I turned and ran out, knocking over a pile of books. Then I got away from the house as quickly as I could, until you told me to stop – and helped me to escape."

"Very good!" said Martin. "You've remembered the telephone number. Now, can you remember the number of the submarine?"

Ahmed thought hard, but could only say that it was three figures and might have been 458: he had not paid it much attention.

"Not to worry. Is there another phone in the house, and if so, has it the same number?"

"No, I don't think there is: they used what they called 'walky-talkies' around the place."

"Yes, I know. It's a sort of phone with no wires," said Martin by way of explanation. "I keep one in the car."

To his surprise, Ahmed corrected him immediately:

"No. Not a mobile phone. These were different. You had to press a button to talk and it would only work over about a mile."

"Did you see mobile phones before coming to Europe?" asked Martin, as the boy seemed so certain.

"I had heard about them," came the reply, "and, of course, I saw Gerald using his. It had a leather case and bleeped as you...."

"Er, Gerald's mobile: you don't happen to know the number of that, I suppose?" asked Martin as casually as he could.

"Oh, yes. We all had to memorise it – but not write it down!" beamed Ahmed, writing it carefully next to the other one.

"This is excellent!" said Martin. "Just one thing more – unless any other ideas occur to either of us. You mentioned some keys; what did you do with them?"

Again the young man, intent on providing value with which to impress Martin's mythical bosses, tried to recall the exact sequence of events during his hectic few minutes in the bunker.

"I – I don't know," he sighed at last. "I think I must have dropped them when I knocked over those books, unless I put them in my pocket – with the scrap of paper I'd written the telephone number on."

"In which case," continued Martin sadly, "they are now at the bottom of the river. Oh well, you can't win 'em all – and I can't see myself nipping round there to try them out, even if you had kept them!"

"Have I told you enough?" asked Ahmed anxiously. "Will they give me my papers? Please tell them I have co-operated!"

"I think," said Martin, somewhat ponderously, "that you have a very good chance, but before we move you out of this area, I want you to help me to bamboozle our friend Gerald."

"What is 'bamboozle'?" queried Ahmed, "And Gerald is not my friend: I told you I would not let him ....."

"Yes, yes. Just an expression," assured Martin hurriedly. "I'll explain in a minute. Now, where do you want to go to? London?"

"They said they would get me fixed up in Leicester. It's a small town over in the west, with plenty of work and plenty of people of my race. Can you take me there?"

Martin had reservations about the availability of work in the 'small' town in question, but could see that it made sense. However, it definitely did not make sense to go to a place where they would expect Ahmed to go – and probably had several 'business partners'. It would be much wiser to go to another town with a substantial Asian population, such as Bradford, he explained. Then, noticing the drooping eyelids opposite, and suddenly himself feeling in the grip of fatigue, decided to leave the nature of his plan for 'bamboozlement' to the morning.

CHAPTER NINE

Andreas Ketels dozed gently on the settee in his expensive home in a much sought-after part of the Wirral. At the age of eighty, he was one of a steadily dwindling group who had formed the hand-picked crew of the 'Retter', each of whom had been personally briefed by Grossadmiral Dönitz in those far off closing days of the war. As Hitler's chosen successor, Dönitz wished to approve personally those charged with the task of carrying on the fight, of bringing about by whatever means presented themselves, the resurrection of the Third, or rather the Fourth, Reich.

"Germany has lost the war. You and many like you are charged with making sure that she wins the peace!"

Andreas still remembered the stirring words, of feeling proud of the bravery, not of himself and his colleagues, who were going to live and deceive and prosper in Japan, in South America or, as in his case, having spent many long school holidays there, in England....but of those who planned the whole scheme, yet stayed behind to face disgrace, hardship, death. It was nearly time for him to be driven to the monthly meeting of the 'High Command', but he continued to dream, to reminisce, to marvel at their success. He recalled the night departure from Lübeck, the last minute conference with the Captain of the XXI class 534 (who shot himself in '48, fearing, it was thought, that he would give away the secret if his mind started to get feeble with old age) and then returning, full of confidence, to supervise the loading of the 'Retter'. What a boat! If only we'd had a hundred of those in 1940 – or even in '43. The gold was already on board, he recalled, smiling to himself. Enough to fund their operations for ever, or so they thought. Why should the metal have broken the rule of centuries? It had half the buying power now of, say, ten years ago. The old man was dreaming now, seeing the precious human cargo, the young boys, fair-haired – just like so many in East Anglia, thanks to their marauding forebears a thousand years before – all excited, some tearful, all quiet, over-awed by the moment, as yet unaware that they were to be submariners and risk the horrible death experienced by so many of their fathers.

"Time to go!" He remembered hearing the order: "Time to go!... Time t..." Ketels awoke with a start.

"Time to go, Sir!" repeated the young driver-cum-bodyguard, whose father had been one of those children the old man had been dreaming about.

"Oh, it's you. I must have dropped off for a moment. What's that stuck in your ear, man? An earring? Get rid of it – and if you're wearing lipstick, take that off as well!"

Kevin Parrish flushed with concealed anger.

"Orders, Sir! We're supposed to look like everyone else, give no hint of our breeding by," he quoted from memory, "higher standards of dress, speech, deportment or lifestyle than that appropriate to our temporary calling."

"I see," replied the old Nazi, icily, "and do I take it that you have recently downed ten bottles of lager and watched a violent video in your avid pursuit of ethnic decadence?"

Without waiting for a reply, he rose from his settee, already regretting his peevish outburst and placed an arm in the sleeve of the coat held by the object of his sarcasm. The latter swallowed his irritation, reminding himself that his moment would come, that soon he could act like this old relic, but with real underlings, with the trappings of power and wealth, able to boast of his lineage. It would be, he thought, like those descendants in America of the Founding Fathers: they, too, had made a perilous journey by sea.

"Take me past the old 534," ordered the passenger peremptorily.

"Is that wise, Sir? We have been asked not to show too much interest in her."

"Just do as I say!" instructed the old man. "There is no reason why *I* should not show an interest. Unlike yourself, I have the honour – and cover – of having been a loyal servant of the Reich, who has served his time as a prisoner."

Without replying, Kevin turned off to take them past the Maritime Museum, outside which could be seen the wreck of U-534, raised at great expense from the Kattegat, where she had been sunk by Allied aircraft in May 1945, attempting to escape, like so many others. The old man chuckled quietly:

"They thought they would find gold and papers and important relics – and they found nothing! They'd got wind of the importance of the cargo, but they didn't realise her rôle! 'Proceed on the surface; fire your anti-aircraft guns if attacked. Draw them away: the 'Retter's' special covering should hide her from their radar, but we must take no chances. Sacrifice your whole crew, if necessary – and hint at your keel being filled with gold. Let them think they are the chosen ones. Draw them away as the hen partridge pretending to have a broken wing: don't let them find the fledglings'. Did I ever tell you about the 'Retter'? Hydrogen peroxide for fuel; nearly 30 knots under water; invisible to radar – 'stealth' they would call it now – able to stay under water almost indef....."

"Yes, Sir. You did – and so did my father. Shall we move on? It's getting late."

"If we'd had fifty Type XVIII's!" continued the old man. "The scientists at Eckernforde put all their efforts into developing them after those rockets failed to tame the British. Most of them were captured in Lübeck Harbour, before they were fitted out. They only needed a small crew, you see – and practically noiseless!"

"Which was the one which surrendered eight days after the capitulation, half way to Tokyo?" asked Kevin, deciding to humour his passenger, from whom he had heard the stories a hundred times.

"That was U-234! She was one of twenty long-range boats, taking the top-ranking party members to South America and Japan. They left it too late, of course....but some of us were successful."

Silence fell, as the old submariner relived that last journey. Off-loading the precious human cargo, including his own baby son, to be collected by English sympathisers just off Blakeney, in Norfolk. Then back down the coast to the final resting-place. It was the gold – they were right, it was the most expensive keel ever made – which had let them down. They'd salvaged it gradually over the years under cover of the wreck of a Spanish galleon, but now it had to be drugs or immigrants.. it was clever, the cover for that, declaring a little, and.. it was the keel, and she was built to stay down for ever... but the gold was falling, so they had to use other ways...and the rockets .... but the gold was f.... The old eyes closed, and Kevin drove slowly off.

"Time to go! Time to go, Sir! Wake up, Sir! We're there." But this time there was no sudden awakening from a dream. The sleep was deep......and permanent. The High Command would have to choose a successor.

The meeting was cut short, the start having been delayed by the need to comply with the formalities associated with a sudden death. In this case, there was no question of foul play: Andreas Ketels had fallen asleep and died, essentially of old age. 'The best way to go', they all agreed, adding, in their private thoughts, 'better by far than the hangman's noose, or an SAS bullet'. The Chairman tapped lightly on the table:

"Can we make it brief, please, Gentlemen. Just confirm all is well or if there is a problem. I'll run down the list. Finance?"

"Gold may rise a little as a result of the slump in Far East share prices: it's a haven in times of trouble. We're watching closely, and will unload more if it rises enough."

"Right! International movements?"

"Immigrants are flourishing. There is pressure building to tighten the regulations, which should squeeze out some of our, shall we say, less well-connected, competitors – and enable us to raise the fee."

"Thank you, Alistair. Let's move on to those connections you mentioned. Police?"

"We're still keeping the women more or less in their place. There's unease about failure to deal with those known to be corrupt – to move to a less rigorous level of proof. On the other hand, we could find more and more people in quite influential positions willing to – er – supplement their income, as they fear for a future without state benefits as of right for the old."

"Thanks. Did you arrange this right wing government for us, Eric?" The Chairman paused for a moment to allow the laughter to subside, and then added: "Don't answer that! Just give us an idea of the political scene."

"The U S of E is looking more and more likely – and when it comes, no country within it will be able to match the influence of a united Germany!"

"Careful my friend: don't fall into the trap of under-estimating the British. Our predecessors did that!"

"We're well advanced with our referendum campaign, Malcolm. We shall be able to bring a whole new meaning to 'forecasting the result' by the time it takes place. The electorate here imagines that only blacks are capable of rigging elections. I can confidently forecast the result we want!"

And so it went on round the table. The Army would support a right wing coup, the Air Force to a lesser extent (but the move towards integration of command was making that less of a problem). Schools were more or less under control now, becoming accustomed to sudden, unexplained, changes of direction dictated by central government. The emphasis on the inculcation of basic values and state-approved religion was very helpful, making it easy to label those who questioned as woolly-minded left wing thinkers (or, better still, agitators).

"I still advise the Movement to change its policy on homosexuals: there is nothing left wing about the concept, and, indeed, it goes well with our approach to women. Many of our most loyal supporters are closet gays, frightened only of being denounced to – ourselves! Can we not....."

"I asked for a brief report, David. Bring this up next time. We could always 'fail to succeed with some manifesto items' – after all those who supported Clinton don't seem to have got much out of it!"

"But votes are not the point: I consider we should really put away our prejudice and...."

"Not now!" said the Chairman firmly, to sympathetic and, in several cases, hypocritical nods from the others. It was all very well for David with his reputation as an ardent womaniser, but for others, anything other than disgust, preferably expressed in a way which was technically illegal by the current law of the land, could spell the end of a promising career in the Organisation.

"Next please: the regions. Any problems?"

"Nothing too serious, Chair, but there is...."

"Can we dispense with these politically correct expressions, John. There is not going to be a female in the chair! You're a Rotarian, you should know better!"

"Sorry, Chairman," continued John smoothly, veteran of a thousand meetings, ready with the timely 'on a point of information', or the terse 'seconded'.

"I also operate at District level, school Governing bodies and, of course, the River Board. One finds oneself slipping into the... ."

"It sounds as if one had recently been talking to one's monarch," sneered the Chairman, to sycophantic smirks from some of the older members, "but do, please, carry on. What is the nature of this – ah – problem?"

Stung by the older man's patronising attitude, John Dalton, Leader-Designate of the Blackwater District Council (and Controller-Designate of one third of England, from Colchester to Newcastle, when the New Glorious Revolution took place), replied in what only he recognised as ageist terms:

"It concerns what my man Gerald describes as a 'bumbling old busy-body' who has been spying on their local base, Hall Farm, for several days, and the recent escape of a young immigrant."

John paused, to be rewarded with a curt request to continue.

"They nearly caught him in the woods near the farm, by enlisting the aid of a local riding school, who were led to believe they were rounding up a hunt saboteur.... but he evaded capture. Gerald blamed the helicopter pilot, and the unfortunate arrival of some ramblers."

"Shock troops indeed!" interjected the Chairman, who found himself entertaining inappropriately sympathetic thoughts about this slippery senior citizen. "And I suppose the aircraft carrier your man whistled up got stuck in the Forty Foot, or whatever the local waterway is called?"

The laughter at this point was general, but John continued doggedly:

"He also posed as a Veteran, using a forged Identity Card carrying the number 534, thereby persuading the Castle to hand over a complete set of documents destined for the latest batch of immigrants. In addition," he continued, by now to an audience no longer laughing at his expense, "he is thought to have followed the van to Harwich."

A babble of consternation ran round the table as the potential significance of all this knowledge in the wrong hands struck home.

"And what," demanded the Chairman after calling the meeting to order, "is 'bumbling' about that? This agent seems to be running rings round your man – er – Gerald. Why is he unable to deal with the matter? Should he be replaced – or does he need authorisation to resort to extreme measures?"

"Things may not be as bad as they seem," said John, but the resultant uproar prevented him from making a fuller explanation.

In fact, there was no reason to assume that the escape of the immigrant was connected, or that the elderly investigator had any notion of the real significance of the information he had (almost certainly unwittingly) uncovered. The meeting instructed John to deal with the matter personally, using any means he thought fit – and, once the threat had been neutralised, to consider carefully what to do about Gerald.

Before agreeing the date of the next meeting, the Council had one other item to consider, indecent though the haste might seem to be. Andreas Ketels had to be replaced, and as there was not even a pretence of 'democracy' about the exercise (for this was a self-perpetuating group) there was no time like the present. Seizing the moment, Edwin, another septuagenarian, recalled his instructions in such an eventuality, and moved with commendable (and unwonted) despatch:

"I propose Andreas's son. He's very sound – can be relied upon to carry on the good work," (This was said to propitiate the older clique), "and is in touch with the younger grass roots element in – er – in ..."

At this point it became clear that Edwin had absolutely no personal knowledge of the man in question, and he tailed off as John helpfully interjected:

"The Fens, in fact." He paused for effect. "You have just instructed me to consider carefully what to do about him."

There was an embarrassed pause whilst this intelligence was absorbed, followed by the Chairman asking for, but not getting, a seconder. In truth there had not been time for the lobbying and machinations which normally accompanied these occasions, during the period between the resignation, assassination, death or incapacity of the outgoing member and the next meeting of the Council.

"I have one or two excellent people to sound out," said the Chairman, "but I should have to be sure that they were willing to serve before moving to a proposal."

Whether anyone was fooled by this pretence that they would be lucky to persuade such talented and self-sacrificing people as he had in mind, it was difficult to tell, but they readily agreed, after the unfortunate experience of their colleague, to leave the matter until the next meeting.

On his way to the station, en route to London and thence to Colchester, John rang Gerald to tell him of the death of his father. He had already decided to confine that conversation to imparting the news, together with appropriate sympathy, merely adding that he would try to drop in 'in a few days' time'.

"I'll keep you posted about the funeral arrangements, but I'm sure you appreciate that it would be very unwise to attend: we don't want people putting two and......."

"Yes, quite. I fully agree, Sir."

Gerald wondered whether to raise the question of his father's successor. As his superior had had the sensitivity not to ask about the 'little problem' (which was still not resolved) he decided to follow suit and not mix business with bereavement. That 'sensitivity' on John's part extended to not telling Gerald that his whole future was under review (not to say his continued existence). By not, at that point, saying that he was about to take over the hunt for the troublesome detective – and would be arriving very shortly – John had also given the impression that Gerald had a few days to sort things out by his own efforts. It allowed him to think that there was no need to remain on the premises, awaiting a phone call alerting him to the imminent arrival of the top brass. Later, John was to regret that omission.

CHAPTER TEN

Martin was woken by the insistent ringing of the telephone. His wife, having failed to raise him when she had rung two or three times during the previous evening, was beginning to wonder whether he was all right. Partly because he had only just woken from a particularly deep sleep and mainly because he could hardly tell the truth, Martin's explanation of where he had been sounded, even to his own ears, somewhat weak. However, they re-assured each other that all was well; that the dog was well ('The dog! the wretched animal hadn't even been fed last night', thought Martin guiltily); that the plants had been watered; that he would get the dry-cleaning when he was next in Safeways.

Ahmed, who had gone to sleep wondering what it meant to be 'bum-boozled', and glad that it was to Gerald that it would be happening, came down to breakfast hoping that Martin would now agree to organise his papers. Promising her a really good walk that evening (but unwilling to leave Ahmed alone in the house), Martin let the neglected animal out into the garden, trying to ignore the air of cowed and injured misery which it (like all Golden Retrievers) was able to generate in the hope of being seen by a passing RSPCA inspector. Mentally adding another two years for cruelty to animals to the five he was likely to get for aiding and abetting an illegal immigrant, Martin settled down to plan the next move.

"As soon as I can get your papers, I want you on your way, Ahmed. It's not safe for you to be in this area and I can't keep you hidden from view here for long."

"I've told you everything I can remember," said the lad anxiously. "What else will they want me to do?"

Martin almost corrected the plural in the last sentence, before remembering that he was supposed to be the front man of a large and powerful organisation. If only that were the case!

"This is what – er – we require from you," he said firmly. "You will ring Gerald on his mobile, asking him to help you. Give him the impression that you are at the end of your tether, cold, wet, exhausted, nowhere to go; that you want to come back; that you will do anything – and you must stress *anything* – he wants if he will help you."

As Martin had begun, Ahmed had felt apprehensive, but as the plan unfolded, his eyes shone at the thought of his persecutor being 'bum-boozled' (Ahmed's version had a certain piquant appropriateness, in view of the lure envisaged by the plan!).

"Will you catch him in a trap – or shoot him as he arrives?" he asked eagerly.

"Don't concern yourself with the details." (Details – a casual shooting – what *was* he doing, for Heaven's Sake?). "I won't be there; you won't be there. We shall ring him from a distance, just to get him well out of the way and make sure he continues looking for you miles from where you actually will be," said Martin, appalled at the thought of tangling with this professional thug in person. "I also want you to record your story on tape, including the reason why you ran away. It will be useful to clobber Gerald with and will enable me to convince others about the whole set-up, as they may not believe me without any hard evidence."

In fact, Martin thought that he might be able to imitate Ahmed's distinctive accent well enough to fool someone who was expecting to hear him. The telephone always distorted the real voice to some extent. These tapes would also provide a useful learning resource.

"Right! Let's be on our way. I'll just check the car and see that the coast is clear, then we'll smuggle you in. It won't be very comfortable, I'm afraid, but you have, alas, experienced a lot worse."

As he was cleaning the back seat and floor of the car, Martin came across a brooch which he recognised as being exactly like one belonging to the friend whose house he had visited recently. Could Ahmed have got hold of it – and dropped it? Had he dropped anything else? A more thorough search did, in fact, turn up a very interesting item: under the passenger seat, Martin found the bunch of keys which the lad had taken from the bunker. He decided not to mention the keys, which he could still not envisage actually using, but thought he might ask one or two questions about the brooch.

Partly for evidence and partly as additional material to enable him to perfect his impersonation, Martin made use of a gadget he had purchased some years before to record from the telephone. Several staff had had nuisance calls and the idea had been to produce recorded evidence, although in fact it had never been utilised. It very quickly became apparent that Ahmed had quite a talent for acting. From his first tentative, whispered 'It is me, Ahmed. Is that you, Gerald?', he successfully conveyed a desperate, frightened, hunted, naïve boy, who saw Gerald as his one 'friend' – the only person to whom he could turn. As agreed, he claimed to be ringing from a call-box near to the old bridge at Crowland, which would divert attention well away from the A 1 and Bradford. Before ringing off on a note of rising panic at the supposed sight of a police car, Ahmed said he would make for Thorpe Tunnel and would ring again to arrange a meeting.

"Now let's be clear on one thing, you cock-teasing little bastard," said Gerald (and it had to be admitted that the first adjective was entirely justified by Ahmed's promises of doing *anything*, if only he could be given his papers), "if you don't show up, I'll personally wring your scrawny little ...."

"I must go! I am not safe here. You must come alone to the Tunnel: if I see anyone else, I shall run away. You must come alone – but please come, please!"

As he flipped his phone off, Gerald smiled grimly to himself and murmured:

"Don't you worry, sonny, I'll be alone!"

He found that the thought of killing the troublesome young Asian, after taking advantage of his trusting nature, stimulated the very satisfying erection which had increased as the telephone call progressed. Such was his condition that he had to remain seated for some time when his assistant came into the room to ask for instructions.

"I think we'll concentrate our hunt round here for that fugitive," he said. "Call in the vans. Ahmed will have run off across the fields and be hiding in a shed somewhere. I'll get stuck into the search myself, too. You can cope here. Don't ring me unless it's urgent – and I may have to switch off if I'm stalking him. Understood?"

"Well, ye-es," said Henry doubtfully. He did not like responsibility and, although he was quick to criticise everyone else in authority, lacked confidence in himself, should there be a problem and no-one to contact (and thus blame if anything went wrong). "What if one of the others goes walk-about? Or suppose someone turns up from H Q? I'm not sure I know how to work the radio link with the plane."

"You'll be fine. You've seen me work the radio, and if someone just 'turns up', tell them to wait. I've got a man-hunt on my hands: I can't hang around on the off-chance that John, or someone, will want to drop in to count the socks."

Gerald spoke these high-sounding words, designed to indicate that he was not afraid of the hierarchy, safe in the knowledge that John had made it clear that he would not be around for 'a few days'. He was also confident that by then he would have dealt with Ahmed.

Admittedly, the problem of the elderly snooper remained irritatingly unresolved, but so far there had been no repercussions from his acquisition of the false papers, some of which, ironically Gerald thought, had been destined for the wretch who was now on the run. It was just as well those two had not got together! Probably the old fool had realised he was batting out of his league, had been badly frightened by his narrow escape in the woods, and would never be heard of again.

Buoyed up by the thought of his forthcoming sexual gratification, to be followed by that exercise of ultimate power, the deliberate taking of life, Gerald set off, supposedly to scour the countryside with the aid of his dog, in fact to await the call on his mobile which would guide him to his unsuspecting prey.

After that, he reminded himself, it would be time to see what could be done about taking his rightful place on the High Command. He had always understood that his father had someone primed to propose him, but presumably he had failed to do so – or the equally doddery colleague entrusted with the task had forgotten! They were all past it, that generation, content to wait for ever. Even he, Gerald, was over fifty now: they needed to get a move on, force the pace. If they waited much longer for the 'ripe plum' to fall, he would be too old himself! For a moment, his mood of gleeful anticipation was overturned by the thought of spending all his life under cover, hidden away in obscurity in places like Hall Farm (what a dump that was!), only to be passed over when the moment came, or die of old age if cautious counsels were to prevail much longer.

"They say there's always someone worse off than yourself, Nero," said Gerald to his four-legged friend. "And that someone is about to get his come-uppance."

At the sound of his name the dog raised his head and gazed, amber-eyed and uncomprehending as his master laughed and shouted:

"His 'come-uppance', Nero, now there's an apt expression for you! His come-bloody-uppance!"

****

The twin objects of Gerald's lust and derision sped north up the A 1 towards Bradford. In order to maintain the fiction of an extensive organisation, Martin had claimed that the papers would be passed to him at a Service Area en route. After about thirty miles, he told his passenger he could sit normally in the back and get to know the nature of the scenery – so different from that of the Fens. Martin also took the opportunity to tackle him about the ring he had found on the floor of the car. As he had suspected, it had been stolen from the house visited by Martin on his return from viewing the farm. It had been given to Ahmed by Gerald, presumably in an (unsuccessful) attempt to gain his friendship. Martin said he would take it back to its rightful owner and asked Ahmed whether he knew why they had targeted that particular house. It was with not a little surprise that he learned of his narrow escape.

"Weren't they taking a risk of being caught by the police?" he asked.

"Caught by the police! They often act as lookouts for them. Gerald boasts about his contacts with the police and the River Board and a firm of builders who were very useful, too."

"What was the name of the builders?" asked Martin eagerly. "Did you see their van, or know which town they came from?"

It soon became clear that Ahmed was only repeating something which was talked about amongst the immigrants. It could be a rumour designed to prevent anyone from 'shopping' the Organisation to the authorities. It seemed highly unlikely that they had many police on their side, but one could not rule out the odd one or two, for there was plenty of money to be made from the immigrants, not only 'up front' as a fee, but also as willing accomplices in theft – one of the services Ahmed had offered in an attempt to persuade Martin to obtain identity documents.

Eventually, having joined the M 62, Martin pulled in to the Services, where he made a pretence of entering the 'Gents' in order to be contacted and emerged carrying a packet which in fact he had taken in with him. Fearing another extravagant display of gratitude, Martin waited until they were back on the road before passing the papers over his shoulder.

"Here you are, Ahmed. I think everything's in order. Take a look."

Forcing himself to be calm, the delighted recipient carefully opened the packet and sorted through the contents.

"It is all there – just as Gerald said it would be!" Then, remembering that these were not from that source, he hurriedly added. "But I think these are probably much better – and you have not had any money for them. I – I don't know what to say. Thank you so much!"

To Martin's relief, the young man lapsed into silence, gradually coming to terms with having attained his goal. For weeks he had endured great hardships, had come close to death, seen others succumb and forced himself, against all reason, to believe that the money his family had paid would not be wasted. What would the future bring? Might he still be caught and sent home? In fact, although he did not realise it, thousands who had no papers and were in theory waiting for their case to be investigated succeeded in 'disappearing' somewhere in the U K – usually in London. Ahmed's chances of getting away with it, thought Martin, were good, unless the sinister organisation he had stumbled across were to make it their business to find him. If they found Ahmed, moreover, they could make him tell them how to find the 'bumbling busybody'.

As they neared the dropping off point, having turned off at Junction 27, Martin felt a touch of fear. He had, by any reasonable standards, been a bloody fool – and it all stemmed from that damned footpath sign!

"Well, this is it, young man. You're on your own now," said Martin as they arrived in Bradford. He nearly added the trite 'Don't do anything I wouldn't do', but realised not only the hackneyed nature of the phrase, but also the wide scope it offered, given the sort of things he had in fact recently been doing!

"No emotional goodbyes, now!" he admonished, noting a certain wetness around his companion's eyes. "Just wave and wish me luck – and here are your final instructions. Memorise the contents: we don't want this to fall into the wrong hands."

With that, Martin handed over an envelope and drove rapidly away. The car was almost out of sight by the time Ahmed had opened the envelope, wondering what more was expected of him. The tears flowed then, as Martin had feared they would (hence his rapid departure) for the contents were a brief message and five ten pound notes. The note read: 'Good Luck! Bamboozle the lot! Martin'.

It was an uneventful journey home. As he drove, Martin considered his next move, hovering between the gung-ho and the lie-lo, but much of the time he felt too drained to do more than concentrate on his driving. It was, in short, a tired old man who turned into his drive to find the house lights on and his daughter's car parked accusingly in the driveway. Normally, he would have been delighted to see her, welcoming her stimulating conversation and enthusiasm and the way in which the house seemed to come alive again and glow – literally, in the sense that every room in the house would have the light on! There was also, however, a sense in which he was a bit frightened of his children: they were both more successful and cleverer than him and absorbed new ideas in a tenth of the time he needed – even when he was capable of doing so. On this occasion, of course, Martin had every reason to be apprehensive, for he knew he had been making a fool of himself and Elizabeth would not be fobbed off with bland comments. Such tactics were all very well on the phone but would never survive a face-to-face encounter.

He had not taken any trouble to hide away the evidence of his recent activities. (Try explaining a 'wet-suit', a house which had hardly been touched in terms of cleaning, to say nothing of strangely worded tapes, if she happened to have pressed the 'play' button!). No; the game was up. Wearily and above all guiltily, Martin climbed out of the car to commence the dialogue with a somewhat shifty:

"Hallo! This is a nice surprise: I wasn't expecting you! Is everything all right?"

CHAPTER ELEVEN

Elizabeth had been about to have a go at her father concerning the state of the house, the fact that he never seemed to be in when anyone phoned and her mother's concern lest he were unwell. However, the forced joviality, the tiredness bordering on exhaustion and the rather pathetic air of a small boy caught in the act, disarmed her – and alarmed her. Perhaps the old boy was unwell, or was going through some sort of mid-life (well, fairly late-life) crisis. There was something else different about him, too, but she could not quite put her finger on it. Being both a practical and a sensitive person, she recognised the need for food – and affection – before questions and explanations, if the latter were likely to be forthcoming.

"What's more to the point," she said, giving him a kiss, " is how *you* are? You look all in. Tea? Or something stronger? Then I'll get you something to eat and you can tell me how you've been managing without Mother. Er – you're not feeling unwell, are you?"

The restorative effects of a strong cup of Assam, combined with sympathy, bacon and egg and his own need to confide in someone, caused the strange tale to emerge. Despite trying not to stem the flow by appearing too critical, Elizabeth could not repress an exclamation when it came to the waterborne incursion along the little River Glave, scene of childhood boating trips on hot summer days, when the only possible danger she could recall was a large, severe-looking swan, sailing majestically towards them, very clearly convinced that it had right of way. Similarly, being 'buzzed' by a low-flying, hostile object brought to mind, not a helicopter gunship, but one of the larger dragonflies, which her father had always referred to as 'four-engined jobs'. And all the time, there lurked unseen this gang of homicidal smugglers!

As the tale unfolded, Elizabeth's concern about her father's health diminished. His colour returned, as did his general animation – and she discerned the 'something about him' which had eluded her when he arrived. He was less bored – or was it....? No; he was less bor-ing! Elizabeth had never consciously thought of her father as being boring – indeed he was quite an out-going type whom her friends always found it easy to talk to – but he led an essentially boring life (as he would be the first to admit). Now that he had recovered from the 'down' of having delivered Ahmed and a long drive with nothing to eat, she could see that his adventures had caused the adrenalin to flow and sharpened him up. He looked thinner (probably on account of his inadequate diet, it had to be said) and if not actually younger, a more 'with-it' version than the last time she had been down, when the similarity to Victor Meldrew was beginning to be worrying rather than funny. The report requested by her mother was going to be difficult to compile – very difficult – but she could reassure her concerning the old boy's physical well-being.

"I suppose your mother suspected something, did she?" he asked eventually. "I didn't think I sounded entirely convincing last time we spoke.....but I couldn't tell her the truth, now, could I?"

At least, thought Elizabeth, he had got that bit right. A fraction of this lot would have made her mother jump on the next plane back. Remembering a canoe-ing trip on the Vienne many years before, her mind ranged over the thought of her father, armed to the teeth, surging down the river, intent on rolling back the jack-booted invaders. A dreadful pun on 'Jerry-actric' rose to the surface of her mind, as she wrenched her thoughts away from phantasy to – something not a whole lot different – the barely believable reality.

"I'll think of a way to stop Mother worrying. What's more to the point is what to do about the H F C gang. Incidentally, Hall Farm is nearly H F C, too!"

"You know, you're right! We must look into that – in fact, I think it's....."

"Hang on, Father, hold it! We are not doing anything, and that includes you. These people are too dangerous and too numerous. We need to think how best to alert the authorities, so that someone can find out the scope of the Organisation and its aims."

"I suppose," said Martin reluctantly, "it had better be the police. I did consider it before, but I wasn't sure if they would believe me."

"More importantly," replied Elizabeth, "they might be working for the other side, if your Asian friend was right about the help they sometimes got. No. I think I might give Patrick a ring and see if he has any brilliant ideas."

"But your brother's in Poland or somewhere, translating poems. What on earth could he do?"

"Well, let's say he doesn't only translate poems. He has certain contacts – and we know he's on our side," replied Elizabeth enigmatically. "Yes, the more I think about it, the more I think he might be very interested."

"Good God! You mean he's a – a 'spook'. Well I'll be damned. And all this time, I've been thinking of him poring over an abstruse manuscript, discovering the Magyar equivalent of spondees and dactyls. He never said he was in Intelligence!"

"The whole point of being a spy is that no-one should suspect you of being one!" said Elizabeth. "And make sure you forget you were ever told anything."

"Well, I'll be damned, Patrick a spy. Who would have thought it? I wonder where he gets it from?"

"You're a fine one to be asking that," replied his daughter with some asperity. "The only reason you've survived the last few days is because no-one could possibly imagine that an elderly retired schoolteacher with an interest in footpaths was the deadly agent they were all looking for. Your camouflage," she added, with a distinct edge to her voice, "could be described as 'impenetrable'! But I rather suspect you've been enjoying it all, and here and there, it has to be said, have shown some talent."

Martin felt he was on ground too weak to permit of a riposte to this last rather patronising remark, so he offered to turn in whilst she contacted her brother.

"Yes, O.K. I shan't have a lot to say, and he may be busy. I think I've a fair idea of the overall picture."

Martin had recounted nearly everything, although he had not wished to compromise Ahmed, so, in his account of the visit to the Castle, he had said that the forged documents were not quite ready. He had nearly owned up when Elizabeth had pressed him about his parting with Ahmed, however.

"Did you hand anything over before you drove off?" she had asked. He had hesitated over the direct lie, his embarrassment being noticed by his daughter, who had added, resignedly – for it was clear that he had risked a lot for the lad who probably saw him as a 'soft touch':

"Come on. How much? How much did he con out of you?"

Martin had lowered his eyes, not (as she had thought) because he was ashamed of his naïveté, but to hide the relief which would have been apparent and replied in a suitably shame-faced (and entirely truthful) way:

"Er – only fifty pounds. I couldn't let him go off without a penny to his name."

"You'll never learn, will you – and have you checked the silver?"

"The silver!" her father replied disparagingly. "You're looking at it, over there: the place is barely worth turning over – and not everyone can afford to adopt high principles."

Once upstairs, Martin checked again that the other documents were still there, then, relieved that he was no longer on his own, fell rapidly asleep.

The conversation between brother and sister, both being mindful of the need to maintain security, was brief and to a previously arranged pattern. It resulted in several other international calls, as a result of which a competent, experienced Intelligence agent was to find himself Lincolnshire-bound the following morning, charged with the task of contacting Martin, establishing the nature of the emergency and deciding what, if any, action should be taken.

Before going to bed, Elizabeth played over the tapes of Ahmed's story and noted his clear expectation of getting papers from her father's 'organisation'. Had he omitted something when telling the story? Surely, the young man couldn't long survive without them? Or would he come back to try and get them? Perhaps the Intelligence Service could come up with something.... which reminded her: someone should be making contact fairly soon, but until then they needed to keep the Hall Farm mob busy. She groaned inwardly at the realisation that that would mean an early start the next morning, put the lights out and went to bed, but not immediately to sleep, as her mind was full of the series of events related by her normally entirely predictable father. Sleep only came after she had decided on a simple – and safe – ruse for keeping Gerald occupied. She would discuss it with her father in the morning. After all, there was no harm in encouraging him a bit, now that the matter had been reported.

CHAPTER TWELVE

Gerald was awake early, having passed a less-than-satisfactory night trying to sleep in his van, which he had parked in a lay-by on a minor road not far from Thorpe Tunnel. On two occasions Nero had woken him, growling to be let out to see off a fox which could smell the supply of dog food inside the van. The cramped conditions, overpowering canine odour and lack of a handy shower, combined to make him wonder whether the prize was worth the rigours of the race. Today should bring the expected call from Ahmed, however, and he would make the little sod pay for all the worry and discomfort he had caused. He drove off to the anonymity of the fast food outlets on the A 1 to have a wash and a desperately needed cup of coffee.

Elsewhere, others were stirring. Gerald's assistant, Henry, had not slept well either – but that was worry, not physical discomfort, for his lack of confidence in himself was entirely justified. He was right: he *was* inadequate, prone to panic, unable to take a decision and stick to it. Why had Gerald gone off and left him? Surely, as leader, his place should have been back at base, not farting around the countryside with that bloody great dog? His train of thought was interrupted by the insistent tones of the telephone. About time, too: he hadn't heard from Gerald for hours. He lifted the phone. Perhaps he had succeeded in getting his hands on that wretched little ......

"Hallo Gerald, where are...?"

"John Dalton here. I want to speak to Gerald."

Henry froze, staring moronically into space as the phone squawked again: the unthinkable had happened. What should he say? The answer was not, in fact, very difficult. All he needed to do was to say that Gerald was not there and offer to take a message, but the information conveyed to John was that he was in the hands of a stuttering incompetent, who seemed unable even to contact his own boss.

"Have you found those two, yet? Is all under control?"

"Er – yes, or rather no. Gerald's out looking and mustn't be disturbed. There's only ......"

"Mustn't?....I'll decide who should be 'disturbed'. Get him on his mobile now and tell him to contact me."

"But he may be stalking Ahmed and the noise will give away his position. It'll be your responsibility."

Henry waited for the reply which would absolve him from all further thought, but the silence lengthened. John had rung off, unwilling to listen to any more drivelling 'buts' from this Fenland fool.

The phone rang while Gerald was in, or to be more accurate on, the toilet. Reception was poor, but Gerald gathered who was ringing and heard a reference to the Regional Controller. He agreed to ring back shortly, switched off and considered his position. Ahmed should have rung by now: he would give him a few more hours, but he couldn't stay out and stall H Q for much longer. Still havering, he moved outside to a point of better reception, where his next course of action was decided for him by the ringing of his phone. A slow, cruel smile spread over Gerald's face as he recognised the unmistakable and agitated voice he had been hoping to hear.

"Calm down! Calm down!" said Gerald soothingly. "Are you near the Tunnel? When do you want me to meet you?"

They agreed that it would be best to wait until it was dark and Gerald uttered appropriate reassurances about his desire to help and his willingness to arrive alone. He also noted the increasing desperation of the fugitive, who would now be willing to submit himself to *any* indignity in order to get his papers. The wait and the discomfort of the night (to say nothing of the risks associated with failing to 'jump' when contacted by the Regional Controller) were all about to pay off!

Now for that call to the farm. Henry would have to stall John, explain that Gerald was following up a recent sighting of the runaway and was confident of catching him in the very near future. He would try to ring in occasionally, but was not to be contacted unless anything really significant happened – such as one of the others finding Ahmed or the meddlesome old buffer. In fact, thought Gerald, as he gave his instructions to his protesting assistant, where he would be most of the time his mobile would be out of range – and he wouldn't be telling them he was at the Tunnel until he'd had a few hours fun. It was a pity he couldn't keep the lad locked up for a month or two, but he had to be seen to be dealing with the matter effectively, so Ahmed's permanent silence was needed. The Movement had retained the Nazi attitude to homosexuality, so he would not take any chances of being expo.... er.. found out, especially at a time when there was a strong likelihood that he would be put up for the High Command.

Replacing the phone, Henry turned to Paul, who was just about to issue forth, accompanied by one of the immigrants, to scour a few more highways and by-ways.

"I'm not taking the rap for this. If that John rings again, I'm not covering for Gerald. He should be here to deal with all that."

"Yes," replied the other guard, "and I'm not sure whether we can trust these other buggers: they're beginning to think Ahmed got away. It's a short step from that to deciding to scarper themselves."

"What? With no papers? They'd be caught and sent home: they won't risk that."

Paul lowered his voice:

"What papers? Christopher up at the Castle told me they'd given them to some real high up, who was checking up on the system. Gerald did his nut when he was told!"

The sharp, intrusive ring of the telephone cut short the two underlings' conversation. Mouthing 'Good Luck!', Paul left the 'strawstack bunker' to continue the search, and Henry cautiously raised the receiver.

"Henry here," he said, wondering who it was this time.

"Still no Gerald! Did you contact him as I told you?"

"Yes, Sir. He was following up a lead and rang me back later to say – er – that he – er – was following up a lead and ....."

"You just said that, man! What did he actually say? Just tell me his exact words: is that asking too much?"

Henry was not up to dealing with this bullying approach, and had already decided he would drop Gerald in it if he got any aggro from H bloody Q. The stutter disappeared, the tone became studiedly neutral – that of a mere reporter of facts.

"He instructed me to stall if you rang again. He was only to be disturbed if someone else found either of the two we're all searching for – Sir!"

Henry braced himself for a tirade, but was pleasantly surprised.

"Thank you. You have been most helpful. I'm glad someone is acting sensibly. What did you say your name was?"

"Henry, Sir!" replied the guard, by this time standing to attention, relieved at last of the burden of responsibility.

"Right, Henry. I shall be along later in the day. I shall also organise some reinforcements. There's no need to bother Gerald with all this. He's obviously too busy. Just keep it between the two of us – O K ?"

"Yessir! Right, Sir! As you say, Sir! Can I....."

"I'll be in touch later. Goodbye!" John allowed his fury to surface as he cut the connection. "What a moron! And who the hell does Gerald think he is? I'll give him stall. Roger!" He called to his assistant and issued a series of instructions. The Fens and these two troublesome civilians would soon be sorted out – and Mr High-and-Mighty Gerald with them!

Elizabeth grinned at her father as she put the phone down after her conversation with Gerald:

"Well, what did you think? How did I do?"

Martin knew his daughter had always had a talent for mimicry – the 'musical ear' inherited from her mother – but he had been staggered by this performance, the fruits of listening to Ahmed's tape.

"Fantastic! Ahmed's own mother would have thought it was him! We can keep this character Gerald – and anyone else at the farm – running round in circles for ever!"

"What a repulsive man. You could hear him gloating – and I was getting worried he might want to go into specifics about the nature of the 'anything' I was offering to do for him!"

"Oh, I'm sure you could have coped," said her admiring father, without thinking.

"Really? With my experience of sexual deviancy, do you mean? Thanks very much!"

"No, no. I meant you would have the intelligence to think of a way of – er – getting him off the subject. You know quite well what I meant. You're just trying to wind me up."

"It's not difficult!"

"Yes, well...what do we do now? We've got Gerald nicely out of the way for several hours."

"We do two things: we wait for someone to come to help us – sent by Patrick – and I , which means not you, ring Mother."

"You won't tell her about all this?" asked Martin anxiously. "She'll only worry," he added solicitously. "You know what she's like."

"Oh, yes. I know what you mean. It *would* be silly of her to worry over such trivial matters as you being chased round Lincolnshire whilst organising the escape of an illegal immigrant from the clutches of Boris Karloff!"

"I don't think that Boris and Gerald are of the same – er – sexual orientation, in fact," objected her father mildly.

"You know perfectly what I mean! Don't quibble over unimportant details. That man is dangerous and you are – well, you're *you*! "

At this point, Elizabeth broke off as she realised from the look in his eye that it had been her turn to be 'wound up'.

"You're impossible – and you know it. However, your James Bond days are now over, so I can truthfully tell her you are in good health, that she has no need to worry and I'm preparing some suitable nourishing dishes, as you were being rather unadventurous in.... your culinary habits," she finished firmly, in response to his raised eyebrow at the word 'unadventurous'.

While his wife's 'agent-in-post' was reporting the agreed, bowdlerised, version of the condition of dog, house and husband (in descending order of importance), Martin made a cafetière of drinkable coffee and browsed through the local paper. He nearly missed the small item on one of the inner pages, his eye in fact being caught by the somewhat fanciful heading 'Fox Overboard'. A dead fox, ran the report, had been found entangled in the mooring rope of a small inflatable dinghy, found near Spalding. A police spokesman said that a local angler had noticed the boat, but there had been no reports of children missing, so it had probably just been swept away from its mooring by the strong current. They urged parents to be careful, as recent heavy rains had swollen some normally placid rivers, increasing substantially the dangers which always applied to some extent. It was claimed that the police agreed with the reporter's suggestion that, as far as the fox was concerned, 'fowl play' was not suspected.

"Well, well," thought Martin, turning his attention to the Telegraph, "if only they knew!"

There were, as usual, several items concerning the strength in certain areas of Europe of the neo-Nazi movement, which now intrigued Martin, and reminded him of the still unexplained interest of Gerald in the war-time U-boat service. He was still reading the Telegraph, studiously avoiding any articles on education in order to maintain the equilibrium of his blood pressure, when Elizabeth finished her lengthy telephone call and there came a knock on the door.

CHAPTER THIRTEEN

Kenneth, the agent from British Intelligence, had had a pleasant, traffic-free drive, broken by a very acceptable 'Early Starter' at a Little Chef near Wansford, having considered calling in at The Haycock, and decided it might look bad on his expenses claim. He was looking forward to a day in pleasant rural surroundings, well away from his boss, with plenty of time to file a brief report, having reassured this member of the public that everything was now in good hands. The lightness of spirit associated with his anticipation of the day became even lighter when the door was opened by an attractive young girl. He didn't quite say: 'Hello. Is your Daddy in?'.... but he came close.

"Good morning, Miss! One thing's certain: you're not Mr Martin Brady – and he's the one I've come to see!"

The 'vision of loveliness' spoke, pointedly not opening the door for him to enter.

"I will enquire whether he wishes to see you. Whom shall I say it is?"

Even the insensitive Kenneth sensed that somehow he had got off on the wrong foot, but never-the-less he continued to march out of step.

"I think it's best if I tell him that myself, my dear. You'll find he is expecting me."

It was the 'my dear' which triggered the cold hard look, accompanied by a curt response that if he failed to produce suitable identification within ten seconds, she would phone the police and have him locked up. It was, therefore, with some relief, a minute or two later, that Kenneth found himself talking to an amiable old boy, very few of whose genes seemed to have found their way into the D N A of the fiercesome female whom he had (presumably) fathered. The story was complex but the clarity with which it was told caused Kenneth to have grave doubts about its authenticity. Would these two quintessentially pampered middle class citizens react so calmly if it were true? What evidence was there to show that 'Ahmed' had ever existed? Even the rubber boat had disappeared, and one could hardly build a report for action of any sort on the existence of an I D card for a firm called H F C. Not only that, thought Kenneth, mentally starting to write that report behind his bland exterior, the man is even a Telegraph reader! Leaning back, he dropped the I D card containing Gerald's photograph onto the kitchen table – or, to be more precise, onto the opened newspaper.

Life is full of coincidences, and the section of the paper on which it fell contained several obituaries, one of which concerned the life and times of one of the survivors of a force which suffered 80% losses in World War Two, namely the German U-boat service. Andreas Ketels, former officer in the German Navy, it reported, who spent several months as a prisoner of war, but later made his home amongst his former enemies, etc., etc., had died peacefully in his chauffeured car. There was more interesting detail but the coincidence in question related to the accompanying photograph – and its immediate proximity to that of Gerald. The likeness was immediately apparent, for the photo was many years old and was almost certainly the one which had caused Ahmed to say that he had noticed that Gerald had been one of those standing on the U-boat.

"I expect you're wondering whether we have any hard evidence to back up our story?" asked Martin, as he carefully aligned the I D card with the photograph in the newspaper.

"Well, old boy," replied Kenneth, relieved that the point had been made for him, "no-one doubts you of course, least of all myself, but some of the people I report to are going to say just that. I realise you have the tape, but they would say that it could have been made by anyone. Th....."

"By me, for example," interjected Elizabeth, in tones which belied any suggestion that she had meant to be helpful.

"Well, since you mention it, yes..... not, of course that I am for a moment suggesting that you....."

"You have just given us some evidence, my friend," said Martin, not being above the odd patronising expression himself. "There it is. Look! They're father and son: it stands out a mile. Not only that. If you read the text, you'll find the U-boat connection. Ahmed was right!"

"Ye-es," said Kenneth reluctantly. "You may have a point there, I agree, but one can't always believe what one reads in the newspapers."

Hurriedly, he added that he would have it 'checked out', in response to the beginnings of a contemptuous curl of the young lady's lip. Martin continued to look thoughtful, searching his mind for something triggered by that remark about not always being able to believe what you read. What was it? Something he'd read recently.

"The fox!" he shouted, causing a temporary alliance between the two younger members sitting at the table, both of whom wondered whether the pressure had finally got to him. "It was in the Local. Where did I....? Here we are, under here, somewhere in the middle of the paper. Yes, look!"

In triumph, he pointed to the story about the discovery of an inflatable boat.

"Yes, this does, to some extent, bear out your story, I agree," said Kenneth reluctantly. "You could go and identify it, perhaps."

"No. Not the boat, you fool! The fox! Don't you see? The bullet might still be in it – a bullet, not shot from a cartridge. That guard had a silenced rifle. I saw it in silhouette although it was dark. Very like a Heckler and Koch G3 fitted with a noise suppressor..... I'm not sure, but whatever it is, it's illegal, so we've got them!"

"And since when did you become an authority on firearms, Father? Had discipline at that school broken down to the extent of the staff being issued with personal weapons?"

"Since you ask," said her father, restoring her faith in his predictable respectability, "I remembered it from a project done by one of my Third Years on the resurgence of the German arms industry. He was quite a bright lad, father worked for ....."

Kenneth thought it was about time he took control, as the only professional present, apart from which, that part of the story had always struck him as being particularly weak. Probably, the old boy was a bit hard of hearing, or had his ears blocked with mud, so just hadn't heard the shot (always assuming he had been there in the first place!).

81

"All right! I'll get the police to check the cause of death – that's if the carcase is still around – and if it *is* a bullet, we'll pay a visit to your farm, claiming we've had a report that they've an illegal weapon on the premises."

Privately, Martin had his doubts, not only concerning the availability of the carcase, but also about the advisability of just 'visiting and asking' at the farm. It might only alert them to the continued threat of discovery, and it would be easy for them to deny having any weapons: they would hardly keep them hanging on the wall for all to see. On the other hand, it was the first time that the man from 'Intelligence' had shown any inclination to take any aspect of the story seriously.

"We can continue to keep Gerald away while you call at the farm, if you like," offered Martin. "That would weaken the opposition. In fact," he added, warming to his theme, "I could organise a diversion while you go in and search."

Repressing the phrase 'God save us from gung-ho senior citizens', Kenneth diplomatically thanked him and pointed out that he was not going in as might a drug-busting squad, merely in the capacity of a Home Office Firearms Licensing Officer, accompanied by a member of the local police force, in pursuance of a report from a member of the public. He also reminded the two civilians that using the telephone system for purposes of deception was an offence – unless, he added hurriedly, to Elizabeth's retreating back – it was on official Government business. He reached for the phonebook to obtain the number of Spalding Police Station, pretending not to hear what had sounded uncommonly like 'pompous prick' as the door closed behind her.

The telephone call from Kenneth, using his Home Office 'cover', caused some consternation within the police force as the fox carcase had been disposed of, there being more interest in the possibility of a boating accident than in the exact manner of the animal's demise. After a couple of hours, however, it had not only been located, thanks primarily to the forgetfulness of one of the cleaners, but also examined. The cause of death was found to have indeed been a bullet, fired (to Martin's smug satisfaction) from a Heckler and Koch Gewehr 3, in all probability fitted with a silencer. As the probable time of death matched that claimed by Martin,

Kenneth's request for assistance in approaching the inhabitants of Hall Farm was readily agreed, and P C Carradine was instructed to help the 'man from the Ministry'.

This information was rung through to Martin's house by the duty sergeant, whose call, unfortunately, was overheard by another member of the force, who realised its importance and passed it to his contact, who in turn rang Hall Farm.

"Are you quite sure you don't want us to organise a diversion, now that you realise they're armed?" enquired Martin. "They've got sophisticated intruder sensing equipment – and a lot at stake, you know."

"Ah, yes. The electronic bulrushes," said Kenneth, who had placed little credence on that part of the story. "Just leave it to the professionals. This is merely a verification exercise. They'll have no idea why we're coming and no reason to regard us as intruders. I doubt somehow that the person who reads the electricity meter has to lay down a creeping barrage in order to approach in safety!"

Kenneth paused after this (as he saw it) witty exposé of the situation and then threw the old boy a bone in the form of a request that, if he did wish to be of assistance, he could cut along to a point near Thorpe Tunnel to see whether Gerald was on his way back. At least, he reasoned to himself, it should keep them (for Elizabeth insisted on accompanying her father) out of mischief.

Reference has already been made to it having been 'unfortunate' that the sergeant's telephone call had been overheard by one of the Organisation's police contacts. What made it disastrous, rather than merely troublesome, however, was the absence of Gerald.

"George here. Clear the decks. The police are on their way with a chap from Intelligence. They know you've got a rifle and will be with you any time now!"

"Christ!" exclaimed Henry. "That stupid bugger Gerald's gone off and left me! What am I supposed to do?"

"Not my problem, old boy. I'm just paid to pass on info. What ever you do, you'll have to do it fast, though. I shouldn't let them find your – ah – 'guests', if I were you….and remember: this call didn't take place!"

Henry gazed panic-stricken at the receiver, as his caller cut the connection. Where was John's number? Should he call Gerald? No: John didn't want him to know he was coming. What was an Intelligence agent doing – and how the hell did they know about the rifles? He would have to do something – they could be here any minute and those illegals must be hidden away. Two of them, who had been out all night, and Paul, were asleep upstairs in the farmhouse. They might wake up and panic!

In fact, Henry was doing enough panicking for all of them, torn between contacting HQ and warning the others at the farm. Still cursing the absent Gerald, he ran upstairs to wake Paul, warned him the police were coming and then dashed back to the bunker to telephone for instructions and help. As he entered the hidden door in the 'strawstack', he heard, this time with relief, the urgent ringing of the telephone.

"Thank God!" he gasped as he snatched up the receiver. "Henry here: who's that?"

It was with a mixture of anger and fright, but above all relief that he heard the answer he had prayed for:

"Gerald here. What's the matter?"

"Everything bloody thing's the matter, for Christ's sake! The police are on their way – with a bloody Intelligence man. H Q are taking over the whole operation ... Oh Christ, I was told not to tell you that ......there's reinforcements coming – and John – and I don't know what to ......"

The rising note indicated a man close to breakdown, on the verge of tears, capable of any misjudgement:

"You've got to get back. Bugger that Asian – or the other guy. Get yourself back here now!"

The reply was terse and failed to reassure Henry:

"Now, get this! I'm on my way and I'll ring again in about ten minutes. Do not on any account ring H Q. I'm not having them take anything over. Just stall the police: say you've only got a shot-gun, or something. And don't ring me. I'll ring you."

A few miles away, Martin switched off his 'mobile' and looked triumphantly at his daughter.

"Well! Didn't I do well!"

"Rory Bremner has nothing to fear," she replied, "but you got away with it. I winced at that southern 'gun', mind you. Only six for artistic impression, but nine point three for effort."

As he set off to brief his colleague, Henry heard the bleep of the furthest sensor and glanced at the VDU: a car was approaching slowly. By this time feeling physically sick, Henry ran across to the farmhouse and shouted up the stairs:

"They're coming! Get down here, all of you! Paul, you take these two and shut yourselves into the bunker. I'll stall these people until Gerald gets here."

"What if the.....?"

"No time for questions. Just do as I say!"

CHAPTER FOURTEEN

Although the man who met them seemed rather out of breath, there was nothing out of the ordinary to be seen by the time Kenneth and his police assistant drove into the ramshackle farmyard. "How do you do, Sir? Are you the owner of this place?" said Kenneth, taking in the general air of neglect, the rusting machinery, old overgrown hay bales and tumble-down outbuildings.

"No, he's on his way – er – should be back soon," mumbled Henry. "If you'd like to wait in the kitchen, I'll get on with my – er ... ."

"Oh, I'm sure you can help us, Sir. While we're waiting, you won't mind answering a few questions, will you?"

It had not escaped Kenneth's notice that the man was agitated, wanted to get away – and, perhaps most surprising of all, had not asked who they were or why they were there. It could merely be that he was unused to visitors, better with sheep than people, a bit shy and awkward..... or it could be that the visit had been expected. As his young, inexperienced colleague, 'on loan' from the police, was not in uniform and looked more like a member of a school Sixth form than part of a two-man hit squad, the absence of curiosity as to their identity was, well – odd.

"I expect you're wondering why we're here, Sir? Here's my identification, and this is P C Carradine. No need to be alarmed – we're just following up a report, which may well be mistaken, that you have an unauthorised fire-arm on the premises."

Henry glanced at the proffered I D cards and mumbled that he didn't know anything. It would be better to wait until his boss came, as he would know all that.

"Yes. We'll wait, but just for the record, do you know if any guns are kept on site? Legal ones, that is?"

Remembering his most recent instruction from Gerald, Henry replied that they had a shot-gun, for the rats, rabbits, etc.

"Good. Quite understandable," said Kenneth, soothingly. "Could you get it for me, please? Then I'll get the owner to show me the licence. I expect everything's in order."

"I – er – don't know where it ....," muttered the hapless Henry, sweating profusely now, unable to meet his questioner's eye.

"Is that it hanging on the wall?" asked Kenneth, pointing at an old 12-bore, the presence of which Henry had forgotten, largely because it was never used, did not work, and was there only as a form of 'decoration', as were the old cooking pots and horse brasses, designed to look harmless and bucolic.

"Oh! Oh, yes. I couldn't remember where it had been put," said Henry lamely.

"You use it to shoot rats, I believe you said. Have you shot any recently?"

At this point, Henry remembered that when one was being questioned, it was a good thing to say as much as possible that was true. With relief, he replied reasonably accurately that, as it happened, his mate – who was also out – had recently had to shoot a fox which had been after the chickens.

To Henry's surprise, his visitor showed considerable interest in this use of the gun, although it was easy to answer the questions: when, where, what had happened to the dead animal.

"And have you any other guns around the farm?"

"No. That's the only one – at least, as far as I know. You need to ask the boss – and he should be here any minute."

Kenneth walked over to the wall and lifted down the old gun. It took no more than a minute to confirm that the relic had certainly not been fired recently – probably didn't even work.

"I don't think," he said, fixing Henry with a penetrating stare, "that you are being entirely frank with us, Sir! This gun is not in a fit state to be fired. Are you sure there is no other weapon – one which fires a bullet, rather than a cartridge, possibly fitted with a silencer?"

The wild-eyed look, the gasp of horror, the stumbling denial, all combined to make Kenneth realise not only that there was almost certainly such a weapon, but that the rest of Martin's improbable story could well prove to be true.

"I think you'd better get in touch with your superiors, Constable. We shall need a search warrant and we shall need to ask this gentleman's 'boss', always assuming such a person exists, a few questions!"

Inspector Green had been worried about the interest shown in the goings on at Hall Farm, but he had decided to co-operate, whilst passing on a warning to his contact. He had long been on the pay-roll of the Organisation as one of a small, but influential, proportion of the uniformed force, who found their shared membership of the Masons a useful cover for far more sinister purposes than mere self advancement and occasional favours or 'blind eye turning'. When he received a call from the young P C whom he had selected as lacking in initiative and unlikely to ask awkward questions, he realised that this Intelligence chap could be about to make waves, big waves, the sort that cause people to drown, especially if those people could be criticised for allowing things to get out of hand.

"Right, Matthew. You get back here. Leave our friend at the farm, keeping an eye on this fellow, and we'll see about how best to follow things up."

"Should I arrest him first, Sir? Or bring him with me?"

"Arrest who, lad? The bogus Environmental Inspector or the farm labourer? No, you can't arrest someone for not firing a gun at a fox, especially as the owner is out! That Intelligence chap isn't carrying, is he?"

"What, a gun, do you mean?"

"No, a loaded banana, you fool. Of course I mean a gun! These people are a law unto themselves – create more trouble than they're worth, half the time."

"No, I don't think so. I'll ask him."

"Never mind. Just get back here," said the exasperated inspector, anxious to get the nosy agent on his own and well away from any direct connection with the forces of law and order. How they dealt with the chap was none of his business, except in so far as he would expect a substantial bonus for buying them time and opportunity.

After the departure of the young policeman, Kenneth and Henry eyed each other speculatively.

"You'll save yourself a lot of trouble – not to say a few years inside – if you come clean," said Kenneth.

"I've nothing more to say," said Henry, who seemed much calmer now, even though he must know that the game was virtually up.

The silence lengthened. Kenneth tried again, acting on the assumption that all of his elderly informant's information could well be correct:

"What about these illegals?" he said casually. "We shall be picking them up and getting them to give evidence before sending them back, to stop anyone else using you and your mates as a route to the West. Are you sure you don't want to tell me about it?"

Henry maintained a sullen silence, but he was not the only person who had heard those last words. The other was Issed, who had been sent from the bunker by Paul to find out what had been happening when the security V D U showed the visitors' car departing rapidly, presumably to summon help as it only contained one person. Having heard the visitor's intentions towards himself, Issed nipped smartly back to the bunker, prepared to follow any instructions designed to prevent Kenneth from carrying out his threat.

There was no longer, it appeared to Paul, any point in pretending there were no weapons on site, so, armed with two hand guns (one for Henry), he and the two Asians emerged from the bunker and moved silently, knowing every inch of the ground, towards the back door of the farmhouse.

"Are you going to tell these people to give themselves up," asked Kenneth, after another silence, "or do I have to search the cellars, the attic, even the....Bunker?"

This sally was rewarded with a look of surprise from the taciturn Henry.

"Ah! I see you thought we didn't know about that! Perhaps now you see that your only hope is to tell me everything you know. Let's start with these smuggled immigrants. Where are they at the moment?"

It was with some quiet satisfaction that Henry was able to answer that particular question:

"Two of them are right behind you!" he said, as the trio entered the room noiselessly. "Don't try anything! Well done,

Paul. Give me that shooter – and don't be afraid to use yours if he tries anything. We can just say he left after a bit, so no-one will ever be able to prove anything."

"I thought you said the police were here? Who's this chap?"

"This, my friend, is a member of Her Majesty's Secret Service – a Mr Black, so his I D card would have us believe. Somehow, I doubt whether he'll be around for much longer, though, so I shouldn't bother getting on first name terms with him."

"You won't get away with this!" expostulated Kenneth, rising from his seat. "You'll spend the rest of your life in prison if anything happens to me."

"Grab him! Get some rope and tie him up – and slug him if he doesn't shut up."

Kenneth struggled in vain as the two wiry immigrants held him until Paul returned with some rope.

"What shall we do with him, Henry? Drop him down the old well?"

"Not a bad idea, but we'd better let H Q decide. In the mean time, if anyone asks, or the police come back, say he went off to look round just after that gormless copper drove off. I don't somehow think our friends in high places will enquire too closely. Lock him up in the brig – he seems to know all about the Bunker, so he can spend his last few hours in it!"

"How come he knows that?" said Paul. "Do you think they caught Ahmed and sweated it out of him?"

"I don't know, but I've no doubt John will persuade him to say! Right! Paul, you'd better get upstairs on look-out. And you two, get him over to the Bunker. I'll come with you. Gag him just in case anyone happens to be in earshot until he's locked up in that inner room. He can shout all he likes there, or scream, if it comes to that!"

The sound-proofing qualities of the bunker were demonstrated as they opened the door, for the last two or three rings of the telephone (which had been trilling its request to be unhooked for the last two minutes) could then be heard.

"Let's get this chap locked away safely, then I'll see who that was," said Henry, taking a bunch of keys from his pocket.

"And check those bonds. We don't want him to think he's in a hotel and start ringing for room service!"

As the door clanged shut behind him, Kenneth could see why his guard had referred to it as 'the brig'. There was no light, no heat, no furniture – and nothing on the damp concrete floor. He had no doubt that he would be missed, and no doubt that Martin and the police knew where to look for him. They would have to move quickly, however, for he also had no doubt that these trigger-happy gangsters had everything to gain from silencing him. Permanently.

He knew too much – and yet he knew too little. Who, or what was H Q ? Was there an absent 'boss' as Henry had claimed? Judging by the regalia, decorations, hangings and photographs he had glimpsed on the way to his 'prison cell', Martin's ideas about the neo-Nazis were anything but fanciful after all.....but were there really people in 'high places' who would protect them.... or even encourage them to go further? Kenneth was no fool, was, indeed a 'professional' as he had rather patronisingly (he now realised) pointed out to Martin. He set about trying to free himself from his bonds and think how he could bargain for his life and/or escape. Surely someone in this organisation would have the sense to stop their underlings from making a terrible mistake. Why in Hell's name had he been so contemptuous of the help offered by Martin and his daughter? What would he not give for a 'diversion' now!

CHAPTER FIFTEEN

The area round Thorpe Tunnel was quiet and peaceful when Martin and his daughter arrived there, having (like Gerald, whom they could not see) left the car some way away. Training jets from R A F Cranwell passed carefully overhead, in long curving sweeps and occasionally evil-looking 'tank-busters', from a more distant American air-base, appeared silently and were gone, to be followed a second later by the explosive thunder of powerful engines. The wild life continued to graze, hunt, buzz or bleat, according to its nature, but mere mortals ducked in fright, thankful that on this occasion the aircraft had all contrived to miss each other.

Having found a suitable vantage point, they settled down to wait and watch, taking it in turns to scan the area with the binoculars. Various vehicles passed below them, but none stopped at the tunnel itself, although a lay-by a few hundred yards away, next to an area of woodland, seemed popular as a 'comfort stop'.

"That place seems to be well manured!" said Martin, somewhat crudely, earning himself a withering look. "There goes another – the furniture van. Where's it from?"

"I can't quite see from this angle, but the telephone number looks like 01428, wherever that is," replied Elizabeth, sweeping the binoculars round to the left. "Oh! what was that.....?"

"It's probably down south – someone will be making a packet, selling there and buying up here."

"Well, well, I think I must be looking at the famous Gerald!" exclaimed Elizabeth. "There's a man standing up, looking at something through binoculars."

"Careful! Don't let him see you – the sun on the lens can give you away. I know: it's what gave me away, I think."

"Don't worry. It's how I came to see *him*: the sun's behind us. He must have moved as I swept past him to look at that furniture van."

"Let's have a look!"

"Hang on. I think it's the van which interests him – enough to make him forget and break cover to get a better view."

"Perhaps the driver's taking his trousers off! If it *is* Gerald, he'd want a good look, or," he hurried on, forestalling criticism, "perhaps the driver looks like Ahmed?"

"He doesn't and... Now, that's funny! There are two other men now, just inside the wood: they can be seen from up here. Where on earth did they spring from?"

"Let me have a look at your watcher: I'll recognise him from his I D photograph, if it is. Thanks ..... yes, it's him all right. He's putting the binoculars down to get something out of his pocket. Hell! It's his mobile phone. If he rings the farm, he'll find out I've been impersonating him!"

"And he'll find out about the....."

"Reinforcements!" they both exclaimed, brains racing to take in what was happening.

"They're being dropped off from that van!" said Elizabeth, getting there just ahead of her father. "And Gerald must have recognised the vehicle as one of theirs, so he....Give me that phone!" she concluded. "I'm going to stop him getting through to the farm."

"But they ....."

"Shush! Ahmed has seen the reinforcements, too, and....."

Martin, watching through the binoculars, saw Gerald pause and press a button on his mobile. During the course of quite a lengthy conversation, Elizabeth managed, the accent never slipping, to convey to Gerald that Ahmed was near-by, had stolen a mobile phone (the number of which he did not know) and had taken fright at the sight of the other men whom Gerald had brought with him – despite having said he would come alone.

Gerald was torn, once again, between duty and 'pleasure'. He tried to reassure 'Ahmed' that he knew nothing of the extra men, that he was trying to find out and could still meet him, as agreed, in Thorpe Tunnel.

"I'm not going down there to be caught by those men. They're probably going there, too. I know where you are. I can see you from here. I'll come to you. And don't use the phone to tell them where I am. If I hear or see you using it, you'll never see me again!"

Elizabeth stopped, cut the connection, and let out a long slow breath.

"That was brilliant!" said Martin. "Let's hope it works. It should give us ten minutes to think what to do. The pace is a bit too much for my creaking mental faculties!"

"It depends mainly on how things are going with our revered professional spy," said Elizabeth, adding in a slightly exaggerated version of the real thing: "No need for you to worry your pretty little head about that, my dear!"

"Time for Gerald to ring in, I think," said Martin.

"I thought you were expecting to gain ten minutes," said his daughter, focusing the binoculars.

"Rory rides again! Here we go – and I'll watch those flat Fenland vowels, this time!" Martin keyed in the relevant numbers and waited for the ringing tone.

"Engaged! Blast it. I wonder who it is. Is it.....?"

"No. He's still sitting there. Just looked at his watch. Now he's looking at the furniture van. I can almost feel the anxiety from here!"

"Ah, at la(h)st! Sorry – last. I'd better get in character!"

Over at the Hall Farm bunker, Henry heard the phone start to ring again....and, down in Essex, John's assistant turned to his colleague.

"They're not answering. I've rung for about three minutes."

"Could be out of order, or there's a problem. Either way, John's not going to like it. I'll ring the plane. He can sort things out when he gets there. Charlie should be there with the reinforcements any time now. Talk about a sledge-hammer to crack a nut!"

"From what I can gather, this chap they're after *is* a bit of a nut!"

Henry had intended to key in 1471 to see who had been trying to get through, but managed this time to pick up the receiver in good time.

"Sorry! We were a bit busy, but all's well now."

"Gerald here. About time, too," grumbled the voice (well nearly) of Gerald, adding: "Put me in the picture."

Elizabeth observed, rather than heard, the conversation. Her father said very little – just the occasional grunt to encourage Henry to continue – but the widening of the eyes and the odd grimace made it clear that the monologue was something more than a detailed run-down on the current state of the Common Agricultural Policy.

"Yes, I see," Martin said eventually. "You've all done very well. You haven't told H Q yet, have you?...No, never mind. Leave that to me. Don't harm him in any way until we get instructions...The well, yes....but no drastic action until they give the word.... Oh, just to double check, which number did they ring from before?... Good, good..." Martin signalled to Elizabeth to write the numbers, ".....2131. O K . I'll be in touch shortly."

Martin was about to ring off when he had a sudden thought.

"One thing more, Henry. It's occurred to me that young Ahmed might ring the farm, or even get someone to ring pretending to be one of us!...Yes, that's right... well, let's agree a simple code. We can change it as often as we like. If the person ringing asks what you should put on a stinging nettle rash.... and the other answers 'buttercups', then we..... Yes, yes, I know that dockleaves are the thing – that's the whole point of the code! An impostor – someone pretending to be one of us – would say 'dockleaves', but we will say 'bu .....' Yes, you've got it! Right. I'll be in touch, so don't ring me!"

"Buttercups!" said Elizabeth scornfully. "Why choose something with a 'u' in it? You could have said 'hollyhocks' or, or ... oh, never mind. What did he have to say for such ages. I'm dying to know!"

"Unfortunately 'dying' could be one of the options," began Martin as he related the disastrous outcome of Kenneth's reconnaissance.

"You've got to do something, Father. You can't just let him rot. Surely they wouldn't kill him in cold blood. They'd never get away with it!"

"Working backwards, no they wouldn't get away with it, but that's of little interest to Kenneth if he's dead; yes, they might – in cold water, to be more exact. Bear in mind that the racket they're in is shared with Triads, Mafia, drug cartels – you name it. And as regards your first point, who was it who recently told me my James Bond days were over?"

"I didn't mean charge in, showing true grit, for God's sake! Think of something. We could ring the police!"

But even as she said it, Elizabeth realised the problem: those friends in high places on the one hand and incredulity on the other.

"Or," she continued, "we could ring his Intelligence people..... yes, I know: we might get the wrong person. Well, I'll get on to Patrick anyway. Give me that phone."

They both knew really that Kenneth could have minutes rather than hours to live; that 'the man from H Q' was on the way; that a group of perhaps half a dozen men had joined the hunt. Moreover, a humiliated Gerald was about to find out what was going on – and could well take precipitate, violent action to make up for his absence at such a crucial time. The logic of the situation, reinforced by Elizabeth's encounter with an answering machine in response to her call to Poland, pointed to the need for a 'cunning plan'.

Martin coughed apologetically and looked anywhere but at his daughter:

"If – and I only said if – we could arrange a diversion, I've got Gerald's keys back at the house," he began hesitantly, "and if I could get to that strawstack, I think I could find the door .... and one of his keys might...."

He tailed off and waited for an outburst of scorn and derision, references to his lack of experience and training, and similarity to 'Q' rather than even the lowest 'field man', let alone 007.

In fact, Elizabeth regarded him thoughtfully and merely said:

"And what, still speaking purely hypothetically, did you have in mind by way of a diversion? Not, of course, that I should let you attempt anything like that on your own, even if there were any possibility of action on the lines you propose."

Martin had, in fact, given some thought to what amounted to a diversion for some time. His reason for getting Ahmed to tape his story had been partly in order to get Gerald out of the way. He had vague plans of driving into the farmyard to have a really good look round, aided by the set of keys which Ahmed had snaffled and believed to be at the bottom of the river. If enough vehicles, all at once, were to converge on the farm, it would be well-nigh impossible for them to deal with an intruder hidden in the middle. The sort of vehicles he had in mind were fire engines, gas detector vans, Anglia Water, the police, the River Board, an ambulance, perhaps – even the odd T V or newspaper reporter. If all or most of those were telephoned and told there was an emergency (leaking gas, electricity pylon collapsing, water flooding out of the raised river bank, etc.), there would be total confusion in the farmyard. One more person, claiming to be, say, an environmental, health or animal rights inspector also called out on (appropriately for the Fens) a 'wild goose chase', would never be noticed, let alone suspected.

Although she had not seen it, Elizabeth could envisage the narrow Fen road, the cramped, muddy farmyard and the confused and inadequate Henry.

"Hmm! You've given this some thought haven't you? What were you like at school, I wonder? It might work at that – the diversion, that is, not you as the White Knight."

"I know what you mean, but one can't involve some innocent by-stander in this. Your young athletic friends for example, or ex-students I could rustle up. One might even contact a member of the opposition by mistake!"

"If only Patrick would ring back," said Elizabeth. "He could pull the right strings and send in someone more – er – well not you , anyway!"

"The only trouble is," said Martin thoughtfully, "the roads would be too blocked to get Kenneth out. Perhaps we shouldn't call quite so many?"

"Now hang on! Nothing has been decided yet. I know you. You'll be hiring a helicopter next and getting me to read you the flying instructions from the handbook!"

"That would be the answer, though, wouldn't it? A helicopter! If only we could get hold of the right people quickly enough."

Conscious that time was running out, they racked their brains for a solution. It boiled down to wondering whom they could trust, for just as some elements of the police were thought to be dicey, so might be others, such as the military, or their M P, or even members of Kenneth's Intelligence organisation itself.

"Did you tell Patrick to ring on this machine, by the way, or," he added, seeing the reply in Elizabeth's face, "is there at this very minute a message on the answerphone at home?"

Quickly, they got to their feet to return to the car.

"Just before we go, is Gerald still sitting there waiting 'goodly'?"

Elizabeth focused on the relevant spot: "Yes. Is it worth another smoke signal to keep him sweet?"

"Wrong type of Indian, but yes. Talk as we hurry along: it'll sound more authentic."

As they made their way back down the hill, 'Ahmed' could be heard pleading with Gerald not to go and leave him, explaining that he had had to double back because of the extra men who had emerged from the furniture van. The aim was to make Gerald think that he was playing a fish on a long line, gradually winding him in, but always risking, by too sharp a 'jerk on the line', that it would snap, resulting in the loss of the catch. In fact a better analogy might have been that of the line being reeled in to yield up an old boot – or even, given events unfolding back at the farm, 'fishing while Rome burned'.

Father and daughter were back home by the time Gerald decided to ring the farm to see if there was any news, so they did not see him shouting, puce with rage, engaged in a pointless discussion of the merits of nettles and dockleaves with Henry, who appeared to have 'flipped' under the strain!

In fact, Henry did well, once having established – by means of the 'stinging nettle code' – that he was in direct communication with the impostor whom Gerald had warned him about. Without giving him any useful information, he discovered where the man was ringing from, including the fact that he had seen the Haslemere Furnishing Company van unloading its complement of 'troops'. The fact that the 'real' Gerald had been told earlier about the expected reinforcements, whereas this one clearly had no knowledge of that conversation, convinced Henry utterly that he had a 'wrong'un', probably the man they had all been trying to catch for several days. In other circumstances, his request that Gerald go down to the Thorpe Tunnel bunker to help issue them with arms would have been seen as a master-stroke, for a bogus Gerald would have crept near to get a good look at the place.

The real Gerald found it altogether a sensible request – something to hang on to in the welter of waffle about improbable herbal remedies. He replaced the phone into his pocket, seething with anger at having been 'stood up' by that wretch Ahmed, who had cost him a very uncomfortable night and delayed the hunt for the elusive bearer of I D 534. As the incident involving a false I D card came into his mind, he recalled that he had mislaid his own. He had been reluctant to ask for a replacement, thinking it would 'turn up', as it would have made him appear inefficient. He had wondered if he had dropped it that night when Nero had put up a pheasant, but he had gone back the next day and there had been no sign of it. He would have to come clean soon – make up a story about dropping it down the well by mistake, or something.

Occupied with such thoughts, Gerald was caught totally by surprise when he was suddenly thrown to the ground and sat upon by two burly men, who proceeded to tie him up whilst preventing him from uttering a word, then gagged him efficiently and hustled him towards the bunker. Apart from breaking his mobile phone, they did no damage and regarded his pop-eyed attempts to convey outrage with contempt. Nothing could be more obvious than that this was the man who had been unmasked by Henry, whose subsequent call to H Q had resulted in their instructions to lock him up after searching him and leave him to the tender mercies of John, who was arriving shortly by plane at Hall Farm airstrip. Had their search revealed his I D card, of course, it is possible that they would have given him a chance to explain himself. There was, to be sure, a set of car keys, but no visible vehicle: that was parked well out of sight, in a spot where the odd bark from Nero would not attract a lot of attention.

Having locked Gerald away, they settled down to await the arrival of ... that same Gerald, meanwhile congratulating themselves on a job well done. There was one small doubt raised by one of the men, though:

"He looks a lot younger than we were told: ugly looking customer, mind you – and he stinks of dog!"

Behind the gag, Gerald strained to tell them what bloody fools they were, but their stupidity did not extend to the tying of knots. In that respect they scored ten for technical merit.

CHAPTER SIXTEEN

There was, indeed, a message waiting when Martin and Elizabeth arrived home.

"It'll probably be the bloody library telling me the book I ordered is now ready for collection," said Martin, as they waited for the mechanism to work its magic. On this occasion, however, his pessimism was unjustified.

"Hi! Dad – it's me. I've got a few days spare so think I'll pop home. Can you meet me at the usual airport? It'll be handy if you want to fit in a visit to Gran. Oh, and would you let Adrian know as soon as possible on 763291 – same code as Gran funnily enough. He can probably help with that other query you had. I'll ring again to let you know the flight number. Cheers!"

"Well, well. He must be worried about being overheard – those friends in very high places, I suppose," said Martin.

"Yes, thank God he's coming: this is getting a bit beyond us two!"

"Can you remember that number, or shall I play it again?"

"Yes, but do you know Gran's code?" replied Elizabeth.

"Easy: it used to be O S O 2 – S O for Southend, in the days when telephone numbers had proper letters."

"And for half a groat you could get drunk, go to the cinema and have a newspaper full of fish and chips. I know! Now, what .. is .. the.. code?"

"And," continued Martin smugly, "before they added an extra '1', so the code is 01702."

"At last! Now let's find out what the limp-wristed Adrian has to say for himself!" said Elizabeth, keying in the number and handing it to her father.

"Don't be so judgmental. He can't help what his name..... Oh – er – can I speak to Adrian, please?"

"What was the name again, Sir?"

"Adrian...A.. D.. R...."

"Yes, I'll put you through," said the Intelligence Service operator after he had verified the significance of the codeword.

The duty officer had some idea of Kenneth's mission, but as the latter had set off having little notion himself of just what was involved, it took some time to brief him on sufficient of the background for him to make sense of the urgency of the immediate situation.

"Right! Leave it with me. I'll get someone down there as quickly as possible. Stay by the phone – oh, and don't tell anyone else about this. As you've gathered, not everyone is trustworthy, however respectable they might seem."

Martin put the phone down with some relief and turned to his daughter:

"Perhaps the diversion won't be needed, after all!"

"Yes – pity in a way: I'm sure it would have worked, and I thought of another type of firm to send in: Dial-a-Pizza..... or Indian or whatever."

"Yes! And a certain poetic justice if the Taj Mahal Take-Away could come to the rescue!"

"I think we ought to ring the farm to get an update. They've probably rumbled us by now, as Gerald will have been able to prove he was the real one after a bit."

"He probably thought buttercups *were* the best treatment for stinging nettles – he's stupid enough!" said Martin, ringing through, ready to get in character.

Martin started to establish his bona fides by means of the 'stinging nettle' code, but was cut short by Henry.

"No need for all that now," he said cheerfully. "The lads have caught that other chap. They've got him locked up at Thorpe Tunnel. In fact if you're still near-by, you could cut along there and 'interview' him. Although," he added hastily, "I'd rather you came back here."

"Yes, well put me in the picture about Ke...." He managed to turn the name into a cough before giving away that he knew it, and continued, "about this chap from Intelligence and John, etc."

Kenneth was no problem, it seemed, and still in the land of the living, but John was expected to land at the farm airstrip in about an hour and a half, depending on head winds.

"Good. With any luck, I might have Ahmed by then. If so, I could get those characters to guard him, too, with that interfering old fool."

"John said that he wanted an 'accident' organised for the Intelligence chap very quickly, so that the time of death would look right for him having wandered off round the farm."

"Must go. There's someone coming!" said Martin, cutting the conversation short following this reminder that any rescue attempt would have to be carried out within the next hour, preferably before the arrival of John.

A series of rapid phone calls established that a helicopter (in preference to a Harrier, the arrival of which might have alarmed his neighbours) would land shortly in Martin's back paddock to collect Gerald's keys. For reasons of later 'deniability', it was agreed by 'Adrian' that Martin and Elizabeth should organise the diversion, enabling two S A S men to drive into a farmyard crowded with unnecessary vehicles, and 'spring' Kenneth from the bunker. There would be time to pick up Henry, his mate and the 'illegals', together with John and company, later. It was essential not to panic Henry – or Gerald if he had managed to get himself accepted by then – into killing Kenneth.

Although well aware of the serious nature of the whole affair, Elizabeth and Martin, one on the regular phone, the other on the 'mobile', quite enjoyed themselves ordering sufficiently expensive quantities of various goods and services to ensure efficient service, all to arrive promptly in one hour's time.

"Here we are! 'Take away food'," said Elizabeth, opening the Yellow Pages. "I could jam the A 15 with these, never mind that narrow Fen road. I'll start with Ali's Kebab House in Bourne, then Eastern Balti in Spalding – they claim 'Local fast free delivery'. By the way who's going to pay for all this?"

"Never mind that. The Intelligence Service should value Kenneth sufficiently to stump up for the odd curry! Rip out that sheet and give me the book. Now, who do I contact to fix that strong smell of gas? Here we are 'For any gas emergency... call free' ... 0800 111 999. That'll save the tax-payers' money!"

Soon taxis, pizzas, the RSPCA ('That reminds me, I must take that dog out!'), the gas, electricity, water emergency services and one or two others, were geared up to descend on

Hall Farm. The keys had been collected and passed to three tough-looking characters, carrying authorised weapons, stun grenades, etc., who were waiting in an anonymous looking van, two hidden in the back, ready to slip into the 'convoy'.

One thing was certain: those stuck out in that Fenland backwater, unable to go back on account of the continuing flow of vehicles, would not want for sustenance – or lack the sound of colourful language.

"I'll just gild the lily by telling Henry that I've ordered some take-away food to be delivered, so that the party from H Q can be fed," said Martin. "It might gain a few precious moments if they're expecting something, even if they do think it's a bit odd."

Henry did indeed think it odd, as such a thing had never happened before: indeed no tradesmen called, although suitably agricultural looking vehicles came and went from time to time. He was also surprised to receive a call, about twenty minutes later, from their contact at the River Board, asking what the problem was. It would have been better had Martin not included that organisation in his list of 'emergency call outs', for it had been heavily infiltrated right across the country. Messages began to flow. Henry was instructed to check back with Gerald concerning his unprecedented and out of character decision to invite a delivery of food.

It would also have been better had Martin not (as he had indeed described it) sought to 'gild the lily' by ringing to say that a van was on its way, for on receipt of this, to him strange, message, Henry sent Issed on a 'quad bike' to intercept the delivery at the main road. About twenty minutes later, a little ahead of time, the first of the vans, bearing a Pizza from Crowland, pulled up to consult his map and was approached by Issed.

The 'hit squad', waiting in a handy lay-by, were less than pleased to see an altercation taking place about a mile from the farmyard, as they realised that there was a danger that the crucial element of surprise could be lost. Fortunately, apart from having no money (hence the altercation), Issed did not have a mobile phone, so was unable to let the farm know why he continued to wait, despite the departure of the delivery van.

Paul, as look-out, was concentrating on the delivery van, so he did not see what happened when another van drove up and parked alongside. He reported this to Henry, who was in the bunker waiting for a call from the plane bringing John.

"Keep watching!" he told Paul. "Gavin from the River Board just rang to ask what's up. Apparently Gerald rang them, too."

"O K. Wait....the second van's moving off, now. Yes, so's the first one. I can see the word Pizza on the side. Good, I hope it's got salami.. I ... Issed's getting back on the bike.... Can't see any package. Did you give him any money?"

"No, I did *not*. Gerald can pay. I've only got a tenner. That's his problem. I can't think what the silly sod's doing anyway. What's happening now?"

"Issed's having trouble starting it. I bet he's forgotten to put his foot right down on the clutch, the dozy berk!"

In fact, Issed, minus his anorak, gloves and crash helmet was tied up and terrified in the back of the S A S van. Those same garments now adorned one of the soldiers who knew perfectly well how to start the bike, but was playing for time, well aware that he was likely to be under surveillance from the farm. Accustomed to taking the initiative and adapting rapidly to changing circumstances, the S A S team had established from Martin that he had informed the farm of the impending arrival of a fast food delivery (unspecifically, as it depended on which one got there first). Martin had been suitably contrite, but as it turned out it made it possible for the bogus Issed to stop and talk to each new arrival, in full view of the farm.

"There's another van coming!" Paul informed Henry excitedly on the intercom. "Issed's got off the bike and is stopping it.... and there's a bigger van starting to slow dow....."

"There's something funny going on, Paul. Send Akbor on the other bike to help keep them there. Hell! The pilot's calling from the plane now....."

Henry put down the intercom and cursed as he struggled with the unfamiliar equipment.

"Where the sodding hell are you when you're wanted, Gerald? Hello! Hello! Come in you stupid bastard!"

His frantic fingers sought to make the connection, each time getting the sequence wrong. The intercom buzzed again. "For Christ's sake! I can't get through to the plane! Can you work this gadget, Paul?"

"There's a string of yellow flashing lights now. I think they're all coming here. What do we do? Shall I drop a couple of 'em? They must be...."

"They must be after that bloody man tied up in the brig. I don't know what to....Christ! The plane's circling: I can see it on the monitor. It must be a trap. I....."

Once again the intercom cut off, leaving Paul gazing appalled as the two quad bikes sped back towards the farm and the plane, which had failed to get an answer to its request for confirmation of clearance for landing, came in on its final approach. The occupants did not notice Paul waving frantically from the top window of the farm, nor did they notice the quad bikes approaching at speed. The pilot, however, did hear from Henry, who managed at last to get the sequence right.

"What the hell are you doing?" cried John as the engine screamed angrily and the small plane levelled off and started to climb. The pilot, however, heard only the panicky screeching of Henry in his ears:

"Don't land! Abort! Abort! For God's Sake don't try to land. There's a....."

But neither the pilot nor John, nor his assistant ever knew what the problem was, for the straining engine failed to gain sufficient lift to clear the tree line at the edge of the airstrip. The landing wheels caught the top of a tree, lowering the nose that all-important fraction, so that, as they climbed from just above the river beyond, a wing caught the highest of the four overhead wires looped between the pylons which stretched northwards for mile after mile back to the main electricity supply plant and south for the industrial and residential needs of Peterborough. The explosion was spectacular and the flash from the stricken plane was the more visible as it coincided with the instant failure of every light in the area.

"Now that's what I call a diversion!" said the leading S A S man, as he skidded to a halt in the farmyard and called out, relying on being mistaken for the Asians, to establish where the opposition was.

It was unfortunate that Paul had been thinking about 'dropping' someone, for as a result he had his rifle raised to upper chest level as he leaned out in response to the call from what he believed to be Issed. He died instantly in a brief burst of silenced fire.

Armed with the knowledge of the approximate position of the strawstack door, Kenneth's rescuers had little difficulty in unlocking it with the aid of the keys provided by Martin. Rapidly donning gas masks, they opened it and hurled in a small but instantly effective gas grenade.

Neither Henry, who was just taking in what he had done, as the lights and monitor screens were extinguished, nor Kenneth, unaware of the whole scene, knew anything of the entry of the gas-masked soldiers. Having now been joined by the third member of their group, the party of six – three standing, three inert over their shoulders – slipped out into the yard. They went unnoticed by the occupants of the various emergency vehicles, taxi-drivers, etc., who had been proceeding in an orderly line towards the farm when they were stopped by the aerial drama and its shocking, mind-numbing result. It came as no great surprise to them, therefore, to see a low-flying olive-painted twin-rotor helicopter suddenly appear (in response to the call from its S A S colleagues on the ground) and hover close to the buildings. They might have been surprised, had they thought about it, by the speed of response, but then the same could have been said for the emergency services who were on the scene 'almost before the plane had ceased to burn' as one impressed reporter later put it.

CHAPTER SEVENTEEN

Apart from the phone call to elicit the fact that Martin had alerted Hall Farm to the imminent arrival of deliverers (in the more literal sense of the word!), he and Elizabeth had had no further contact, so had the same reaction as everyone else to the sudden failure of the electricity – shock and irritation. It did not occur to them that it might be connected to their own recent actions. No electricity, so no T V.....so no evening news bulletin containing brief details of the crash of a light plane, understood to have 'got into trouble' en route to Hull. The telephone, however, was still working, as a result of which Martin was preparing to set off for Stansted Airport (in response to a brief call from Patrick) still unaware of the success – one might almost say 'devastating success' – of the operation.

They had decided that it would be best if Elizabeth stayed, in case her mother rang, and to discover anything the authorities thought fit to tell them about the operation at Hall Farm, especially the well-being of Kenneth.

"Are you going to take the H F C identity card to show him?" she asked. "And what about the tapes of Ahmed?"

"Those tapes need to be kept safe. Put them in the freezer. I seem to remember that being used in some book I read, so that no-one would find them."

"Unless they'd read the same book, of course," said Elizabeth drily. "I'll get the card, then. Is it upstairs?"

"I think I put it in the basket on top of the fridge. Have a look."

"Now that's much safer. No-one can ever find anything there! Is this it – oh, no, that's slimy old Gerald. This is more like it. An international super-spy brilliantly disguised as a doddering old fool, I D number S U B 534. Why did you choose that num....Hey! That must have been why the chap at the Castle reacted to it – S U B...sub-marine! And we know Gerald was keen on U-boats and," she rushed on, pursuing the train of thought, coming perilously close (from the point of view of the 'High Command') to adding two to two and making five, "....and that old boy we think was his father was in U-boats during the war."

"Yes," said Martin, having caught up at last. "I asked Ahmed if he could recall the number on the U-boat in the photograph, but he couldn't. I think he said there was a 5 in it, but....."

"But it doesn't matter!" said Elizabeth impatiently. "We can get these S A S people to go and get the photo!"

"Well, yes, but for all we know they may have blown it up by now."

"Fusing the lights the while?" said Elizabeth facetiously, and then stopped short. "Actually that... Oh no, it was just a coincidence – I hope! To change, or rather revert to, the subject, why *did* you choose that number?"

"I just altered Gerald's. His was S U E 5 8 4, and it was easy to alter them by erasing or inking in parts of letters. It might be interesting to find out about U-534, I suppose..... if it existed. I must get going, though, or I shall get into trouble for being late."

"Yes. Given the sort of people Patrick seems to be able to conjure up, he'd probably have you shot for dereliction of duty. Leave the research to me – reading history at Magdalen may not have fitted me for much, but for that, I think I can say it did."

After her father had gone, having left instructions concerning the dog and a request to give his love to her mother when she rang, Elizabeth gave some thought to the nature of the conspiracy, or if not that, criminal organisation, which her father had stumbled upon. How widespread was it? Clearly Gerald looked elsewhere for instructions – and had contacts at the Castle and among the police. There was a branch in Harwich; the men who were dropped off by the furniture van came from somewhere, possibly from wherever the telephone code served; a helicopter was available from a nearby base at very short notice, and there seemed to be several H F C vans around; surveillance systems and loaded rifles implied that they had plenty to hide. Was their secret the traffic in illegal immigrants, or were they just one aspect of profitable business engaged in by..... by what, or whom? Perhaps Patrick could throw more light on it – could and would? Would he have pulled those strings in order to bring to justice minor criminals? Well, perhaps, to protect their father, who was clearly way out of his depth, even if the old devil seemed to be coping quite well, and was far from being intimidated. Indeed, it would be better if he *were* more frightened, she thought, hoping that the Hall Farm lot would never find out who had pretended to be Gerald and created the spurious 'stinging nettle' password.

"Now," mused Elizabeth, "who do I know who's a walking authority on U-boats?"

Martin set off for Yaxley to join the A 1 with a spring in his step. He always enjoyed the hassle-free experience of meeting his son at Stansted. It was an easy drive on the recently improved A 1, followed by the A 14 and then that least used of motorways, reminiscent of the best French autoroutes, the M 11. As the sign to Duxford came up, he was reminded of his wait on the bridge when he tracked the H F C van to Harwich. It was only a few days ago, but so much had happened it seemed quite a long time. What, he wondered, drew them to Harwich? Probably to arrange to process more unfortunates like Ahmed – those who survived that far. And what was *he* doing now? Had he managed to get a foot on the ladder – or had he landed on a 'snake'? He would have enjoyed hearing about Gerald, tied up by his own side! Martin continued to run over recent events and speculate about the success or otherwise of his diversionary tactics, until he saw the turn off for the Airport and concentrated on getting into the correct lane, to proceed, still unpressured by traffic (what a contrast with Heath Row!) to the car parks set aside for arrivals.He had a good hour to wait, as the flight from Prague was slightly delayed, so he rang Elizabeth to let her know he had arrived and see if there was any news. The modern, spotlessly clean, uncrowded concourse had a calming effect, so he was brought up short by his daughter's excited greeting.

"It's all happening here!" she began, somewhat to his alarm. "Did you hear the news on the way down?"

"No – I....."

"You didn't? The plane crashed, killing all on board – that's why we've still got no electricity. Julian rang to say that....."

"Julian? Who the Hell is Julian?"

"Oh, you know who I mean! Adrian! Anyway he rang to say 'mission accomplished', but I've no other details. Except one: he said the S A S asked to have a special word of thanks passed on to whoever had organised the diversion. Apparently it went like a dream – or a nightmare, depending on whose side you were on!"

"So Kenneth's all right? What about Gerald and his mates?"

"No details. All too secret, it seems, but he must be O K if 'mission' was accomplished. Anyway, well done us, eh? Tell that fat slob of a son of yours that with time and good leadership, his men could have a lot to offer!"

Martin found it difficult to take in the latest events, and could not imagine how or why a plane, presumably the one bringing the Area Commander, had crashed. However, there was more to come from Elizabeth:

"Also," she continued, "I've been busy on the U-boat front. I rang a friend in Sussex – more on that in a moment – who is an authority on such matters. Apparently one can walk round the old 534, if one is so inclined!"

She paused for both effect and breath.

"Walk round it?" The response was satisfyingly astonished.

"Yes. It's at the National Maritime museum at Birkenhead, having been raised from where it was sunk in 1945. It was thought to have important Nazi relics, gold, etc., as well as top party officials. They were all trying to escape from the Baltic, or Kiel, or somewhere at that time, but this one didn't make it."

"Didn't make it? Were there any survivors?"

"Yes. They nearly all survived, it seems..... and the official line is that there was nothing superspecial in the wreck when they brought it up. Mind you, if you believe that, you'd believe anything! I'm going up there to have a look."

They exchanged a few more words on the subject and then Elizabeth returned to a remark she had made earlier.

"There's one other thing, which might interest Patrick, if he doesn't know it already. You know I rang that friend?"

"Yes, the authority on....."

"Yes, Gareth. Well, he lives in Haslemere....and the code for Haslemere is 01428 !"

"Ye-es," said her father, wondering whether he was being particularly thick.

"Don't you remember? That was the code on the furniture van which brought the reinforcements! So it was probably the Haslemere Furniture Company – which is H F C!"

"Well, yes, but there is such a thing as coincidence, and you can't be sure it was called that."

"And is it just coincidence that Hall Farm is H F – probably followed by C for Company?"

"'Cultivation', in fact, if I recall the sign correctly," said Martin, "presumably to go with the mushroom beds over at Thorpe Tunnel. You could have a point, but not all H F C's can be bent."

"Maybe not, but they're suspect. What about these from the Yellow Pages? Holbeach Floor Covering; Hacconby Farming Company; Health Food Centre – that's Boston; Hereward Freight Company; Huntingdon Football Club....."

"Come off it. Every town beginning with 'H' that has a Football Club can't be helping to smuggle immigrants in order to balance the books! I'll pass on the tip, though. I suppose it would be convenient for vehicles to move from one area to another without exciting interest....like a Hull or Harwich Fishing Co. lorry going to Hall Farm. It'd be taken to be a local one at each place. Anyway, I must go. Take care!"

Martin replaced the receiver and, before setting off in search of a cup of coffee, sat down to ponder this latest intelligence.

He wondered whether the S A S had shot the plane down with a hand-held ground to air missile, but it seemed a bit strong and might have been seen by all the 'visitors' – always assuming they had arrived. Presumably they had, as the diversion was said to have been very effective. He had been a bit concerned when they had rung to ask whether he had told the farm. It had sounded as though something was amiss. Then there was the U-534: no wonder the young man at the Castle had asked respectfully if he was on it, when he saw the I D number. Mind you, one would have to have been well over 70 – the Germans were dragging in very young men by the end, but not, as far as he knew, under 5! The recruiting age was getting down to primary school level in some of these African countries these days, mind you..... and it was all too literally true that modern weapons were so light and easy to use that a child could master them. There was something else that the chap at the Castle had said. What was it? Something which related to the submarine – although he hadn't known about it, so the comments went above his head at the time. Probably didn't matter, anyway. Back to the present; time to go to the arrivals area.

"Might even," thought Martin, setting his wristwatch alarm, so as not to appear too geriatric by being still asleep when his son arrived, "doze off for a few minutes...." And he did, allowing his adrenalin-laden, overloaded system to calm down.

He was woken half an hour later by the insistent bleeping at his wrist, a bit stiff in the neck and feeling in need of a thirst-quenching drink, but otherwise far better able to face the world. The drink and a 'wash and brush up' would have to wait, however, as the Prague plane was down and the passengers would shortly be clearing customs. Eagerly, he scanned the arrivals, remembering the many times over the years that he had sat in the same spot, welcoming one of his children, or a foreign exchange student (most of whom seemed to exhibit an almost total unwillingness to communicate in any language, particularly English). In due course Patrick strode round the corner, instantly recognisable by the confident, almost loping walk, although the clothes marked him as 'Euro-man', along with the hair-cut.

To Martin's faint surprise, he waved from a distance and smiled, calling out 'Hi! Dad' from a short way away and putting down the shouldered bag in order to shake his hand. Having expected the usual British reserve and comparative difficulty in getting his son to communicate general gossip and small talk, Martin found himself surprised, given recent events, at the banality of their conversation. This was explained in the midst of what could only be described as a welcome, almost conventional, interest in the welfare of his mother, sister – and even the dog. Seeing the look of puzzlement on his father's face, Patrick continued the

113

catechism, but inserted an instruction to act normally, and not let this look like anything other than a holiday visit. Martin realised then that he was a form of cover for his son, who presumably thought they might be watched, or overheard.

"And don't look round!" added Patrick out of the side of his mouth. "We'll talk in the car....So, how are things? Still enjoying retirement – getting some of the decorating done?"

"Oh – er – yes, thanks. I've been using my new PaintMate: it's really good on ceilings. I've nearly finished the dining room and....."

"That sounds par for the course – nearly finished. You haven't lost your touch, then – nothing like nearly completing something!"

"I'll nearly finish you in a minute!" said his father, joining in with what he feared sounded like false laughter, but hoped was good enough to convince 'them', wherever they were.

In fact, he need not have bothered as the two shared sufficient features and mannerisms for there to be any doubt as to the meeting being genuinely father and son, as opposed to an occasion for 'clandestine business'. The hidden watcher contented himself with a quick photograph and then lost interest.

Still uncharacteristically discussing the merits of PaintMates and paper-hanging, they proceeded towards the parking ticket machine (without, to Martin's regret, having stopped for any form of refreshment) and joined the numerous people making their way to their cars. Martin had for years found it difficult to keep pace with his son (mentally as well as physically) but he found himself tending to move ahead as they emerged from the lower level.

"It's over there," he said, leading the way.

"Don't rush, Dad. I don't want to catch up those two ahead. Just take it steady."

"Are they spies?" whispered Martin, thinking it safe to refer, at least obliquely, to recent events which had presumably resulted in his son deciding to return to sort things out.

"Good Lord, no. The Honourable Anthony Laurence Burton-Latimer would be most insulted to be taken for a spy! He's just obnoxious, filthy rich, spent four years patronising those who were not from the top rank schools when we were at Cambridge – and less than happy when I got a First and he didn't!"

"What does he do, now?"

But Martin's question remained unanswered, as the object of their discussion turned, caught sight of Patrick and came towards them with a beaming smile of recognition.

"Paddy, you old devil! How's the world treating you? Still raking in the royalties on those poems?"

Patrick replied civilly and explained that he was taking a short holiday at home.

"I thought life was one long holiday for you – academic Poland can't have the stress endured by those of us who toil in the old 'Mille Carrée' – or have you moved into other fields these days?"

Was it his imagination, or was there a slight edge to that last question, wondered Martin, as he allowed his hand to be grasped in a probing, but unrequited, Masonic handshake, and debated whether to ask if the pompous twit of a merchant banker worked in Takeaway Catering. ('Meal Carry' indeed! – or perhaps it was a 'caff'' called the 'Square Mille', he continued silently to invent whilst exchanging conventional banalities).

"And are you a Cambridge academic, too, Sir?"

"No, L S E actually," he found himself replying. "I've recently retired – from teaching."

As Martin imagined, both the first reply, and certainly the second, were sufficient for him to be dismissed as of no further interest to Burton-Latimer, who parted from them in a haze of easily resistible charm and expressions of the desirability of the two young men 'getting together some time'.

"I see what you mean!" said Martin as they smilingly waved farewell and Monty (as he reprovingly reminded Patrick that he was known to his friends) rejoined his companion who was obviously the chauffeur. "I was tempted to ask him if he was related to Joyce Grenfell's 'Lumpy Latimer', just to see his face! And as for the 'Square Meal': I ask you!"

"I could almost feel the mutual disdain!" said Patrick. "But he's big in the City – or so he would have us believe."

As they were leaving at the same time, it was not surprising that they found themselves a few minutes later side by side at the traffic lights which controlled the big roundabout at the junction with the M 11. Glancing across to his left, Martin was reminded of his daughter's suspicions.

"If Elizabeth were here," said Martin, "we'd be following your aristocratic chum! He's travelling in a suspect vehicle!"

"A Renault Espace? Isn't that carrying francophobia a bit far?"

"No, the name on it – Harlow Ferry Cars....H F C! She has this theory that the reinforcements were probably dropped off by the Haslemere Furniture Company – and Hall Farm is really Hall Farm Cultivation and....." Martin continued his explanation as they moved round to the next set of traffic lights.

"Can you pull over for the Services, do you think? I could do with a coffee and there's nothing on the M 11."

"So could I. I thought you were in a hurry to get to – to wherever you want to go. Is it home, by the way? Oh God, these South East drivers. Can't the bloody fool see I want to get across?"

Patrick laughed, to the surprise of the driver of the articulated lorry, whose face was suffused with incipient road rage caused by his encounter with the bucolic 'Sunday driver' who had got into the wrong lane.

"You haven't changed, I see! Just go on round again – it was my fault. I should've told you sooner. I ought to make a phone call and you haven't got the mobile."

"Me, too. I'd better ring Elizabeth. When shall I tell her to expect us?"

"I'll let you know after those calls. I might want to stop off in Cambridge – but not for long. You sit over there, Dad. I'll join you in a few minutes."

CHAPTER EIGHTEEN

In fact, Patrick was nearer twenty minutes and returned with a wry smile on his face.

"I've been brought up to date on certain of your recent activities," he said, having first made sure that no-one could overhear them. "As your son, I am appalled, but in my – er – other capacity, I should like to congratulate you...and ask for your further assistance."

He paused and then added:

"Before we go any further, we should like you to sign the Official Secrets Act, to which end I have arranged for a brief meeting at my College with an appropriate person. Is that all right?"

There was no doubt in Martin's mind that it was not as a parent he was being addressed, that he had little option but to co-operate and, even after the forthcoming ceremony, would only be told as much as it was good for him to know. Facing him was not only a formidable intelligence, but also a steely resolve and – yes, that was it – the habit of command.

"Well, yes, of course; whatever. Are you going to pin a deputy's badge on Elizabeth, as well? She's au fait with everything, and has a much better memory than me."

"Don't worry about that, Dad. It's not a problem. Now let's....."

"You mean she's already signed it, don't you? Bloody Hell, I've been living in a nest of spies all these years and never....."

A dreadful thought occurred to him:

"Don't tell me your mother is at this very moment inserting a hatpin at the base of some Third World dictator's spine?"

"Far more likely to be undermining our own government's attempts to achieve a favourable Balance of Payments, if I know Mother...and I haven't said that any of us is a 'spy' as you so indelicately put it...any more...." he stifled his father's objection, "any more than *you* would be if you were to do your civic duty by continuing to help to investigate what could well be an aspect of neo-Nazism."

Put like that, there was little more to be said, so, at the latter's suggestion, Martin handed the keys to his son and settled back to get another half hour's recuperative slumber on the journey to Fitzwilliam College. He came to in time to marvel, as he still did each time he saw them, at the mediaeval splendour of the colleges as seen from 'The Backs'.

"Lifts the old spirit, doesn't it?" grinned Patrick, noticing that his elderly parent had surfaced.

As they drove along, he had glanced across from time to time at the nodding head, the hair even thinner – and certainly greyer – than he had remembered it and silently wondered how the Hell the old boy had managed to outwit such a murderous scheming bunch.

"The Backs? Yes, it sure does. When I'm here, I can't imagine how people can rave about Oxford....until I go there again!"

"Oh, Oxford certainly has something," said Patrick turning into the car park at the front of Fitzwilliam, "but not as much as Cambridge!"

"Don't let Elizabeth hear you say that!"

"The poor, deluded soul. Right. Now leave this to me. The College has put my usual room at our disposal, so I'll leave you to wait a few minutes in the Porters Lodge while I brief these people. Then someone'll come and get you, to be 'sworn in'. That O K by you?"

"I'll give Elizabeth a quick ring; I forgot to do so at the 'Services'. Then I'll wait in the chapel. I shall feel a bit less 'spare' than standing around, looking like everyone's grandfather. Shall I say we'll be there in – what? Two hours?"

"Make it two and a half, then she won't worry if we're a few minutes late."

About ten minutes later, Martin was collected, warned about the significance of his actions in signing the Act, and was then, at last, ready to engage in an in-depth discussion, which was really a form of interrogation, interlarded with some explanations and many more references which went over his head, as the little group hammered out the way forward.

"To keep our options open," said Patrick, "I gave instructions that the guy who was in the bunker – the one who told the pilot not to land – was not to be allowed to regain consciousness for the time being. He was in an inner room, so never saw the S A S open the main door. He was suddenly rendered unconscious by the gas grenade, so we can feed him any story we like, bring him round where we like.....or," he nodded at his more 'hawkish' colleague, "we could stop him coming round at all."

"Surely he's not high enough up in the Organisation to lead us to anyone. We already know his boss: he's trussed up, oven-ready, in this Tunnel place. He'd've been taken out if he'd offered any armed resistance, so ....."

Martin tried to keep all expression off his face as they debated the fate of the wretched man, for in his capacity as the spurious Gerald, he had come to regard Henry almost as a colleague – a bit simple, unable to cope when things got difficult, but surely not so evil that he had to be exterminated. However, Martin knew it was not he who was going to be taking that decision: he waited in silence.

"I agree he's of no great consequence (although doubtless his mother loves him), but you're quite right, Bernard, to home in on the one who really matters – Gerald, who's suffered the indignity of being captured by his own side."

Martin recognised the technique of making the person whom you intend to persuade believe that he it was who had thought of it first!

"Haven't they worked that out yet? They only had to get the farm to ring the relevant mobile number, then, when the one at Thorpe Tunnel rang, it would be obvious who was the real Gerald and who was the impostor."

"I have been advised," replied Patrick," that when they entered the Tunnel bunker, using Gerald's own keys, of course, they found him still tied up, next to his inoperative mobile phone, which must have got broken at some point. There were no signs of the famous reinforcements, who must have just abandoned him to his fate. I gave instructions that he was to be told nothing and kept there until we decided how to deal with him."

"I think he should get a taste of his own medicine. Drop him down a handy well: he was quite happy to see Kenneth go that way!"

Once again the 'hawkish' approach was advocated by Bernard, and once again the voice of reason, or perhaps it should be called 'guile', raised the intellectual level – not that that was difficult, in Martin's view, with Bernard around.

"No, we'll stick to your original idea, Bernard, and use Gerald. He could be very valuable alive and working for us."

"Out of gratitude? He'd be too frightened of the Organisation to stick to any bargain he made with us and if they just left him there, they can't regard him as too much of a security risk. Presumably he doesn't know anything really worthwhile, but I agree he should be kept for us to sweat out of him what he *does* know."

The last few words caused Martin's scalp to tingle at the thought of being 'sweated' by Bernard, whose ancestors probably worked over Guy Fawkes in order to unmask the other plotters.

"I haven't crossed all the 'T's' yet," said Patrick, ignoring Bernard's failure to realise that – from *their* point of view – it was not Gerald who had been left by the 'reinforcers', "but I think we can persuade Gerald to work for *us*. I think we can ensure that, from his friends' point of view, he comes out of this smelling of roses."

"But the man is an absolute liability!" expostulated Martin, unable, despite his earlier resolution, to keep quiet. "He was conned into effectively deserting his post, failed to keep in touch, left his incompetent assistant to carry the can, as a result of which the regional boss, or whatever he was, has been written off! He smells more like the stuff you put *on* roses: they'll crucify him!"

"I'm glad to see that *someone* in the family can see the main picture," said Bernard. "Welcome aboard!"

Martin was struck with an instant feeling of contrition at having let down his son, and disgust at finding himself lining up with the bloodthirsty and, to put it mildly, unsubtle Bernard.

"I only meant..... "

"And you were quite right, Martin" said Patrick, using his father's given name for, as far as the latter could recall, the very first time.

He carried on, mildly amused by the look of surprise, which owed as much to the 'Martin' as to the endorsement of his father's expression of dissent. "That is our lever – his fear of his present bosses finding out what really happened. Our other lever is his love of his fellow man, or, as the Greeks might have put it, homophilia. Again, he won't wish his superiors to be made aware that the plane crashed because he was trying to entice young Ahmed to the Tunnel for his own sexual gratification."

Patrick paused while his slower-witted audience took in the beauty of the scheme.

"It could be said," said Martin, relieved that his outburst had been turned to advantage, "that you have him by the short and curlies!"

"Yes, it might work," said Bernard grudgingly, "but only if you could produce any real evidence."

"But we can, Bernard, and we can persuade Gerald to provide us with some more, too. No.....," Patrick hurried on, as he saw a gleam in his colleague's eye, "not by wiring him up to the light, but by getting him to enunciate certain appropriate phrases, out of context, and then getting our tame Ahmed impersonator, or rather impersonatrix, to provide suitably incriminating questions. The technical boys should be able to construct something which would ensure an instant death sentence for Gerald."

"No court of law would convict him on that sort of evidence," said Bernard authoritatively, drawing on his knowledge of police procedure. "You'll have to do better than that!"

Even Martin, however, could see the obvious, but it was the fourth member, Ralph, who spoke, almost for the first time.

"It's not the courts who would have to be convinced, but the neo-Nazi High Command, and they won't be quibbling about the 'burden of proof'. Not only that, we only have to convince Gerald. Providing he thinks his colleagues would believe the tape, he'll work for us. Yes, it's brilliant. Let's get to work crossing those 'T's'!"

'T'-crossing revolved around the construction of a scenario which would explain the destruction of the plane, the escape of Kenneth (without Henry being aware of it) and the death of

Paul, whilst preserving, or rather enhancing, the reputation of Gerald. At this point, Ralph took over and quickly set in motion the brainstorming session.

"First of all, some easy bits. The immigrants must have taken fright and disappeared, followed by Paul, who has to be the person who fouled up."

"Yes. He must have rushed into the bunker, knocked out Henry (who therefore remembers nothing and is a bit confused), given dud instructions to the pilot and then......"

"..... fled, realising he would have to answer with his life for killing the occupants of the plane."

"The only trouble is that Henry wasn't hit; he was gassed," objected Bernard.

"If we decide on that story," replied Ralph, "we make sure he gets a hefty clout before we bring him round: if it genuinely causes concussion, so much the better. Now, what about Kenneth? Did Paul let him out – or overpower him when he burst in to finish him off?"

"One of the Asians could have freed him – before running away, that is," suggested Martin, tentatively.

"Possibly," said Ralph encouragingly. "Keep the ideas coming: any other suggestions?"

"We must remember," said Patrick thoughtfully, "that Gerald himself does not necessarily have to have been jumped by the reinforcements: that could have been (as the two who locked him up thought) the person impersonating him. Bear in mind that Henry thinks he was talking to the real Gerald most of the time. That could be useful in developing a story which puts Gerald in a good light and is backed up by Henry."

Martin made the occasional contribution, but most of the time he struggled to keep up as Ralph and Patrick rewrote history, searching for a way to divert any blame from Gerald, whilst ensuring that Henry, if questioned by Gerald's superiors, would confirm the tale.

"Henry would never stand up to a professional interrogation," said Patrick, "so we have to make sure that he believes the tale which Gerald will spin him – and feels indebted to him, loyal to him, flattered when asked by Gerald to be his personal assistant in his new job."

"What new job? He'll be lucky to keep the old, never mind a new one," exclaimed Bernard, dead on cue.

"I think," said Ralph slowly, "that Patrick is ambitious for our new friend – wants to see him get on in life. Am I right?"

"We said earlier that we wanted him 'covered in roses'," said Patrick mildly. "We can't predict the course of his career, but we can do our best to get him trusted – even twist things so that the recently deceased Regional Controller is seen as trying to take over Gerald's operation and, in the process, causing a monumental balls-up."

"Including his own death," said Martin. "Talk about poetic justice!"

"If the story is that the real Gerald was riding to the rescue, who are they to think is (as far as they know) still tied up in Thorpe Tunnel? And who do they think that *we* think he is?"

The discussion continued too rapidly for Martin, who was still trying to get his mind round the implications of Ralph's questions when he became aware that all three were looking at him.

"Sorry! I was just trying to work that last bit out. Did I miss something?"

"Yes!" said Bernard nastily. "Your death!"

Martin stared at the grim-faced trio in astonishment (mixed with some alarm and the beginnings of anger)."My what! Come off it. I've managed to stay out of their way – and in any case...."

"Don't worry about it, Dad," laughed Patrick. "We'll find a stand-in on the night. The point is that Gerald can report to his superiors that, on opening up the mushroom farm, he discovered someone tied up – and then acted decisively to get rid of the evidence."

"But surely I – that is, this person – would be missed. There'd be relatives. Some explanation of why he he'd been watching the farm would be needed."

"It is never," said Ralph, "difficult to convince someone who *wishes* to be convinced. They thought all along that they were dealing with an amateur, someone who just happened to be nosy, was working on his own, but, by sheer luck – his own bad luck, it will now appear – started to peel back too many layers of the onion."

Ralph continued to develop the scenario. The man knew too much to be allowed to live and, under Gerald's skilful questioning, gave away the fact that he had told no-one what he was up to. His only relative was his sister, who lived in Canada, and his neighbours in a large faceless estate in Peterborough thought he went off bird-watching (as, indeed, had been his habit until he started taking an interest in Hall Farm). He had (Gerald would report) grown quite animated when he explained how he had followed the H F C van all the way to Harwich, where he had lost it. Gerald would be able to add, with the superior smile of one of the Gods, that the brief excitement afforded to the poor old bugger probably made up for the curtailment of his existence, which was unlikely even to be noticed until Christmas, when he was in the habit of making his annual telephone call to Canada.

As he drove steadily home from Cambridge, Martin ruminated on the disturbing similarities between the fictional 'busy-body' and himself, the real life one, whose neighbours also thought he went dog-walking (and bird-watching) and whose boring life had likewise been injected with excitement. He, too, could have had 'bad luck', been caught by Gerald and quietly disposed of. He shuddered and glanced across for reassurance at his son, who lay back, eyes closed, running through a series of ingenious scenarios to explain how Gerald, the resourceful, dynamic master planner, had reacted to finding Kenneth locked up at the farm. Had he already been released by the bungling Paul? Had he still got him locked up, planning to claim to the police when they came looking for him, that he must have wandered off and fallen down that well? Behind the closed eyelids, the formidable brain created and rejected, wove webs and summoned legends with which to confuse his opponents, only too aware that the passage of time would very soon start closing off options.

CHAPTER NINETEEN

An emergency meeting of the High Command had been arranged to take place two days later: it was going to be a sombre one. Their number had been reduced by two, the first by natural causes, the second in an unexplained plane crash on a routine flight to one of their outlying units somewhere in the Fens. Moreover, they knew no more than could be gathered from news reports, in addition to a comment from a police sympathiser (unconfirmed) that a member of the Intelligence Service had visited the farm just before the crash. They knew, too, that John had arranged for a van-load of reinforcements to travel north, only to be recalled, having achieved little, as soon as the nature of the disaster had been discovered. Word had also been sent to Vienna, who had already arranged to send a man to check on certain rumours concerning the British section.

The information had been passed to the unit on Mersea Island, near Colchester which, like so many others, used as its hidden base one of the government underground bunkers, known only to a very select few since the early nineteen-forties. Those few had been approached to form the core of the 'resistance movement', set up to carry on the fight after the expected German invasion. This particular outpost consisted of a large garage, built ostensibly to house a single-decker service bus for what became the Eastern National. Although quite large, its size was more than tripled by the extensive underground chambers, reached from a hidden trap door in what appeared to be an inspection pit. Ownership of this building had passed to the River Board in the sixties and the secret of its hidden accommodation had been passed from father to son. It was, perhaps, paradoxical that the present guardians of that secret, just like their equivalent in the Fens, and throughout much of the land, now owed allegiance to a structure dedicated to the re-emergence of that same German National Socialist organisation it had originally been designed to combat. Hitler, of course, and his senior colleagues, would not have seen anything odd about this, for all along they had cherished hopes of an accommodation with the U K. Right up to the end, with Russian armies within striking distance, they continued to hope that the British would realise that the real enemy of Europe lay to the east, that they would abandon the foolish pact with Stalin and help to drive them back. The common enemy was Communism, and there were those who sympathised among the British aristocracy, including, many thought, not only the recently dispossessed monarch, but also those who had been entrusted by a gullible government with the task of setting up, and commanding, the embryonic resistance movement. Who could be less suspect of being in command of a bunch of poachers than the landowners who were their traditional enemy?

By the nineties, of course, many such subterranean complexes, having been first decommissioned then re-arranged as (still secret) local seats of government in the case of a Russian nuclear attack, had been sold off to a 'suitable' bidder. One such was Thorpe Tunnel, owned quite openly by Hall Farm Cultivators. Others, like Hall Farm itself – and the old bus garage at East Mersea – remained secret, and actively engaged in the long-term service of those who still schemed to bring about one Europe under the leadership of a strong, re-united right wing Germany.

It was to this area that Vienna's man 'Larry' (Monty to his friends) was driven, after his encounter with Patrick and his elderly uninspiring father. He, too, like Patrick, had sat back in silence, running over in his mind the events which had caused him to return hurriedly to England. There had been some faint suggestion that Patrick Brady was not quite what he seemed and had it not been for the obviously genuine nature of the father/son meeting, Monty would have been extremely suspicious. He had, in fact, arranged for a photograph to be taken of the person who met him – although in the event that had been a waste of effort. He had long been aware that Patrick engaged in the odd bit of low level intelligence work for H M G, under cover of his (very genuine) academic pursuits. Monty, himself, did likewise, gaining useful contacts thereby, but there had been disturbing reports coming to him that someone, somewhere, was getting together a task force to investigate aspects of the neo-Nazi Movement which could result in them being panicked into unwise action.

The H F C car swept on towards Colchester, where it turned off onto the B 1025 to Mersea Island. As so frequently happened – twice a day in practice, depending on the height of the tides – they were brought to a halt at the Strood, where a line of vehicles waited for the flood tide to subside and render the Island accessible. An impatient man by nature, Monty looked up in annoyance as the car slowed, but was reassured to some extent when his driver pointed to a man moving towards them from a River Board Landrover which was parked on the other side of the road.

"Good! They may have a message for me: I'll stroll along and have a word as if I'm asking about the tides."

Remembering to point occasionally at the causeway and the marshland surrounding it, the two men spoke for rather longer than was required to establish whether the tide was still coming in, for there was indeed a message, bringing news of recent happenings. 'Monty' Burton-Latimer returned slowly to his car and sank into the back seat, plainly a worried man. He was shocked to hear of the death of John, one of the most able members of the Council in his opinion, and worried by the escalation of interest in Hall Farm from that evinced by an elderly busy-body to the involvement, however tentative, of the Intelligence Service. Could there be someone pulling strings in the background – or were these strands unconnected? Of more immediate importance, what should be done to ensure that the secrets of Hall Farm be kept, despite the presence of police, crash investigators, reporters and even T V cameras?

The sea water having now receded from the roadway, it was possible to continue the journey, ostensibly to the motor cruiser 'Python', which Monty kept moored in a channel just off East Mersea, for his local cover was that of a wealthy 'winter sailor' (as those who seldom ventured forth were disparagingly known to the natives). In his absence, an eye was kept on the boat by a firm from West Mersea which was home to hundreds of such vessels. It would not have amazed Elizabeth that the firm was called 'Henry Farley Chandlers' and made use of vehicles bearing the letters H F C.

As soon as he had rowed across to the well appointed craft, Monty set about communicating with a number of influential members of the Movement, using his link to the powerful transmitter set in the 'Garage Bunker', a few hundred metres away on dry land. However, no-one either knew exactly what had happened, or had much idea of how to proceed, apart from hoping to hear from the local unit commander, always assuming that person (name of Gerald, apparently) was still both alive and at large.

"What's this chap like, Malcolm? Is he up to dealing with a situation like this?"

"Well, I don't think John was very impressed: he wasn't in favour of his replacing Andreas when Edwin proposed him. In fact, he was on his way to take over as things seemed to be getting out of control."

"A bit early to be organising a replacement wasn't it? The old chap was barely cold!"

"Yes it was, Larry, but I think Edwin had been asked to put him up, as a favour to an old friend, handing down, father to son, you know!"

"Oh! He's the son, is he? Well, well. Now's his chance to show what he's worth – if he's in a position to do so, that is. I have one or two connections in the area; might make a social call and contrive to meet this chap. We can afford to write off that set-up. The important thing is to make sure no-one gets wind of the Harwich operation."

"John wasn't too worried about that, but there was some report about one of our vans being followed. They suspected the same chap they saw checking on the farm with binoculars – very amateurish, just nosy."

"When was that?" asked Monty, far from totally reassured.

"About a week ago, I think. One of their immigrants went walk-about around the same time."

"Any connection?"

"No. No question of that, but as far as I know they hadn't found either of them by the time of the plane crash."

"Which, again, had no connection, I presume?" asked Monty whose inclination was never to rely on coincidences being quite what they seemed.

"Well, hardly old boy! Bird-watching snoopers and stateless lads living rough are unlikely to be operating ground-to-air missiles. This Intelligence chappie *might* have put a spanner in the works, but it would be a bit, shall we say, unsubtle and more likely to *stop* them finding things out than ......"

"There's no question of our own people having caused the crash, I suppose?" asked Monty. "To do just that – stop H M G from finding out what we're about. Was the agent killed at the same time?"

"You're always looking for conspiracies! Planes *do* crash from time to time – and I shouldn't let your opinion of the leadership be too widely known, or we might be reading *your* obituary!"

"Which is another way of saying that you agree with their, or rather, *our* capacity for ruthless action when needed!" replied Monty. "I may be various things, but naïve I am not, nor squeamish. Such action might, for all I know, have been entirely appropriate. I shall therefore be just as suspicious as the opposition if it transpires that their man conveniently perished before he could make a report. We desperately need more information."

Having not yet worked out just what he was up against, 'Monty' Burton-Latimer failed to appreciate that what he did not need (but was likely to acquire) was a large portion of disinformation. He was not, however, one to let the grass grow under his feet, so made further phone calls to arrange his transportation to and accommodation at Wothorpe Castle. The current owner, like his immediate predecessor, enjoyed a substantial subsidy from the proceeds of the neo-Nazi Movement for doing little more than provide a respectable front and condone various dubious, not to say downright illegal, activities. This both ensured his current high standard of living and promised a position of power, wealth and influence when the long-planned unification of Europe took place – not under a weak, vacillating democracy, but under firm, efficient leadership, patriotic in the real sense, able to move on the world stage with the confidence of the Germany of 1940.

In the mean time, to keep the great ideal alive, money was needed, to buy continued loyalty as son took on the torch from father, especially as those who took over became distanced from their forebears by time. They were held together by the secret they shared rather than by blind obedience to a 'führer', or by pseudo-religious concepts which sought to continue the fight pursued by the 'chivalrous' in the mediaeval Crusades, against the race deemed to have put to death the Son of God. They had become, of course, little more than a secret society, akin to the Mafia, or the Triads, seeking to benefit themselves by the age-old methods of theft, intimidation, blackmail and assassination. The anti-gun lobby had their full support; they championed those who suffered from the freedom of the press; they looked with approval at the reduction of local democratic influence in favour of powerful regional assemblies; they looked forward to the minor twist which would be needed to make the National Curriculum an effective means of child indoctrination. All that was needed was 'enlightened' leadership, the emergence from the shadows of those who had grown from the seed sown so effectively in the very last days of the Second World War. That seed had been carried under water and nurtured by the many who sympathised with the Great European Ideal, which had foundered against the unholy alliance of the then leadership of America and Russia – two of the small group of bullies in the world playground.

Thus thought the likes of Monty, John (whose light had gone out when his plane struck the Fenland pylon), the current Lord Wothorpe, and others on whom Patrick was engaged in foisting the corrupted (in more than one sense) Gerald. The latter was incapable of appreciating anything other than his own personal situation, caring little for ideals, whether 'Great', 'European' or related to ethnic cleansing, but was none the less dangerous when wielding a gun. He would not be the first member of a ruling group, if he could become accepted, who lacked the intellectual powers required for efficient discharge of his duties, however. History could show many examples of the lunatics being given the keys to the asylum.....and some examples of those lunatics being ultimately controlled, for a few years, by a woman or man who was, in all senses of the word, 'rational'.

As he sped westwards from Colchester towards the M 11, Monty came to feel that his short term aim was to meet this Gerald and form a view concerning his competence. Someone had to take over from John, but on the face of it, this fellow's experience was very limited, even if he was the son of one of the 'founding fathers'. His present command was little more than a muddy outpost, boasting a permanent staff of what? Three plus a few 'illegals'? On the other hand, he was acquainted with the set-up at the Castle, well to the north of the region, and regularly visited the all-important operation at Harwich. He was in a position to call up helicopter support – although one wondered whether he had botched that manoeuvre, just as one wondered to what extent, if at all, he was personally responsible for John's plane crash. Had he managed to do anything about the visitor to the farm, whom their police sympathisers had identified as an Intelligence agent? Which reminded Monty: a bonus payment should be made in that direction, to ensure continued loyalty to the cause.

Subject to his being unexpectedly impressed by Gerald as a result of meeting and talking with him, Monty thought it would be better to appoint Roger, John's deputy, to command the Eastern Area. There was, however, no reason to raise him to the High Command, a post for which he, Monty, was far better fitted, although it would increase the risk of his being rumbled, and, in any case, he had his eye on even higher things. No, on the whole he preferred to manipulate the Council members, be the puppet master, so to speak, maintaining his ability to move in diverse circles, including the Security Service itself, at present only at the lower levels.

At Wothorpe Castle, Monty was greeted by the butler, shown to his room and told that, as requested, an office had been put at his disposal. The Agent for the Estate, Philip Proudfoot ('Another possible contender for preferment within the movement,' mused Monty), was away, as was His Lordship. The latter was in fact a distant cousin who, whilst being his host and the ostensible reason for the visit, did not get directly involved. He was not expected, thought Monty wryly, to 'dirty his hands' in the day-to-day business of murder and mayhem. As a result, only the young assistant, Christopher, was available to run errands.

Monty visited the Castle rarely. Despite having some good shooting, first class venison and salmon flown down from the Scottish estates, it was, in his opinion, uncomfortable and inconvenient. One had to keep disappearing into secret passages to avoid the paying public, and his host's I Q was only, in Fahrenheit terms, marginally above the far from stifling temperature deemed suitable for the well-being of the fabric: neither managed to rise much above sixty.

Duty called, however, and Monty settled down to catch up on various items of business, including the latest on Hall Farm. The only additional piece of information came from the police contact, who could give a welcome reassurance that the bunker had not been discovered. As the disintegrating plane had brought down the telephone wires, it was quite possible that one or more of the staff (including the odd 'illegal') might be inside, unable to emerge as the failure of their surveillance system made it too risky, and unable to communicate with the outside world by telephone. They hoped to restore telephone communication fairly soon, but as there appeared to be no-one at the farm, it was not possible for the police to exert pressure to get the matter treated with any urgency: only the owners of the farm, or their 'friends' could do that. Monty was not worried about the survival of anyone trapped in the strawstack bunker: it was built for that very purpose and kept provisioned against any eventuality. He had not expected, however, to be faced with the communication problem.

"We'll see what we can do about restoring the telephone link in the morning," he told Christopher. "In the mean time, I must be told immediately we hear from Gerald, or anyone else on his staff. Get me a link to Northern Area: I'll get them to send someone who can pretend to be an insurance assessor. Have you got any spare keys for that 'bunker'?"

"No, Sir – at least not as far as I know. We didn't go there at all. In theory they just supplied us with fish; not, that is, from the farm, but they went there as well and brought us the passport photos and then....."

"Yes, yes, I see," said Monty. "There must be one of them somewhere who will have the sense to get in touch shortly. I'll ring round one or two people to see if they know of any spare keys. If the worst comes to the worst, we'll have to get hold of a J C B and dig them out on some pretext or other, but we'll give it twenty-four hours and hope something turns up."

CHAPTER TWENTY

Unknown to either, the two high-powered young men who had met and sparred verbally at Stansted a short time before, were now only a few miles apart. One, Monty, hoped to receive some information, the other, Patrick, was working hard to provide it. On arriving in the area, Patrick had dropped his father off at his home and gone on to Thorpe Tunnel, where a by now very apprehensive (and, it has to be said, rather noxious) Gerald was still tied up, just as he had been when left by the two who had apprehended him. They had been rapidly withdrawn when the whole operation ran into the ground with the fatal plane crash.

Awaiting Patrick in the Tunnel bunker was Kenneth, fully recovered from his experiences at Hall Farm and bearing no great good will towards Gerald (not that the wretched man had had any part in his treatment, or even knew who he was). Patrick had instructed that Kenneth bring with him a discreet two-way communicator so that, despite controlling the course of the interview, he could ensure that the only visible contact was Kenneth, who would do the talking. The fewer who knew that Patrick was more than an international academic, the better – and in that context he had wondered whether the condescending (but, he acknowledged, far from stupid) Burton-Latimer had heard that he might have 'branched out'. As Patrick knew, Monty himself had on occasion been helpful to the Intelligence Service, so would have a few useful contacts.

The hand which Kenneth was asked to play was a strong one, but he played it well, only occasionally needing a prompt from his hidden mentor, via the tiny speaker inserted into his ear. Having been carefully briefed by Patrick, who was situated in an adjacent room to monitor the proceedings, Kenneth moved in on Gerald, who was appalled to discover that he was now in the hands of the opposition. Whilst he required some evidence (newspaper report, photographs, etc., of the plane crash) he readily grasped that one of the options open to his inquisitor was, quite literally, to do *nothing* – to walk away and forget about him for a week or two. All the forensic evidence, and their own belief, would confirm that he had been left to die by the two members of the reinforcement team. In due course, they might work out that they had killed the wrong person, even if they failed to discover how, as Henry had been captured also (so could easily be made to 'disappear') and Paul was dead. Only if H M G could see a very positive advantage in keeping Gerald alive would they do so. He, Kenneth, who brought total realism to his expression of anger on this point, would be more than happy to mete out to Gerald the fate the Organisation had been prepared to arrange for *him*. There was, after all, little difference between being dropped down a well and being left to moulder in a mushroom farm.

A by now terrified Gerald offered to change sides, inform on all his contacts, give them all he knew about the immigrant-smuggling operation – anything. He would never have suggested killing a member of the Intelligence Service had he been put in the picture, but that fool Henry had only gibbered on about stinging nettles, and obviously had failed in the simple task of arranging the landing of the plane. He would make sure that Henry paid any price they wanted if they would only let him, Gerald, go free and carry on working for them. He could give them contacts in places they would never have *dreamed* of.....At this point, Kenneth languidly responded that he presumed he was referring to the Castle and that Gerald had really very little to offer which they did not know already, unless he could provide fuller details on the submarine connection.

It soon became apparent that Gerald was wary of telling them all he knew, lest he then be considered expendable, and be left quite literally to rot. Responding to the instructions passed to him, Kenneth now pointed to the cassette recorder which had been, quite openly, registering their conversation.

"What do you think your superiors would say if they were to receive a copy of you agreeing to work for the other side?" he asked his prisoner.

"They'd kill me, but why should you want to tell them. I can be more use to you on the inside than....."

135

"No, they wouldn't," said Kenneth. "They would regard it as something said under duress – and start feeding us dud information. You could convince them that your true loyalty still lay with them, and then go on to prove it in some appropriate way."

"Well, I – er – I wouldn't. I mean it wouldn't.....my loyalty, that is. You could rely on me to...."

"To do anything to save your foul-smelling skin!" Kenneth completed the sentence threateningly. "No, *that recording* will not ensure your continued co-operation with us..... but *this* one," he paused to insert another cassette, "should do the trick."

Any fight that had still remained in Gerald evaporated as he heard Ahmed's voice, and his own setting out in graphic detail just what the lad was expected to do in return for the older man's help. He could imagine only too well the combined effect of a revelation that he was not only homosexual but had, in effect, caused the death of John Dalton and compromised the entire operation in order to indulge his, to them, unacceptable passion.

"How – how did you...? He said he was....." Gerald's voice died away and silence fell in the room as the tape came to an end.

"Just leave him to stew for a bit," came the instruction to Kenneth. "You've done well. He'll do anything you tell him in the future. Leave him and come next door so that we can plan the next phase."

Kenneth emerged from the interrogation room, shutting the door firmly behind him on the thoroughly dejected and demoralised figure still tied to his chair, sitting miserably in his own excrement.

"Whew! The smell in there!" he said, removing the tiny speaker from his ear. "He's ripe for plucking – do you want to take over, now?"

"No. You're doing very well. I don't want him to see me, as we might meet at some time and one cannot rely on a fool like that not to give the game away. Give him a few more minutes, not longer as we have to get him moving, and then this is the plot."

Patrick proceeded to set out the 'life-line' which Kenneth was to offer. It was, in many ways, an attractive proposition. In return for selling his soul to the devil (incarnate in the form of Kenneth), Gerald was to report to H Q in terms of a scenario which bore about as much relation to fact as an incorrect choice in the T V panel game 'Call My Bluff'. If presented persuasively and in a transparently honest manner, it had a seductive ring of truth about it.

Patrick made Gerald and Kenneth go over and over what was supposed to have happened, and was not satisfied until he heard Kenneth report (with some disgust) that Gerald's swagger was returning. Gerald now enjoyed seeing Kenneth's discomfort as he described the latter's cringing whine as he was lowered into the well, head first. Kenneth (he would claim) had later recounted the sensation of pounding in the ears, bulging eyes and the last thoughts as he struggled to hang on to the life-retaining breath. Gerald even embellished slightly, describing how he had drawn the attention of the emergency services away from the yard by telling them he had seen a figure staggering towards the river, thus enabling him to slip unnoticed inside the strawstack.

By this time, Gerald had come to half believe that he really had shown that cool resolve and instant grasp of a dangerous situation expected of someone worthy of promotion. He had got over his surprise at being told that they already knew who his father had been (although he had the feeling that some of his contribution concerning the numerous children, like himself, who were brought over by submarine at the end of the war, came as news to them). After an extensive wash and a change of clothing, with the sentence of death lifted and the prospect of his re-instatement, Gerald was not only ready to play his new rôle, he was looking forward to it.

"The big factor in our favour," said Patrick as he settled down to listen off-stage and, if necessary, pass instructions to Kenneth concerning the response required from Gerald, "is that they won't wish to believe that their organisation has been penetrated to the extent that it has. That renders them – or most of them – essentially gullible. The interpretation of events which we are feeding them is one which will be music to their ears, music designed to lull them to sleep, or at least encourage them to relax their guard."

The star of the forthcoming show acknowledged the signal from his erstwhile tormentor, who had now become his 'control' and reached out purposefully for the telephone.

"H F C. Can I help you?"

"Gerald here. Put me through to David."

"I think he's rather tied up at the moment. Can I pass on a message?"

"No, you can't. Untie him, and put him on the phone NOW!"

The new Gerald was drawing on histrionic talents never before suspected. His eyes shone, his voice crackled with command and, despite himself, even David (who had been privy to John's less than complimentary comments), was impressed. As the tale unfolded, David realised he was out of his depth. Someone more senior needed to hear all this, and decide how to proceed. That lah-di-dah so-called banker who had just flown in from Eastern Europe was the best person to pass this particular buck to.

"Hold on, Gerald," he interrupted, "I'll get in touch with our Larry. He's somewhere up your way at the moment. Do you know him?"

After a fractional pause, Gerald replied that he didn't know him, then added for good measure:

"Is he reliable? I don't want some cock-eyed cowboy who imagines he can ride in and put the world to rights knowing sod all about it!"

David winced at this scarcely veiled reference to his late boss – and both Patrick and Kenneth tensed at this show of aggression, wondering if Gerald had gone too far.

"If you're referring to John, I'll have you know he....."

"John's out of it!" snapped Gerald. "I asked you about this Harry. Can you, or can you not vouch for him?"

Battered by the bullying treatment, anxious to pass the matter on and appalled by the callous attitude of the caller, David backed down, becoming if not servile, certainly acquiescent.

"It's not Harry, it's Larry – and yes, he's reliable. He reports direct to the High Command. I'll get him to ring you. Are you at the farm?"

"No, Thorpe Tunnel. And tell him to get a move on."

"I'll inform him," said David, without inflection, adding, as the phone went dead, "and I hope the tricky bastard stuffs one of those bloody pylons right up your Fenland fanny!"

Back at Thorpe Tunnel, Kenneth and Gerald, partners now in deception, whooped for joy.

"Bloody marvellous! You sounded like everyone's pet hate: a right little shit on the make. I can think of a few like that on *our* side!"

A strange look passed over Gerald's face: not 'hurt' exactly, but … reproof.

"But I am on your side now," he said.

Patrick, listening in the next room, smiled and said quietly to himself:

"I do believe you are and so do you! Now for the big one – this Harry/Larry."

CHAPTER TWENTY-ONE

There was rejoicing, too, at the Castle when the news came through that Gerald was not only all right but seemingly had everything under control.

"He insists on meeting you, apparently," said Christopher, who had taken the message from David.

"Really!" said Monty. "And how is it he's heard of me – still less knows I'm here?"

"David thought you were the best person to contact in the circumstances – and Gerald was acting pretty high-handed."

"Was he? Do you know him, by the way?"

"No," said Christopher. "I've only been here a short time, but the others do. They haven't said much about him. He usually calls in the van to collect papers and....."

"Unless he sends an elderly fraudulent stand-in?" interposed Monty, enjoying the younger man's embarrassment.

The latter had been going to say that his colleagues had also said that Gerald was normally very quiet and that he was amazed to hear that he had been 'uppity' with someone from H Q – and equally surprised to hear that he had sorted everything out, rather than wait for 'them' to tell him what to do. As it was, this information, which just might have rung a warning bell in Monty's mind, was not conveyed, for Christopher, crushed by the reminder of his gullibility, stood in red-faced silence.

"Well, as it happens, I want to see *him*," said Monty, after a brief pause, "so you'd better set it up."

Christopher paused, wondering whether he wanted Gerald to come to the Castle, or would prefer to go to him.

"Well, get on with it. I have other matters to attend to before I fly back. I have no wish to spend another night in a freezing cold, crenellated cubby-hole!"

Monty's experience of the mediaeval delights of the 'Old Tower', a room whose only merit lay in its total inaccessibility by members of the paying public, had not left him in the best of moods.

Christopher hurried off, reflecting that however high-handed Gerald turned out to be, he could hardly be worse than this miserable sod. He duly rang Gerald at Thorpe Tunnel Bunker and agreed with him that 'Larry' (the name used by Burton-Latimer within the Organisation) would be there in about two hours. He, Christopher, would bring him in his own car, a white Honda Civic, and call back for him later.

Acting on Patrick's instructions, Gerald was very calm, reasonable and efficient – just the sort of person for whom Christopher would like to work, in fact.

"Things are a bit hairy around here at the moment," concluded Gerald, "so if you hear anything interesting, give me a buzz."

"Will do!" replied Christopher, flattered at being paid the compliment of treatment as an equal, especially from someone with a reputation for not being afraid to tell H Q to get off their backsides.

In fact, 'Larry' was far from pleased at being expected to crawl around in some damp mushroom-ridden cave and demanded to know why Gerald was not coming to *him*.

"Because, *Sir*," replied Christopher, "you did not ask me to arrange that; you left it to me, and I've agreed it with Gerald. He won't be happy to have the meet altered, and there's not much time, anyway. I said I would bring you, which I trust is to your liking."

Christopher paused and then, fresh from his confidence-boosting encounter with Gerald, added:

"The bus service is not very good out here in the sticks."

"Let's remember one thing," snapped Monty. "I do the jokes around here – and next time check before you make arrangements. How far is this – er – tunnel?"

"It'll take about twenty minutes – and it's a bit muddy," said Christopher, eyeing the highly polished Italian ('poncy' was the adjective which occurred to him) footwear sported by Larry. Perhaps, he thought, homophobically confusing the meaning, the name was short for Lothario, a name he recalled having looked up in a dictionary and found to mean a 'gay seducer'.

The timescale made possible a small amount of rehearsal, the setting up of recording, photographic and video equipment, all available in the Bunker, and the agreement between Gerald and Kenneth of a procedure in the case of a tricky line of questioning. The ploy agreed was that, if he could not think of a good answer, Gerald was to flap his left hand. The gesture would be seen by Kenneth, who would be watching on CCTV. He would contrive a noise, such as would give Gerald an excuse to leave the room to investigate, gun in hand, closing the door behind him.....and Patrick would provide instructions on how to respond.

The other aspect of the arrangements concerned the preparation of that lethal Ground Control Approach operative, Gerald's assistant, Henry. He, along with the body of Paul, and the comatose Kenneth, had been bundled out of the strawstack bunker by the S A S team and helicoptered away.

In accordance with Patrick's instructions, Henry had been kept unconscious until this moment, as a result of which it was possible for him to be brought round by Gerald and told that he had been carried from the bunker over to Thorpe Tunnel, where he had remained out for the count. He had been given a suitable bash on the head to give credence to the notion that Paul must have unaccountably decided to take over the landing procedure after rendering Henry and Kenneth unconscious. As would be expected, Kenneth was under guard and able to confirm to Henry that he was now working for Gerald.

Henry was full of admiration for his immediate superior (whom he had earlier criticised for having left him to stew on his own) as he learnt of the problems he had encountered, and his cleverness in 'springing' his colleague and the prisoner from the bunker under the very noses of the emergency services. He was also impressed by the casual way in which he related the despatch of the elderly snooper, whose body would eventually be found somewhere near Cromer, believed drowned off the north Norfolk coast whilst looking for a lesser-spotted shrike. He it had been, apparently, who had made the hoax telephone calls before being so efficiently unmasked by Henry – and left to die by John's bungling group of thugs. Gerald (supposedly) had elucidated the fact that the old fool had told no-one what he had discovered, but had denied all knowledge of the documents, even when subjected to 'persuasion'. It was to be Gerald's conclusion that the visitor to the Castle was a different person altogether. At present this was left unexplained, but Patrick had plans for Gerald to evolve a plausible theory later. The odd 'loose end' was not to be wondered at: it often occurred in real life.

Monty arrived in good time and fastidiously negotiated the muddy path down to the level of the old track, from which the rails had long since been removed. Watching on the closed circuit T V, Patrick let out a low whistle as the image of the person known to them so far as 'Larry' registered on the screen.

"My old man was right. He *was* travelling in a suspect vehicle!" whispered Patrick to Kenneth. "That's none other than our old friend 'Monty' Burton-Latimer. No wonder he's so filthy rich. He must be quite high up in the Movement – and he's quite well connected in our own Intelligence circles, too. He's no fool, so we'll have to be careful."

"Shall I nab him – sweat him a bit?"

"You sound like another colleague of mine! No, not for the moment. We want to find out all we can first, see where he leads us and, with any luck, get him to support Gerald for the post of Area Commander."

"These pictures and the voice recordings should be all we need to reel him in when we want, anyway," whispered Kenneth, to Patrick's approving nod and signal for silence as the encounter began.

Monty listened for some time in silence, making notes and observing Gerald, who was well aware that if, on reflection, his story did not hang together, it was unlikely that he could be protected from the long arm of the neo-Nazi movement. Eventually, Monty signalled him to pause and then asked him to go over certain items:

"Just so that I can brief the Council without looking a complete ass, old boy, could you go over your encounter with Paul? They'll want to be quite sure why you felt it necessary to kill him."

"I had an option, of course – let him kill *me*! As I let myself into the bunker, he came through from the inner room. I could see Henry slumped over the radio and started to ask what was going on. Then Paul turned his gun towards me....." Gerald stared straight ahead, seemingly reliving those few seconds.

"He shouted: 'I've fixed Henry and now it's your turn!' I just stood there for a moment, flabbergasted. I had no weapon, facing a madman, the outside crawling with people. Paul had the Intelligence man lying on the floor in front of him, still tied up and, like me, expecting a bullet at any moment."

"And then the lights went out?" queried Monty, glancing at his notes.

"Yes. I suppose I owe my life to the pilot's failure to clear that pylon. I was able to jump Paul, wrest his gun off him and then, sensing that he was about to open the strawstack door to escape, got in a lucky shot in the dark before he gave the game away to those outside."

"Did you fire a burst, or just one shot?"

"What is this? A murder enquiry? I..... " expostulated Gerald, frantically waving his left hand in order to gain time – time during which a noise was heard, in the fashion pre-arranged.

"What was that? Stay here! I'll go and investigate."

Gerald drew his gun and moved fearlessly (not difficult, given what he knew about the noise!), showing coolness, determination and the ability to take over when it was needed. Despite himself, Monty was impressed. There were certain aspects on which he would like to question Henry, especially on the period before the unwelcome visitors. He wondered whether it had been sensible of Gerald to leave Henry to cope. Also, should he have been aware that Paul was so unstable? On the other hand one has to delegate....hmmm.... Perhaps a chat with Henry, who sounded a fairly simple soul, might throw light on the sort of chap that Gerald was. It was a pity that....

Monty's train of thought was broken by the return of Gerald to report that it had only been the Intelligence agent, knocking over a pile of boxes.

"Now, where were we? Accounting for the possible waste of ammunition, as I recall. Well, the empty shells in the bunker should give a fair idea: I didn't check very closely before disposing of him down the old well, but I doubt whether more than one or two struck home."

"Never mind about that!" said Monty (whom Gerald had to remember was 'Larry' as far as he was concerned). "I didn't realise you had that chap here: I'd welcome a word with him while I'm here."

As Patrick had calculated, the realisation that Kenneth was available to corroborate details and check for new-found 'loyalty to the cause', deflected the course of the debriefing. The next move had been planned, too.

"Not wise," stated Gerald firmly. "I don't want him to know too much about the Organisation – and it's better if he doesn't know who *you* are. He'll work to me only: I'm the one with the drop on him, and I shall vouch for him."

Gerald raised his hand, still holding the (unloaded) gun: "And, should it prove necessary, I will personally take care of him," he added, menacingly.

"Do stop waving that thing around," said Monty, deeming it wiser to accept what was, on reflection, good advice. "Is Henry available, by any chance?"

Gerald smiled: "I have to find him first. Then you're welcome to chat to your heart's content."

"But I thought you said you'd rescued him?" queried Monty, starting through his notes, with the beginnings of a frown of irritation.

"It's complicated, isn't it?" laughed Gerald easily. "Both he and the agent, whose name, by the way, is Kenneth, have to be 'found' as far as Her Majesty's Government is concerned. I shall search an out-of-the-way barn over by the airstrip, aided by my trusty hound Nero....and lo! having sought, I shall behold those two, trussed up by Paul, beginning to despair of being found."

"You seem to have thought it out very well," conceded Monty, "but make sure you don't get the stories mixed up."

As in fact there were two other versions of 'the truth', Patrick, listening to the exchange near-by, heartily endorsed Monty's warning.

"You'd better run over this interfering busy-body again," said Monty. "He's somewhere in the North Sea at the moment, isn't he?"

"Running over him is not such a bad idea!" said Gerald. "No, he's in fact awaiting onward transmission. I haven't had time to give him a maritime burial. In fact, you might be able to help me there. I've no authority over that bunch of 'enforcers' sent by John and I don't want to involve more people than necessary. Could you get the two who actually *saw* the old boy to come up here and transport the body to the coast?"

"Yes, certainly. Good idea," said Monty. "There's a bit of a vacuum in command. Will be until they appoint a successor to John, which needs to be soon."

He paused, wondering whether Gerald would propose himself, whether he had been trying to impress with a view to such a move. After all, he was the son of one of the recently deceased members of Council. Gerald, however, had been prepared for this situation, so he merely shrugged and replied that the obvious move was to confirm the deputy, David, in the post. As far as Gerald knew, he seemed to be quite sound. ('Nothing like damning with faint praise', Patrick had said).

"Right!" said Monty. "I'll report briefly to the High Command that you have everything under control here, then some time I'd like a few words with your assistant, Henry. Can that be arranged?"

Both Patrick, listening in and Gerald himself, noted the tone – not deference, but not arrogant bullying either, more one of acknowledging the authority of the commander on the ground, who knew better than him (Monty) just what was possible and the implications of actions by outsiders. In that last attitude, Monty was more correct than he realised. Gerald knew *much* more about those implications: things were far from being as they seemed.

Monty, however, was very relieved. Secrecy had been maintained. The police could be told that Henry had had no idea that Paul had acquired a rifle until he had threatened the Intelligence agent. Gerald was equally astonished and none of them knew what had happened after the plane crash. They could only assume that Paul had fired at the plane, as he seemed to have gone berserk, causing the pilot to take fatal avoiding action. When this scenario had been explained to Henry by Gerald, the former (anxious to forget his own descent into panic) had been delighted at the blame being doubly fixed on Paul. The 'true' version (as Henry believed it to be, and as it had been told to the Organisation) blamed Paul – as did the 'fictitious' version given to the local police inspector, who was only too happy to make token efforts to track down the missing farm labourer, whilst accepting uncritically the innocence of Gerald and Henry.

CHAPTER TWENTY-TWO

A couple of hundred miles to the north-west of the Fens, a hastily summoned meeting of the Council which oversaw the Organisation in England received with relief the preliminary report from 'Larry' and agreed to meet again the following evening to enable that gentleman to report in person. On the agenda was the Fen Affair in general, and the matter of replacing recently deceased members, in addition to that of the appointment of a new Area Commander for the Eastern Region. The Chairman was known to have a 'favourite son' – not in this case an expression denoting an actual family relationship – and Edwin was understood still to be attempting to peddle his candidate, although respect for the very able and sadly missed John (who had been killed whilst attempting to sort out the mess which had developed in the Fens) made it unlikely that the remainder of the Council would accept Gerald, however well connected he might be.

Meanwhile, Patrick was reviewing the forthcoming meeting between Monty and Gerald's assistant, who was still a bit groggy from having been kept drugged into unconsciousness until it had proved expedient to revive him, a condition not helped by a hearty knock on the head, designed to give credence to the tale of an attack by Paul. He was, however, in a fairly suggestible state, grateful to Gerald for having rescued him from the strawstack bunker, supported his unconscious body in the water as they floated down the river Glave, and brought him to the safety of Thorpe Tunnel. ('It might sound unlikely, but it could actually happen!' Patrick had said). The mythical river trip had (so Henry had been led to believe) been made even more difficult by having to ensure that Kenneth, whom Gerald had had to render unconscious lest he cry out, also be kept from drowning. This feat of initiative and strength (carrying the inert bodies to the van and from it to the bunker at Thorpe Tunnel) greatly impressed Henry, who had completely forgotten his earlier sentiments concerning Gerald, from whose fundament – in Henry's opinion – the sun now shone brightly.

Given this state of mind, it was not going to be difficult for Monty to be fed a form of corroboration of events leading up to the crash, devoid of references to Gerald's unsupportive, and, as it turned out, fruitless, absence and failure to respond to his superior's order to get into contact immediately. Henry had also been primed to refer to John's insistence on horning in on the exercise, resulting in their frightening away Ahmed, just as he had been about to give himself up to Gerald.

Monty, having concluded his debriefing of Gerald, asked if he could make use of the bunker's toilet facilities, so he was out of the immediate area when the phone rang. Patrick got Kenneth to fetch Gerald to answer it, attaching a small listening device to monitor the call simultaneously. It proved to be a very excitable Christopher who, on driving back to the Castle, had spotted what looked remarkably like the chap who had claimed to be a member of the Organisation, and to whom he had trustingly handed the batch of forged documents a few days previously. He had followed him, and his dog, across several fields, having abandoned his car, and was now keeping watch on his house. By this time, Patrick knew what the address would be: that of his own father, who was now in deadly danger. Hurriedly, he wrote instructions for Gerald, who continued the conversation appropriately.

"Well done. Keep watching. Follow him if he goes out again. But on no account approach him, or do anything to harm him. For one thing he may well be dangerous, and for another, we think it's probable he was reporting to John, was in fact sent to check on operations in this area."

"Oh no!" bleated Christopher. "I rang the Agent before ringing you – and he said he would take care of him. I was to stay here to keep a look-out while....."

"How long ago did you ring him?"

"About five minutes. I'll tell whoever comes not to take any action – on your instructions."

"Do that! I'll get over there as quick as I can. Don't let him out of your sight, and be careful!"

Gerald cut the connection as instructed by Kenneth, who ushered him hurriedly back into the other room so that Patrick could ring his home number.

149

"Dad? Now listen carefully, don't ask questions and do exactly as I say."

"Right! Well, what do you want?"

"Put on that dreadful yellow-coloured anorak and take the dog out. Go towards....."

"But I've just got back from taking her – and why *that* anorak? It's in the...."

"I said 'Don't ask questions'. Trust me: it's important. Get moving NOW! Go down the lane and across as if you were making for Thorpe Tunnel. No violent hurry; your usual pace, but keep moving. Right?"

"Well, you know best, I suppose. Shall I...? O K, O K, I know: no questions. I'm on the way!"

"Whew! Thank God for that!" said Patrick. "Now let's get hold of the S A S! They can earn their pay."

As Patrick started to put through a call to R A F Wittering, Ned Swinnerton and his assistant, Brian, were setting off from Hadding, a village not far off the A 1 near Wansford, in response to a request from Philip Proudfoot, the Agent at Wothorpe Castle. Ned was a big man by any standards, who claimed to be descended from Will Scarlett, 'second to none for strength and sturdye limm', whose attributes were attested to on a plaque above the west door of Peterborough Cathedral. Like the man from whom he claimed ancestry, Ned was a gravedigger in addition to running the local smithy, Hadding Farriers, and was often to be seen in or near the churchyard at Fotheringhay. The connection with the long gone sexton of Peterborough Cathedral was enhanced by the fact that one of the 'two qveens.. hee had interd', Mary, Queen of Scots, had been beheaded at Fotheringhay. The castle was now little more than a mound, and of the extensive buildings of the Abbey, there remained only the western half, the Parish Church. The magnificent collegiate church, rebuilt in the 1440's on a massive scale, shrank to half its size following the destruction of the eastern half and the College in 1575. By then all the chantry priests, whose task had been to pray for the souls of Richard II, Henry IV and Henry V, had been dispersed. It was not until the 1920's that excavations took place, but even they did not discover everything that lay beneath what was now a grassy platform situated between the present church and the river.

Handed down over the ages, perhaps from the days when it was an important centre of support for the House of York, was the secret of the underground chambers and narrow tunnel which emerged close to the present course of the River Nene, its mouth covered by some tumble-down stone-built farm sheds, which housed the tools of the grave-diggers' trade. It was from there that Ned had extracted the tools of his other trade – that of an active 'soldier in the field' for the Organisation. He and his father before him had followed the lead given by a member of the local 'gentry', allegiance to whom they put higher than that to God, Queen or Country (believing that all three would, if they only knew what was good for them, welcome such action). The array of hand guns, rifles, ammunition and explosives was impressive, although the selection carried by Ned and his assistant – and their mien – appalled Christopher when they caught up with him, guided by his 'mobile'.

Not long after his second call – to Gerald – Christopher had been surprised to see his quarry, sporting this time a bright yellow anorak, set off again with his dog. Keeping in touch from time to time by phone, Christopher followed him warily, finding little difficulty in keeping the gaudy garment in sight, until joined by the massive blacksmith and his smaller, but sturdy, cold-eyed assistant. Thinking that 'Central Casting' could hardly have done a better job if asked for two murderers, Christopher demanded, and was shown, their H F C identity cards (which, in their case, related to Hadding Farriers Castings, the name on the van).

"Where's he gone?" said the big man, who, like his sixteenth century forebear, could be described as being 'of mighty voice and visage grim'. "You're too far back here: he's given us the slip."

"Don't worry. He's easy to follow...Yes, he's in sight again. Look out for the yellow anorak....and there's the dog. He's following the footpath signs – obviously comes this way often. Hey! You're not supposed to shoot him! Put those things away! Gerald said he might....."

"Just shut up, sonny. I know who I take orders from – and it ain't you, or yer precious Gerald. Right Bri! Take this – and drop 'im if he starts to make a run for it. And, that goes for you, too, if you get in our way!"

Christopher quailed before the venom and the vicious-looking rifle onto which 'Bri' was carefully fitting a telescopic sight.

"And you can give me *that!*" Ned snatched the mobile phone with which Christopher had started to warn Gerald.

Frightened and completely out of his depth, Christopher followed, willing the elderly walker not to speed up, wishing he had never spotted him in the first place.

It was then that nature took a hand, in the form, once again, of a game-bird. This time, however, it was not a pheasant, whose intervention had earlier saved Martin from discovery, but a partridge, which scurried across the path of Sherry, causing her to set off in hot pursuit, still attached by the lead to her master. The movement of the dog could not be seen by the two men who were stalking Martin, but the sudden rapid movement of the yellow anorak was all that was needed for both to come rapidly to the firing position, Brian slightly ahead of his boss. The sharp cracks of high velocity bullets rent the air, one puncturing the yellow anorak and felling its wearer, another speeding over the falling body into the thicket beyond. The sound of shots and subsequent effect was heard and seen by Kenneth and Gerald, both of whom broke cover from about two hundred metres west of the fallen figure.

"Christ! They've shot him!" exclaimed Gerald. "And all I've got is this piddling revolver, which," he added, in mounting disgust and sudden fear at his exposure to superior fire-power, "isn't even loaded!"

He dropped flat and turned to see Kenneth zig-zagging rapidly across the open field, brandishing a small hand-gun.

"Don't be a bloody fool! Drop flat. For Christ's Sake! No! Drop!"

Kenneth, however continued unharmed towards the fallen man, oblivious even of a tall menacing figure, now visible at the far side of the field, rifle in hand, holding by the arm another who gazed as if mesmerised at the crumpled yellow garment, its motionless contents and the two lifeless farriers.

From his uncomfortable position in the thick hedge, Martin raised his head cautiously. He had been frightened into staying down by the two rapid shots, fired from just above his head by his burly captor, who had first held him whilst his mate removed the yellow anorak, and then sat on him, enforcing total immobility and silence. Shocked and bemused by the sudden ambush, Martin took in the scene and tried to summon the energy and will to escape whilst he had even half a chance. One moment he had been proceeding as instructed, accompanied by..... now that was another thing. They'd taken the dog!... And then wham! He was thrown to the ground, not a word spoken, his anorak and bobble hat removed and, quite literally, sat on by a muscular lout with a rifle and hard grey eyes. They had remained like this for a few minutes until..... Yes, hadn't he heard two more distant shots, fractionally head of the other two? He watched as his recent assailant led another man rapidly towards the crumpled yellow shape.

Corporal Charlton growled at Christopher to stand still, then went forward to speak quietly to Kenneth, who was removing the tell-tale anorak after checking for a pulse.

"Where'd they get him?"

"No problem – slap bang in the middle of the back. The body armour did its stuff, but the force of the bullet knocked him down. It looks as though he hit his head on a flat stone. Ah! He's starting to come round now."

"He'll live....which is just as well for that silly little prick over there!" muttered the corporal. "Keep him looking dead!"

The corporal moved towards the terrified Christopher, narrowing his eyes mercilessly:

"I get the feeling you're about to attempt to escape, or make a sudden movement which unfortunately will look to me just like someone drawing a gun!"

"No! No! Don't shoot! I tried to stop them. They – they – wouldn't..... I said Gerald had told me to just follow. You've got to believe me! Ask Gerald. Oh God! He's not... I mean..... Whose side are you on? Gerald said he might be one of ours after all. It was the Agent's – Proudfoot's – fault: he sent for those two. I only......"

"You only set him up, is that it? Don't worry: he's dead so you'll die too, along with Proudfoot," said the corporal dismissively, as he was joined by Kenneth who was satisfied that the other soldier had now recovered sufficiently to stay 'dead'.

"Please! They all told me he was a spy. I said he was genuine. Was he working for H Q – or for Dalton? Was he..... right at the top?"

"Be quiet, man. The less you know the better," said Kenneth, watching the corporal move back and bend down close to his now fully conscious mate, as Christopher collapsed in self-pitying tears.

"So it works – the flak jacket? " he murmured quietly, making sure that Christopher could not hear. "Not a bad test! You all right, Pete?"

The other S A S man, who had substituted himself, as instructed, ('earning their money', Patrick had called it) for the elderly 'non-professional', grinned ruefully and replied quietly, without moving:

"Yeah. I'm O K. A bit sore and I've got a headache, but nothing that'll stop me from sorting out whoever set up this scam! What happened to the chap who shot me?"

Corporal Charlton drew a finger meaningfully across the throat of his supine colleague.

"And the other one? He fired, too, I guess....God! You've been busy. Are you in the clear?"

"The guy running this'll fix it. Probably it never happened!"

At this point, the 'wet work' being – for the moment, at least – at an end, Kenneth decided to take charge and called out to the corporal:

"Can you go over and tell that 'rambler' we don't need any help, please? I'll keep an eye on this lad."

Kenneth had noticed that Gerald was starting to make his way towards them and realised that it was essential that he should not be seen by Christopher, for whom Patrick had 'other plans'.

As much to Kenneth's surprise as any one's, the corporal raised his rifle and sent a bullet spinning into the grassy slope just beyond the advancing Gerald. With gratifying rapidity, the latter threw himself to the ground as the supersonic crack sounded inches over his head.

"That should curb his curiosity! Now, what do you want done with this worthless little shit?"

Charlton turned towards Christopher, only to see him crumple to the floor.

"Well, would you believe it? He's gone and fainted. Was it something I said?"

CHAPTER TWENTY-THREE

Kenneth gave a resigned sigh at the thought of rebuilding Gerald's faith in the good will of his new masters after having had a gun turned on him, and got out his mobile phone to report the success of the recent exercise – and the body count – as he walked towards the spot where they had left Martin. Although he did not show it, Patrick was appalled by the turn events had taken, not least by the danger to which his father had become exposed. There seemed little doubt that the pair from Fotheringhay had set off intending to exterminate the impostor, on whose orders it was not quite clear. It might have been a 'Thomas à Becket syndrome', with his father cast in the rôle of 'turbulent priest'..... but who had been the Henry the Second? The Agent, Philip Proudfoot? His intellectually challenged employer? A central, so far unknown, figure? The only suspect with the perfect alibi was the slippery Burton-Latimer, who was about to return to the Castle, where they must be surprised at the cessation of reports from Christopher.

"Give me a minute to think this through, Kenneth. Meanwhile, see how my father is. From the sound of those two S A S men, he may have been a bit shaken up: they don't sound the nanny type and will have had to act quickly. Ring me back in, say, five minutes – and don't let Gerald or, of course, Christopher, see Martin. I'm not sure if it's safe for him to go home yet. That depends on who's running the show, if anyone, from their end."

Kenneth rang off and trotted back to Martin, to find him looking his age, feeling the cold, and still shaking from a form of delayed shock

"Here, take my coat. You look frozen. Sorry about that. We had to move quickly when we heard they'd sent someone to follow up a sighting by that young lad you saw at the Castle. Their team consisted of two blacksmith-cum-gravediggers..... and ours (apart from me and Gerald who arrived just after the shooting) consisted of two members of the S A S. As you'll have gathered, one of them shot the two from the Organisation, who'd come hell for leather in a van from

Fotheringhay, as soon as they opened up on what they thought was you!"

"S-s-sorry. C'can't s-stop sh-shivering. Must be getting old! W-where do you want me to go, now?"

"I'll have to check with Patrick. Can you stand, walk about a bit, flap your arms? We'll get you in the warm as soon as we can – but....."

"Wait!" said Martin. "Where's Sherry? She may have been frightened by the bangs and taken off. I'll call her."

Motivated by concern for his dog, he struggled to his feet, trying to control the shaking.

"She'll be all right," said Kenneth reassuringly, although now that the animal had been mentioned, it occurred to him that it hadn't been around for the last few minutes. "I'll just check with Patrick, then I'll round her up."

Patrick had thought through part of his strategy, but still had no knowledge of the extent to which the Castle had been in touch with any higher authority. He should be able to get an accurate idea from Gerald, but that needed time – time to tell Gerald what to say, what line to take, and then time for him to pass the information back.

"Tell Gerald to get on the phone to the Castle, saying he's heard from you and asking for Burton-Latimer – that's 'Larry' to them. He may not be there yet, so Gerald's to insist on them getting hold of Proudfoot. He's to take a tough line with him. 'Who the hell authorised this? Three people dead; Christopher scared shitless (that bit's true, anyway) and will have to be got out of the country pronto; when H Q realise what's happened, the life of whoever was responsible won't be worth a nickel, as they've shot this important agent; papers on him show he was working for the very top brass, checking on efficiency; etc., etc.'. When we let him, Christopher can claim he reported all this, but was told he was an idiot..... that sort of thing; O K?"

Kenneth assimilated the instructions as fast as he could, explaining that Gerald was about three hundred metres away – and probably pretty scared, as was, he reminded Patrick, his own father.

"Oh God, yes. Poor old boy. Put him on the line... Hello, Dad! It's all under control now. Sorry you had such a fright. How are you feeling?"

"Well – er – a bit sort of groggy, you know..... not quite up to 'Shoot out at High Fen', I suppose..... but we're worried about Sherry: no-one's seen her since the – er – incident. She's got a tag on, but....."

"She'll turn up, Dad. The point is how are *you*? Can you cope on your own for a few minutes... while Kenneth gets things moving for me?"

"Yes, O K," said Martin, who was beginning to feel a little more human after hearing the familiar voice. "I'll start looking for Sherry."

"Don't you go and get lost, too! Keep the others in sight, so that we can get you home as soon as I'm sure it's clear. Take care!"

Back at the Thorpe Tunnel bunker, Patrick cradled the phone and looked down at his notes. There were getting to be too many loose ends, too many 'disappearances', which might make someone suspicious. The supposed body of the impostor would have to disappear; the two S A S men who had implied to Christopher that they were members of some Organisation hit squad would have to disappear – with no clear indication of who had summoned them; Christopher would have to disappear, lest he once again see Martin – but not before he had (more or less) explained how the Fotheringhay farriers had met their end. Possibly the Organisation could be relied upon to put about their own story, prompted by Gerald. A shooting accident? Surely not both of them at once? A vehicle accident – but what about the bullets? They could have been shot by rival drug-runners and left in the van: something like that had happened a few years before in south Essex. What about his father – did he need round-the-clock protection, or would he have to 'go on holiday'?

The priority was to get Gerald accepted by the higher echelons of the Organisation. For that, the key was that wretch Burton-Latimer, who must have finished talking to Henry and now be beginning to agitate at having been left incommunicado, without transport. Time to get Gerald and

Kenneth back here, to Thorpe Tunnel – the quicker the better. He stretched out a hand to the phone:

"Kenneth? Those soldiers came on motor-bikes, didn't they? Good. Well I imagine they left them pretty near...Right, one of you on each: it's only about a mile cross-country to here. Get Gerald to explain to 'Larry' that Chris, as instructed by the Agent, had gone after the 'impostor'....and that a bodyguard appeared from nowhere when the guys sent by Proudfoot shot him....Yes, that's right – and that he said he would take care of the bodies.....What..? No, four in all. There's a dead 'rambler' as well from Chris's point of view! Get him to tell Proudfoot to organise transport for Larry – and tell him just to say that Gerald's man is on his way to report...and that he, Chris, is getting the hell out of it, as it's all gone wrong.....Yes, then tie Chris up and blindfold him thoroughly. I don't want him seeing the so-called dead come back to life....Yes, he might not come round from that faint!...Then tell the corporal to take him to the Fotheringhay van. I'll get a couple more blokes from Wittering to meet him there.....Oh, and tell the other soldier to give me a lift back to my old man, who's fussing about the dog! See you shortly!"

After a, quite literally, hair-raising journey on the back of the two motor-bikes, Gerald and Kenneth arrived back at Thorpe Tunnel, the former having been briefed by Kenneth as they jogged and scrambled the final fifty or sixty metres. Patrick met Kenneth, who had arrived, as arranged, just ahead of Gerald after slipping out unseen by Monty and Henry. He reminded him that Gerald was to say he had given Kenneth instructions to advance across the field and find out what had happened from Chris (whom he had seen standing with the man who had fired the shots). If Chris were questioned later, he wouldn't be surprised to hear of Gerald's mistake – nor, given his own doubts as to whose side the assassin was on, would he be surprised that Kenneth had not said Gerald was hidden in the hedge on the far side of the field.

"Is that all?!" gasped Kenneth, as he struggled to take on board the rapidly adjusted scenario.

"That's the best I can do in the time available!" said Patrick as he set off. "If Gerald gets asked who his helper was, he's to say it was the Intelligence man, who had thereby proved to his satisfaction that he was loyal to the Cause... and that he then sent him to look for Chris's car. That'll explain his absence, although in fact I want you in the inner room, near the phone, monitoring what goes on. I'll be in touch."

Patrick set off rapidly to rendez-vous with the motor-bike, which, after a short, exhilirating run, dropped him close to the spot where Martin had been 'bush-whacked'. To his surprise – and concern – there was no sign of his father, who should surely have heard the approaching engine, even if he had moved some distance away during the previous ten or fifteen minutes. Wondering whether the old boy had fainted or something, Patrick set off to look for him in the immediate area, sending Pete down the track in case he had decided to go home.

Having been told not to let the others out of sight by his son, Martin was surprised to see most of the party suddenly disappear on the motor-bikes, leaving only a gagged, bound and blindfolded figure propped up against the far hedge. After getting enough strength back into his wobbly legs to start moving, he set off, warmed by Kenneth's anorak, to search for Sherry. Not liking to whistle or call out in case he drew unwelcome attention to his presence, he walked on, following the route taken by his substitute. A few minutes later, he heard the first motor-bike returning and hurriedly dived for the hedge, uncertain who was friend and who foe. He watched him load up the blindfolded figure and set off down the track, then cautiously started to raise himself upright to continue the search. He failed to complete the movement, however, not because he was aware of the advent of the second bike, but because his eye was caught by the familiar brown feathers of a partridge, eyes closed in death, facing him from the ditch. The cause of death might well have been fright, or shock: the agent, however, was patently clear, for the bird's tail feathers were firmly clasped between the rigid jaws of the elderly Golden Retriever. Against all the odds, for the first time in its life, the dog had managed to catch its life-long prey, but there was no smile of success in the eyes, no slowly wagging tail, sure of receiving the benediction of 'Goo-d Doggy' and the instruction to 'Drop it!'

As he slowly examined the motionless animal, his recently regained equilibrium draining away, Martin realised what had happened. The first bullet having pierced the yellow anorak, the second had passed over the falling body and struck the dog just as its triumphant jaws clamped themselves round the fleeing partridge.

It was thus that Patrick came upon the 'elderly busy-body', scourge of the enemies of the State, gazing fixedly, seemingly more shocked by this tableau than that of the recent human slaughter.

"Oh, no! Poor old Sherry," he said, bending down close to his father. "Are *you* O K, though?"

"She's never caught one before. I hope she knew. I shouldn't have let him take her: she tried to help me – but I couldn't......"

"It wasn't your fault. It was the only way to save you. We heard too late to do it any other way. Sorry, Dad. They spotted you, and followed. Those two thought it was you they were shooting: you'd found out too much and someone panicked. Thank God we got there in time!"

But Martin could only think of the unfairness of the thousand-to-one chance of the second bullet striking the innocent animal, merely doing the job it was trained for. He sat there, stroking her head, and muttering:

"Poor old girl: you caught it. You really grabbed it that time..."

Suddenly, he broke off and looked up, appalled by the thought:

"What about your mother? What do we say? She asks about the dog every day...and she's always telling me off because Sherry's so trusting when I talk to her and say I need a new pair of gloves – or....."

"Yes, I know, you old fool....and ask the animal if she's read the menu: 'Roast Dog'. Never mind Mother for the moment: how are *you*? You've been roughed up, found... this, and....."

"I should never have accepted those documents, that's what must have done it. I bet someone from the Castle recognised me and wanted to get the rest of the documents back. It was just a game then and I wanted to know what he meant by 'the other one'. Yes, that was it, that's what he said. It must have been the other submarine! Tell Elizabeth: she..... Oh, hell! I'd better get Sherry home. Give me a hand up, old boy!"

With the help of the S A S men, Patrick got his father and the stiffening dog, still clasping its feathered prize, back home, where a message from Elizabeth awaited them to say she was on her way back that day and wished to be met at Peterborough. He also got them to place the dead gravedigger and his assistant in the back of their van, having rung his immediate superior in the Intelligence Service for clearance for a simulated 'drug gang assassination' (two gunshot victims to be discovered in a burnt out van in a local quarry). Of the blacksmith's long remembered ancestor, it was recorded 'no doubt his sovle doth live for aye in heaven'....but one had to be less confident in Ned's case.

CHAPTER TWENTY-FOUR

Monty's patience had been sorely tried by the time Gerald got round to dealing with the matter of transporting him back to the Castle – achieved by a brusque phone call which resulted in one of the estate workers who was not 'security cleared' arriving in his Lordship's Landrover. Monty and Gerald travelled together, unable to talk beyond a whispered:

"The shit seems to have hit the fan good and proper, Larry. I'll put you in the picture as soon as we get there. Proudfoot's cocked it up: Christopher got in touch with me....."

"What the hell's going on?" asked Monty, when at last they could talk in the Agent's office.

Gerald explained all he knew (or rather all he was prepared to lay claim to by way of knowledge) to 'Larry', while Proudfoot, to whom Gerald had spoken earlier on lines laid down by Patrick, stood, his eyes assuming a hunted look as the catalogue of disasters unfolded.

Monty grew increasingly nervous as he realised his proximity to the 'field of battle'. It was not his habit to lead from the front; indeed he took great care never to be directly involved with the nefarious activities which provided the funds to keep alive the long term aims of the pan-European neo-Nazi movement, a substantial sum from which found its way into his own pocket.

"Right! Well, this is not the time to apportion blame. The main thing is to inform the High Command. I need to get over to Liverpool as soon as possible." He turned to Philip Proudfoot. "When's the next train from Peterborough?"

"Er – it's – that is, you might do better from Grantham. I'll get Christo.....Oh, no, of course. I'll see what I can....The train, that's it, the train......"

Gerald, who seemed to flourish as a 'double agent', saw his chance to re-inforce his dynamic image.

"I can whistle up a helicopter within half an hour – much better than...." His pitying look was more effective than finishing the sentence, which could only have continued on the lines of: '....waiting for this silly bugger to organise anything!'

Monty accepted thankfully, anxious to get well away before anyone started investigating the recent spate of violent deaths, and also keen to advise the High Command that the Eastern Area, bereft of a leader, was flying apart in a series of unco-ordinated, even mutually destructive incidents. There was no longer any doubt in Monty's mind who was the best person for the job: Gerald. While they were waiting, Gerald discussed with Monty the best way to get Christopher out of the country, both wondering, but not articulating the thought, whether it might come to removing the young man in a more permanent sense.

"Are you sure that old boy was working for John Dalton? He didn't tell me – and we worked pretty closely together," said the Agent. "You thought he was a spy," he added accusingly, turning to Gerald. "That's why you were hunting him....."

"No, no!" said Monty, impatiently. "They caught that chap. Gerald's got him stashed away somewhere, waiting for the two that caught him to come and dispose of the body. That's right, isn't it, old boy?"

"Yes, Larry. There was a period when it looked as though it might have been the same chap.... but John was, well, from my point of view, interfering – from his point of view quite legitimately checking on all of us. He didn't tell me – and he didn't tell you, Philip. I'm sure the High Command will understand why you had him shot; it's always a risk when the left hand doesn't know what the right hand's doing. Don't you agree, Larry?"

Proudfoot winced at the confident use of the first name by this – this – *peasant*. He had nurtured hopes of moving higher in the Movement, saw himself as an obvious candidate for John Dalton's job, and eventually, perhaps, a seat on the High Command....then, who could tell: a regional governorship when they made their long-awaited move?

"Yes, yes. I'm sure they'll understand," said Monty, with palpable insincerity, adding enigmatically: "I'll see they're fully briefed, with everybody's contribution recognised."

The helicopter was about five miles away when the phone rang again and was picked up by the Agent.

"Proudfoot. Who's speaking?... Christopher! Where have you b... What do you mean? Yes, he's here, but he's not your.... You cheeky little devil! Make your report now – and to *me* or I'll see you....."

"One moment, Philip. Let me have a word.....Hallo, Chris. Larry here. Can I help? We're fairly well in the picture, but your own perspective would be most valuable."

Charm and authority oozed from the well-fed smoothie, but Christopher was adamant.

"I don't trust Proudfoot. Those vicious killers of his threatened me when I told them we suspected the chap in the yellow anorak might be working for the top brass. They gunned him down before anyone had a chance to question him – and now I want Gerald to get me out of the country. Put him on the line. There's something else I'm only telling him."

"Over to you, it seems!" said Monty ruefully. "You seem to inspire the lad with confidence – and we need his report."

The last phrase was by way of an explanation to Proudfoot, who saw his authority being usurped by, as he saw it – with much justification – the gormless nonentity, Gerald. A dreadful thought struck the tall, competent-looking confidant of his Lordship, to whom so many owed their livelihoods: this 'Larry', who had the ear of the High Command might recommend.... He, Philip Proudfoot, reporting to Gerald? Doing his bidding, even accepting a lesser job? Stuck in that Fenland slum, ferrying immigrants....Never! He sat down, defeated, to contemplate his fate when it became known that he had had one of the most senior men in the Organisation killed: that bloody Ned and his.... Proudfoot buried his head in his hands as Gerald took over the phone and calmly reassured Christopher that he would be kept hidden for a day or two until arrangements could be finalised.

"You've got them there! The bodyguard....Yes, I gathered they found conclusive evidence....Yes, quite, but they gave you the..... Oh, I see. Hang on a minute!" Gerald turned to Monty with a grin. "The chap who was the 'minder', who shot these two from Fotheringhay, has various documents which he'll give to Christopher as soon as he has clearance." (Patrick had instructed that time be gained to forge something suitable). "Apparently," Gerald continued, relaying

Christopher's words, "our man had expected to hand them to John, so had to keep them when the plane crashed. The bodyguard's done well to realise the importance of these documents – although he failed to protect his charge, so has to face that music, of course. One other thing: Christopher will only give them to me. I ought to hand them to John's successor. Can you get someone to give me instructions – and perhaps you have contacts across the Channel I can liaise with concerning young Christopher?"

"Yes. Good!" said Monty. "Something's going right for a change! Hang on to those documents when you get them. Who knows? You might be needing them!"

"O K Christopher," said Gerald, returning to the phone. "Stay where you are. I'll get across as soon as possible and we'll take it from there. Don't worry; you're in the clear!"

Gerald contrived to look blank, as if the significance of Larry's reference to the possibility of his 'needing' the documents had been lost on him. Neither Monty, nor Philip Proudfoot, the Agent for Wothorpe Castle Estate, was fooled, however. The latter, indeed, rose slowly to his feet and, muttering that he had a few things to see to, left the room just as the clatter of the approaching helicopter called a halt to the conversation.

"I suggest you hang on here for the time being," said Monty, casually, "just in case I need to confirm any details."

The same insouciant charade was played out, this time without the mute participation of the devastated, disillusioned and, by now, clinically depressed, Philip Proudfoot.

As soon as he was alone, Gerald availed himself of the direct line to communicate with Thorpe Tunnel. He permitted himself cautious optimism concerning the outcome of the 'election' of a successor to his father – and even more confidence concerning his imminent elevation to controller of the Eastern Area.

"It's becoming very clear that someone needs to be appointed to stop us – or rather 'them' (just a slip of the tongue, sorry!) – from pulling in several directions at once, and indulging in more mutual annihilation!" Gerald concluded.

"I hope," said Kenneth, with a hint of steel in his voice, "that the slip was not Freudian – for your sake."

"Don't worry, you've got enough on me to ensure my loyalty, which I think has already been amply demonstrated. Even your 'controller', whoever that is, couldn't have stitched up Proudfoot like I've just done. I know which side my bread's buttered..... and, like Christopher Robin, I *do* like a little bit of butter on my bread!"

"I think you've got your ditties in a bit of a twist there," said Kenneth, "but talking of Christopher, have you managed to arrange anything?"

"Larry has agreed to put me in touch with one of his Continental cronies – and I imagine we can work the immigrant route in reverse, or just send him conventionally under a false name."

"O K. Well done. I expect we'll be in touch again, soon. Where will you be?"

"Waiting here for good news – then wherever they send me.....but I'll keep you in the picture."

****

The agenda of the special meeting of the High Command, in Liverpool, had the receipt of Monty's report as its first item, together with discussion of appropriate action, followed by the appointment of a replacement as Controller for the Eastern Area of England ... and then the appointment of two Council members.

Death, assassination, removal of evidence, torture and blackmail were no strangers to the hard-bitten group, who followed the twists and turns – including the 'turning' of the Intelligence Officer known as Kenneth – with interest rather than horror.

"Has this chap Gerald got firm evidence of his double agent accepting our money?" asked one.

"Yes. Apparently the chap co-operated fully – was anxious to prove how we could 'fix' him if we wanted to. Gerald's got photos, tape recordings, the lot! He played hard to convince, kept saying H M G would never believe it, so he might as well kill the chap.... making him work desperately to suggest more and more damning evidence against himself! I was impressed, to be honest – didn't expect to find any signs of intelligent life in the Fens at all, let alone a man of his calibre!" replied Monty, staking his reputation on his protégé.

"Well, he comes from good stock!" said Edwin. "I propose we...."

"One thing at a time, please," said the Chairman firmly. "We shall be coming to that under item 3. Can I take it we're agreed, then? Larry's man to take over the Eastern Area with immediate effect. No dissenters? Right! Now for the next item...."

"Excuse me, Chairman," said Monty. "May I break off to inform him, please – or would you? It really is essential that someone gather up the reins before the wagon crashes into the ravine!"

"Go ahead, Monty.... I mean Larry, sorry! Not that I'm giving away anything unknown to all of us, as I'm sure you appreciate! We don't need you for the next item in fact, so I know I speak for all of us in saying a hearty 'Thank you' for sorting out this mess, for coming back so promptly..... and," he added, a little archly, "should there be any need for support for any project which affects you personally in the future, you can rely on us."

To nods of approval and a broad, conspiratorial wink from Edwin, Monty rose from the table and paused as the Chairman added chillingly:

"This new chap has our approval to deal with – er – Proudfoot in any way, and I do mean *any* way, he thinks fit. Do I make myself clear?"

Monty nodded, gathered up his papers and left to telephone Wothorpe Castle, hoping he would encounter Gerald rather than the disgraced Proudfoot.

He need not have worried. As the phone was ringing, Philip Proudfoot parked his car on a farm track not far from the Mallard public house at Little Bytham. The name owed nothing to the frequent sightings of wild duck in the area, for the sign depicted the famous steam engine which had hauled trains at over 100 miles per hour in the 1930's along the nearby length of track, the fastest stretch along the whole of the King's Cross to Edinburgh line. The driver knew there was no point in even *trying* to stop the Intercity in the thirty seconds which elapsed between the man stepping onto the track and the slight bump he felt as the engine fulfilled Philip Proudfoot's desire to end it all. He slowed whilst he reported the incident and got clearance to continue south, accelerating to well over the 1930's record speed in order to arrive on time at Peterborough.

CHAPTER TWENTY-FIVE

Peterborough station was also the destination of Patrick, in his case by road, en route to meet his sister who was travelling back from Birkenhead after the completion of her research into U-534. Her tour of the rusty hulk, refloated some years before, had been interesting, but it was the small museum which had proved of greatest value, in particular an aerial photo, taken by one of the planes which had sunk her. The picture showed the boat speeding defiantly on the surface, anti-aircraft guns firing (to good effect, it might be added). As she gazed at the old black and white print, it came to her. The U-boat was making no attempt at concealment; rather it was inviting attack by the planes....it was drawing them to itself.... leading them, leading them *away*. Yes, that had to be it! Leading them away from the real prize – the *other*, invisible, submerged U-boat, with its precious load. The U-534 was a decoy; the stories about its cargo of high Nazi officials, gold and 'sacred' emblems had no truth, as those who laboured to refloat it found to their disappointment.

Excitedly, she related the tantalising tale to her brother, whose habitual flippant cynicism was stilled as he recalled the recent remark made by Christopher to his father: '.... the other one, were you on the other one?'

"Brilliant!" he declared. "But how did it elude the enemy? Our radar was pretty effective by then, and what seemed to be all the others were eventually caught on their way to Japan or South America."

"That's the point! I'm sure this one didn't go that far! I. G. Farben are known to have been developing a protective screening – what we would now call a 'stealth' covering – to make it invisible in all senses. Not only that, the latest U-boats could travel fast under water, possibly, in a successful prototype, nearly 30 knots – and they could travel in virtually complete silence at 2 to 3 knots. I think they brought a more precious load than gold, although that as well, doubtless." She paused for effect.

"Go on, go on!" said Patrick, his mind racing with the possibilities of her theory. "Spit it out!"

"They carried *children*. Yes, children, like your friend Gerald, who must have been inserted into the community by sympathisers at all levels of society (and God knows there were plenty about, from the highest in the land downwards). They've bided their time, built up an organisation, turned to crime for finance, and Father, meddling old fool that he is, stuck his walking-stick into the ant-hill, or whatever simile you like!"

At this point they turned off the main road and Patrick broke off from speculating on the possible survival of Nazi 'water babies' to explain his concern about their father. His sister was shocked by the story, and dashed in to see him as soon as they arrived back at the house (observed by one of the hidden S A S soldiers, whom Patrick had arranged as protection for all of them 'just in case').

To the concern (and irritation) of both of his children, Martin, as soon as his son had departed to collect Elizabeth, had left the warm room, the whisky and the comfortable settee, to go out into the drizzle, dig a large hole in the orchard and carefully lay both dog and partridge therein. He had just finished the gruesome task as the car turned in and appeared, gaunt, tired, wet and miserable, covered in mud – and stubbornly guilty.

"You, you... Oh, Father!" said Elizabeth, torn between delivering the comfort he needed and the tongue-lashing he so richly deserved. "Why couldn't you leave it? Come on; you'll make yourself ill. Take those wet things off. Patrick! Run a bath and talk some sense into him!"

Between them they got Martin into a bath and outside some hot soup, but a series of ominous sneezes showed that recent events had combined to render him *hors de combat* – and make it impossible to provide a reassuring bulletin for his wife when she rang for news. Even half the truth was enough to start her talking in terms of returning home early, a course deplored by her son as he would have to provide protection for her as well.

"Try to get her to stay there!" he whispered. "Things could get very nasty if they happened to discover I'm involved, or who Dad is. There are too many loose ends to be absolutely sure we're fire proof."

171

To himself, Patrick added that if Burton-Latimer ever paused for real thought, he could start asking some very awkward questions.

"Come on, Dad, let's get you out of those wet things. And by the way, what did you mean when you said you shouldn't have taken the documents?"

There was a pause while his father sipped a hot Lemsip, then he looked almost sly and said:

"Can you keep a secret?"

"Oh come off it! You know I can... now, give!"

"Well, I gave one set to Ahmed... I know it was illegal, but he had had such a rough time and....."

"What documents, Dad?" asked Patrick, his patience beginning to wane. "Where did they come from?"

"From the Castle. I didn't mention them before because I shouldn't have kept them, or given them to......"

"Kept them? Where are they now?"

"Upstairs, under the bed. There are two other sets. I suppose it'll all have to come out now..... but I want Ahmed kept out of it."

Patrick dashed upstairs and opened the package with growing delight. He rushed past his father, calling out:

"You're brilliant! Any more little secrets like that? I'll just set these up so that they were 'found' on the body of the dead 'you' – that is whoever one assumes was wearing the yellow anorak – and strengthen Christopher's hand when he's negotiating his escape from the country! I got him to say there were important documents, which I was going to have forged. Now we've got the real thing! I'll be right back. You've done really well!"

The praise did more for Martin's morale and general well-being than any drugs, baths or blankets, and he clambered thankfully out of his sodden gear as his son began to brief his 'troops'.

The telephone call with France did not go well. Torn between telling the truth, concern for her father, loyalty to her brother and a desire not to worry her mother, Elizabeth failed to reassure, admitting first that the dog was not in the best of health, then that it had unfortunately been shot by mistake when pursuing a partridge, finally that her father had been

172

rather shaken and had a bit of a cold. Given that it had been like getting blood out of a stone to arrive at what was presumably the truth concerning the dog, Jennifer half expected that her husband's 'slight illness' would turn out to be terminal by the end of the conversation. There seemed so much opposition to her returning early from the course that she resolved to depart with as much despatch as possible (whilst appearing to agree to wait a day or two to see how he was feeling).

"He dotes on that animal really," she said. "She's his only companion now that I'm working and he's retired. They commune together and he walks her off her feet. He'll be thinking it was his fault; I know him. Is he having her cremated, do you know?"

Elizabeth had stopped short of telling her mother about the burial scene and had implied a 'normal' shotgun incident, with the dog getting in the way of pellets intended for the partridge (which was the 'authorised version' for the neighbours). She was, in fact, concerned about her father's tendency to cover up his feelings, but recalled that his main worry had been that his wife would be upset, so should not be told, lest it spoil her 'holiday'.

After conveying strict instructions that she was to be told immediately if Martin's health or mood deteriorated, Jennifer rang off and straight away contacted the British course leader to say that she would have to leave the next day as her husband was unwell – and the dog had been shot. They were very understanding and offered to make all the booking arrangements for her – although regretting that she would have to pay the full fare herself, virtually the same as the cost of a return ticket, as she mentioned to her hosts that evening. They were a French family, the Cazaux, whose daughter had been an 'exchange student' with Elizabeth some years before.

"They ought to pay in the circumstances. I'll have a word with them if you like," said the husband.

"Oh, don't worry. It's only money....and a dead dog hardly counts as a 'bereavement', does it?" said Jennifer, so the Frenchman shrugged his shoulders, and rose to refill the glasses, the conversation turning to a discussion of pets and their foibles.

Mrs Pateman had worked at the Castle for about eleven years, ever since her husband had been killed in a road accident. He had worked as a general labourer and driver, helped with the 'shoots' and earned good money, some of which, he had once told her, was 'for keeping me mouth shut – and you'll do the same if you know what's good for you'. This had been in response to a question she had put when he had been called out late at night and had returned with a badly bruised arm and ripped jacket. After his death, they, or rather the Agent, had been very good to her, fixing her up with a job collecting money at the front desk.....with a substantial bonus for 'extra duties', the performance of which had thrown light on her husband's advice, and, very recently, had caused her to discuss the carvings of Grinling Gibbons with an old chap who had contrived to show her his H F C identity card. She was sharp-witted and could remember his face quite well enough to recognise it again when, as now, she found herself staring at his photograph.

The tragic suicide of Philip Proudfoot, who had been so good to her, had thrown the staff at the Castle into a flat spin, but after all those years, Mrs Pateman had become his unofficial personal assistant in matters to which most of the staff were not privy. She therefore took it upon herself to open an envelope addressed to him containing the 'deliberate error' in the spelling of his name as Proudefoot, indicating that this was Organisation business. The envelope contained three photographs and a note saying they were to be passed on to 'Larry', as he had requested. They had been taken a day or two previously at Stansted Airport, and showed the subject (Patrick) talking to another man, agent number 534, whom she knew had caused Mr Proudfoot a lot of worry, possibly to the point of driving him to take his own life.

Mrs Pateman rang her contact number and was rapidly connected to Larry, whom she had met during his recent brief stay at the Castle.

"Could you describe this photo to me, Mrs P?" asked Monty breezily. "It's two people, you say, one of whom looks a bit like the chap whom you passed on to Christopher. Is that right?"

"It doesn't look a 'bit' like him, Sir," said the lady, bridling at the over-familiar 'Mrs P' and remembering she hadn't taken to this lah-di-dah chap, by whom she sensed her Mr Proudfoot had felt in some way threatened. "It *is* him – but I don't know the young man with him."

A dreadful thought was creeping unwillingly up on Monty at the mention of a young man.

"Did you say the note mentioned Stansted Airport? Does it give a date as well?"

It did – and the description of the young man fitted perfectly.

"Bloody Hell!" ejaculated Monty, as a cold feeling gripped him, only to be succeeded by a hot flush of fear and anger combined. "The tricky little bastard!"

"I beg your pardon!" said Mrs Pateman starchily. "I'm only trying to be of help. There's no reason to......"

"No, no. You've been *most* helpful, Mrs – er – most helpful. I didn't mean to be....you just took me a bit by surprise. Now please don't mention this to anyone else. I may ask you to do a little investigating for me, for additional – er – that is a generous expense allowance. Could you manage that, do you think?"

In mentioning money, Monty had pressed the right button, for Mrs. Pateman's widowed mother seemed to be a constant drain on her resources, and she still suspected that this old chap had in some way 'done the dirty' on Proudfoot.

"Well, that depends, of course, on what you want. I mean I'm not, well, I'm not normally one to pry into other people's business, but....."

Despite his anxiety, Monty could not repress a slight smile as he recognised the phrase of the inveterate snoop. This one, he thought, could be a very useful pair of eyes. They agreed that she should commence immediately to find out all she could, starting from an assumption that his surname was Brady, he lived somewhere a mile or two east of Thorpe Tunnel and had a son called Patrick – the one in the photo.

"I shouldn't go to the actual house after you've discovered it," said Monty. "I don't want to risk alerting them." (And there might be a body-guard, he thought, but decided not to mention it to his new colleague).

"I expect that man from the Fens would have a good idea where they live. Shall I....?"

"No, Mrs Pateman, I think we'll leave him out of it – for the moment, that is. One other thing. Don't be surprised if you hear he, that is the father, has just gone away, or is in hospital, or has recently met with an accident. Any background would be useful, though."

In the event, one did not have to be Sherlock Holmes (or Miss Silver, for that matter) to locate the house: the local telephone directory showed Brady, Martin as being the only one in the immediate area, at 57, Southorpe Lane. Half an hour after her conversation with Burton-Latimer, Mrs Pateman was on the way, rehearsing in her mind a series of questions to put to householders at the *other* end of the village.

It only needed one friendly, garrulous person, and Mrs Pateman struck oil at the third house.

"Oh, no! Mr Brady is *much* older – he's retired now, used to be at the Grammar. It might be his son you want, but he's away most of the time. They did very well, went to....Yes, there's a daughter as well.... Gracious me, no. *She's* still teaching. I saw her only the other day when she called round for some eggs...."

Mrs Pateman thought at this point it would be a good idea to prolong the conversation (not that it seemed to be difficult!) by asking if she, too, could buy a dozen....if that was possible. It was, but it took time, during which Monty's personal spy was deluged with information, some of which she found time to commit to paper whilst her source broke off to answer the telephone.

Among the trivia (as they appeared to Mrs P) she learnt that Mrs Brady – a very nice woman, who.....etc., etc. – was away at the present, in France, on a course. That was why she had been stocking up with eggs, for her husband.... . Mrs Pateman agreed that she 'knew what men were', and established that her talkative friend did not know where in France, had, indeed, only a rather hazy idea of 'France' as a concept. She also established that Mr Brady was on his own this week and – this as a result of the telephone call which had interrupted the flow

– her friend Mrs Chadwick had just heard that the dog had died... so he wouldn't be out walking it if she called round... but her friend had seen the son, so he wasn't on his own after all, which was nice, as it's always upsetting when.....

Mrs Pateman, who now knew everything except the colour of underpants her prey was wearing, agreed that Mr Brady would be unlikely to be taking the dog out in the circumstances, and extricated herself, accompanied by Mrs Tolliver, the jolly gossip, who insisted on carrying the eggs to the car.

Unaware of the explosive nature of the information in her possession, Mrs Pateman took her time – a little shopping, some carefully set out notes – before contacting the man whom she knew only as 'Larry'. She reasoned that it would not do to make the task look too easy: that might reduce the amount she could expect for 'expenses' (which, she reminded herself craftily, could include those eggs). Also, she had no knowledge of the nature of recent events which had led up to the suicide of her boss.

The information that (although Mrs Pateman had not actually *seen* him) the subject of the photo was still alive, was going to galvanise the Organisation into action, and the news of the dead dog came as useful confirmation to Monty when he received the report. However, the fact onto which he latched was the absence on a course in France of Patrick's mother. Posing as a researcher from the Department for Education and Science, he soon found out from County Offices which establishment they used for their residential language courses; also that there was a (mixed) party of secondary teachers there now. International directory enquiries led to the secretary at the 'Institut Pédagogique'. She had herself made the booking and confirmed that Mrs Brady was on her way home, via Stansted Airport. As a result, she could not speak to the 'education officer' who needed to check certain details in order to process her expenses claim.

"Right, clever Dick, let's see what use your first class degree is when you hear we've, or rather 'they've', got your mother!" said Monty to himself, as, still based in Liverpool, he prepared to set up the abduction of Martin's wife, preferably before she left the Continent, but with a fall-back at Stansted

Airport, where, he assumed, she would be met by a member of the family.

CHAPTER TWENTY-SIX

Christopher, the Agent's assistant, was by now in hiding in Thorpe Tunnel Bunker, a move organised by Gerald. However, when the latter heard from Larry that he was to assume command of the Eastern Area, he rang the Bunker to inform the young man (who congratulated him warmly) and say that Larry had agreed to take care of arrangements for his, Christopher's, untraceable departure from the country. This was to be followed by 'adoption' by, probably, the Dutch branch, where an Englishman loyal to the Cause would be a useful asset.

"I shall be a bit busy," said Gerald, using the understatement to demonstrate his ability calmly to take the pressure, "so I'll have to leave it to you to liaise direct."

Christopher duly rang the number which Gerald had given him and asked to speak to Larry:

"Speaking. Who's that? ..Ah! The chappie who 'always said that the man he gave the papers to was genuine'?"

"Er – yes. But I can quite see why ....."

"And saw him ruthlessly gunned down by our own men?" continued Monty, who had just discovered that some form of switch and/or pantomime must have been played out among the hedgerows.

"Yes. I reported all that to Gerald," said Christopher. "He said you would get me out of the country. Why are you....?"

"All in good time, laddie," came the reply. "First of all, tell me *exactly* what you saw....then I will tell *you* that you were the audience for a little playlet, written, produced and directed, I have no doubt, by an old Cambridge acquaintance of mine, who works in his spare time for British Intelligence!"

"I – I don't understand," said the hapless Christopher. "I saw him fall... and.. were the other two pretending to be... ?"

As he asked the question, Christopher felt the vomit rise in his throat at the recollection of the two bodies, heads damn' near blown apart, blood, brains and tissue exposed on the bright grass.

"They were dead I tell you. Dead!" Christopher's voice rose to a shriek.

Recognising the unwisdom of having wound the young man up when he was too far away to control his actions, Monty sought to calm him down, saying that he, Larry, had found a way to control the opposition and was expecting a call from some friends in France in the very near future by way of confirmation, at which time he would organise the Continental end of Christopher's translation.

"In the mean time, sit tight and don't breathe a word of all this to *anyone*."

****

The two 'heavies' who had been sent to Charles de Gaulle airport to kidnap Jennifer were disappointed when the announcement failed to bring a middle-aged English lady called Mrs. Brady to the information desk. They had no photograph, so had hoped to 'flush her out' by that means. They did not despair, however, as presumably she was leaving it to the last minute, had been delayed, or – just possibly – had passed through the gates before they got there.

"What about that one?" asked the junior of the two. "She's on her own, looks English – we can check by reading the labels on the case – and is about the right age."

"But why didn't she respond to hearing her name – if it *is* her?"

"Perhaps she's a bit deaf, or was in the toilet or something. I'll get them to try the announcement again; you watch her carefully, and wander near to look at her cases."

This time, the message included the first name of the target, Mrs Jennifer Brady, and had the gratifying result of making the lady stop, listen hard and start towards the Information desk, only to change her mind and join the crowd moving forward, as the flight was called immediately after. The reason for these movements was that she had intended to go through and then check on the announcement, which had not sounded quite like her married name (not surprisingly, as it was Radley) but was definitely Jennifer.

'Heavies' are not known, in whatever country or cause, for their finesse or ability to analyse, plan and stalk their victim. Jean-Paul was no exception to that generalisation and he had been told to watch for signs of recognition when the announcement was repeated.

Mrs Radley was able to dine out for many months on the strength of the story she had to tell of being asked to accompany the burly French 'customs man' to a back room, where she was told to empty her bag and show her passport. She stood there, worrying about missing the plane, wondering why they thought her name was Brady and listening to the muttered conversation between the two, after which one departed, presumably to ring his superior. He then returned twenty minutes later, wild-eyed, to indulge in excitable French which she was unable to follow. It was at this point in her telling of the story that Jennifer (Radley) still recalled her indignation, for, without a word of explanation, still less apology, the two men 'really rather rough-looking, one would never have taken them for Customs officials in *this* country!'... had literally thrown down her passport and run from the room! And that, the story continued, had not been all...... .

****

"Not to worry!" said Monty on being told that, because of the mistaken identity, the real Mrs Brady must have slipped past them at the last minute. "We'll pick her up this end, at Stansted. It may be all for the best. The secretary was quite sure she'd checked out. She'd made the booking herself, the day before. If she doesn't turn up at Stansted, it'll mean she was warned – in which case we'll have to unmask the source. Tell your men to hang on and see if someone like her, *exactly* like her this time, arrives late. Meanwhile, I'll double check with the Institut and the airline."

The virtual collapse of the chain of command in the Eastern Area meant that it was extremely difficult to get hold of any operatives. Monty tried to contact Gerald at Thorpe Tunnel, but was told he was 'not available' by Christopher, who answered the phone:

"He said he'd let me know where he was, once he'd managed to take over his new job. He was off down south somewhere. If you locate him, can you tell him to get in touch as two blokes are on their way here and I don't know what to do with them."

"Really!" said Monty. "They must be the two who 'arrested' the impostor. Gerald asked for them to come and dispose of the body ......but as he isn't there, they can do a little job for me while they're waiting for his instructions. I know Gerald would approve. Give me the number of their mobile!"

Explaining that they would have to get their skates on to arrive before the plane, Monty sent the two members of the reinforcement team from Haslemere back down the A 1, across to the M 11 and on down to Stansted Airport with instructions to abduct Mrs Brady. They were travelling in a fast car, so he considered it should be possible to get there in time, as in fact proved to be the case.

Monty was delighted when they reported that they were in position and that the plane was due to land shortly, about eight minutes behind schedule. He had, by this time, checked with the Institut Pédagogique, who confirmed the lady's plans, the flight number, etc., and had spoken to the Departures desk. There a bored young man, unimpressed by any Englishman, even one who (for a Customs official) spoke excellent French, glanced down the passenger list and confirmed the presence of a Mrs Brady.

"Mais, bien sûr, prénom Jennifer.... elle a failli de manquer le vol, mais....."

As it happened, acting on different information a little later, Patrick was told the same thing, this time by a different, but equally unimpressed young man, who read the notes made by his colleague, finding them most useful in saving time – time more profitably spent applying himself to the much more rewarding task of chatting up an attractive blonde who claimed to have mislaid her ticket.

As a precaution, Patrick arranged for two armed agents to observe his mother's arrival and give the 'all clear' to Elizabeth, who, still unknown to Jennifer, was meeting her. Thus it was that four athletic-looking men (two from each side), all carrying guns, all prepared to abduct, maim, kill, disable, and then disappear, found themselves waiting and watching in the arrivals area at Stansted Airport. Also there (but aware of only two of the four) was Elizabeth, who had come to meet her mother, with strict instructions to do as she was told by the body-guards, who had made themselves known and were in direct contact by phone with an anxious Patrick.

The reasons for Patrick's concern had begun when Elizabeth had popped out, having seen the state of the fridge, to get some eggs. It was a short step, given the communicative skills of Mrs Tolliver, to discover that someone had been asking questions about the family. Moreover, the sharp-eyed lady was able to add that the enquirer worked at the Castle, there being a staff parking permit on the windscreen, exactly the same as the one her daughter's boyfriend's uncle had on his – and he had worked there for.....Elizabeth had cut short the conversation and rushed home to report the disturbing news to Patrick.

"Somehow they're on to Dad," he decided. " Never mind for the moment how. If it's Burton-bloody-Latimer behind this (and I must assume it is) we've got major problems. He's a nasty bit of work – won't stop at anything – and he's no fool. I'll double the guards on this place and we'd better get Mother back here."

"Surely they wouldn't......" Elizabeth's voice betrayed both shock and fear as the perils of their situation opened before her.

"Too damn' right he would – if he found out where she was, which is highly unlikely, mind you."

But Elizabeth recalled the garrulous Mrs Tolliver, as she expressed surprised pleasure at seeing her. 'As I was only saying just now, it was nice your brother was around, what with your mother being in France and the dog and everything. Men are not very good on their own, I always say and that lady from the Castle said the same thing. Funny them not having any eggs up there, though.....'

"I think they'll know by now," she said, sadly contemplating the significance of the phrase 'as I was only saying just now'. "What *have* we got into?"

In a flurry of phone calls, Patrick set up as much protection as he could, including a team to intercept his mother at Charles de Gaulle Airport, which arrived too late.

"We have one advantage," he told Kenneth. "It's safe to assume they don't yet know that *we* know that *they* know that I – and my father – are involved. I've had no warning from Gerald, though, which could mean he's changed sides.... I agree, I agree, but it *could*. It could mean that Burton-Latimer suspects that Gerald is working for us, so has deliberately left him out of it....or it could mean that B-L arranged for this woman to ferret about and report direct to him. Let's hope it's the last scenario."

"Why, for God's sake? Surely the whole point of having an agent in place is to get prior knowledge of what they're doing? If this Latimer chap leaves Gerald out of it, we've had it!"

"I know what you mean," said Patrick, " but in the longer term we don't want them to suspect Gerald, so if he *hasn't* been told, and we know anyway, we're better off. The trouble is that Burton-Latimer may take a long hard look at the fable he's been fed, and suspect practically everyone."

"The trouble is he may grab your mother. Never mind the long term," Kenneth grimly reminded Patrick, who fell silent, fingers surreptitiously, and uncharacteristically, crossed.

****

Mrs Radley had enjoyed her flight. A fuss had been made of her on account of her unpleasant treatment at the airport, which had caused her nearly to miss the plane, being ferried out to the runway just before it took off and then upgraded to First Class. The large gin to steady her nerves, followed by two glasses of wine, was more than enough to induce a mood of theatricality, so it was with glee that she swept down upon her staid and astonished husband: an audience at last!

"You see before you," she proclaimed in ringing tones with a suitably expansive gesture, "Mrs Jennifer Brady! New wives for old! Pick up the car keys... I'm yours for the price of a....."

But details of the tariff were never vouchsafed, to the short-lived relief of her embarrassed spouse – and disappointment of most of those within earshot. At the mention of the name of the person they had come to abduct, the two Organisation 'foot-soldiers' exchanged a quick glance and then closed on their prey.

"Mrs Brady? Would you accompany us please, there's been a mix-up with your ....."

A second such approach was too much for the unfortunate lady, however, who let out a piercing shriek and swung her hand-bag to such good effect that the bogus official, caught completely unawares, fell to the ground. In the process, his mackintosh opened, rather like the classic 'flasher', exposing his weapon – metallic rather than phallic, but none-the-less alarming to Mrs Radley, who shrieked at full volume:

"He's got a gun! Stop him, Oliver! Help! Help! Kill him - he's ... No! Don't shoot. Ahhhh!"

And with that Mrs Radley crumpled to the ground as the panicky gunmen started to run for the exit, one loosing a shot into the air to ensure a free passage.

As luck would have it, the stray bullet struck a child's helium-filled balloon which had lodged in the steel 'rafters', causing a sharp crack which the two men took to emanate from a hidden sniper. Both turned, guns at the ready, as they realised their chosen route led to the lifts rather than the loading area outside.

The men sent by Patrick to prevent such an approach were in two minds, for no word had come from the daughter, watching out of sight on closed circuit T V, to the effect that this Mrs Brady had emerged from behind the screens. Also, they were loath to declare themselves to the extent of drawing their own firearms. Frustrated and irresolute, they could only observe the rapid departure of the opposition, thankful that the attempted kidnap had failed.

Stansted, however, is regularly patrolled by security police, armed with sub-machine guns, alert for any terrorist threat. It was towards two such men that the bungling pair had turned, on finding their route blocked and (as they believed) under fire from above. They were in no state to react sensibly to the appropriate shouted warning, the result being all too predictable. They were cut down by a burst of automatic fire, each receiving several bullets in the chest. One was pronounced dead on the spot, the other, Gordon, underwent a successful operation at the East Herts General Hospital, Harlow, after which he was placed in a recovery room, still asleep.

The two British Intelligence agents had been in danger of making themselves conspicuous by *not* joining the crowd which thronged towards the scene of the recent action. They, like Elizabeth, had continued to watch the emerging passengers, hoping that the real Mrs Brady could be got away as soon as she had collected her luggage, under cover of all the excitement...... but they were disappointed.

CHAPTER TWENTY-SEVEN

At the start of the news item concerning a 'shoot-out' at Stansted Airport, Gerald was only mildly interested, there being no reason to connect it with the Organisation. When photographs of the two 'terrorists' appeared on the screen, however, he found himself gaping like an urchin with its face pressed to the sweet shop window, for there they were, the two who had held him captive in the Bunker!

"Couldn't have happened to two nicer guys!" he murmured to himself. "Saves me from having to do the same thing, but what in Hell's name were they doing there? And who sent them without consulting me?"

A telephone call to Thorpe Tunnel, answered by Christopher, brought him up to date – and made him realise how close Larry was to unravelling the web of lies in which he had been enmeshed by Kenneth and his unobtrusive behind-the-scenes manipulator.

Monty, for his part, although he had never seen them, had little doubt that the two dead men in the news were his 'hit squad' and even less that Patrick had acquired an informer within the Organisation which had enabled him to keep one step ahead. Mrs bloody Brady must have been warned, so had never got on the flight, which had been booked as a decoy. Somehow they had got to the K L M / U K Air clerk who had misinformed him – or hacked into their computer and altered the information. Who, then, was the traitor that bastard had 'turned'? Monty reviewed the events of the past few days, trying to sort impeccable fact from the illusionist's patter. What could be relied upon? He knew that the man in the yellow anorak had not been Patrick's father. So who *had* he been – and was he *really* shot...by whom? Had any of that ever happened? Who had actually witnessed the events....or, more relevantly, *claimed* to have seen them happen? Monty forced himself to face the worst possible scenario – that the traitor was Gerald. If that were so, he, Monty, would have to go back to the High Command, before whom he had argued so forcibly for Gerald, indicating clearly his support for an appointment, not just as Area Controller, but to that august body itself. Surely it wasn't? No, it couldn't have been him: he didn't know about Patrick's father; didn't know about the move against his mother at Charles de Gaulle; didn't know what sort of brain he was up against. At least he hadn't cocked things up like that fellow Proudfoot, thought Monty, continuing his train of thought, which led to the ghastly conclusion that the Agent had walked under a train because he believed he had ordered the killing of one of the Organisation's top men – a man who had probably never existed, had never been killed, and had certainly not been a member of the Organisation!

Who, then, knew enough to warn Patrick and give him time to spirit his mother away, minutes ahead of her would-be abductors? Mrs Pateman? Hardly. She it had been who had discovered the vital facts. Not, of course, that that was conclusive: that 'knowledge' had resulted in two more deaths – on the wrong side. Christopher? Could be... in fact... Monty ran the events past his mind's eye casting this time Christopher in the rôle of double agent. By Heaven, it is! Only Christopher knew in time to warn Patrick. It had been Christopher who had supposedly stood by the assassin as he gunned down the Fotheringhay pair – or, more probably, tied them up and removed them from the scene. After all, who had actually *seen* them dead? Gerald? No, he'd been shot at to keep him at a distance! The Intelligence agent whom Gerald thought he'd 'turned'? Yes, perhaps. He'd better warn Gerald not to trust him until they were sure, and get his help in eliminating that bastard Christopher before he could do any more damage. Or, wait! Perhaps he could be used to pass on dis-information until Patrick realised his man had been rumbled.

The 'Fen Affair' had taken up so much of Monty's time since his return to England that he had so far had no opportunity to carry out the main task with which he had been charged by the group to membership of which he aspired, the Grand Central Council. Based in Vienna, they controlled national High Commands throughout the world and had recently become concerned at reports from Britain of impatience amongst those who served in humble circumstances – the Geralds of the movement, facing retirement and contemplating the dubious benefits of having waited and waited, for about forty years, for the coup that never came. For years they had been held in check by their fathers, who had held high rank and enjoyed authority (if only briefly) at a very young age. As a generation, they had gambled and lost – but at least they had 'lived'. Now it was the task of the next generation to keep in check the young firebrands, to make them serve in lowly positions as drivers, Water Board labourers, clerks, foremen, etc., buoyed up by their secrets, additional income and the promise of wealth, respect and power over the colourless ordinary people. Always that promise – one that those under thirty could see had proved illusory for their fathers... the middle generation, who would never personally benefit, a significant number of whom wished to return to the gaming tables and gamble all, once again, on a right wing revolution. Monty had been told to weigh up the situation and influence thinking towards caution, to discourage Britain from going off at half cock, thereby alerting society to their existence, and setting the Cause back another thirty to fifty years.

The Continental view was that there was no need to undertake any risks – that the course of history was with them. They noted the re-unification of the two Germanys, the collapse of the great enemy, Russia, the compliance of France and the surely unstoppable emergence of a United States of Europe. They noted too the clumsy democratic systems which could easily be subverted by men of vision, for whom the end of the eventual fulfilment of the great Nazi dream justified any means. The growth of support for the 'Right' would easily lead to the emergence of politicians loyal to the Cause, of which there were many (either by genuine conviction or under some form of duress). The pressure on jobs, houses, welfare, etc., caused by the inflow of Eastern or Middle Eastern peoples was already being turned to the advantage of the heirs of the Third Reich....despite their involvement in that traffic as part of their criminally inspired money-raising activities. Just as there is no stronger supporter of law and order than the retired bank robber anxious to protect his ill-gotten gains, so the policies of these bandits bristled with Draconian measures against crime, with deportation, with death or disfigurement for 'offences against the state', with the creation of sub-classes such as women, only tolerated if needed to render some service and with simplistic loyalties to flag, symbol or physical fit. Those who were not for them were deemed to be against.

Monty forced himself to consider the advisability of immediate and unannounced departure, to avoid being dragged into the swirling waters as the British – or, at least, the Eastern Area – ship foundered, betrayed within and weakened by a series of small, but spectacularly unsuccessful encounters. On the other hand, to return having accomplished nothing, and possibly be seen as having failed to prevent (or worse still, helped to bring about!) a major disaster, would put paid to his hopes of ...... No. He would have to get in touch with the High Command before leaving the Liverpool area. His new protégé, Gerald, would have to win his spurs by stabilising the situation. Once he had been alerted to the danger represented by Christopher, he should be all right.....and Monty would make sure he got the credit for the unmasking by passing the information through the High Command.

The Chairman agreed to a meeting, but was far from happy to hear that the Fen business was still not under control. There seemed always to be a development which would solve everything – followed by news that matters were now worse. It was encouraging however, that Larry had now pin-pointed the rotten apple responsible for the latest debâcle so things should run more smoothly. As regards the hawks versus doves debate, it was, the Chairman cautiously admitted, true to say that there were plans to use the forthcoming national referendum to generate a climate more suited to a pro-active approach. Well, yes, to effect a transfer of power to a group dominated by sympathetic..... Yes, yes (crossly by now) one could call it a form of coup – but only once there was no risk of failure.

Monty, mindful of his brief, which did not include the transmission of direct instructions, forebore from pointing out that phrases such as 'no risk of failure' could be seen as the product of complacency. Parallels of a sort could be drawn with the Maginot Line, the defoliation bombing by the Americans in Vietnam, the Bay of Pigs escapade and the Argentinian decision to occupy the Malvinas, safe in the 'knowledge' that there was little which Britain could actually do about it.

"You plan to fiddle the result, I gather?" said Monty.

"Let us say we expect it to be a very close result – and that as 'Chairman' I shall need to exercise my casting vote," came the reply, delivered in a distinctly repressive, but confidently amused tone, for this was becoming too much like an interrogation for the speaker's liking. "If you want details – and nothing is absolutely final yet – I suggest you request a copy through channels, so that the High Command may deal with it appropriately."

In fact, the plan was for the result to be a larger 'No' than could easily be believed, followed by the exposure of the many unsuspecting minor agents who had followed instructions to act in a fraudulent manner. This in turn would lead to a crisis situation which could only be resolved by a second referendum. Those who had helped to uncover the first 'fiddle' would be held in reserve to do a similar job, should it be needed, but all their projections had pointed confidently to there being no need to intervene. Not only would there be a resounding (genuine) 'Yes', but also the mobilisation of right wing groups, hitherto opposed to European Union – and their consequent success at the polls on a tide of righteous indignation against the 'moderates' – would ensure sufficient 'democratic' voting power to bring in martial law. The latter would be needed to stabilise a situation which the British neo-Nazi movement had plans to thoroughly destabilise. Aspects of that, thought the Chairman, smiling to himself as he saw his ambitious, scheming colleague prepare to depart, would make paratroopers dressed as nuns seem very small beer! And then there was the 'Retter'... but after over fifty years would it really still work? John had sworn it had been meticulously maintained...... .

"I don't want that Christopher taken care of for the moment," said Monty, interrupting the older man's train of thought. "He'll be useful as a channel of dis-information. Can you let Gerald know he's not safe, though?"

"Gerald? Oh, yes, I shall be briefing him fully on the 'Retter', now that he's to be on our committee, so I'll pass on your suspicions."

"More than suspicions: I'm certain," said Monty, nettled by something in the tone of the last remark... and not happy with what amounted to a refusal to be open about the plans to force the pace. "That was a quick decision on the appointment, then?"

In reality, despite his claim to certainty about Christopher having been 'turned', Monty was aware of a niggle at the back of his mind which told him that, with Patrick involved, he would do well not to believe it had been snowing until he was living in an igloo. However, he was pretty sure of Gerald – and to admit now to this pompous old fool that he might have been wrong was more than he could stomach.

"Yes," said the Chairman. "Your recommendation won the day. He wouldn't have been our first choice had John been – er – available: he didn't think a lot of him, in fact. Gerald's come well out of this mess, however: seems to be able to command respect from the younger element, which we need."

Yes, thought Monty, with another frisson of worry, including friend Christopher, which was not as great an endorsement as he had thought! But he held his peace.

****

Martin's wife, Jennifer, had still not been located by the Organisation, which was convinced that British Intelligence had been warned and was keeping her in a safe place. The latter, however, were convinced that, despite the shambles at Stansted, some section of the Organisation had kidnapped her – possibly on her way to Charles de Gaulle Airport, possibly from the Institut – and were keeping her as a trump card.

Patrick was wary of showing his hand. He knew that Monty was a spy, but he had to be able to prove it to his superiors, not all of whom he could trust. Moreover, because of the presence of traitors, everyone was to some extent suspect – including himself. If accused, Monty would try to put together a case to prove that he, Patrick, was the real spy and either succeed or at least gain sufficient time to counter-attack. If he could gain leverage by threatening his mother, as he certainly would if backed into a corner, Monty could still turn the tables.

Both Patrick and Monty, mobilising their considerable resources, continued to search for a (genuinely) harmless middle aged school teacher, who remained blissfully unaware of her predicament, recalling, as she sped along the autoroute to Calais, the way the previous evening had ended. Henri Cazaux had been some time refilling the glasses, whilst his wife and Jennifer discussed pets. In fact, realising that his English guest was worried about the extra expense incurred by returning from her course ahead of time, he had been busy.

"It's all arranged!" he had announced when he eventually returned. "You stay here this evening; we go now to collect your luggage; you leave with our good friends, Marc and Georgette Loriot, first thing tomorrow morning!"

"But Henri...perhaps Jennifer would rather....." demurred his wife.

"Would rather pay for a plane ticket? Of course not: it would be ridiculous when they are driving to England and would enjoy her company. Do you not agree?"

He looked to Jennifer for approval and received it, noticing that she bit back the comment which had risen to her lips. "And don't worry about the ticket. I have a friend who works there – and he has promised to arrange a refund. These things can be done if you know the right people. Shall we go and get your luggage?"

Hélène apologised for her husband's high-handed action, but reassured Jennifer that the Loriots were very 'sympa' and would take her wherever she wished to go. Did she wish to telephone home to explain the change of plan? As Jennifer had been at pains to keep from her family the fact that she had decided to return, that was not necessary.

They did not see anyone when collecting her things and her room-mate, Miss Priscilla Plant, did not notice their absence when she returned at two in the morning to fall, fully clothed, onto her bed, where she slept as for dead (dead drunk was nearer the mark) until after ten the following morning. Miss Plant, when capable of mental effort, assumed that Jennifer had left as previously arranged to catch her plane. No-one asked her if she had left the night before, and if they had, they would have been no better off, for her memory of the entire evening was a blur. She recalled that Jennifer had talked of visiting friends, but had no idea who or where they were, whether she had in fact gone to see them or at what time she had departed in the morning. Miss Plant explained that she was a 'heavy sleeper' to the course director, who felt quite light-headed from the alcoholic fumes which remained behind as she, suffering the unaccustomed effects of a hang-over, carefully left the room.

And so it came about that Jennifer, very fortunately for her, eluded the attentions of predators and protectors alike. By nine the following morning, she was on her way, still expected on the midday flight for, in accordance with the well known Irishman's law, Henri Cazaux's airport friend had put his back out, bending down to pick up his brief-case and had spent the next few hours in agony, failing, therefore, to take the appropriate action concerning Jennifer's change of plan. During what became a crucial period, she remained booked in. This inaccuracy was compounded by the desk clerk misinterpreting a note concerning the apparent success in locating the lady, resulting from his observation of what he took to be Jennifer being escorted to an interview room by men who had claimed to be security officials, when getting him to put out a call for her.

The procedures for double-checking operated effectively, but the actual people who dealt with the phone calls from Monty – and, indeed, from Patrick – failed to pick up the error. When more stringent checks were made as a result of the failure of Jennifer to arrive at Stansted, the foregoing became apparent. Both sides knew she had not travelled KLM / UK Air, both suspected the other side had her somewhere..... but neither had a clue as to her whereabouts.

"They *will* be surprised when I turn up!" said Jennifer brightly, as the helpful French couple approached King's Cross station, having driven up from Dover. "It'll give Martin something else to think about, in stead of brooding over the dog. I do wish he would get out a bit more. Life in the country can be rather, well, 'humdrum', as we say. Thank you so much! No, I can manage, really. I'll ring from here and get someone to meet me at Peterborough. Now remember: you're always welcome! 'Bye!"

****

"Mother!" exploded Elizabeth. "Where have you *been*? We've been....Wait!....I – er – there's someone at the door," she invented desperately to gain time to consult and consider, calling out to the security guard with her hand over the mouthpiece. "It's my mother on the phone! She seems to be all right, and is, I think, at King's Cross. What shall I tell her? Where the hell is Patrick when he's needed?"

Lazing upstairs in a foot of herb-laden hot water, unaware that his wife had been told that he had caught a cold and was cast down by events, Martin heard the note of concern in his daughter's voice, and reached for the cordless phone which, as a matter of routine, he always took with him when having a bath.

"Hello, dear! How are you? Not long to go now – how's it going?"

"Martin! Where's Elizabeth gone? And never mind me..... How are *you*? I was so sorry to hear about Sherry..... Look, I can't talk now. The train goes in five minutes..... Can someone meet me at Peterborough in about an hour? If not, I'll get a taxi."

At this point, Elizabeth raised the receiver once again, realising that she would have to decide whether to tell her mother about her pursuers (always assuming she was still unaware of them) and whether to persuade her to stay put, get on the train..... or what.

"Oh, Hell!" she said despairingly to the guard, who had come running, revolver at the ready, on hearing her shout. "Father's on the other phone. That's all we need!"

She was just in time to hear her father swallow his surprise at hearing that his wife had returned early, manage to avoid delving into the murky waters of what she had been told and merely reply hurriedly:

"No. I mean no problem...... we'll be there..... see you soon."

"Elizabeth! That was your mother! Did you tell her to come back? I said I didn't want her bothered. I'm quite O K and..... anyway, I must get dressed and collect her."

195

"I think, Sir," said the Intelligence agent entrusted with ensuring their safety, "that she is the one to worry about. There have already been two attempts to abduct her. Let's hope she gave the opposition the slip just as much as she did *us*! The best thing – if you feel well enough – is for you and your daughter to drive in to the station with a couple of us following. That'll leave two to keep an eye on this place. Meanwhile, we'll try to get in touch with your son."

Shocked by the news that there had been attempts to kidnap his wife, Martin did as he was told and, on the way to the station, listened without interrupting as Elizabeth put him fully in the picture.

"Bloody Hell! They must have a Hell of a lot to hide. How on earth did she avoid them? Where can she have been if the people running the course haven't been able to find her?" ·

"At least that murdering bunch of Nazis haven't been able to either," said Elizabeth. "But what shall we do if she's not on this train?" she added, voicing everyone's concern as she swung the car round the roundabout and headed back to the station.

"Ten bloody minutes," said Martin, glancing at the dashboard clock. "Those two over there could be the opposition – or, more likely those!"

"Stop being silly!" said his daughter. "What about the two who have just drawn into the car park?"

"Yes, they look pretty tough.....but aren't they our two lads?" objected Martin. "Oh, all right, you win! If anything happens to Jennifer, though, it'll be all my fault. I should never have poked my nose in....." His voice tailed off and he turned away to hide the tears of worry, of regret ....of love.

"Come on, you old fool," said his daughter, placing a consoling hand on his arm. "Let's go and meet her – and don't let her see you looking like that. Your job is to look cheerful, brisk, surprised, but *pleased*, to see her; not too cast down about Sherry..... just a few minor local difficulties. Nothing to worry about. O K?"

Martin responded well to the advice, almost literally shaking himself out of his gloomy mood.

"You're right. Thanks. As regards the dog, it won't be difficult. I'm ashamed to say that all this with your mother has completely driven Sherry from my mind....."

"I should damn' well hope so, too!" replied Elizabeth, leading her father firmly into the station.

CHAPTER TWENTY-EIGHT

As the new Eastern Area Controller, the order should have come to Gerald to arrange the murder in hospital of Gordon, the surviving half of the hit squad which had come to grief at Stansted. He could at least have tipped off Patrick, even if refusing to implement it would have been too compromising. In fact, it was given by Monty direct to the local commander at Haslemere, (who was also worried about being linked to the Lincolnshire killings) with a request to make *absolutely* sure by using someone who could recognise the victim.

"One other thing," added Monty, "have you heard about that Christopher – the lad at the Castle? No? Well, he's the one who's been tipping off the opposition. I want to interrogate him: the Chairman asked me to organise someone to pick him up. Can you cover that as well?"

"We'll take care of that, Larry," came the reply, "providing we can despatch the bastard slowly and painfully afterwards: he's caused the death of one, shortly to be two, of my best men."

"O K – but let the Chairman know," said Monty. "And no balls-ups on this one: there's been enough mistaken identity recently. Let's get it right for a change!"

Monty's remark was not well received, as the 'Mrs Brady fiasco' had been orchestrated by this same 'Larry'.... but a recent recruit whose record appeared to be suitably scruple-free (and could recognise Gordon) was duly despatched to perform the grisly task before Gordon could pass on, whether willingly or under the influence of drugs, information which might incriminate others. As one of those 'others', Monty was particularly keen to guarantee the man's permanent silence.

Masquerading as a hospital porter, the assassin, one Kevin Goode, gained access to the relevant area with ease (aided by a consultant loyal to the Cause). Whilst there were advantages in the fact that Goode could recognise Gordon, the converse proved counter-productive. Gordon gave the appearance of being asleep when his murderer peered in the window, but in fact he was surveying his surroundings through half closed eyelids... and recognised him. He also noted the man's expression, which, combined with his knowledge of the way in which the Organisation operated, forced him to the unpleasant conclusion that he was about to be sacrificed. He was still unable to talk, but rage and fear combined to create readings of pulse, brain activity, etc., which caused the nurse who came to check on him to scribble the results hurriedly, dropping her ball-point pen in the process, before departing rapidly to get help.

By the time his system was found once again to be stable, Gordon had made up his mind. He would write a 'confession', hoping thereby to get lenient treatment (including a new identity). After all, they hadn't in fact killed anyone, and surely information about the body in Thorpe Tunnel Bunker, and this chap 'Larry' who had set up the attempted kidnapping, would be sufficient to bargain with. The trouble was there was so little time if, as he suspected, the fake porter had instructions to silence him....and though he had the ball-point pen dropped by the nurse, he had no paper, and could barely move.

Kevin Goode had to work a long shift before seeing his opportunity – the brief descent into slumber of the policeman detailed to sit on guard outside Gordon's room. His attack was swift, silent and lethally effective: Patrick had lost a vital link in his quest for clearly demonstrable evidence of Monty's real loyalties.

That was the bad news, but it was more than outweighed by the good, when it was flashed through to Patrick: his mother had been found – or, rather, heard. Somehow she had evaded Monty's agents. The other good news was that Mrs Pateman had been located – not difficult with Mrs Tolliver's excellent description, combined with the type, colour and number of her car, including the tell-tale parking permit for the Castle. She was 'singing' loudly about 'Larry' whose description fitted Monty perfectly, even down to the rather prominent ears (which he was more than happy to have compared to those so often highlighted in caricatures of the heir to the throne). The only link needed was proof that the 'Larry' who could be identified by Mrs Pateman, if that lady were shown Burton-Latimer in a 'line-up', was the same person who had arranged the attempted abduction. Patrick still hesitated to make his denouncement, knowing what he was up against. It had to be water tight, and it had to be soon or the traitor would 'do a Lucan' – probably aided by some of the same people who had helped that gentleman to evade arrest.

Patrick was right: Monty was on his way back across the Channel, by train to Leeds, thence to London (King's Cross), by Underground to Liverpool Street and from there by the boat train to Harwich. By one of life's weird coincidences, he was walking across the concourse just as Jennifer put down the phone and hurried to catch her train to Peterborough. She was looking ahead, searching for Platform 3 and ran straight into him, her own modest weight boosted by a substantial suitcase on wheels.

"Sorry!" said Monty, quintessentially English, displaying that nation's absurd habit of apologising for someone else's clumsiness.

"No, my fault. I – I must dash..... The train....." panted Jennifer.

"Wait!" said Monty, rubbing his knee. "You've dropped your paper."

Jennifer smiled her thanks at the nice polite gentleman with the protruding ears; what a difference from those rude Parisians! And so the two passed in mutual ignorance, hunter and hunted colliding and splitting apart like atomic particles in a chemical reaction. Perhaps Patrick's superstitiously crossed fingers had worked after all – or may be, for once, the devil had failed to look after his own.

On the other hand, Monty's luck held in respect of Gordon's failure to get hold of any paper to complement the ball-point pen found tightly gripped in his stiffening fingers. The body had been wheeled to the morgue prior to the performance of an autopsy to determine the cause of death. Patrick had little interest in the result of that examination, for he had no doubt that the gunman had been murdered by his own side, the method being of purely academic interest at this stage. He was equally uninterested in the bed-sheets which surrounded the corpse. In that, however, he was making a big mistake, for, by a superhuman effort, the wounded, almost immobilised, patient had contrived to scrawl upon the starched white cotton sufficient key words to link together 'Larry', Thorpe Tunnel, Gerald, Mrs Brady, H F C and the neo-Nazis.

Gordon's determined effort to revenge his death deserved better than to be bleached into obscurity in the hospital laundry – and so it proved. The orderly whose task was to strip away the bedding noticed the biro marks and looked more closely. As he deciphered the writing, he grew both excited and nervous. The guy was thought to have been 'got at', so the writing would probably help to find the assassins, but whoever drew attention to it might well find themselves in deep water (literally, wearing the proverbial concrete overcoat).

By a happy chance, the porter had not long before read an article drawing attention to the decline of the word 'secret' in the Secret Service, citing as evidence the publication of the name of the head of the Service (a far cry from 'M') and the provision of a telephone number, available through Yellow Pages. It even quoted the number, going on to 'rubbish' the idea by means of an imagined conversation which began 'U K Export/Import, Boris speaking.....'. He placed the sheet where it would not be disturbed on finishing his shift and went home, resolved to ring if he could find the article but too nervous of being identified to risk Directory Enquiries.

Whilst this delay gave Monty more time to make himself scarce, it was unfortunate for him that the porter had to post a small parcel – for it was while waiting in the queue at the Post Office that he saw a poster giving him the very information he required. Careful to disguise what he was writing, he copied it down: 0171 930 9000. Then, having posted the parcel, he made for a vacant telephone. In fact, it was just like ringing any other business answer phone:

"This is the M I 5 Phoneline. If you have information which you want to give to the Security Service, please hold the line and an operator will speak to you."

No pressure was applied for him to identify himself and at the end (having only related the contents, implying that it was written on paper and being vague about the author), he was thanked and asked if he would either give a number where he could be contacted or, failing that, ring again in about an hour. The call was timed and its location deduced as being a public phone booth near the East Herts Hospital, at Harlow. There were sufficient keywords in the message for its contents to be rapidly conveyed to Patrick, for whom the location – close to the hospital to which the two gunmen had been taken from nearby Stansted – was the clincher.

"Could he have written something before they got to him?" he asked the ward Sister when she came to the phone.

"Well, it's true he had Nurse Macaulay's biro gripped in his hand when we pulled back the sheet – but he couldn't have got hold of any paper without asking, and he never regained the power of speech, so...."

"What about the bed-clothes? Did you check them? Or, rather, would you please do so?" he asked, with mounting excitement.

The public-spirited porter rang back as requested, to find that all seemed to be known except the actual location of the sheet, which he gladly supplied.

Knowing the difficulty for his superiors of being confronted with a denunciation by one member of the Service of another – deciding which one is the traitor before taking positive action – Patrick had been waiting until he had some 'proof' which he, personally, could not have manufactured: this was it. The Director was convinced, and the hunt for the Honourable Anthony Laurence Burton-Latimer was on.

****

Monty rubbed his knee where the clumsy woman had rammed her overloaded suitcase into him and contemplated the spreading urban sprawl of Colchester as the train left for Harwich. He had considered leaving the train and taking the bus to Mersea Island to get aboard his boat, but felt he was too well known in the area for safety. No; a rapid, anonymous departure was required before the Department grew suspicious – encouraged by that fellow Brady. If only he'd managed to get his hands on the wretch's mother – doubtless just as dreary a person as the father.....and how the hell had *he* run rings round Gerald? He'd better ring Vienna to get fixed up with somewhere to lie low until they could stabilise the situation. They'd be worried by the hawkishness he had detected amongst the British leadership, especially if they intended to activate the 'Retter'. The bloody fools! All they had to do was sit back and wait. Look at the recent successes of the National Front in France: extra payments to 'racially pure' parents, even! And all in the precious name of local democracy. There was plenty of time to make the odd telephone call before passing through passport control to the ferry......but the reflective calm of the moment was shattered by the information thereby gained. Monty learned that he was, without realising it, 'on the run'. Had he continued and boarded the ferry, he would have suffered a similar fate to that of Crippen, and been caught by a radio message and detained on board ship.

"I'll get back to my launch and sail her across," declared Monty, wishing he had followed that course an hour earlier

"Too risky," came the reply, "and as you seem to have failed to bring the British round to a policy of patience, there is a little job we want done before you leave."

"Before I leave!" expostulated Monty, recognising the criticism implicit in the reference to his 'failure'. "You've just said I could be picked up at any moment. I'm sure John Dalton's replacement can organise something this end – he's only just down the road and we've been working together lately."

"Yes, that should make it easy. He's the one you're to contact. Get him to hide you for a day or two on the 'Retter': tell him you know more about it than he could learn from a visit, despite what he will have found in John's safe, which is true – or will be shortly. He's sure to be interested enough to come to Harwich. Now, listen! This is what you are to do."

****

With the office door locked, and instructions not to disturb him, Gerald settled down with a large mug of coffee and a few biscuits. By applying the combination of numbers, number of clockwise and reverse turns of the dial – and the all-important pause after the third and fifth digits – he was able to open John Dalton's safe. He noted the substantial amount of money and wondered whether it was accountable, skimmed through the notes on staff (including a far from complimentary comment

203

on himself which, presumably, had not been given a wider distribution!) and lifted out two fat files. The first contained a large number of short typed notes and cuttings of varying length taken from a wide range of publications, going back over many years. They were numbered with the prefix R P, followed by a letter, two numbers and then another one, two or three numbers. Given the contents, it was not difficult to work out that the letter referred to the country – F for France, for example. The next two numbers gave the year and the final series the identification. Key words were highlighted, so that B 98 64 was presumably cross-referenced to 'bunker' and ran as follows:

'Bunker sale. A nuclear bunker buried 300ft below ground at R A F Ash, near Manston, Kent is close to being sold. The bunker has two control rooms, a fire station, sewage works, accommodation and a maze of corridors.'

A slightly earlier item contained several words deemed worthy of cross-referral and was a letter to the Times, again from Kent, which ran: '..... at Referendum Party functions is the fear that if Britain enters the E M U, which Helmut Kohl advocates, it will mean the surrender of all control over fiscal and social policies.....'

The last section was underlined in its entirety and read: '..In effect Britain will become a province of an undemocratic European Union dominated by Germany.'

The other file contained very different material, all neatly typed and bound, with the prefix S T T. They were a series of plans, all designed to create civil unrest, the latest relating to the forthcoming Referendum on European Monetary Union. Gerald read on, fascinated, while his coffee grew cold and his biscuits remained untouched. The extent to which the leadership appeared to be able to call on sympathisers was an eye-opener. Key positions throughout the Kingdom were in their hands – in our hands..... no, dammit, in *their* hands, for clearly he, Gerald, was held in such low regard that he would never have gained the recognition his abilities and breeding demanded, had he remained loyal to the Cause. Kenneth, he mused, would be delighted with this! He read on, noting references to the 'Retter', to plans to sink a ferry, having issued a warning supposedly from the I R A, to an attempt (which was planned to fail) to blow up the House of Lords on November the Fifth. Again the aim was to manipulate public opinion by making them believe the worst of other (especially left wing) terrorist groups, to observe the incompetence and weakness of the legitimate government of the day..... and then to be receptive to firm action, especially the imposition, 'temporarily', of martial law.

In all cases, there was an army of adherents, each small group unaware of more than a handful of like-minded people, throughout the land. The pattern of Hall Farm, the Castle, Fotheringhay, the helicopter near Peterborough, was repeated nation-wide, with similar units... at East Mersea, in Essex, for example and, of course, Haslemere in Sussex. Infiltration of the police was a feature, as was that of the River Boards, Water Authorities and Sea Defence Boards. It was clear, too, that extensive use had been made of the secret depôts set up in the 1940's and the 'Resistance Freedom Fighters', whose expertise and potential for murder and disruption had never had to be put to the test against the expected German conquerors. Everywhere, it seemed, could be found facilities such as those at Hall Farm (the strawstack bunker), Thorpe Tunnel and the ancient passages at Fotheringhay, the secret of which had been lost with the sudden death of the two blacksmiths and their immediate superior, the Agent at Wothorpe Castle.

Constant reference was made to the 'Retter', and Gerald turned with mounting interest to the relevant Appendix. Although he had picked up parts of the story over the years – hence the large photograph of a submarine in the inner room at Hall Farm Bunker – he was fascinated by the account, only his eyes moving as they scanned the yellowing pages. He had been part of it, over fifty years ago, one of the babies loaded on board this triumph of advanced engineering, incorporating all the latest technical refinements which came just too late to win the war.

Capable of staying under water indefinitely, of high submerged speeds, silent running at 2 to 3 knots and shrouded in a radar resistant 'stealth' material, the Retter (the 'Saviour'), boasted a keel made largely of gold and contained boxes of documents designed to put pressure on British collaborators. It also had torpedoes, of course, and even the ability to fire rockets from a submerged position. There had been three major technical hopes as the war turned against Hitler – rockets, submarines and the destructive potential of splitting the atom. It was clear from these documents that in the 'Retter' they had developed two of these to form a powerful threat: a threat which, it appeared, still existed.

"Of course!" murmured Gerald to himself. "Just off Harwich: the gold didn't come from a 16th century wreck at all. I must pay a visit – go back to the womb, as it were!"

He returned the files to the safe, having made a few brief notes for his report, and emerged, stretching, to be told that a person identifying himself as 'Larry' was very anxious to make contact.

CHAPTER TWENTY-NINE

As he listened to Monty's insistent request for sanctuary on the 'Retter', Gerald started to feel out of his depth. What line should he take? It was not practicable to ring his 'control' from the office, so he decided to set up a meeting some way away in order to give himself time to unload his information and get guidance on how to cope with Larry, who had not given a return number – not surprisingly as he was ringing from a (very) public booth in the Stena Line waiting area.

As it suited both parties, Gerald quickly got Larry's agreement to meet at Harwich, Parkeston Quay in about an hour and set off, clutching his mobile phone. After about ten minutes, he pulled off into a well-screened lay-by and set about the task of tracking down Kenneth, who told him to drive on, ready to pull in again, to get instructions before meeting Larry. Kenneth debated whether to warn Gerald that they were officially aware of Monty as a spy, but thought it best to leave the timing of that as a decision for Patrick.

In due course, briefed by Kenneth on Patrick's instructions, Gerald drove into the Harwich International Ferry car park, where he was rapidly joined by the harassed, sweating Larry, who urged him to get him out of sight as quickly as possible.

"Vienna told me I was blown," he gasped. "That bugger Brady, it must be. Those incompetent fools made a total *balls-up* of snatching his mother. You've got to hide me on the 'Retter' until they can set up a safe route. Are you in the picture about the sunken sub., over there?"

Monty flapped his hand in the general direction of the open sea, hoping his protégé would accept what amounted to instructions without counter suggestions or too much checking back with his High Command. Monty's orders from Austria were to immobilise the Retter's 'weapon to end all weapons' (as it had seemed back in 1945). The first step was to get on board. Thanks to his relationship with Gerald, that was going very well.

Patrick had correctly foreseen that Monty must have been warned that he was being hunted, but had been unwilling to take the excellent opportunity offered of picking him up, lest it point too clearly to Gerald as the source of information. In fact, they had completely lost Monty and feared he had managed to quit the country. "Tell Gerald to see what he wants," had been his instructions to Kenneth. "If he wants to be hidden, O K. They'll have several places in the area, and Gerald will know where he is, so there should be no real problem. Gerald can get advice from his local staff if he's not yet fully au fait with all their codes, local commanders, etc."

In fact, Gerald had often visited the H F C establishment in Harwich Old Town, towards which he now took Larry, although only since examining the documents in John's safe had he realised the full depth – in every sense of the word – of that operation.

Back in 1945, the un-numbered U-boat known as the 'Retter' had sailed with U-534, escaping under cover of the diversion provided by the sinking of the latter. It had voyaged as far as the North Norfolk coast, where it had unloaded the precious human cargo before returning to a pre-determined spot a few miles off-shore from the port of Harwich. That spot was not far from a flashing marker – a small light-ship in effect, easily visible from the cross-channel ferry as it wound its way slowly down the narrow channel in the estuary. Many years before, about four hundred, in fact, one of the supply ships of the Spanish Armada had foundered at the spot, sinking a surprising depth, for there was a sort of underwater ravine into which, by chance, the stricken ship had finally fallen, together with its cargo. The right to dive and retrieve treasure had been acquired before the war by a local landowner who had been sympathetic to the Nazis.....and the sleek, fully operational, gold-laden U-boat had been carefully manoeuvred to lie alongside the ancient wreck, enabling comings and goings to take place as if for the purpose of salvaging the 16th century remains.

Entry to the submarine was effected via the rocket-firing 'port', for the boat (a fore-runner of the much more powerful Polaris) was able, or so the scientists claimed, to despatch rockets from beneath the sea. All this Gerald had gathered in theory as he perused the secret documents. Now he was about to see it, courtesy of Clarence, whom he had known for years to be in charge of the salvage operations which (supposedly, as it turned out) produced a steady trickle of gold, coins, cannon balls, etc.

The arrival of the car (which appeared to contain only Gerald) was monitored by one of Patrick's men, placed near the H F C offices after the place had been identified as 'dodgy' by Martin. This was convenient, as Gerald had not been able to break off and report his movements whilst with his 'guest', who was presumed to be crouching on the floor in order to escape detection.

Shortly after their arrival, Gerald and Monty boarded the sea-going launch used to 'service' the salvage operation, their docking at the diving platform being photographed by a hastily routed reconnaissance aircraft.

"Now we give old Klaus a buzz," said Clarence to Gerald as they made fast in the centre of the substantial concrete platform, covered not only to keep out the weather, but also prying eyes, so that it resembled the process of docking in one of the old Channel port U-boat pens (which had influenced the design). "Your friend can step out now. He'll not be seen."

"Klaus? I thought his name was Stanley," said Gerald, recalling the details in the file. "How long does he stay here at a time?"

"He's Stanley the same as yon toff is Larry – but there's only four of us come here regular, and he's Klaus to us. You'll see!" he added with a knowing laugh.

"And who relieves him – you?"

"Hardly! I'm a respectable fisherman and antique dealer, aren't I? No, there's no relief for old Klaus..... and you can take that whichever way you like. Here we go!" he added, as an answering buzz came from the depths. "One at a time. I'll have a quick word on the old ship-to-ship so he knows what's up, then you go first. I'll stay up here."

Clarence stepped across to the intercom, from which emerged a crackle of noise concluded by a sharp word and a muttered:

"Cantankerous old sod!.... He's ready," said Clarence.

"But not 'willing and able'?" asked Gerald who had heard the tenor but not the words of the exchange.

"You could say that – but he'll do what he's told. Can't say I blame him, the life he leads. Just step in and spin the wheel to make the seal tight..... then press the down arrow and wait until you see a green light. That'll mean you've arrived and are secured to the airlock. You unbolt the hole in the floor – and provided all is well, you climb down to the good ship 'Retter'!"

Feeling extremely vulnerable, Gerald stepped inside the small 'bathysphere' and turned the locking wheel. In due course, a green light appeared, which he took to mean it was time to press for 'down'. Apart from a slight rocking, there was little sense of movement as the chains which raised and lowered the globe moved slowly, powered by electric motors top and bottom. The bump as it met the casing of the last of the ill-fated German submarine navy caused Gerald to fall against the side, bruising his head and adding that discomfort to the mounting claustrophobia and the chill which had crept over his under-clothed body as they descended.

"That miserable bugger could have kitted us out for this," he grumbled to himself as he bent to release the hatch, pausing to wonder whether the equipment was still safe.

It was with considerable relief that he stepped down to the warmth of the submarine and took in his surroundings. The shining gauges, brightly lit and quite spacious interior, with its table containing the remains of a meal for one, the flags and badges of the long gone military might of Hitler's Germany..... all this he barely noticed, for the scene was dominated by the single shining eye of the septuagenarian? – octogenarian? – whose bent frame and pale visage confronted him.

The stream of sailor's German which issued from the twisted mouth was too rapid for Gerald to follow, but the foul stench of the Ancient Mariner's breath and the spittle as the tirade continued, caused him to push the old ruin away and move past to gain breathing space. So this was Stanley, he thought, servant of the 'Retter', the 'Saviour', who must have been here for – surely not since.....? God, it was possible! His thoughts were interrupted by a buzz from up top which caused the noxious creature to turn to move slowly up the ladder to make secure the hatch in the sphere. Presumably that was what the old wreck had been on about, thought Gerald: one was supposed to secure the base of the craft before entering the submarine.... again poor briefing by Clarence. There seemed to be scope for tightening up on John Dalton's staff, thought Gerald, conveniently forgetting that that was precisely what the wretched man had been doing when he met his end.

Steeling himself to cope with Klaus's company in the confined spaces of the aged submarine, he indicated a desire to use the intercom and spoke to Clarence.

"I'll take a look round with – er – Klaus, then I'll come up and Larry can return..... yes..... a few days, I said, not a few hours. We can't organise his escape that quickly. No; it's a bit cramped down here, so I think it's best if I come up first....He says what? He'd rather do it that way? Good – about ten minutes, I imagine. Will you have a word with Stanl...with Klaus? My German's a little rusty. Oh, does he..... well, have a word all the same, will you. Here he is."

Gerald passed the receiver to Klaus and removed himself to the other end of the immediate area, while Clarence carried out his wishes. He found the meaningful (uncomplimentary) glances and the knowing cackles extremely irritating, as they clearly arose from comments far from appropriate concerning their new boss. The sooner he was out of here, the better, gold or no gold, he thought, as the conversation concluded and the aged caretaker signalled him to follow.

There was no doubt that the engineers had built well. Some repairs and strengthening had been carried out, but everything appeared to be in working order. It seemed unlikely that the torpedo tubes were clear of external obstruction, and one had no way of knowing how easy it would be to reconvert the rocket firing arrangements, should plan S T T 4 be thought desirable. Indeed, after so many years it would surely be unwise to risk the shock of actually firing a rocket. Gerald noted the markings on various boxes which appeared to contain warheads, and did his best to reproduce in his notebook what looked like Russian and Arabic letters on six much newer boxes. The freezers contained plenty of food, a small desalination plant took care of drinking water needs and there were both an air-line and a power cable leading to the diving platform.

Before leaving, Gerald noted that the firing mechanism for the rockets was protected by a form of combination lock, akin to a wall safe. Klaus indicated that he did not have the number, much to Gerald's relief, for the man was not fit to be trusted with a bow and arrow, never mind an untested, archaic and probably highly volatile underwater version of the 'V 2', with God only knew what in the warhead! H M G would have to decide what to do about this threat to the environment parked at their back door – and the sooner he passed on the information, the better. Time to return topsides for fresh air, dry land, and instructions.

Monty had been trying to think of a way of getting Gerald out of the way to have the 'Retter' to himself, so he was delighted when it was proposed that he go down and Gerald come up. He heard Clarence say a few hours, but did not hear the correction from down below. Clarence, for his part, did not *forget* to make this clear to 'Larry' – he had his own reasons for quite deliberately allowing him to continue to think that his sojourn in the 'Retter' would be only a matter of hours.

Gerald sniffed the air appreciatively as he stepped from the deep sea 'lift', and allowed Monty to seal himself in.

"See you to-morrow," he called as the hatch closed, adding to the sound-proof globe, "Good Luck with Klaus!"

"On the run, is he?" said Clarence. "You can always tell.... had one years ago, poor bugger. Klaus was younger then..... He's matured with age, just like a ripe Camembert!" He laughed unpleasantly as he saw Gerald's nose wrinkle with the recent memory. The very thought of spending a whole day in the company of that...that...crone was enough to cause a nauseous shudder.

"Heard the forecast?" asked the boatman, continuing with evident glee. "By this time tomorrow they reckon Force 10: you'll not be seeing yon toff while next week."

"Did you tell him?"

"Not bloody likely! We never do... had one chap – very upper class – bit like 'im. Only lasted two year; less than that in 'is right mind."

"Two years! Down there on his own? Surely he...."

"Oh, he'd have been all right on his own – books, letters, videos, we even put bets on for them. No, it's Klaus: they can't stand 'is 'abits, you see. When 'e eats, 'e....."

"Spare me. I'd rather not know. You can't get up-wind of someone in a submarine. Doesn't anyone try to do something about him?"

"Are *you* going to? No, it's too late... he's just rotting away, and mad as a hatter. Lives, if you could call it that, for the 'Retter', thinks of himself as a sort of High Priest."

"He's certainly 'high'," agreed Gerald. "Larry'll be upset if we don't get him away to the Continent pretty soon."

Clarence's chuckle was suppressed, emerging as a cross between a snort and a bark. He'd seen it all before..... like the other fella he'd been talking about..... just disappeared one night. They could come up for a breath of night air when no-one could see them....but there was always the risk in daylight of a distant telescope, or aerial photo's. There'd been a plane overhead earlier – often was round here – and they couldn't risk being seen when they were on the run. Mind you, the price was high.... high, yes!

Shortly after returning from the Retter, Gerald left Harwich old town and stopped after about two miles to phone in his report, only to be told to drive on and pull in at another, better hidden, lay-by where Kenneth was waiting. In due course, all the details, including the reproductions of the markings on the newer rockets, were made available to Patrick, together with Gerald's brief summaries of the contents of the two fat files from John Dalton's safe. The information was dynamite and Patrick instructed Kenneth to get hold of the complete details as soon as possible.

From information already supplied, however, it was clear that the Organisation had, mainly from the former Soviet Union, obtained modern rockets, almost certainly now armed with a powerful nerve gas or, perhaps, droplet-spread anthrax germs. Whilst the original rockets were unlikely still to be usable, these new ones, if the projection facilities were intact – represented a significant threat, or last ditch weapon. It was one of Patrick's staff who came up with the probable reason for the prefix S T T which applied to the scary scenarios involving chemical warfare directed at London – and always blamed others in order to create chaos, suspicion and mistrust of the legal authorities. It was, she suggested, short for 'Shake The Tree'.... and was contrasted with the evidence of steady success throughout Europe. Those items justifying a waiting game, showing that history was on their side, were given the prefix R P; surely that must be 'Ripe Plum', she had added, to general agreement.

It was not quite so easy to decide what to do about the underwater arsenal, however. If faced with a direct threat, it would be better to blow it up to prevent a missile launch, but no-one could be sure that such a move might not seriously contaminate the ocean, risking the creation of that very civil panic which the Organisation hoped, in the S T T plans, to turn to their advantage.

"We have to assume that they wanted to get Monty on board," said Patrick. "He could've got away, but we know he deliberately missed the ferry and then contacted Gerald. The question is: why? What's his mission? Remember, he must have been sent over here. By chance, he and I met at Stansted, both very much on 'business', both claiming otherwise."

"Surely he could just have been warned he was rumbled – and didn't risk being caught on the ferry? The 'Retter' was the obvious hiding place: we'd never've known without Gerald."

"Perhaps," said Patrick, "but he was ahead of us, and good intelligence from our own Secret Service was, indeed still is, available to him. The other point is whether he was deliberately misinformed by his own side, frightened into running to Gerald for help, and whether Vienna was unimpressed by his contribution to the British scene... to the point of giving him last minute instructions concerning his mission whilst he's under the waves. The crucial thing – and we've nothing to go on – is whether Monty is there to make it easier to 'shake the tree', or to remove the effectiveness of that ultimate weapon, lest it be misused by the British leadership. Time may tell – in the form of instructions to Gerald from Vienna and Liverpool."

"We may not have time," said Patrick's chief. "I want a strike force ready at a moment's notice – but I want it to appear to be an accident. How about a rival submarine? No-one would know what had happened if we ran a night attack."

"Daytime is better," opined Patrick, "for an accident. Oh, yes, it is... something on these lines: three planes on a training flight; one gets into trouble. The pilot gallantly stays with it long enough to clear the populated area, ejects just before it crashes into the sea..... at the very spot where there is an insignificant treasure-seeking operation on a 16th century wreck."

"A wreck loaded with bugs and modern high explosive?"

"Easy! We load up the sacrificial plane with bits of Second World War mine casing...... then those bits will be found, and appear to have caused the massive explosion. What a happy chance! Another miracle, better than the parting of the waters of the Red Sea."

"It could work!" said a colleague, whilst another added drily: "It wouldn't be the first time a plane has crashed conveniently. With modern guidance techniques, the hero could bail out several miles away."

"Or never have been on board at all!" added the Chief. "Get it set up ready to go, using some suitably obsolescent fighter plane."

"Are you implying, Sir," interjected the only military man present, "that we have any other sort?"

CHAPTER THIRTY

Christopher and, to a lesser extent, Henry were feeling abandoned. Monty had promised to organise the disappearance of Christopher from the area and to contact his Continental colleagues to find a suitable position.... but he seemed to have gone to ground himself. Gerald was too busy, perhaps too elevated, to concern himself with low grade operatives. They couldn't stay indefinitely at the Thorpe Tunnel bunker: their absence from the Castle and the farm, respectively, would soon look very odd.

"Why don't you come with me to 'suss out' Hall Farm?" said Henry. "If the coast is clear you can stay there. Give me a hand around the place.... perhaps drive down to get the next batch of immigrants."

"I can't be seen around here!" said Christopher, appalled at the thought of settling down for a lifetime of obscurity in the Fens, playing second fiddle to Henry, "but I might try my luck down south. Is it Harwich you go to?"

"Yes, but you'd have to be *told* to go down. You couldn't just drop in. If you wait a few days, Gerald'll get things organised again. Surely it's worth having a look..... but stay here if you prefer. I'll ring you if the bunker's untouched."

"And suppose they're waiting for you – what then? I shall be sat here wondering what's happening."

"So come and see! I know a cross-country route, along paths and through the wood. You can get quite close to the farm without being seen.....Good, let's get moving. Use those spare gumboots: it's quite muddy in places, but take your shoes as well."

And so the two young men set off in an easterly direction towards Hall Farm, carrying a basket of mushrooms as 'cover', a modern day version of the wolf striding out for Little Red Riding Hood's grandmother (for the basket contained Henry's gun in addition to the innocent fungi).

Playing, quite unwittingly, the rôle of the far from street-wise maiden in the same fable, Martin had set off to go into town. Much as she loved him, Jennifer had found him a bit of a nuisance 'under her feet all day', and had urged him to go for a walk to get some exercise, even though it was not made necessary by having to take the dog. They had compromised on his walking into town to go to the cash machine and get his hair cut. With the virtual incarceration of Monty, Patrick had removed the permanent bodyguard, although they had a number to ring if they saw anything suspicious. So it was that Martin, having been put off by finding four people waiting at the old-fashioned 'barber' he insisted on patronising (despite the lack of appointments and uncompromising nature of the styling), found himself in effect committed to being 'out' for the next two or three hours.

It was not surprising that his steps took him towards the wood, but he didn't *have* to carry on to the 'secret path' which led to Hall Farm. Given the operation of 'Sod's Law' on such occasions, it could be said to have been almost inevitable that he was just about to remove the false brushwood screen when Christopher and Henry caught up with him. He turned at the noise and the obvious mutual recognition precluded the possibility – by either party – of a muttered greeting and departure.

"But you were....I saw..." Christopher lapsed into open-mouthed silence, but his colleague had his pistol out in a second, for it was clear that this was no chance encounter with a genuine member of the rambling public.

"Stay back!" Henry commanded Christopher. "You'll be in my field of fire. Now, I don't know how you know him, but I'm pretty damn' sure he knows too much."

"Put that away for God's sake!" cried Christopher. "We don't want another balls up like last time: this is – er – one of our most senior people. He's....."

He turned to the petrified Martin, who was conscious only of his stupidity in failing to stay away from danger: no bodyguards, no-one knew where he had gone, no hope of playing the innocent old fool, the rambling rustic..... and no convenient body-armoured stand-in.

"You must believe me!" continued Christopher, who was in fact overjoyed to see that 534 was alive and well. "I'd no idea they were going to shoot: I tried to stop them, but they threatened me. They wouldn't believe you were genuine.... I told them... and then the others found you were bringing a report! Old Proudfoot was shattered.... he walked under... but you must know all this! I'm so relieved. You see they blame me, too, and I suppose they're right, but *please*," Christopher ignored his colleague's firing angle and actually fell to his knees before the astonished Martin. "I swear I meant you no harm!"

"That's all right. I understand. All in the line of business," said Martin, keeping a wary eye on Henry, who did not seem to be a fully paid up member of his newly founded fan club.

"Er – what are you two doing here?" he asked, reasoning that by taking the initiative he might forestall the same question being put by one of *them*.

"We're on our way to the farm," said Henry, who had still not lowered his gun. "And how come if he saw you shot, you're not dead?"

Blasphemously, Martin recalled that he was not the first person to be asked to explain himself in such circumstances. 'Good question' came to mind, along with 'Doubting Thomas' and 'Ye of little faith'..... but, after a barely perceptible pause, during which his brain raced like a ship's propeller as it rises clear of the water, he replied:

"You've heard of body armour? Plus the fact that they didn't get a second chance; we were expecting some such move. Now, you get on your way – and take care. Report what you find in the usual way.... and do you think you could point that thing somewhere else? I'm somewhat under-dressed for the occasion!"

Martin smiled in what he hoped was (literally) a disarming manner, and bent down to give a helping hand to his chief (and possibly only) disciple.

Christopher grasped the proffered hand eagerly and stood to look his generous, brave, truly *venerable* leader firmly in the eye:

"Tell me what I can do to make up for it. Let me prove my loyalty!" he exclaimed, melodramatic in his appreciation.

Martin had great difficulty in reciprocating the direct gaze, and was spared the task of formulating an appropriate response (being, as a schoolteacher, unused to praise of any sort, let alone the fulsome variety), by the interjection of Henry, who had at least postponed sentencing of Christopher's idol for the gathering of medical and psychological reports:

"That'll keep! We're off to the farm, and you're off to... wherever you sprang from. Got a vehicle somewhere?"

"I tend to use public transport whenever possible," said Martin loftily. "It's better for security. There's a bus due along that road shortly, so I'll wish you two lads good luck and – er – keep up the good work!"

"Do you live round here, then?" asked Henry.

"Good Gracious, no," said Martin. "I, well, I get around. Back to London, now. We may meet again, of course, but my work takes me to various places."

If only he had said 'Bristol' or 'Worksop', rather than 'London', thought Martin a moment later, for the delighted Christopher almost yelped his request:

"London! Let me come with you. Larry said he would arrange for me to get clear of this area – of the country, even...... but *you* could do that. I mean, I could help you, work for you, if..... that is ....if you'll have me."

The lad was so genuine and Martin, like many in his profession, was essentially an optimist where the young were concerned, so found himself assuring Christopher that he would do what he could. Realising that he had to explain how he came to be walking, with no car nearby, Martin claimed to be about to catch a local bus to Peterborough and thence by train to London, King's Cross; if he wished, Christopher could accompany him. He was, he felt, being sensible (rather than just pushing his luck) as in this way he reinforced his credentials as a member of the Organisation. He should be able to make an excuse to use a public phone before too long and then warn either Gerald or, better still, Patrick what was happening. Being accompanied by Christopher, Martin thought, would ensure that he was not attacked by other members of the Organisation.

In fact that was not quite the case. Thanks to Monty, Christopher was a marked man and at that very moment, two thugs from Haslemere were on their way to South Lincolnshire, charged with the task of bringing the young man, preferably but not necessarily in one piece, to a spot where he could be interrogated. The Chairman had been contacted by the Haslemere commander and had agreed to let him send his men to deal with the traitor whom Monty had unmasked: for such people the Organisation had no mercy.

The first opportunity for Martin to telephone one of the 'very important people whom only he knew' occurred at Peterborough station. Handing Christopher fifty pounds, he told him to join the queue for tickets, whilst he used the phone to make suitable arrangements for his reception in Holland. With relief, Martin turned towards the phone booths, only to pause as he realised that he was unable to remember any of the most suitable numbers – not that for Gerald, for Patrick nor for their special security guard. Cursing this evidence of advancing senility, Martin rang his own home, hoping against all the odds that it would be one of his children who answered. In the event, he was faced with his own answering machine and prefaced the rather alarming message with an instruction to get the information to Patrick, or Elizabeth, or the Security Service guard as soon as possible. Although his wife was very efficient at checking for messages, he had no means of knowing when she would return to the house. He emphasised that he was in no danger and requested that someone with instructions on how to deal with Christopher meet the next train at the London terminus. Should there not be time to arrange things by then, he would go on to Liverpool Street, where he would take the next available train to..... Harwich. Surely, he reasoned, that should give enough time, even if his message did not get to the right place for several hours.

Christopher was in the queue for some minutes, during which – as luck would have it (good or bad, depending on one's viewpoint) – he was spotted by Harvey, whose colleague from Haslemere, Michael, had gone to collect the pre-arranged Avis rental car from the nearby office. Surreptitiously, Harvey studied the photograph, hoping that Michael would soon return to confirm his opinion and decide whether to snatch him, follow him, or ring for further instructions. To his surprise, Harvey saw Christopher purchase the tickets and then move to rejoin a travelling companion – an old boy with a worried look who had just finished telephoning. The worried look transferred itself to Harvey, however, as he saw the pair converse briefly and then move through to the trains, just as the public address burst into life announcing the imminent arrival of the G N E R non-stop service to King's Cross.

"Come on, Michael, you dozy bastard!" said Harvey to himself. "They'll have gone in a minute and we ought to be on that train – and we need instructions about the other chap, who's probably Christopher's controller. How the Hell can I let him know?"

The noise of the incoming train galvanised Harvey into action. Desperately, he scribbled a few words on a scrap of paper and turned to a fairly 'with it' looking middle aged man who was waiting to meet someone.

"Excuse me Guv'nor, but my mate, name of Michael, has been delayed. Could you give him that when he comes looking for me, please? He's a tall dark chap, wearing a green anorak, long sideburns, earring in his left ear, heavy brown boots and a tattoo on the back of his right hand. That's my train! Can't wait. Can you do that, please? Gotta dash!"

Michael completed the formalities at the Avis office, strolled over to look at the vehicle, dumped his anorak, containing the papers, in the back and then returned to the forecourt to collect Harvey – who was nowhere to be seen. He nipped through onto the platform, which was virtually deserted, nearly everyone having piled onto the recently departed London train.

"Where the ... oh, the 'Gents', I suppose,' he muttered. But he wasn't there, nor in the cafeteria. Returning, somewhat puzzled, but not yet alarmed, to the forecourt, Michael started as he was accosted:

"Are you Michael, by any chance?"

"Who wants to know?" came the aggressive reply, as Michael continued to stare with mounting frenzy around the waiting area.

"Sorry! It's just that I thought I saw a tattoo on your...."

"Now look here. I don't know what your game is, but I'm busy and if you don't want a tattoo where it hurts most, you'd better make yerself scarce. Savvy?"

"Well, really, I was only....." spluttered Harvey's outraged courier, as he retreated, deciding he would think twice before approaching anyone else, even if they fitted the description to a 'T' (including an anorak, which this unpleasant lout, it had to be admitted, did not seem to own). He stuffed Harvey's hastily scribbled message into his pocket and sat down to wait for his brother, aware of the continued presence of the tattooed man, who, he related later, buzzed backwards and forwards (by then wearing a green anorak and talking urgently into a mobile phone) for about ten minutes like the proverbial blue-arsed fly.

On the journey to King's Cross, Martin was regaled with the life history of Christopher, whose father had been killed in a boating accident when he was about three, after which his mother (helped financially by the Organisation) had brought him up on her own. At the age of sixteen, she had taken him to see two men who had told him that his father had been brought as a baby to England in a German submarine, that he was a member of a 'master race' and was assured of a steady well paid job, and eventual power and wealth if he was willing to take the oath of allegiance to the Organisation. In exchange for following orders, he was installed originally in an insurance office and then, when his mother died of a brain tumour, was invited to join the staff at Wothorpe Castle. Clearly, the Organisation, his only 'family', enabled him to keep faith with the memory of his father, and seemed to offer much in return for very little. The recent incident involving Martin had been the first time that Christopher had come across the really seamy side of the Organisation. He had obviously been badly shaken by the violence, bloodshed and manifest illegality of that occasion. He knew the theory that the ends justified the means, that once in power they would abolish crime and make the land safe for all to travel in, but the reality of maiming and killing was a very different thing.

Forged passports to help Asians could be seen as a valuable service if you wished to delude yourself, rather than a criminal racket, thought Martin, with a feeling of moral superiority, which quickly gave way to one of guilty understanding as he recalled his own recent dealings with Ahmed!

The young man enjoyed his work at the Castle, referring with pride to the important people who had visited over the three months he had been there, most of the time fetching, carrying, driving and running messages. As someone who had taken the oath, he was trusted and picked up a lot from conversations behind him in the car, from telephoned messages and faxes. Many of the names he mentioned surprised Martin (and many more would have caused a ripple in Intelligence circles). He was anxious to progress in the Organisation, to prove his willingness to die, if necessary, for the Cause – or, more specifically, for ......

"What should I call you, Sir? I mean we use first names mostly, as you know, like Philip for Mr Proudfoot, and our Area Controller is – er – was John... but I can't really use your I D number....."

"As you will have gathered, Christopher," said Martin gravely, "I operate outside the usual network. Only a handful at the top, the very top, know me and know my name. I should like to look on you as...as a nephew in a sense. There may be occasions in the future when I shall call on you to do something for me as I feel I know you and can trust you."

"You can, you..."

"No. Let me finish," continued Martin, warming to his theme, "Others will merely know me as '534'. If you discover that they also know my full name, you will know they have, like me, a special rôle within the Organisation. You might come across me using other names, but I have decided to include you among that small group who know me. My name is Charles – Charles Hastings: on occasions such as this, call me Charles, but don't let on that you know the rest. All right?"

The young man was, well, delighted, flattered even, but something more. They had been talking quietly, insulated from the others in the half full carriage, but, mercifully, Christopher managed to restrain himself from carrying out the act that he felt was appropriate – to kiss the signet ring which shone dully on the 'papal' finger. In stead he relapsed into silence for the last ten minutes of the journey, contemplating his good fortune and sensible of the great honour which had just been conferred upon him.

Their arrival at King's Cross was somewhat anticlimactic. There was no sign of a bodyguard, a courier or even a placard. Martin ambled along the platform, hoping to be approached by a representative of H M G, unaware that he and his companion were being followed by the similarly disappointed Harvey, who was expecting the back-up *he* had requested in the note to his colleague, Michael.

"I'll get a taxi!" said Christopher, helpfully, noticing that his idol was obviously tired as he was walking so slowly. He dashed off, giving Harvey the problem of deciding which one to follow and returned in triumph five minutes later. By that time, Martin had worked out that he should have taken the opportunity to do a vanishing act, as opportunities during the onward journey to Harwich would be difficult to engineer. Panting after Christopher, trying to keep out of sight, came Harvey, uncomfortably aware that if he were to lose the young man, his life would not be worth living.

"If I ever see that old bastard I asked to pass a note to Michael, I'll murder him," he thought. "He *must* have come looking for me. You can't rely on anyone these days."

As he watched the two walk towards the approaching taxi, Harvey realised that 'make your mind up time' was here. Had Christopher been on his own, he could have taken him – killed him if that was the only way – but he couldn't be sure about the old boy with him. Could he be from the Organisation? Doubtful. From M I 6? If so, they must have been let down, as someone had clearly been expected.... but not by Christopher, come to think of it. Could he force himself upon them – 'Mind if I share your taxi, gents?' – and then hi-jack the cab? In the end, he decided to risk relying on their declared intention, easily overheard, of going to Liverpool Street. The risk proved justified and it was with relief, prompting him to give a substantial tip to the driver, that he arrived in time to see the pair, fortunately still walking slowly, as they moved towards the queue for the ticket office.

Martin was getting worried. What could he do if they arrived and there was no one to meet them at Harwich? It would be easier to disappear here in London – pretend to go to the toilet and then, once out of sight, just 'take off'? The same ploy would have no chance of success at a small station. On the other hand, it would be a pity to throw away his special relationship. Perhaps Patrick could make use of it? In addition to that, he was loath to disillusion the young man, to say nothing of putting him seriously at risk. No. He couldn't leave him to be 'disposed of' by the S A S, for Martin realised that now that Christopher knew him, he might, if allowed to roam freely, see him again. He might see him with Patrick, with dire consequences. Surely Jennifer would realise the importance of passing on his message – unless.... his blood ran cold. Supposing she had been in a car accident, was unable to get home, was at this very moment in intensive care?

"Are you feeling all right?" asked Christopher solicitously, for the old boy was looking distinctly grey around the gills. "I'll get the tickets; why don't you go and have a cup of tea or something?"

And so it was that both Martin and Harvey decided there was just enough time for a quick call, whilst the object of their surveillance, unaware that he was on the Organisation's hit list and relying for his safety on what amounted to a phantom agent, stood unconcernedly in the queue for tickets.

CHAPTER THIRTY-ONE

"I'm back!" called Jennifer as she opened the front door, expecting that her husband would have returned and could give her a hand unloading the car, which was groaning with supplies from the local Sainsbury's.

"Oh, well, at least he's getting some exercise," she thought, moving into the living room to check for messages on the answerphone. Jennifer sat down part way through, took some notes towards the end – and then played it over again to make more notes. Although a born worrier, for some reason she reacted only with calm efficiency to the astonishing contents.

Somehow, over in France, she had known she ought to get back and now she realised what they had been keeping from her – or part of it. She had been right: he had sounded shifty..... and was obviously much more deeply involved than she had been led to believe. Could it be, she wondered, that Patrick had returned to help, rather than 'happening to be taking a few days off'? We'll see, she decided, finding the contact number referred to in her husband's message and dictating the contents of his plea for help.

By the time an S A S man arrived, Jennifer had put the frozen goods into the freezer, packed an overnight bag and was in the process of gathering a change of clothing for Martin.

"Sorry about all this, Madam," he said. "There's no need to worry: we're following up the message and can get someone to your husband very soon, now."

"Good," replied Jennifer. "Too late to catch them at King's Cross, though?"

"Well – er – yes, but plenty of time before they arrive at Harwich. Can I give you a hand with....."

"Yes, you can as a matter of fact. I must just finish packing, so can you get the rest of the groceries out of the car before we leave?"

"Before we lea... Er, where were you thinking of going?" asked the soldier, by now feeling pressurised by events, and picking up the plural pronoun with distinct unease.

"I am not *thinking* of going anywhere. I intend to go to Harwich, and thought that you might prefer to come, too, if you have been assigned to be my 'minder'.... but I'm quite happy to go on my own. I shall be ready in about two minutes. There's a phone in the kitchen: leave the stuff in the car if you prefer."

"Now hang on, Miss. You can't go rushing off to Harwich. It's – well it might be dangerous and...." Corporal Johnson was used to calling the shots but he quailed before the onslaught:

"Firstly, young man, it is not 'Miss', but Mrs Brady. Secondly, I was unaware that I had been placed under house arrest..... and thirdly it is precisely because I realised that my husband was in danger that I decided to go to Harwich to be of assistance. It was also why I would have preferred to have you along, but by all means stay and guard the house if those are your orders. Now, if you will excuse me, I'll finish getting my things."

"Bloody Hell!" said the corporal, but very quietly, under his breath. "Women!"

He moved into the kitchen, rang his section leader for instructions, and was told to accompany the lady but keep in touch. Perhaps she had a 'mobile'? The vital piece of equipment was visible on the kitchen table, so Corporal Johnson reassured his contact on that point as well as on the enquiry as to how the 'little lady' was taking the news.

"Oh – er – very well...."

"No hysterics – you don't need a female to...?"

"No, no. Quite the reverse: enough already if you know what I mean!" replied the Corporal, raising his voice to conclude the conversation as Jennifer came down the stairs. "That's all agreed, then. We'll get going and you'll contact us en route." Smiling encouragingly, he turned to Jennifer:

"That's all settled, Mrs Brady. I'm to accompany you – if that's what you wish, of course – and they'll keep us fully informed. Shall I carry that?"

"Thank you!" Jennifer smiled sweetly. "The name's Jennifer, by the way, and *you'd* better drive as we need to get a move on. I'm really quite looking forward to this with you to protect me: I was dreading having to go on my own!"

The corporal accepted the car keys, the flattery and the change of personality with relief and they set off towards the A 1, Jennifer calmly reminding 'Jacko' that his superiors would not have the number of her mobile, so she had better let them know while he concentrated on his driving.

"Yes, that's right, the Audi.... the A 14, yes.... Newmarket. Yes I'm fine and Jacko is an excellent driver. Yes, I'll tell him. Bye!....Your friend asked me to say the sun is shining down there and the driving conditions are very good," Jennifer said as she put the phone down and settled back, outwardly cool, calm and collected, apparently to enjoy the ride.

Slightly flushed with embarrassment, Corporal Johnson, who could recognise sarcasm when he heard it, made a mental note to thump the afore-mentioned 'friend' when he got back.

A short time after his mother had telephoned through the contents of Martin's answerphone message, Patrick was considering its implications. He wondered briefly how it had happened that his father had 'bumped into' Christopher and another man (who had to be Henry) and then set about analysing the new situation. As he was well aware of Monty's present concerns and location, he was not surprised to learn that Christopher felt abandoned. Indeed, he himself had forgotten the young man who was now, Mrs Pateman and Monty having been 'neutralised', the only person who knew enough to work out the family connection between 'busy-body' and Intelligence Officer. He had relied on Monty and Gerald between them to get Christopher out of the country, as much as anything to avoid having to take more drastic action to remove him from the local (and possibly even global) scene.

Even as Patrick contemplated the advantages of continuing to string the chap along, allowing the Organisation to install him in Holland, whilst keeping in reserve the ability to manipulate him, Kenneth telephoned. His news was that the Haslemere unit had despatched two thugs to deal with the traitor, Christopher, one of whom had been left behind for some reason at Peterborough station. The latter (Michael) had rung Henry at Hall Farm, who had, fortunately, rung Gerald as Area Controller. There was, Kenneth added, an old boy with Christopher, who (Gerald had said) sounded just like the one who had collected the documents from the Castle! What, Kenneth concluded, should he tell Gerald to do?

"For now," said Patrick, "tell him to send a couple of men to shadow them. Presumably, they now know, or will shortly from this other guy from Haslemere, where they are. I've just had that confirmed as Liverpool Street station. I want Gerald to appear to be co-operating fully in the search. I'll organise one or two things this end and then put you more fully in the picture."

Patrick was right: the Organisation did now know where the pair had got to, thanks to a call made by Harvey. Both sides just managed to get a team of armed operatives to Liverpool Street in time to follow both Christopher, who had no idea he was under surveillance by either side, and Martin, who hoped he was being joined by his own.

****

Gerald's two men had no reason to suspect that their presence was known to the Security Services, for whom they believed Christopher to be working, together with (almost certainly) his elderly companion. One positioned himself where he could keep an eye on their 'prey' whilst the other, furnished with a helpful description, set off to make contact with Harvey.

Patrick's three men had hoped to be able to identify the opposition with reasonable confidence but the presence on the train of Army personnel returning to their barracks at Colchester made the task extremely difficult, although they found them useful as 'cover'.

"We've got to find a way of getting Martin away from this Christopher," said Patrick's boss. "The other lot could move at any moment."

"They won't move until told to do so by Gerald," said Patrick, "and we can control that. I don't want to spoil the hold that Martin seems to have managed to get over Christopher if I can help it: there could be a useful long-term asset there."

"Well, it's your father, so if you think it's worth the risk....."

"I agree we should separate them. I'm trying to think how best to do it, not taking risks," said Patrick, rather more sharply than was perhaps appropriate when speaking to one's superior, a sign that, despite the outward calm and logical approach, he was feeling the strain.

"At least your mother's in good hands," said the Chief's personal assistant, seeking to lower the temperature slightly. "She's got an excellent bodyguard and there's no way the opposition can know where she is."

"True," said Patrick. "They can't be that far away from Harwich by now, with Johnson driving.... In fact. Yes. I've got it!"

One usually pays attention to an announcement containing one's own name (or that of a close relative) and Martin was no exception. He was paying careful attention when it was repeated:

"Will Miss Elizabeth Brady, believed to be travelling with Mr J C Carrier, please come to the Customer Service Manager's Office, which is situated at the rear of Coach B."

Surely Elizabeth was not on the train? And her companion J C..... Not for nothing, it turned out, had he wasted so many hours doing crosswords. It had to be Christopher, the carrier of Christ, of J-C; in other words – J. C. Carrier. Slowly, Martin rose to his feet, smiled at his companion, to whom the message meant nothing, and, saying he'd be back shortly, strolled towards the rear of the train. There he found one of Corporal Johnson's three colleagues, who introduced himself as 'Dave' and said:

"Well done, Sir. And to reassure you that you can trust me, I'm told to tell you that Candy Island sounds much better."

Martin grinned at this reference (which only someone in the family could know) to his father's unshakable belief that this was the name of the location near Southend which everyone else knew as 'Canvey' Island.

"Good!" said Martin. "What are my orders, then?"

"You return to your seat and tell sonny boy he's to carry on to Harwich, where he will be met by 'the man from Hall Farm'. I hope that makes sense."

"Yes. It sounds O K. That way, Ger – er – that man won't see me."

"Not only that, Sir. You'll be out of the way if there's any unpleasantness."

"Oh, yes," said Martin casually, sensing there was some aspect of this which he was unaware of, "are you expecting much trouble?"

"Well, Sir, with three of them on the train, all out to get this lad and three of us told to protect him – and you, of course – things could get quite lively!"

Martin's mind raced. For some reason 'they' were after Christopher – must have followed them onto the train. But surely Gerald could protect him? Unless he didn't control these men, or would attract too much unwelcome attention if he called them off and allowed Christopher to escape.

"Well, I must get moving," said Martin. "Have you identified these three, yet?"

"We're pretty sure about two of them, but haven't pinpointed the third yet. It should be easier after all these soldiers get off at Colchester. Mind you, *we'll* be more obvious, too, if they're looking out for us."

Martin returned thoughtfully to his seat and leaned forward confidentially towards Christopher.

"There's been a new development," he said. "As you know, Proudfoot sent two men to kill me. We foiled that attempt but I've been told others in that group are still trying and at least two, possibly more are on this train. No, don't look round. There are a lot of military types on board at the moment so it's impossible to spot them. I shall get off at Colchester, which should divide their forces, but as you've been seen with me, and are known to have been present when their two, those 'blacksmiths', were gunned down, suspicion has fallen on you, too."

"I feared something like that," said Christopher, "so did Gerald and Larry. That's why they were going to get me out of the country. Can't I come with you, Charles?"

"You're most in danger, at the moment, near me," replied Martin. "Carry on to Harwich and don't trust anyone except Gerald. If he's not there for some reason, mingle with the crowd, make a dash for it and go to ground. Then ring this number," he added, handing over that for his own mobile phone. "Identify yourself as – er – Mr Bearer and I'll send help. Just leave a message if it's switched off."

Christopher gripped his hand in silent thanks as he palmed the piece of paper, realising he might never see 'Charles' again, but could always count on him as a powerful friend in a very high place.

The train drew in to Colchester, where a large number of passengers alighted, including Martin, whose departure was seen by Corporal Johnson's colleague with relief..... and by Harvey with indecision. Should he abandon Christopher to the other two and follow the old man? Or should he stick to his orders which related only to the traitor in their midst, whose actions had cost the lives of two of his mates at Stansted? He had little time to decide, for the train would soon move off, there being only a handful waiting to get on. In desperation, he moved forward to speak to one of Gerald's men who had joined the chase at Liverpool Street.

Harvey's obvious interest in the elderly agent and subsequent actions were observed by Dave, who was now confident he knew all three of the opposition. The next move, however, came too quickly for Dave even to think about countering it. Just before the whistle blew, one of Gerald's two men ran to the nearest door and jumped down onto the platform. Dave gave his colleague the pre-arranged signal, and he moved past, giving the impression that he had just joined the train, to the seat opposite Christopher.

"This seat taken, mate?" he asked the wary looking young man, who shook his head and resumed staring out of the window, wondering if his new companion would turn out to be his executioner. In the mean time, Dave slipped his mobile phone from his left-hand pocket – the one without the loaded pistol – to warn his superiors by text message.

Patrick had sent instructions to his father to descend at Colchester, go to the Cafeteria and wait to be picked up by someone who would identify himself by a reference to 'Candy' Island very early in the conversation. It had seemed straight-forward enough, and Corporal Johnson was even now on his way (his route to Harwich taking him very close to Colchester). The message from Dave, however, that his father had been followed by one of the thugs from the Organisation, was received with considerable alarm. Shortly, both his mother and father would be at Colchester station, potentially exposed to violent action. The odds were much too even for Patrick's liking: one against one, both armed.

"Put me through to Johnson, now!" commanded Patrick.

"Johnson! It's H Q. The subject got off the train as arranged, but he was followed. I'll give you the description as soon as I can but he's almost certainly armed and probably believes subject to be working for us. Extreme sanction authorised if necessary, bearing in mind the safety of the general public. Got that?"

"Yes, I think so, dear," came his mother's voice. "I am sure Jacko will be able to deal with it. Er – E T A approximately six minutes. Any instructions for – er – 'subject' when we meet him?"

"Mother!" exclaimed Patrick in exasperation, startled out of his careful anonymity. "You – you're – for God's sake take care! This chap won't do anything other than keep the old boy under observation. Tell Johnson we're sending a back-up team; he'll know the priorities. And Mother!"

"Yes, dear."

"You're something else!"

"Thank you dear.... I have the impression that you are, too. Shall I give 'subject' your love, when I see him?"

"Er – yes, of course," said Patrick, to the amusement of his hard-bitten colleagues, "and tell Johnson to identify himself by referring to – oh God!", he paused in further embarrassment at having to parade a family joke with his mother in her present mood, "...'Candy Island' at some point."

"Is that both God and Candy Island, or just Candy Island, as in 'Swansford' for Wansford, dear?"

"The latter, Mother! Now just do it.. *please!*"

"Wilco. Over and out!" came the reply, eliciting a spontaneous burst of clapping round the table, which drowned Patrick's incipient apology for his parent's 'mili-ternal' style. By this time, Jacko, despite the forthcoming danger and the need to concentrate on getting to the station as quickly as possible, had given up trying to keep a straight face as he thought of the incident coordinator's embarrassment at finding his own mother on the line, unable to prevent her from putting him firmly in his place.

"Don't worry, Ma'am. Your husband'll be all right."

Jennifer did not trust herself to reply and tried to stop her hand from shaking as she severed the connection.

CHAPTER THIRTY-TWO

The Chairman was distinctly worried. Various reports he had been receiving concerning the Stansted incident made it clear that H M G had been just as puzzled by the non-appearance of this woman whom Larry had been pursuing as had the Organisation. It transpired that she had received a call from her daughter the night before she vanished (this information had been expensive to obtain, and was thought to be accurate), as a result of which she had decided to go home to her husband who was upset about their dog, of all things. It seemed the chap was a bit inadequate and unable to look after himself when she was away. Bloody effete English, he thought scathingly. Need proper leadership – always have. If only..... But back to the point, he reminded himself. She had not been 'tipped off' any more than had H M G..... in which case this young man whom Larry had told him was leaking information was in the clear, or at least should be given every opportunity to establish his innocence. It looked as though this Monty/Larry chap sent over by Vienna had made a balls up and tried to blame it all on this young lad. The trouble was that the Chairman had authorised what amounted to a death warrant. That Haslemere lot could well ignore Christopher's pleas and protestations and.....and the slow and awful death would be *his* fault. Well, partly his fault – in fact not really anyone's except that chap Larry, who seemed to have disappeared off the face of the earth. Larry seemed likely to have contacted that new member of Council, thought the Chairman.... and put in a call to Gerald in Colchester.

Despite having to be patched through to Gerald on his way to Harwich, it was no time at all before the Chairman was utterly convinced of his error in ordering Haslemere to go after Christopher, and fully in agreement with leaving Monty in his submarine timeshare until the whole matter had been resolved. It was one thing, however, to take the decision to call off the troops and quite another to make it effective. The two from Haslemere had been split – and Harvey did not have the mobile phone. Unless and until Harvey called in, he could not be given fresh orders and might well go so far as to shoot Christopher if he thought he was about to flee the country. To compound the communication problem, the man who left the train to pursue Martin took the mobile phone, thus making it impossible to contact *his* partner, who continued, with Harvey, to follow the 'traitorous' Christopher.

****

Martin had been less than happy to leave the train, although he could see that it made sense. Despite the fact that the young man had been instrumental in setting up an attempt on his life, Martin felt responsible for him. It was bad enough to allow him to believe that he was some sort of Nazi messiah, risen from the dead, omni-present, omniscient, omni-every-damn-thing, who only vouchsafed his name to his chosen people. To then abandon him to the S A S or, worse by far, his own people who believed he was the traitor in their midst......that was, well, sacrilege. As he mused on these lines, standing in the queue for refreshments, Martin was unaware that yet another employee of the Organisation had him in his sights (not literally, fortunately, but that might be only a matter of time).

Barry, the afore-mentioned employee, had had little time to consider his recent move, for, whilst their orders had been to follow both men, nothing had been specifically said as to what they should do if they split up, or, indeed, what they were supposed to do when they all arrived at their destination. The answer was to ring in for instructions, so he nipped outside to gain sufficient privacy, and was still deep in telephonic conversation when Corporal Johnson came running down the platform.

Such was the speed of events that the corporal had dashed from the hard-driven car just before H Q (a different voice this time) rang through the description of the Organisation's agent who was pursuing Martin, to enable him to identify the opposition.

Although not by nature what one might call 'agent material', Jennifer in defence of her husband was proving a formidable threat to the forces of misrule and disorder.

Realising the value of the information she had just been given, she hurried from the car after the recently departed Jacko.

Armed with his description, it was not difficult for Jennifer to spot Barry, who was in the process of explaining on his 'mobile' that he could not tell his partner that there had been a re-think on Christopher as they had become separated. He was also having difficulty in getting sense out of Gerald concerning the elderly chap whom he had followed into the Cafeteria.

"Hang on!" he said, desperate for precise instructions, "He's talking to a chap who just dashed in – could be one of theirs, or ours, if it comes to that. He's obviously not pleased to see him, doesn't trust him, is moving away..... the other chap's following. The woman on the till looks bothered: she's.....Oufff!"

Gerald took the phone from his ear at the sound of its hitting the ground and turned to his assistant:

"Something's gone wrong. The phone's dead and Barry was on about some chap who'd just dashed in. I need a full team at Harwich, and I don't want another Stansted episode at Colchester station. Is there someone nearby you could send to find out what's up?"

"Well, there's Mrs Banstead: she lives quite near and does the odd bit of work for us, but she couldn't help Barry if he's in real trouble."

"Fine!" said Gerald. "Right, do that, then join us at Harwich. Barry may have just dropped the phone for all we know!"

In fact, the Organisation's operative was in considerable trouble having been sent sprawling by eight stone of concentrated venom, after being disorientated by the inhuman screech which drew Jacko's attention to the fracas just outside the door of the Cafeteria. Jennifer, who seemed to have inflated herself like a cat arched and spitting to repel its canine opponent, was attempting to render the unfortunate Barry sightless by means of a wicked-looking weapon, which she had removed from her foot. Dazed by the attack from such an unexpected direction, Barry was no match for Jacko, who emerged to protect the 'defenceless female' from his depradations.

"They sent his description," panted Jennifer, "and he was on the phone, telling them all about you. Then he was going to shoot you both.....so I... Oh Martin! Are you all right? This horrid man was....."

"I never bloody touched her," gasped the indignant Barry. "She came at me like a – like a mad thing. She ought to be locked up: she's barmy, that's what!"

"We'll let the law decide that!" said Jacko, sitting firmly on the battered and indignant thug.

He was pretty confident that a search by the police, who had been called by the lady on the till, would rapidly reveal the presence of a concealed, unauthorised hand-gun. That, combined with Jennifer's claim that he had attacked her, would be sufficient to ensure that this particular member of the Organisation took no further part in hostilities for some years to come.

For his part, Martin was quite speechless as he and his now trembling wife clung together. After a few moments, he led her gently to a table, to which the helpful assistant, the one who had called the police, brought both tea and sympathy.

"That dreadful man!" she said. "And your husband was having trouble with another one just before. I think they must be rival gangs, Mafia or those Chinese: no-one's safe nowadays. It's the drugs – they're all on them, killing each other and Goodness knows what. Would you like anything else, dear? A whisky, or – or do you need a doctor?" she added, solicitously.

"No. No thank you. I'll be all right..... now," replied Jennifer, finding her voice at last and holding Martin's hand tightly as much, one felt, to stop him going off somewhere as for the feeling of comfort.

"I think I'd like a whisky, please," said Martin, beginning to recover from the trauma of being approached by someone with the wrong codeword, for the whole point of it was that it was *not* 'Canvey' as Jacko had said..... but *Candy* Island. That difficult situation had suddenly changed into what had appeared to be an attack on his wife, who had no business being there at all but had certainly caused the resolution of that phase of the affair in no uncertain fashion.

"That'll be two pounds, please. Any ice?"

"Er – no thanks.. I seem to have....." Martin had handed all his money to Christopher, who had had to spend most of it on tickets, the taxi, etc., and found (not for the first time) that he had to turn to his wife for help.

"Here you are," she said with a resigned grin, raising her eyebrows expressively at the assistant's words as she accepted the coins:

"Men! They're all the same!"

By the time an S A S back-up team arrived, the police were dealing with Barry and a helpful, but shrewd, woman officer was taking a brief, unrevealing, statement from Jennifer, supported in its inaccurate detail by both Jacko, who 'happened to be passing', and Martin, whom she had arrived to meet in the family car ('just outside in the short term car park, Officer').

Mrs Banstead arrived unobtrusively and observed Barry's predicament. There were various other people about, including a tough looking character, whom she took to be one of the opposition, an elderly couple who appeared to be understandably shaken by the goings on and several other on-lookers like herself. The best source of information, she decided, was the lady behind the counter who had obviously been there all along and seemed to be quite enjoying the excitement.

"Oh yes, dear," the latter replied to Mrs Banstead's enquiry. "I saw it all. That dreadful man suddenly attacked that poor woman just outside the door and..... No, he came in here and ordered a coffee – which is still on that table over there, untouched!"

It was clear that not drinking the dubious beverage was seen as another sign of anti-social behaviour on Barry's part by this witness, who continued to explain how she had thought he looked a bit odd ('on drugs, obviously, like so many of them these days!'), although she had been keeping an eye on the other one at the time.

"Oh!" said Mrs Banstead, hoping to hear something which made some sort of sense. "Did he have an accomplice?"

"No, dear, he must have been from a rival gang, the other one, because he broke off from attacking the old man who was sitting on his own over there, when he heard the shrieking."

"Good Gracious!" said the bemused Mrs Banstead. "What a time you've had! Was the old man hurt?"

"Nothing much. He managed to get away from his attacker and comfort his wife, who ......"

"His wife?" interjected Mrs Banstead, too sharply, forgetting she was supposed to be a passing customer. "You said just now he was on his own!"

"No need to take that tone!" said her informant huffily. "I'm quite sure she was his wife, because he didn't have any money when it came to it .... and that'll be eighty pence, if that's all you're having."

Despite apologising and purchasing a distinctly un-Scandinavian looking 'Danish', Mrs Banstead was unable to make much more sense of the affair and her report was not going to convey any useful information whatsoever, failing in particular to mention the apparent inconsistency of the impecunious old man and his wife departing trustfully together with the former's erstwhile 'attacker' driving their car. In pursuance of her orders to find out all she could about the older man who had accompanied Christopher, however, Mrs Banstead did manage to prise one piece of valuable information out of the Cafeteria lady. She had distinctly heard several references to a place with which she was familiar in South Essex, namely Canvey Island. In addition to this, the Organisation knew from Barry that the S A S man who had held him down until the police came was not welcomed by this man (a fact confirmed by the Cafeteria lady). Despite – or, in reality, because of – its lack of clarity and reliance on the fanciful utterances of the Cafeteria lady, Mrs Banstead's hopelessly confused report was later accepted by the regional boss (Gerald) and, to her surprise, she was complimented on its depth and helpfulness.

In accordance with his orders, and their wishes, Jacko had set off to drive the by then calm and content couple home. He was able to report that after about ten miles they were both sleeping peacefully in the back, which made it possible for Patrick (after asking a colleague to contact his sister and suggest that she return home as soon as possible) to give his full attention to the situation at Harwich, Parkeston Quay, where the London train had now arrived.

Trailing 'minders' from both sides, in addition to the still out of touch Harvey, Christopher descended from the train and moved with the crowd towards the International Ferry departure area and, he hoped, sanctuary in the form of the familiar face of Gerald.

CHAPTER THIRTY-THREE

Still hoping to be contacted, Christopher joined the queue for passport control, as did his leech-like companion, Mike, who could feel the tension building as they neared the young, sharp-eyed, though seemingly casual, Passport Control Officer.

As the only 'General' present, Gerald should have realised that failure on his part to make a move would result in precipitate action by Christopher. Without a 'script', however, Gerald was useless under pressure, so he had still taken no action by the time Christopher found himself three places from the front of the queue. Still hoping to be contacted, Christopher fumbled in his pocket, muttered something to the effect of having forgotten his passport and walked rapidly to the nearest exit.

Feeling that all eyes were on him – which was not so far from the mark, as Gerald had brought two more to help shepherd the young man away from harm – Christopher approached the double doors, which slid open invitingly. Beyond lay the darkened platform, the rails straight ahead, to the right a few small offices, piles of boxes and empty trollies and to the left a yard, on the far side of which could be seen various storehouses and an alley leading up into the town. Even now, had he had the sense to walk along to the Stena Line offices and make some irrelevant inquiry, Christopher might have retrieved the situation, but the urge to get away was too strong.

Turning left, he broke into a trot along the deserted platform, about fifteen metres ahead of Harvey, who, having followed casually through the sliding doors, turned to his right, moved behind a pillar and swung round, bringing his gun to bear. At Gerald's shout of 'No! The plan's changed!', Christopher turned, relief at hearing the voice turning to shock, as he took in the levelled gun and felt the impact of the bullet penetrating his chest.

Even as Christopher fell, Gerald shot his killer, moving out from behind the pile of boxes to do so, then making good his escape before anyone could take in just what had happened.

The first person to reach the fallen Christopher was one of Gerald's men, to whom Christopher gasped:

"Tell Gerald that 534 was genuine. He's one of our top men and....."

He coughed as the blood welled in his throat and the fear showed in his eyes as he realised he had been fatally struck and fell silent.

By the time the ambulance came, the Organisation men had all disappeared, leaving Mike, as the dying man's supposed travelling companion – and a priest who happened to be just behind in the passport queue and had been alerted to the probability of trouble by the young man's evident fear as he waited. Just before he breathed his last, still in the speeding ambulance, Christopher seized Mike's arm in a fierce grip and said:

"My money: it's.... give it to... I owe him... tickets....and tell him..."

"Tell who? Who is it?" said Mike urgently.

"Charles," came the reply, clear and distinct. "Tell Charles. He'll....."

"Charles who? What's his other name?" asked the priest, realising the end was at hand. But they found the reply, though clear enough, puzzling, as was the almost sly, knowing look:

"You don't know! They don't know; he was right! Charles said they......" And, strangely content, knowing he had kept faith to the end, the young man died.

There was no reason for the media to link the unprovoked attack on a middle-aged teacher on Colchester station with the shoot-out between 'rival drug gangs' at Harwich, but they soon discovered that the (unarmed) victim had been a colleague of the Agent at Wothorpe Castle. A spokesman for the feudal seat claimed that they had no explanation of either event, and no reason to link them – although the younger man had not reported for work for several days.

The very public nature of the two incidents, and their relative propinquity, made it inevitable that connections were sought between the Stansted and Harwich deaths, but the more significant connection between Sussex and Lincolnshire was not picked up. Mrs Jennifer Radley might have drawn attention to the fact that a Mrs Jennifer Brady – surely *the* Mrs Brady – had been attacked elsewhere in Essex, had the report she read not referred throughout to Mrs Jackie Brady and described her as 'middle-aged', an epithet clearly (in Mrs Radley's view) inapplicable to someone who could be mistaken for herself.

Malcolm, the Chairman of the British High Command, was furious, a sentiment intensified by his personal guilt at having sanctioned the pursuit of Christopher. He communicated his feeling in unequivocal language to the Grand Council in Vienna, pointing out the trail of deaths and confusion that had followed wherever their man, Larry, had seen fit to meddle.

For his part, Larry remained unaware of the drama played out so close to his temporary maritime residence, the seas around which had been too rough to permit Clarence and his friends to return and deliver him from the malodorous Klaus. The task required of him by Vienna had been to de-activate the missile launcher permanently and render harmless all the rockets, torpedoes, nerve gas shells and any other explosives which the British High Command might be stupid enough to consider using in order to hasten the moment when they could take power. He had done his best, but was out of his depth when it came to the more recently imported weaponry of Russian origin. However, they would have to decide what to do about that when he reported in. In the mean time, having little better to do and anxious not to give his companion any opportunity to make conversation, he passed the time looking through files, boxes of papers, newspaper cuttings, etc., which was how he came across the photograph.

"Klaus!" he shouted. "Come here....Stop! That's near enough. What do you know about this?"

At the sight of the black bushy moustache and arrogant stare depicted in the photo, Klaus started to cackle uncontrollably, inserting between these bursts of hilarity phrases which appeared to imply that this person had spent two years with Klaus before departing. For someone who was himself a raving lunatic, to make signs implying that the person depicted went round the bend was, to say the least, distasteful – especially as he looked remarkably like......

"Oh, clear off, you cretinous old ruin!" cried Monty, pushing the spindly arm away as it quivered towards the photo. Klaus fell backwards, failing to prevent himself from striking his head sharply on the edge of a protruding strut.

The silence, though welcome, seemed to be deeper, and longer, than Monty would have expected.

"Klaus! Come on, get up and tell me who thi......Klaus? Oh, Christ, now the old fool's died on me! Trust him to..... Oh, well, at least he's stopped that bloody cackling."

He had, but Monty soon found that whilst Klaus alive could be said to be aromatically challenged, the stench of his maturing corpse in the confined quarters surpassed description. Not only that. Monty had not yet found out how to operate the 'bathysphere' from below, which prevented him from getting a breath of fresh air even though the heavy seas were now subsiding, making it safe to use.

"Gerald!" he shouted at the steel cavern. "Where the Hell have you got to? Get me out!"

****

"It's me Mother. I can't be long now. I'll be down later on – give you a ring from King's Cross then. Anyway... how are you?"

Jennifer was delighted to hear her daughter had managed to get away, not least because she was a bit worried about Martin:

"I'm fine, dear. No ill effects, at least...."

"At least what? Did you get hurt in the brawl – not having nightmares or anything? Why not take a 'tranque': it'd calm you down if....."

"No, nothing like that... it's your father, really. He was fine yesterday; well, a bit quiet, perhaps, but considering he'd been kidnapped by that awful man, that wasn't surprising. I think he may be worried he'll be back, but we're very well protected, so....."

"Worried the chap'll be back? Didn't you see the news? If he'd gone on to Harwich, Father might've been caught in the cross fire! Incidentally, the awful man, as you call him, didn't kidnap him the way I heard it – and anyway, he's dead!"

"Dead? Oh good! No, we went straight to bed without looking at the T V. Well, well; that should set his mind at rest."

"Ye-es," said Elizabeth, "but don't you think he might just be upset about Sherry, still? He's a sentimental old so...er.. so-and-so. Not that," she added hurriedly, "We aren't all very sorry about it, of course."

"Yes, it could be that, I suppose," said her mother doubtfully, "but he seemed to be better last night, tired but not, well, as deflated, if you know what I mean. Anyway, I'll tell him as soon as he comes in from the garden. Now, how long will you be staying? It's just that there's nothing in the house, so I've got to go shopping. Is there anything you fancy?"

They discussed menus and other practicalities for a few more minutes then arranged a probable meeting time.

"Martin!" called Jennifer, as she returned to the kitchen, "Mar..... Oh, no! Where's he gone, now?"

She bent over the hastily scribbled note to find that he had come in from the garden while she was on the phone and decided to go for a walk 'up the hill'.

"He'll be worrying himself sick," she thought, "and then he'll go off like last time with one of those bandits, or something."

Fearing the worst (whatever that turned out to be) Jennifer rushed upstairs to look out of the window and saw with relief that her husband was returning down the 'hill' (which was little more than a gentle incline, although it gained in stature from the flatness of the surrounding countryside).

"Thank Goodness!" she thought. "He's coming back. We'll have to get another dog. I think Elizabeth was right when she said he was still upset about Sherry; probably blames himself."

Jennifer, however, was only half right. Martin did blame himself, but it was the death of Christopher which had exercised him, ever since he had got up early, read the account and seen the pictures in the morning paper. He had said nothing, but lapsed into near silence, giving rise to his wife's concern. To have claimed to be the great 'Charles', Christopher's protector, a power behind the scenes on whom

246

the young man could call in time of trouble, had been deceitful, taking advantage of one of life's victims. Had he, even at the end, clung to the belief that 'Charles' would avenge him? As he walked, Martin ran over in his mind his recent encounter with Christopher, and as he walked and thought, he remembered the young man's naïve trust, his horror at coming into contact with casual murder and his relief when he realised that the person he had so cleverly followed had not, after all, been killed. Martin dwelt, too, on his own success in gaining a hold over a member of the Organisation. That could have been a useful asset. It would have made Martin himself of value as Christopher's contact......and that puffed up, patronising hyphenated swine had, quite wrongly, accused the lad of being a traitor and set him up to be gunned down within yards of sanctuary. Moreover, that same Burton-Latimer, he strongly suspected, had run to Gerald for help in evading the law – and was almost certainly hidden in the submarine which Elizabeth had deduced when investigating U-534.

"Oh, there you are!" said Jennifer brightly. "Nice walk? ..... Elizabeth rang, and do you know what?" She hurried on, not waiting for a reply. "Apparently it was on the news last night. That man who recognised you's been shot! So you needn't worry any more. There was a gun battle at Harwich and....."

"Yes. So I saw. Lucky I got off at Colchester, given what happened. Actually my man was pretty harmless, but when bullets start flying about they're no respecter of persons. Are you off out, then?"

"Yes. Elizabeth's coming down later and the stocks are a bit run down, so....."

"She's coming, too, is she? That's nice."

"Why? Is Patrick coming? No-one said! I'll get enough for four in that case. When did he say he was coming?" asked Jennifer, adding with some asperity. "I'm only the cook; no need to tell me!"

"Oh – er – I thought *you* said he was coming. Perhaps it was him. I'm not sure," said Martin, who had only very recently decided to ring his son to get him down to bend his ear on the subject of Burton-Latimer. To be more accurate on how best to make sure the said B-L suffered the torments of

Hell, rather than succeed in using his many well-connected acquaintances to wriggle his way to a cushy billet.

Jennifer was pleased to find that her husband seemed to have cheered up after his walk and asked if he wanted to come shopping with her (secretly hoping he would decline, as she was looking forward to being a bit extravagant and taking her time browsing round Queensgate).

For his part, Martin was keen to set up a meeting with his son to discuss certain proposals, so welcomed the chance to ring him in his mother's absence.

"No, thanks. You carry on; I've got one or two things to do, the first of which is to make some coffee and finish reading the paper."

"You're feeling better for that walk," said Jennifer. "We could see about getting another dog soon; what do you think?"

"Well, they get you out, I suppose, but they're rather a tie. I'm in no rush, really. Anyway, you get cracking: it's perhaps as well if one of us is here in case Elizabeth rings."

As soon as his wife had gone, Martin seized the phone and rang his son.

"Oh! It's you, Dad. Everything O K? How's Mother?"

"We're both fine, thanks. She's just gone to Peterborough, so I thought I'd......"

"She must be feeling better, then! A spot of retail therapy, is it?"

"Not entirely. Elizabeth's coming later...and if you do, too, she'll be cooking for four, so..."

"Me? I'm a bit tied up at the moment. There are still quite a few loose ends, as I'm sure you realise, but I could probably manage to get down in a few days," said Patrick, thinking of the can of worms he had caused to be opened up by denouncing Burton-Latimer.

"Yes, quite," replied his father steadily, "which is why I'd like you to come down. I have some information – and some thoughts – on the subject of our hyphenated mutual acquaintance which would be best conveyed face to face .... mine to yours, to be more precise."

"Well, I didn't say which particular loose ends I......" demurred Patrick, with perhaps just a hint of irritation in his voice.

"No, you didn't; nor did you say 'full fathom five he lies' for that matter," persisted Martin. "I should like to pass on a few....."

"How the Hell did you know where he .....?" asked Patrick, surprised out of his customary care concerning the transmission of information.

"I didn't, well not to be absolutely sure, but I do now!" replied Martin, triumphantly, "But more importantly, you may recall that I spent several hours with Mr Bearer recently, during which time I ...."

"Mr Who? And please don't use tricks on me like that last one, by the way .....Oh, yes, I follow – Mr Bearer. Why? Did he say anything particularly revealing?"

"It's not for me to decide what is or is not 'revealing', which is why what I have to pass on needs to go direct to you: why I need debriefing and am requesting a 'meet' to that end," continued Martin, his tone altogether crisper, quietly persuasive, not to say insistent.

Reluctantly, Patrick agreed to come down, adding that if his father considered there was a degree of urgency and that what he had to say might bear directly on certain matters of which they were both aware..... he would find the time. What he meant was: 'It had better be worth my while'.... as they both well knew.

"I'm back, dear!" called Jennifer. "Can you give me a hand with these?"

'These' referred to the vast pile of groceries she had abstracted from Waitrose – whose share price, Martin was wont to declare, started to rise whenever she was spotted entering their car park.

"Right!" said Martin moving to the back of the overladen vehicle. "Did you get enough for Patrick? Oh! Silly question: there's enough here to feed the five thousand!"

"Don't be silly – and anyway, surely the whole point was that it only needed a few loaves and fishes? Is he coming? Any particular reason?"

"Oh, I think he just wanted to make sure you were all right," her husband replied. "They worry, you know!"

****

249

"Would you say, Mother, that your firstborn and his father are, shall we say, not in full agreement about something at the moment?" asked Elizabeth later that evening.

"Well, I know what you mean," said Jennifer, who, like her daughter, had been hearing sounds of verbal strife from the other room. "Do you think I ought to go in and....."

"No! I do *not*! Leave them to it," replied Elizabeth. "In fact, it's not Father who's getting het up. Come to think of it, he seemed different to-day: more positive, sharper, not quite so – er – more ....purposeful."

"You're right, dear. I've known him like this before. I remember once I thought we should be walking the streets by evening: he set off to take issue with his Head about one of his students. This lad had been very rude to another member of staff (a 'self-important pseud', in your father's opinion) and they were talking of rewriting his University entrance reference. Martin was furious, but he kept himself under control, demanded to see the Head – almost forced his way in – and argued logically, calmly and...implacably. He's got quite a good analytical mind, really – or he had, anyway. He's seemed a bit like that all day – well since he went for that walk, this morning. He was quite different before, verging on the depressed, which is why I rang you."

"Well he hasn't got any students, now – unless that dog had assumed tutee status, that is!" said Elizabeth, distractedly operating the remote-control to indulge in a bit of 'channel-hopping'.

"You owe me!" said Martin. "The department owes me.... No, you listen! I didn't ask to join your mob... well all right.... but I didn't answer an advert: I was persuaded, as a responsible citizen. I've given you a lot of names, some of which clearly surprised you, and I tried to set up an 'asset' in Christopher, only to have him assassinated by his own side because of this fellow Burton-Latimer's casual, lethal, incompetence."

Patrick sought to 'set the record straight' by reminding his father that they had set out to deceive Monty, and had succeeded; that the aim – insofar as there had been one, when it came to the involvement of the phantom agent 534 – had been to wrong-foot the Organisation, to get them chasing their own tails as it were. The story, one could say, was more one of H M G's success (including, he added by way of diplomacy, Martin's own contribution) than of Monty's incompetence.

Martin, however, was not to be deterred. He had decided that morning to avenge his trusting acolyte: an eye for an eye would do fine, a plus being a slow and painful eye if attainable in Monty's case. He was well aware, however, that the Intelligence world had no time for sentiment, including revenge. The plan he proposed was supported, therefore, by recommendations such as 'value for money' (the taxpayers), deniability, and continued security. It steered clear of any form of 'deal' with Burton-Latimer, whatever knowledge or influence he might have.

"We don't want him being made Keeper of the Queen's Pictures, do we?" Martin had asked, maintaining a calm persistence, countering argument with reason, practical advantages against the risks associated with later discovery.

Eventually, Patrick offered the nearest he was prepared to come to a concession to his implacable parent.

"Right!" he said. "If, and only if, they agree, I will try to get the Task Force to listen to your plan.... with *you* presenting it. They may take the view that we owe you that, and this material you've just given me should help your case, but it must be understood that the whole procedure is covered by the Official Secrets Act, and that you will not be involved in the decision-taking. Don't expect me to help you; don't blame me if you get a verbal mauling."

"Done!" Martin thrust out his hand: "Sold to the old fool in the wheelchair! When will it be?"

"Hold on, Father, hold on! They may not even agree to hear you out: don't get over-excited. On the other hand ..... it's not a bad plan, so marshal your arguments, stick to what you know – which is not, I have to say, absolutely the full picture – and, well you'll know you've done your best for this Christopher, even if he did try to have you neutralised!"

"It's not a question of....." his father started to protest, only to be firmly sat on.

"Come off it! I know you. But you're dead right not to admit it, and that secret will be safe with me. Let logic prevail!"

Jennifer and Elizabeth were relieved to find that the two men seemed to have resolved their differences, and noted the friendly, but business-like, exchange as Patrick left early the following morning:

"I'll be in touch then, Dad. Be ready to make yourself available, but .....well, you know!"

"Don't worry, I've got the message..... and Patrick!"

"Ye-es?" said his son cautiously.

"Thanks!"

"You may not find much to thank me for, if it comes to it," said Patrick, thinking of the ordeal which lay ahead if his father were called to make a presentation before his hard-headed, high-powered, uncompromising colleagues, "but...... Good Luck!"

CHAPTER THIRTY-FOUR

"And what," asked Elizabeth, once her mother had departed to take her son to the station, "was all that about?"

"Oh, nothing much: I've agreed to go to London for a debriefing, if they want me to," replied Martin.

"You seem to have taken a lot of persuading!" replied Elizabeth, making it abundantly clear that she knew a good old-fashioned lie when she heard one. "Was my brother in the business of 'pulling rank'? He really is a bit much!"

"No, I wouldn't say that," said Martin. "More a matter of presentation than substance, one might say. In fact, I must get on with putting together a report. Apparently they might want me to present it in person."

"Can't he do it? You're, well.... a bit – er – out of practice, aren't you?" said Elizabeth.

"The phrase you're looking for is 'past it'," said Martin cheerfully, "and cocky Sixthformers can be pretty daunting, too, believe me: I'll survive if it comes to it."

Elizabeth surveyed her father, and recalled that he had kept his cool and continued to exude an air of competence, and the thought struck her that the boot just might have been on the other foot – in which case.......

"I'm beginning to think you might, Father. Will we all be walking the streets in the near future?"

"Be what?" said Martin, settling down with a pad of A4.

"Oh, nothing; just something Mother mentioned."

It was as well Martin had decided to get cracking on his presentation, for the summons came late that night. He would be met at King's Cross station, near the 'Arrivals Board' at 10.30 the following morning. The driver would know his name... and would ask if he wished to go to 'Candy Island'.

"I suppose," said Elizabeth scathingly, on being told the ridiculous codeword, "the whole encounter will be captured on 'Candied Camera'! You're enjoying this, aren't you?"

Some might have called Martin's smile enigmatic; the word which occurred to his daughter, however, was 'smug'.

"I think you look very nice, dear. Nothing like a clean white shirt, I always say. Have you got a hanky?"

"Oh, Mother, really. He's not trying to get a job. One thing you will need, though."

"What?" asked her father, falling into the trap neatly.

"Your 'Old Person's Railcard' – no need to bother about proof of age!......and Good Luck!"

"Have a nice day, dear, and don't go off with any more strange men this time," said Jennifer, giving him a farewell kiss.

"At least that leaves me free to pursue strange women!" replied Martin as he reversed out of the driveway.

"Well," said Elizabeth to her mother as they both watched Martin depart, "at least he's no longer depressed. I only hope he's up to presenting this famous report....."

"Oh, he'll be all right," said Jennifer, confidently. "It's only to Patrick and one or two friends, apparently. It'll do him good to have a day in London, and the ticket's paid for!"

Elizabeth debated whether to voice her suspicion that the 'friends' in question were likely to be the type that are only ever referred to in inverted commas and might not be all that amiable, but decided not to spoil her mother's day, contenting herself with:

"So you're not worried about the 'strange women', then?"

"I think," replied Jennifer, with feeling, "that Olga will need more than a long cigarette holder and a split skirt to get your father going!"

****

"Good of you to come, Martin," said the Director. "You probably know most people here, so let's get straight to the main business. The floor is yours."

Martin glanced round the room and recalled the advice his first Head of Department had given him: 'Don't give the buggers an inch or they'll run you ragged'. To his relief, the easy habit of a thousand such encounters had not totally deserted him, as he found when the door opened to admit a latecomer, who looked round to find someone sufficiently senior to receive his apology.

"Seat over here," said Martin briskly. "You've only missed the warm-up act. No harm done! Now, give me two minutes without interruption to set out the bare bones, then I – or, I hope, one of you – will respond positively to those who express doubts, reservations and good old-fashioned ridicule."

The group relaxed slightly, recognising that Martin had seized the initiative and was making it clear that the floor was indeed his, however briefly. The Director smiled slightly to himself, thinking that one or two of his colleagues might live to regret it if they tried the last of the possible reactions the speaker had listed: this Martin might be out of his depth, but he'd learnt to swim in some quite rough seas and had no intention of drowning unaccompanied.

"As I see it," began Martin, "the best way to protect the duplicity – in its literal sense – of Gerald is for it to be absolutely clear to the Organisation that H M G has no idea where Monty is. Looking at this from their point of view, the best way to prevent Monty from being found and 'encouraged' to implicate many others...." At this point, Martin glanced at Bernard, whose one track mind caused a predictable flicker of interest to show in the carefully blank attitude he had elected to adopt, ".....many others, would be to eliminate their Honourable colleague rather than allow him to testify, or do some form of deal. The next best thing to *that* – for I have to assume that, unlovable though he may be, he has friends in high places – would be for H M G to be hoodwinked into believing that he had died. In such circumstances, it would be respectable for us to cease searching for him. Instructions to Gerald could be to organise a suitable scenario whereby Monty, attempting to escape the long arm of you lot, comes to, if not a sticky, certainly a fairly public, end. As we would in fact be prepared to believe anything, including his being eaten by a python whilst visiting the zoo, the incomparable Gerald should gain even more Brownie points and confound anyone in the Organisation who suspects he lacks star quality. Having successfully achieved Monty's official death, the Organisation can keep him hidden in some suitably remote spot – for ever more."

At this point, Martin paused and took a sip of the water thoughtfully provided by his son, both to revitalise the 'vibes' with which he was willing the group to accept the logic of his argument, and to allow the picture of Monty the submariner to swim to the surface of all those who knew where he was at present......which meant everyone except, in theory, himself.

"For Monty to be kept incognito," Martin continued, "under what would have to amount to some form of 'house arrest', would mean that the Organisation rather than the British taxpayer would cover the cost of his keep: a saving of, say, £50,000 a year in an open prison, or more if he's guarded from ex-colleagues bent on ensuring his silence.... to say nothing of the probable costs and possible embarrassment of a trial."

Martin paused again, consulting his notes.

"There's another aspect of Burton-Latimer, however: he's no fool. I met him, disliked him, was dismissed by him as a 'nobody', a rôle I have spent years perfecting," (a slight lightening of the atmosphere, even the odd chuckle, greeted this self-deprecatory interjection) "...but thought him a dangerously able adversary ....."

"May I ask why you considered him, well before he was found to be an active neo-Nazi, to be 'an adversary'?" interrupted the suave career Civil Servant, who had been less than enthusiastic when told that the meeting would start with an address by a 'very recent recruit who had special knowledge to contribute', and had not liked the lack of respect shown to him when he had arrived a couple of minutes late.

Martin found a pause helpful, partly to rest his throat, which was beginning to feel the strain, and partly to remind the meeting of his opening 'contract' of two or three minutes to develop the structure *before* the barbed comments. He regarded his questioner thoughtfully, the pause just long enough for both the Director and Patrick to wonder whether the interruption had stopped the flow, even disconcerted the old boy to the point of reducing him to silence.

"I had hoped to complete the case for the prosecution before the onset of a very proper and necessary descent into detail," Martin continued calmly, "so I would ask you, for the moment, to accept the relevance of my answer, even if it escapes you. He left Stansted Airport, turning east at the main roundabout, in a taxi owned by a firm called 'H F C' . I pointed this out as making him 'suspect' to the member of the Security Service with whom I was travelling at the time."

Patrick smiled broadly, as did Ralph (whom Martin remembered from the meeting at Fitzwilliam College) and the group, including the now even sourer-faced questioner, remained silent as he finished developing his proposals.

"Monty, I assume, is no fool. He thought Christopher was working for *us*. As soon as he finds that all is not immediately well, despite the young man's assassination, he will start to examine the whole series of supposedly unconnected events – and suspect Gerald. He already knows about the Brady family, of course, but the key to the whole affair is Gerald: he must be protected. The best way to achieve this is for Gerald to be Monty's keeper, thus ensuring total censorship of any letters he might wish to have sent to the British, or European leadership. It would be preferable if the arrangement had the full agreement of Monty's Continental masters. Should problems arise, such as Gerald having to hand over to a 'genuine' subordinate, Monty would have to be silenced to prevent him from getting word out to those above Gerald in the hierarchy. In short, Gentlemen, although not exactly an apologist for Mr. Burton-Latimer, I propose he should not be brought to book by H M G, despite the considerable evidence of his real allegiance. Get the Organisation, specifically Gerald, to be, in effect, his gaoler. Get *them* to foot the bill for his food and housing, and pretend to believe whatever smokescreen is put up to cover the official disappearance of this much-respected and very smooth operator."

Martin sat down, fighting to control the tremor in the hand that reached for the glass of water, as the Director rose to his feet.

"Thank you, Martin. Succinct, logical, perceptive, persuasive ......but as you are not fully au fait with all the aspects, there may be problems not yet taken into account. I think I should clear the air, or rather expand Martin's security clearance, to cover the 'Retter'. You referred to the probable desire of the Organisation to keep Monty hidden. You were right: he is at present on board a World War Two U-boat, known as the 'Retter' (the 'Saviour', as you may realise, in German), which has lain submerged since 1945 – perhaps the longest maiden voyage on record! It is the reason for the depôt you discovered at Harwich – another H F C, of course.... clever of you to have spotted that so early on. The enterprise is under the control of Gerald, in his new job as Eastern Area Commander. Right! Other points, please .... Percy?"

Martin looked up to meet the far from friendly eye of the task force member with whom he had already crossed swords.

"I, too, am no admirer of Monty, but you seem to be condemning him to a lifetime, which could be suddenly curtailed, banged up in a steel coffin just off Harwich. His lawyers would argue that his crimes, though considerable, do not merit such an extreme penalty. What would you say to that, Sir?"

"I would say, Sir, that Burton-Latimer's failure to consult Christopher's lawyers before condemning him to immediate death absolves any of us from the need to apply Judge's Rules, or whatever safeguards apply in ordinary cases. I would also say that *we* are not doing anything. My proposal is that Gerald be given the kudos for suggesting something which any other member of the Organisation is likely to come up with, for as long as this odious creature is out of favour. He will, in effect, be not unlike Lord Lucan – missing, presumed dead."

"To reinforce that point," added Patrick, "Monty gained no friends in Sussex when he sent those two, without consulting their immediate boss who later had to have one of them murdered by his own man in the hospital. Added to that, I know from Gerald that the British Chairman wrote to Vienna complaining about Monty, as a result of which they are quite happy to have him left on the 'Retter'. He's run out of allies: no-one wants him around."

Martin was delighted with the way things were going: a few more minutes and he could relax. He could feel the dynamism draining away, realised why he had retired: dominating was too damned tiring!

"There is one cloud on the horizon, Toby," said Ralph to the Director, his voice quiet in a room suddenly stilled. Percy looked up, recognising an ally....and Martin's heart sank. Ralph was no fool: without his approval, the scheme was doomed, and he would for ever feel he had let down Christopher in death as well as in life.

"Not everyone is aware of Christopher's last words," Ralph continued, glancing across at the Director. "He mentioned another agent by name and until we can track that person down and find out what he knows, what Christopher told him, whether he had one of his men helping Monty, for example, we cannot be sure whether we are in fact one step behind. I have to counsel caution at this juncture – to consider, repugnant though we may find it, a deal with Monty..... his freedom for that name."

"Sorry, Martin," said the Director. "Need to know, and all that. Your scheme is grand. We even know now that Vienna want to check on the 'Retter', to make sure that Monty had defused the weapons. They'll find he has – or, rather, that by then *we* will have done....but the important thing is that they've no plans to bring Larry, as they know him, back with them."

Martin could feel fatigue creeping over him, but knew, too, that one more effort was required. He sat, head down, shoulders hunched, gathering his strength.

"Hrrmm!" the Director cleared his throat. "Well, I'm sure you would all wish to join me in thanking ......"

"If you were to locate this Charles.....," interrupted Martin, sitting upright now, speaking slowly but distinctly.

"I don't think," said the Director, glancing with disapproval at Patrick, "that I mentioned the name, which remains *highly* classified... but please carry on."

"You didn't Director, and what is more, neither did I, until now. So how do *you* know it?" Martin gazed accusingly at the great man.

"Just for the record, Director," said Patrick, "Martin did not hear it from me: it's the first time I've heard it mentioned. Perhaps we could ask him how....."

"Christopher said it in the ambulance," said the Director repressively, "but he said it in the hearing of only two people. Which one did you get it from?"

There was a shocked pause, as it dawned on those around the table that whilst they were aware that both the priest (who might even have been a Nazi sympathiser) and the S A S man had travelled with the dying man, only those two – and the Director, who had immediately put the highest possible classification on it – knew precisely what the dying man had said.

"Neither," said Martin with a smile, "but I'll offer 50 to 1 he wouldn't tell them the surname!"

It dawned on his son first.

"You old bugger!" he said. "It was you, wasn't it? You were 'Charles'. You couldn't just be 'Agent 534' all the way from Peterborough to Colchester! And only you know the surname, too!"

"Me, and, as poor old Christopher was led to believe, the very top level of the Organisation! So he kept faith to the end. I told him he might come across me using other names and he was only to trust, if it came to the crunch, another person who knew my *full* name. That's the relationship we had: that's what poor bloody hard-done-by Monty loused up. Christopher wanted something to believe in: that was the appeal of his neo-Nazi 'family'. I was pretty confident he wouldn't have divulged the other name, which, by the way, was 'Hastings'. To him it was .....sacred."

There was a different sort of silence now. They all recognised what it had cost Martin to explain, realised the depth of his anger and contempt for Monty, to whom the name 'Charles' would have meant nothing, although he would have strung them along with some tale or other as a bargaining counter. The Director's glance moved round the table. Wordlessly, each man present nodded briefly, Ralph making also a slight movement of his open palm, to signify the removal of his objection.

"Thank you, Martin. Please leave us now. You must be exhausted. My secretary will find you coffee, I'm sure."

Dazed, drained, yet somehow uplifted, Martin stood, gathered his papers and left, looking at no-one. He didn't even notice that they all stood as a mark of respect as he left, resuming their seats as the door closed behind him, and the Director said:

"Unless anyone has any further points to make, please signify if you are in favour of ...... 'Operation Hastings'."

CHAPTER THIRTY-FIVE

Monty did not find it surprising that the first return trip in the 'lift' was taken by Klaus, Clarence having instructed his assistant, Norman, to remove the body and wait for him to come up to stow it on the tender. After so long shut in, first with the ghastly Klaus alive, later with his decomposing flesh, Monty was desperate to be the second load. However, when Norman reported that a boat was approaching from the seaward side, he reluctantly agreed that Clarence would have to go next (as the two wily boatmen had calculated, before inventing a phantom 'visitor'). Monty's feelings, however, when Clarence then told him over the ship-to-ship that the danger had passed but they had no instructions to take him off, ranged from the incredulous to the murderous, the latter when he detected in Clarence's tone not only that he was enjoying the conversation, but that it was the first of many similar to come. Had Klaus, many, many years before seethed beneath the waves with impotent rage? And the man in the photo.... what was it the old ruin had said? Had he, too, suffered for weeks, months – even years, before..... before what?

Monty sat down to consider his options and do some serious thinking about the events which had combined to place him down here, out of favour, out-manoeuvred at every phase. The hand of that devious sod, Brady, was clearly behind it all, but surely, now that Christopher had been disposed of (that much was clear from the newspapers he had seen) the High Command should be able to move effectively. Why, then, were they – and that had to include Vienna – leaving him to rot down here? He deserved to be fêted, not forgotten; what had gone wrong?

It was some time before the awful thought struck Monty that he might be out of favour because he had been wrong about Christopher....and that for the same reason he was still being out-played, namely that *someone else* was the informer making it possible for Brady to act the puppet-master. He remembered then that he had originally considered and rejected the possibility that Patrick had 'turned' Gerald:

rejected it not because it was so far-fetched, but because it would have been so embarrassing to have had to go, cap in hand, to that pompous bugger, Malcolm.

"So where do you go from here, Monty," he asked himself. "Come on. You're brighter than that ..... that.....'nobody'. Just look at his father – what a *boring* little man!"

And so Monty hatched his plan. He would write to the Chairman, Malcolm, telling him that he now realised that someone else was the 'mole', not Christopher...and that he, Monty, would only divulge the name, together with some other important deductions concerning the happenings at Hall Farm, *in person*. The sealed letter was duly received by Gerald following the next maintenance visit, together with a report that Larry seemed very low, had asked when he was to be allowed to go, but didn't argue or shout, just sat, staring at nothing.

The same information caused Patrick to warn Gerald that Larry was not to be trusted and might try to escape if given half a chance. He also had a different letter written to be passed on to the Chairman, in which the Retter's 'prisoner' complained about his treatment, about the incompetence of the British High Command, hinted that he would be taking his view direct to the Grand Council and that he, Larry, was 'not without influence'.

"Monty's no fool," said Patrick to the Director. "He'll work out, when he either receives an unhelpful reply – or none at all – that his letters are being intercepted. From that he will strongly suspect Gerald, and be able to work out most of the rest."

"Perhaps another visit like the last, when we defused the weapons, only this time we don't bring him round again after injecting anaesthetic gas into the 'Retter's' airpipe?" suggested Bernard.

"I'm sorely tempted," said Patrick, "but he can't do any harm where he is, and his sudden death might alert the Organisation that we're on to them..... and cause them eventually to suspect Gerald."

"You have to admit he's dangerous while he lives. I bet your old man would want him snuffed out!" said Bernard, remembering the implacable venom which had led to Operation Hastings.

"Perhaps," said Patrick, "but no-one's asking him. *We* have to decide, taking, I hope, the long view and weighing the risks against the possible gains."

"All right," said the Director. "Are we all agreed to wait and see? But," he added, "let's agree, too, that if the situation deteriorates suddenly, as it well might, Monty is to be – er – 'snuffed out' by appropriately unattributable means."

****

The midweek maintenance visit to the 'Retter' – outwardly to the diving platform over the wreck of a 16th Century transport ship – was usually undertaken by Derek and Stuart. Clarence saw them off from the H F C office, with a reminder to take care on entering the submarine.

"Remember this guy could tip over the edge just like the last one, so be on your guard."

"Yeah, yeah. Bit before my time, he was. This one's more likely to top himself from what you said last weekend. ... but I'll be ready, in case."

Derek slipped a small automatic from his pocket to show his boss, and set off with Stuart at the helm and his load of fresh fruit, newspapers, videotapes and (Monty's special request from three weeks previously) an exercise bicycle.

There was no immediate answering 'buzz' on the intercom this time, however, so Derek tried again, looking meaningfully at his partner.

"D'you think he's ill?" Stuart enquired nervously.

"Could be. He's not out in the garden, that's for sure. I'll take a spare intercom unit in case the other's bust. O K, here goes; I'll let you know the score in a few minutes."

Derek opened the hatch gingerly, gun in hand, as he entered the 'Retter', calling out:

"Larry! Larry, where the..... Oh Christ! You stupid...."

As he had half expected, and had warned Clarence, Larry had had enough. He swung slowly to and fro, suspended from a strut at the far end of the section, an empty bottle of whisky on the surface which passed for a desk. Sadly, for he couldn't help feeling sorry for the guy, Derek pocketed his gun and moved to perform the gruesome task of cutting down the body.

"Dead on cue," thought Monty, moving out from behind his visitor and raising the heavy spanner to bring it down with all his strength on the back of Derek's unsuspecting skull. The latter fell, clutching onto the dangling, death-like scarecrow dressed in Larry's usual garb and causing the crudely made dummy to disintegrate in the process.

"Now for the other sucker!" muttered Monty, reaching for the intercom.

"Stuart!"

"Here... what's up? Is he..."

"Yeah, dead to the world, you might say. I'm sending him up first. Pull the body out and send the lift back down, then I'll come up and contact Clarence. Ready?"

"God, the poor bugger. After all that.... Yes, I'm ready."

Monty grinned evilly to himself as he cut the connection. So far all had gone according to plan, including his imitation of Derek, to whom he had listened carefully on earlier occasions. Between the impure sound and the nature of the news, he had relied on Stuart failing to notice the deception. He activated the 'bathysphere', checked the safety catch on Derek's gun, arranged himself suitably on its floor and waited, as it rose slowly through the water, for the unsuspecting Stuart to pull him out at the top.

It took about half an hour to shoot Stuart, return to the 'Retter', secrete Derek's body in one of the empty torpedo tubes (if only he had thought of that as a relatively smell-proof storage place for Klaus!), return to sea level, load Stuart onto the tender for later disposal .....and set off towards Holland. All he needed was time. The longer no-one knew just what had occurred, the better chance he had of getting to Vienna and telling his story in the right place. Set against his information concerning the 'turning' of Gerald (now in an influential position within the leadership), the murder of a couple of low-grade operatives would be seen as fully justified.

Back at the H F C depot in Harwich, Clarence occupied himself with various tasks, including a bit of shopping, and arranging the clandestine receipt and resale of suitable artefacts (for the 16th century wreck had in fact long ceased to supply anything which could explain H F C's continued presence). On this occasion, however, he had told his men not to be too long as he was expecting a routine visit from the Health and Safety Executive, who would want to check all their equipment. It was not so long, therefore, before he became aware that they had not yet returned and activated his shore-to-ship radio link, only to be met with ...... silence.

A quick scan through his binoculars was sufficient to tell him the tender was not in view, and cause him to report the matter to Gerald before welcoming the H & S E inspector. The latter passed a somewhat inconclusive two hours with a very distracted man who kept breaking off to indulge in brief, uninformative telephone calls, which consisted largely of 'No, not yet. I'm busy with the Safety Inspector... No, I've no idea'.

****

Patrick was having a brief, but genuine, holiday at the family home when the news of Monty's escape came through to him, by which time the double-murderer-double-agent, sought for different reasons by both the organisations for which he worked, was well out into the North Sea, maintaining strict radio silence and, so far as he could judge, completely unobserved.

"Trouble?" asked Martin, as his son replaced the receiver gravely.

"No reason for you not to know, I guess," came the reply. "Monty's given them the slip and is on his way to Holland in their maintenance launch."

"Will he make it in such a small boat? Surely he'll drown – and good riddance!"

"Oh, he's got a pretty good chance: some crossed from occupied Holland to Harwich during the Second World War in much less suitable open boats. It took some time – and this one isn't fast either – but they made it. I *told* them to be careful: he's ruthless and intelligent, with nothing to lose."

"Why didn't he make for the Essex coast and get through to the senior men in the Organisation?" asked Martin.

"Because he's as far out of favour with them as he is with us, and if, as I suspect, he had to kill some of them to get out of the 'Retter'....they'll want to see him dead as much as we do!"

"Oh! We want him dead, too, do we? I thought he'd become a sort of protected species, kept caged up with the odd bottle of wine poked through the bars from time to time!"

Patrick ignored the dig and replied quietly:

"If he gets through, we, as a family, will be prime targets of the Organisation, second on their list after Gerald. We have to get to him first....and, yes, the Director ordered that he be 'rubbed out' – no, 'snuffed out' was the term used by Bernard, if I remember correctly – if there were any development such as this. Don't worry: they remain convinced by your eloquence and concern for the Privy purse!"

"Bernard! That moron! Monty would run rings round him. Can't we do anything?" asked Martin.

Patrick noted, but didn't comment on, the plural pronoun, for he found it helpful to talk through ideas with someone, and there was no time to convene the full task force. Positive action was needed now.

"Can't you just scramble a fighter, armed with air-to-sea missiles – an Exocet or something..... or send a fast patrol-boat after him? He can't outrun them, or even reach territorial waters, can he?" suggested Martin.

"The trouble is that we're not supposed to know what's happened. As far as we know, Burton-Latimer died in the wreck of his boat – the Python, strangely enough, given your reference to us being prepared to believe an accident at the zoo! That means that if we go after him, his objective would be achieved, namely, the unmasking of Gerald. No, he's in more danger from his own people, who believe they've everything to gain by having him killed."

"I presume you got Gerald to organise the decoy boating accident? So," continued Martin, as his son nodded in confirmation, "why not get him to propose an Exocet? They must have access to weapons like that, surely?"

"Well, yes, probably," said Patrick, "but it'll be dusk shortly, and some innocent seafarer might see it skimming over the ocean, followed by the flash on impact!"

"Hmmm! Yes, it wouldn't be very discreet. I see what you mean ..... but if it was carried out by 'terrorists' – which is what they are – and on the High Seas, H M G wouldn't be involved. It's better than doing nothing!"

"True," said Patrick, "but we have a little time to try and improve on it. Remember we need to turn a blind eye, which means not going after Gerald. If he's too involved and the attack on an innocent British boat is too obvious, we might have a problem."

"Couldn't the 'Retter' set sail for one last glorious mission? Bags of poetic justice there!" said Martin. "Even if the torpedoes didn't work, they could ram this tub, then scuttle the sub!"

Patrick recognised the suggestion for the flight of fancy it clearly was, but even as the thought crossed his mind that the ancient warship had in fact bristled with modern rockets (now defused by both sides!) he remembered their provenance: they were Russian. That meant that someone in the British Neo-Nazi High Command had contacts who could, perhaps, purchase not just a weapon, but its use – could buy Monty's assassination, in fact.

"You've given me an idea! Thanks Dad. I'll need to get on with it now, or Monty will get clear away. You won't be needing the phone for a bit, will you?"

Martin took the hint and left his son to plan Monty's second fatal boating incident, remembering the 'need to know' principle which meant he would be excluded from these high level matters, which included arranging for an AWACS plane from near Lincoln to pinpoint the target as it battered its way across the North Sea.

In a short time, Patrick's instructions to Kenneth resulted in a proposal from Gerald to the Chairman of the British High Command.

"Surely a Russian pilot or ship's captain could be persuaded to go after Larry, Malcolm," said Gerald. "I have no personal contacts, I'm afraid – not much call for them in the Fens – but those rockets on the 'Retter' covered in Cyrillic lettering must have lined the pocket of some high-up in Georgia, or wherever."

"Good point, Gerald. I'll get on to them. We can't have this chap appearing suddenly in this boat of yours: open up a right can of worms.... to say nothing of his having murdered its crew. What happened?"

"We don't know any details yet, but Clarence's men must have got careless and allowed Larry to overpower them; I did warn them he was a tricky customer. The main thing is to make sure he never makes Holland – but discreetly. Have they got a fast ship in the area which could ram the bastard?"

"I'll check, Gerald. It could be expensive, mind you: these Ivans are hard bargainers.... but they deliver, with no questions asked. It's a changed world from my day. Never thought I'd be teaming up with the old enemy! Let you know how I get on. If it's no go, you should be able to rustle up a Harrier – at least, John claimed to be able to. Check his records."

****

Monty was enjoying himself. After his spell in the 'Retter', to feel the wind on his face and experience the thrill of deep sea travel was almost magical. Perhaps the laugh which escaped his lips might have been described (had there been anyone nearby to do so) as a touch unbalanced, but six hours out from Harwich, he could permit himself a little mild hysteria.

"The game's up, Patrick!" Monty shouted at the waves. "Gerald's goose is cooked – and thanks to that dreadful Mrs P, I can tell the exterminators *where to find your dreary little parents!*"

Even as he roared this challenge from the darkened cock-pit, Monty felt his world almost literally turn upside down, his ability to reason nullified by the tearing crash as the reinforced sail of the giant Russian submarine, equipped to smash the ice beneath the polar seas, rose like the horn of a huge black sea-bull and tossed the tiny craft in the air. Gored from below, it sank beneath the surface of the sea in seconds, as did its hit-and-run attacker, several of whose crew considered it to have been the easiest way to get a substantial share of £200,000 that they had so far had the good fortune to come across.

Before accepting the commission from the neo-Nazi Grand Council, the Russian contact – who was not above hedging his bets – had checked with British Intelligence to establish the degree of displeasure the proposed action would incur. Their almost total indifference to the fate of what they claimed to be a drug-running vessel, crewed by members of the gang, came as a slight surprise. Perhaps, the Russian thought, extra money could be earned in the future by warning them about their 'enemy within'....but, for the present, it seemed that those on board had run out of friends.

Malcolm, the Chairman of the British neo-Nazi High Command, received the whole-hearted endorsement of all its members for his forthright action.

"Thank you, Gentlemen... it was Gerald's idea, in fact. Well worth the money; completely discreet. And whatever may have gone wrong lately, we can rest assured that our operations can continue with our security completely 'watertight'.... if you'll excuse the expression!"

Despite certain little local difficulties in Britain, the Vienna-based Grand Council, to membership of which Monty had aspired, were very content with the way things were going across Europe. They were convinced that their turn would come, confident that they appealed to sufficient young people to ensure the succession, as it were. They were pragmatic and ruthless, an attitude often euphemistically referred to as 'business-like', and conscious of the need to control the hotheads.

"Apparently Larry had already de-activated nearly all the weapons in that wretched submarine our British colleagues are so proud of. He'd done a thoroughly professional job, according to the team we sent in. They were most impressed," said the President. "Now we have a report that he shot his way out and tried to escape across the North Sea! It seems they managed to do a deal with the Russkies, who had one of their big subs in the area which made a detour and sank him. Perhaps our men should have brought him out when they went in to check?"

"Better to have let sleeping dogs lie, I think: he'd already been officially presumed dead, as you know, President – a 'boating accident' organised by our British High Command, which completely fooled the British Security Service. The last thing we want is to draw their attention to that set-up off Harwich. No, the re-appearance of Larry would have been a serious embarrassment to us, as he, himself, would have been the first to realise had he been in his right mind."

"Oh! Was he no longer.....?"

"Completely, President, I regret to say. Malcolm showed me an absurd letter he'd written complaining and threatening to contact you – and the maintenance team had reported him as being seriously depressed shortly before he made a run for it."

"I see what you mean. Pity. He seemed quite promising, might even....oh, well, these things happen. At least there was no breach of security and Malcolm's very impressed with the chap who took over the Eastern Area. Comes from good stock he tells me: breeding will out, I always say! Now, turning to other matters: this business in France. Can we agree our policy for the elections? It all looks very promising!"

****

The news that Monty had been 'sunk without trace' filtered back to Martin after a few days, but the violent events of the previous weeks had left little more than a slight scar on the flat, peaceful Fenland scene, in the form of a number of pieces of the light plane which were in the process of sinking beneath the fertile soil. In accordance with policy decided at the highest level, the many firms sporting the initials 'H F C' continued to trade, including those under new management such as Hall Farm Cultivation.

The footpath signpost which had proved so disastrous for the Organisation had not yet been interfered with again, but it was now checked daily by Martin as he exercised the new puppy. Quite often, however, his thoughts strayed, running over aspects of recent events.... regretting the death of Christopher, wondering how Ahmed had fared, recalling the success of the 'takeaway diversion'..... reliving the fear of discovery when he was spotted by the low-flying helicopter .....and .... and where had that dog got to?

"Here Jacko! Here! Sit-tt! Good doggy. Right; let's get back and see if we can get some decorating done, shall we? No more excuses now, are there?"

As he arrived at the back door and started to remove his gumboots, Jennifer came out to tell him that she had taken a phone call in his absence from a very high-powered lady who described herself as 'Sir Somebody Something's personal assistant'.

"Would you ring the number I've written on the pad, identify yourself and ask to speak to Ms Patterson – as soon as you return from your walk," said Jennifer, her whole being radiating a desire to know who these people were, whilst letting not one interrogative word pass her lips.

"Ah!" said Martin, provocatively. "The delectable Pattie: I wonder what she wants."

"Pattie!" exclaimed Jennifer scornfully. "I suppose her boss is 'Knightie' to you! Who on earth are these people?"

"I have absolutely no idea," said Martin, laughing, "having never heard of either of them. Like you, however, I can't wait to find out – but not before I feed Jacko, and make us both some coffee."

"La Patterson won't like being kept waiting, dear, to say nothing of the good baronet. I'll make the coffee then you can ring whilst it's brewing."

In fact, although he affected indifference, Martin was a little worried by the message. Had the Organisation tracked them down, rung only to set up a 'snatch', or to make sure they were alone? Should he check with someone before ringing back, or was he exhibiting paranoia?

"Right, dear," said Jennifer, "there's the number. Off you go!"

Warily, Martin waited for his call to be answered, wondering whether the boffins had managed to develop a supersonic note which could be passed down the phone lines and turn the listener's brain to mush, not that his was any great shakes these......

"Room 303; can I help you?"

"Yes, I hope so," said Martin. "I've been asked to ring this number and speak to a Ms Patterson."

"And you are....?" came the carefully modulated reply.

"Before we go into that," said Martin unhelpfully, "I should like to know to whom I am speaking, and the reason for contacting me."

"If you are Mr Martin Brady," said Ms Patterson coolly, "I explained to your wife that I am Sir Toby Hillman's personal assistant. Are you in a position to speak with him now?"

"What sort of 'position' would you consider appropriate? At present, I'm standing up – and still have no idea who you or your boss are, or, indeed, whether you really are who you claim to be."

"One moment, please," replied the P A, trying hard – well, quite hard – to keep the exasperation out of her voice. She reported the exchange to her boss, who was highly amused and asked to be connected direct to the Fens.

"Martin! Absolutely correct of you to want some confirmation of my bona fides, especially in view of your own success in imitating Gerald when talking to Henry! Toby here: I was privileged to be on the end of your recent presentation concerning B-L, and should like to pop down to see you if it's convenient, to discuss a small project which might interest you. Can you spare me a few minutes?"

"I – er – B-L? Oh, Burton-Latimer.... I see, so you're Toby... Are...?" But at this point the penny dropped and Martin's face flushed in embarrassment. "You must be the 'Director'. Sorry. My wife didn't quite catch the name; she thought your secretary said – er – something different," he finished lamely.

"Oh, don't mind Mollie: she probably gave her the full works; quite correct, but it just confuses people! 'Sir Toby Hillman' gets one a better seat in a restaurant, but it's of little use otherwise! Can you give me a few minutes, then?"

"Yes, of course. I can come up to London any time."

"Rather come down to you if that's O K – more discreet if you see what I mean. How about this afternoon, 3 p m? No need for any elaborate identification as we've met before."

"Yes, right. 3 p m. I'll be there – I mean here."

"Good. 'Bye for now." The Director put the phone down and grinned at his scandalised assistant. "See what I mean, Mollie? He has a way of disconcerting people without meaning to. I plan to make use of that talent – and the fewer of our people who know, the better!"

"Well, dear," said Jennifer, who had listened in exasperation as her chances of upward social mobility receded to zero, "you made a right hash of that! I'll get the poor man some tea when he arrives. Will you pop into town and buy a cake? And don't be wearing those old trousers when he gets here. It's interesting his knowing that nice Mr. Burton-Latimer. Such a shame he was killed in his boat the other day."

"What," said Monty cautiously, "do you know about Monty – er – about Burton-Latimer?"

"Oh, nothing really. I recognised his picture with the obituary. No doubt at all, with those ears. Definitely the same chap. Very polite, a real gentleman."

"Where did you meet him?" asked Martin, with mounting amazement.

"At King's Cross," came the reply. "I bumped into him, literally, as I was running to the train when I came back from France. I don't know where he was going – down to Mersea, perhaps, where he kept the boat. Of course we had nothing in common, didn't know each other. Just a chance encounter ..... but it's strange that Sir Toby happens to know him, too, isn't it?"

Martin could only utter a strangled noise of affirmation as he contemplated his wife's latest revelation and imagined Patrick's face when he told him. Mind you, he thought mischievously, it should be interesting to see how the Director copes with Jennifer mentioning that she bumped into Burton-Latimer when the resources of both sides were frantically trying to find her. What with ramming Monty with her suitcase and flattening their hit man on Colchester station, she made Rosa Kleb look like a dinner lady! Which made a change from one or two dinner ladies he could think of who looked like Rosa Kleb.....

"Now," mused Martin, "what was it ....? Ah, yes. Trousers and cake, then for this 'discreet' meeting. I hope the Director isn't disappointed: it may very well be kept secret from most of the Intelligence Service, but it's most unlikely to escape the attention of that worthy soul of indiscretion – our Mrs Tolliver!"

THE END